MONSTER

"*Monster is, from the start, a character-driven thriller with a fantastic message. It can't be pinpointed into any conventional genre, making it all the more creative. The characters are both believable and heartwarming, while the story is well structured and action-packed. You will not find many better books from a young author-it is well worth the read.*"
– Stephen L., 20

"*When I said I wanted to read Monster, I didn't know I would be begging my mom to let me use her kindle for "just a few more minutes" every couple hours. I fell in love with everything about the book. The characters, the plot, everything was just perfect. The whole plot line gave me chills. It was an extraordinary experience and so well written that I could picture it all in my head. I could feel the characters agony, their happiness, and their fear. It is hard to find truly good book in our society. With Monster, I think found that truly good book.*" – Isabel Caroline, 16

"*Where do I even begin with this novel? That is was a stunning read? That it is the sort of event that I can measure time by? For me, there is a "Before Monster" and an "After Monster", before Monster was a time when I was so blissfully innocent of how much anguish I could bear while waiting for the next chapter update for us beta readers. It was a happy time. I cannot even begin to remember how many times I buried my face into a pillow, or clutched at my heart in a futile effort to rip the heart aching pain that Monster gave me out. Monster is a painful read, don't be deceived. It hurt on levels that struck even harder than a fictional novel normally should because it was so real. There are matters in Monster, hardcore, heart aching, matters that are very real and present in our world today. While crying over Mir, I was also crying over the uncountable who die in abortion clinics because they aren't classified as humans. If you are looking for an easy read, a read that will leave you as happy as a butterfly in a valley of whatever your favorite flowers are, you might not want to read Monster. It hurt me in ways that will probably never heal; I hold it in a list of my favorite emotionally damaging novels. There are things in this world that once you*" read, or watch, or see, or hear, you think, "well, I'm not going to ever be the same again" and Monster was, undeniably, one of those things." – Ashley Tahg, 18

"Mirriam Neal's Monster is a work of art. Her ability to weave a story into a beautiful, intricate web of deep, entirely loveable characters is displayed flawlessly, and continuously dragged me back for more. The story brought tears to my eyes and a smile to my face, and left me feeling like I'd been mugged by a pack of killer kittens. She left it all on the page, and this marvelous work of heart has inspired my own writing to new heights. Monster has a place of honor on my bookshelf, and I can't wait to go back and read it again. Mirriam changed my life forever. If you ever get the chance to read Monster, JUST SAY YES. But don't expect to ever be able to do anything else ever again ever." – Hannah Stewart, 18

"An emotionally packed rollercoaster ride! From beginning to end, the plot twisted and turned unexpectedly and kept me guessing until the very end. The characters came alive, and I cheered for them, cried for them, rejoiced at their triumphs, and wept at their sorrows. Even though this is a futuristic book, Mirriam Neal has done an incredible job of bringing the characters and the story to life. Thanks to her inventive imagination and skillful pen, the plot feels like a very real possibility that could happen in the near future." --Ashley Swartwout, 19

"The novel is, from the beginning, gripping, intriguing, and creepy in that not-horror movie but still downright frightening sort of way. I absolutely LOVE the underlying political dispute; what, or who, defines 'human'? This novel makes a person think. The honesty is thought-provoking and the portrayal of this controversial dispute SO well executed. I'm addicted to it." - Caroline Blankenship, 17

"I absolutely LOVE Monster!!! The theme of the book is something that I was instantly drawn into! I fell in love with Mir from the very start and I cried at the sad parts and laughed at the funny parts. The most amazing thing about your book is that it is not like most books out there today. *Your book is easy to read, yet has depth and meaning that most other authors cannot reach. The plot was also totally unexpected, which I love!" – Allison J.*

"This book is by far one of the best books I have read in a very long time! The plot was understandable and intriguing, the characters were relatable and loveable, and the moral of the story is very thought provoking. The writing style is captivating. I laughed, I cried and I enjoyed every minute of reading! I would recommend it to everyone!" – Sierra Fitzwalter

"I just finished Monster, having started it somewhere between 8:30 and 9:00 this morning! I did NOT want to put it down! I don't normally read this genre. It just isn't my type. I was torn between horror and fascination several times. The thing that makes it so scary is that it is so real. I was blown away by this book! Mirriam did a FANTASTIC, WONDERFUL job writing it. I hope this is all coherent and cohesive; I'm afraid my brain isn't at peak efficiency right now." – Melody M.

"Monster is…absolutely amazing." – Lydia H.

"It's just so amazing, epic, brilliant, magnificent, fantastic, marvelous, wonderful…any word you could possibly find to describe pure genius!!!!!! I wasn't really able to start it until last night because we had been busy all day, so I stayed up past 3:30am reading its awesomeness, but I wasn't able to finish it until today after school. Mir….I think I need to keep him. No, scratch that. I know I need to keep him." – Kaytie S., 17

To Lee Chang Sun, for bringing Mir's soul to life.

Dedicated to my forever King and savior.

*"Damaged people are dangerous.
They know they can survive."*
- Josephine Hart

I have never left this place. I have always been kept here by the doctors. They tell me that billions of people died – places were left empty and quarantined – and the doctors are looking for a cure, trying to make sure it never happens again. The world is back to normal, they say, but for how long? They want to save lives by destroying mine, so I died here. I always die here.

Chapter One
Year: 2053

In a remote part of North Alaska, at a WorldCure Medical Research Facility.

"Doctor Stewart, would you step into my office for a moment, please?"

Eva looked up from the microscope as the voice came through the speaker on her desk. She straightened and groaned as her back muscles protested, stiff from an hour of bending over.

She left the room and strode down the white, gleaming hall to the office of Dr. Ross, the head of the Research Department. She smoothed the wrinkles from her lab coat and knocked on the door.

"Come." Dr. Ross did not look up as Eva came in; instead he remained behind his desk studying the transparent computer screen in front of him.

She stood and watched, waiting for him to look up and speak to her. He was a formidable man, and not only because he was tall. He kept his head and eyebrows shaved – less to take care of, he remarked once – and his eyes were pale and watery. He looked, in fact, as if he had been raised in a dark closet.

"Ah, Doctor Stewart." He looked up – *about time,* Eva thought. "Thank you for coming. I wanted to speak to you about upping your pay grade." Eva's eyes widened and she folded her arms, waiting for him to continue. "How would you like to become a Handler?"

Eva stared at him. A Handler meant she would be given access to Beneath. A Handler meant she would have her own Subject to work with – her studies would leap forward. She would no longer be hampered by working with previous research; she could make her own discoveries. This would give her a chance to truly find the cure for Morbus.

"Well?" Dr. Ross looked at her with an expression that would have required a raised eyebrow, if he had had any eyebrows to raise. "Are you going to answer me, Doctor Stewart?"

"I would like that very much, Doctor," Eva finally managed. She curled her fingers in eagerness, but kept her bearing professional. Professionalism was extremely important in her line of work and she adhered to it with rigidity.

A pleased smile broke out on Dr. Ross's face. "Good. Excellent. If you will just hand me your card, I'll update it."

She unclipped the card from the collar of her lab coat and handed it over, watching as he placed it in a slot on his desk and typed a command into the computer. There was a click and a beep, and he handed her card back. "Congratulations, Doctor Stewart. You have great potential, and I know you will do equally great things. Now." He rose from the desk and moved around it, walking forward to shake Eva's hand. "I'll take you down Beneath and introduce you to the warden."

"Yes, sir." Eva followed him out of the office and strode down the labyrinth of white corridors lit with fluorescent lights. When she had first arrived here at WorldCure, she had been overwhelmed by the antiseptic smell of the whole place, but now she was so used to it that when she went outside and breathed in fresh air, it was almost strange.

At the end of the third hall a scanner was embedded in the wall by a steel door. Dr. Ross paused to swipe his card into it. The bolt slid aside and the door clicked open an inch. Dr. Ross opened it the rest of the way and Eva descended the flight of steps behind him. Strips of dim white light ran along either side of the concrete ceiling. They reached the bottom, and Eva blinked as her eyes adjusted to the darkness; she'd never been Beneath before, and the main facilities where she worked were always flushed in harsh white.

"Warden," barked Doctor Ross.

A man appeared from a small, dingy-looking office to the left. He was short but muscular, and his mouth looked as if it had been frowning since the moment he was born. "Doctor Ross," he said stiffly. His eyes flicked over to Eva. "Is she a new Handler?"

"Yes, this is Doctor Stewart. Doctor Stewart, this is Brenton, our Warden."

Eva nodded politely at the warden, who continued to scowl. "You know there's only one Subject left without an official Handler, right?"

Dr. Ross frowned. "Who?"

"Who do you think?" Brenton snorted. "Tiger."

"A-ah." Dr. Ross looked hesitantly at Eva. "Doctor Stewart, I apologize, but you may have to wait until we can procure a Subject other than Thirteen."

"Why?" asked Eva. "Is something wrong with Thirteen?"

"Not exactly," said Dr. Ross at the same time Brenton said "Only everything."

"If the Subject is defective, why do you keep it?" she asked, raising one eyebrow.

Dr. Ross sighed and ran a hand over his face. "Thirteen is an unusual Subject."

"I'll say," grunted Brenton, crossing bulky arms over his barrel chest. "It's escaped twice and both killed and seriously injured six guards in the time it's been here."

"Twice?" Eva asked incredulously. "Six guards? A Subject escaping is almost unheard of, and Thirteen has managed it twice?" She looked back at Dr. Ross, whose eyes were narrowed at the warden.

"Thirteen has been here since it was an infant," he explained, turning his gaze back to Eva.

"How old is it?"

"Early twenties."

Eva could not hide her surprise. "And it's still alive?" Most Subjects did not survive their first few years in the facility, regardless of their age. They were lucky if they lasted twelve months.

"That is why we cannot afford to dispose of it." Dr. Ross's voice was clipped. "It has been our most successful Subject and is extraordinarily resilient to our tests. We have never had another Subject like it."

"I see. What's the problem with it, then? Why are you reluctant to hand it over to me?" Eva planted one gloved hand on her hip.

"It's dangerous, ma'am," Brenton said. "Like I told you, it's killed a few people, and it wasn't pretty. Ripped one of their arms clean off, snapped another's spine – and no offense, ma'am, but you're a woman and a small one at that. Frankly, you can't handle Tiger."

Eva stiffened and glared at Brenton. Their eyes locked until she was sure he knew exactly what she thought of him. "I would like to see Thirteen, if you don't mind," she said with words encased in ice.

"Of course," said Dr. Ross, "as long as you understand the dangers." He led her down the dimly-lit corridor. Their footsteps echoed faintly off the concrete walls as they passed one steel door after another. Each door had a faded number on it, painted in white.

They stopped when they came to the door marked 13.

"It's no coincidence its number is thirteen," said Brenton, who had walked behind them. "It's unlucky, that one."

"Please open the outer door," was all Eva said, her tone as frigid as the air around her. She shivered. "Why do you keep it so cold down here?"

Brenton shrugged and typed a number into the keypad by the door.

"Colder temperatures slow down the Subjects' physical and mental functions," Dr. Ross explained. "Not many of them need it – most of them are semi-comatose at all times, but we find it practical."

Brenton grunted. "There."

The outer door slid open with a harsh, grinding sound, and Eva took a few steps forward. Behind the outer door was another one made of six-inch-thick plastiglass. The cell was dark, and it was difficult to judge how large it was. "Where is the Subject?" asked Eva, squinting for a glimpse of it.

"It usually keeps to the back, unless it's gone crazy," said Brenton. "Just wait. It knows you're here, trust me."

Eva waited. Minutes ticked by, and she began to wonder if there was anything in the cell at all. She was just about to ask Brenton if there was any way he could make it visible when two small spots of light appeared at the back of the cell.

"What is that?" asked Eva, leaning forward to get a better look.

"It's looking at you," said Brenton.

"Its eyes glow?"

Dr. Ross answered. "It was an experiment with phosphorescence. A study suggested that properties in the phosphorescence might have dimmed the effects of Morbus. It did not work well enough, so the experiment was considered a failure, but it still appears in the Subject's eyes when its heart rate is elevated over one hundred."

"What is Thirteen's serial number?" asked Eva, still staring at the two spots of light in the darkness.

"6223-4897," said Brenton. "See it, can you?"

Eva squinted at the darkness. She was sure she could see a three, a dash, and part of a four in the darkness. "Yes, but…"

"It's probably crouching," said Brenton. "It does that a lot. Thirteen was tattooed on the chest, and it turns out that whatever you doctors did to make its eyes glow also lights up its tattoo. Makes it easy to spot when it's not hiding, but when it crouches like that you can't see it."

"Interesting." Eva took a mental note of Brenton's information. "Does any other part of it fluoresce?"

"It has a couple scars, actually," said Brenton, leaning against the wall with his arms crossed. "On its shoulder blades. Those light up too. That's why down here, we call it Tiger."

"I'd like to look at its chart, if you don't mind, Doctor," said Eva.

"Certainly."

Eva followed him out, glancing back only once as the outer door slid closed over cell thirteen – and the burning eyes.

Chapter Two

"So, have you made your decision concerning Subject Thirteen?"

Eva looked directly at Dr. Ross. "Yes, I have. I want it. Its vital signs are good, body mass and structure much better than the other Subjects." She had pored over Subject Thirteen's file well into the night, impressed with how it handled treatments that killed or rendered useless most other Subjects.

Dr. Ross nodded, his expression a mixture of approval and lingering hesitance. "Very well. But you are required to have at least two armed guards with you at all times."

"I do not want Subject Thirteen shot," objected Eva.

"I agree. It would be a shame to have it killed, but I cannot risk one of my staff being hurt by it."

"Then let the guards carry tranquilizers," Eva said, straightening the card clipped to her coat.

"Subject Thirteen has been shown to have a..." Dr. Ross furrowed his brow, "an elevated metabolism."

Eva raised her chin. "Then make it Sedamine. That would take out a bull."

The two doctors looked at each other for a moment. Dr. Ross nodded and held out a hand. "Let me see the file."

Eva handed it to him and watched as he produced a pen from his pocket and signed above a line on the first page. Retracting the pen with a click, he handed the file back to her. "Thirteen is all yours."

"Thank you," said Eva. She gave him a smug smile and turned to walk into her office. Hands on hips, she surveyed the area that had become her life. It was a square room, twenty-five feet on all sides. Her desk sat on one end, and several tables were placed strategically for maximum efficiency and movement. Lamps for lighting, shelves bolted into the chart-lined walls full of antidotes, and works-in-progress. This was her lab, her research room – but now she would be doing much of her research in the Procedure Room beneath.

She smiled.

Now she could get somewhere.

Eva made her way Beneath as soon as she finished her lunch.

"Warden," she barked as her shoes scuffed the concrete floor.

The door to his office opened and he walked out, looking at her as if he would rather she were anyone else. "Yeah?"

"I would like Subject Thirteen taken to the Procedure Room, please."

"Yes, ma'am," Brenton mumbled. He picked up a walkie-talkie and held it to his mouth. "Two guards at cell thirteen." He clipped the walkie-talkie back onto his belt and walked down the hallway. Eva followed with brisk steps.

Two guards waited outside the cell, heavy-duty tranquilizer guns already pointed at the door. Their eyes darted to every corner and their stance was uneasy. Apparently stories about what Thirteen had done to previous guards were handed down through respective security generations.

"Hang on," said Brenton, walking over to the keypad by the door. There was a red button above the square with the other numbers.

"What are you doing?" asked Eva as he poised a finger to push it.

"We have the sound-barrier on," the warden explained. "We do it so we don't have to hear it when Subjects are making a lot of noise. I have to make sure Thirteen's not in one of its moods."

Eva nodded. She'd read about the Subject's 'moods' in the file last night. Though physically in the best condition out of all the current Subjects, Thirteen was classified as 'volatile, unstable, and mentally traumatized.' It was prone to attacks that included screaming and violence.

"Go ahead," she said, and the warden pressed the button.

Sound immediately spilled from the speaker in the middle of the door, and it took Eva a moment to distinguish what the noise actually was. She realized it *was* screaming, just as the file had said, but it was like no screaming she had ever heard before. It was animal. She was surprised that Thirteen still had vocal chords with which to scream if it was in the habit of throwing fits like this.

Brenton turned the button off as sounds of hollow pounding began to burst from the speaker. "Well?" he asked Eva, sticking his hands in his pockets.

"Please sedate it," said Eva.

He nodded and began typing in a new code. "We had special gas chambers installed in the cells of the more violent Subjects. It releases a heavy sedative through the air vents in the ceiling."

"A wise move," Eva conceded. "How long will it take?"

"Until it's sedated?" She nodded. "About twenty seconds. The vents will clear the air after, so it's safe to go inside."

"I would like to watch," she said.

Brenton sighed and typed in another code. The outer door pulled open, and this time Eva could make out a figure in the darkness. Subject Thirteen's serial number glowed brightly, and its eyes turned to match. It took her a moment to realize that the pounding she'd heard before was Thirteen slamming its head against the walls of the cell.

A faint white blur appeared from several vents in the ceiling, gas silently filling the cell. Thirteen stopped thrashing and in the darkness, Eva watched the number on Thirteen's chest lower as the Subject slid to the floor.

"There," said Brenton. "It's safe to go in now."

Eva nodded and motioned toward the guards. They tensed and raised their guns. The plastiglass lifted and Eva waited outside the cell while the guards stepped inside and lifted Thirteen by the arms.

Eva stepped back as they half-dragged, half-carried the Subject down to the end of the hallway where the Procedure Room sat waiting.

The Room was concrete, like everywhere else Beneath. But, unlike the other rooms, it was full. Workbenches, shelves, racks. The walls were lined with instruments. A sink stood in the corner for sanitary reasons. The floor sloped gently inwards toward the middle, and in the center of the room was a large grate-covered drain.

"Please strap him to the table," she ordered, though the guards were already doing so. Apparently they had done this many times before. During normal procedures, thick straps went around the Subject's ankles, thighs, wrists, chest, and neck to prevent thrashing.

But Thirteen was different, and Eva watched with slowly rising eyebrows as the guards worked to hook Thirteen's harness to bolts placed four inches apart on the sides of the table, buckling them down with nervous hands.

The harness looked fairly medieval, but that did not keep it from being effective. It fit around the Subject's upper body with two stiff, thin pieces of metal down the sides, and buckles connected all the way around like belts. The Subject's arms were pinned to its sides and buckled with several other straps, and there were several thick loops in the back so the Subject could be hooked to a wall or machine.

It weighed almost twenty pounds, and made escape nearly impossible for whatever Subject wore it, not that many Subjects had the strength or willpower to attempt an escape. As far as Eva knew, Thirteen was the only one who wore a harness at the moment.

"Leave me room to work, please," she said. Caution was commendable, but there was such a thing as overdoing it.

As Eva put on her tight surgical gloves, she studied the Subject strapped to the table. She knew specifics from its file: male of mixed origin, early twenties, six foot one, 170 lbs. It had pale uncut hair - almost white - due probably to lack of sunlight. Its eyes were Asian in shape, but shone a startling blue underneath the phosphorous. Its face also told of its unclear ethnicity – a thin, well-cut face, a full mouth, and a strong nose that looked as if it had been broken at least once.

I wonder how much scar tissue I'll have to work around, Eva mused as she swabbed disinfectant across the back of Thirteen's neck. She uncoiled a thin black cord from the wall. One end resembled a plug with needles for prongs; the other end was attached to a large monitor screen on the far side of the room. She walked the cord over to the Subject and carefully inserted it into Thirteen's cerebral cortex.

The screen came to life, registering the Subject's vital signs. "Perfect," murmured Eva. She circled the table and raised it so it stood diagonal to the floor. The Subject's eyes were half-closed, heavy with sedative.

Eva lifted a clipboard, complete with fresh paper and pen, from a nearby table. In her other hand she picked up a syringe filled with a clear liquid called stressamine, 'stress' for short. It was a simple serum, designed to measure the strength and endurance of a Subject in order to know how much it could physically handle.

The two guards at the door shifted uneasily, and Eva glanced over to see them shooting nervous looks at one another.

"It is not necessary for you to remain here," she told them in a clipped tone. Quite honestly, she saw them as a nuisance. There was no way the Subject could escape, and she did not need two extra disturbances.

The first guard snorted. "No offense, *Doc*, but the last time that happened two bruisers were killed and the doctor was turned inside-out on the floor."

The mental image made Eva's spine tingle. "But surely that was before you added the extra restraints," she said, motioning toward the Subject that was so well-strapped to the table. She wondered if she would have to undo some of the restraints simply to do her job.

The guards hesitated for a moment, but the moment was brief. "We'll be right outside the door," said one, and as he left the other added, "If you need us, the panic button is right there." He motioned to a red button under a glass case on the wall.

"Thank you," Eva said impatiently. "You are excused."

He nodded and left the room, closing the door behind him. Eva breathed a sigh of relief. *Alone.* Now she could concentrate. She inserted the vial of stress into the Subject's bloodstream and waited. It generally took thirty seconds to a minute for the serum to take effect.

Her eyebrows rose when Thirteen's glassy eyes flew open, glowing as the Subject's muscles strained and tightened. A sheen of sweat broke out over its skin and the Subject began to writhe, struggling against its restraints.

Quick metabolism, Eva noted. Dr. Ross had mentioned that.

The Subject gasped, and the gasp became a growl. Its veins stood out from its skin, blue and purple under the white light of the room. Eva wondered if it would actually manage to escape the restraints. She looked over at the monitor. Vital signs were battling high levels, from heart rate to muscular control. *Keep calm, Eva, this is the normal reaction.*

The drug's effects never lasted long, ten minutes at the most. It was often a prelude to surgeries or medical experimentation, and had proven very effective in measuring Subjects' endurance. As a student she had been allowed to watch during several procedures, and was familiar with the routine.

She watched, her pen jotting down notes on the paper as the Subject battled, helpless, against the overwhelming physical demands. Eva was surprised to note how well Thirteen resisted the stressamine when compared to studies of previous Subjects. She had read about Thirteen's high performance in its file, but it was different witnessing it firsthand.

Because the Subject had an abnormally fast metabolism, the stress wore off in under eight minutes. Thirteen sagged against the restraints, its hair plastered to its forehead with sweat. Eva knew stress produced so much sweat that Subjects often became dehydrated afterwards, so she crossed the room to the cooling unit and brought back a bottle of filtered water.

Carefully – she did not want to have her hand bitten off – she pushed the Subject's head back and tilted the water into its mouth. Thirteen swallowed several mouthfuls and watched her, panting, as she withdrew. Too much water in the Subject's system could dilute the drugs and hamper her research.

Eva looked over at the monitor again – heart rate was slowing back down, it was already below eighty. Muscle tension was easing, the blood flow slowing to normal. Satisfied, Eva marked it down on the clipboard and put it back down on the table. Now for the real work.

Chapter Three

I hurt. I always hurt. And I scream because there is nothing I can do to stop it. When the new doctor was near me I could smell her scent. It was a sweet lie. Her hands were gentle but only brought more pain. The scent of the new doctor is danger. She will kill me. Do I want her to kill me? I don't know, I don't know...if this is all there is... I don't think I would mind dying, but I would mind being killed. I've come so close to freedom; I have felt the blood on my hands, the blood of anything in my way. My blood, when they tell me with more pain, always more, to never try to taste freedom again. I just want the pain to stop, even if it means breaking my own head open. Or the new doctor's.

Eva arrived at work early the next morning, excited by yesterday's proceedings. She finally felt she was getting somewhere, like she had been handed a map after wandering endlessly with no idea where to go.

She unlocked her office and began her work before the rest of the faculty came. It was a short walk from her living quarters to her office – the entire facility was divided into halves. One half served as the actual research facility, and the other half housed everyone who worked there. When you agreed to join a remote team like this, you had to sign a large stack of papers and agree to live on-site for purposes of practicality and keeping the project away from civilian eyes.

Eva had not hesitated when she signed. This was for her parents, this was for herself. She had no one to miss her, she was attached to no one, and all she cared about waited for her at the North Alaskan research facility. Years of schooling – high school from eight to twelve, college from twelve to sixteen, and six more years of medical college – all for this.

She had signed with a flourish.

The clock on the wall ticked slowly as Eva ran tests on Subject Thirteen's blood. She had to diagnose how many foreign substances resided in it before she could proceed with experimentation. So far she had counted thirty-eight non-organic elements in blood that had once been Type O Positive but was now so mingled with drugs and chemicals that it could not rightfully be placed in a 'type.'

Eva's eye was pressed close to the glass of the microscope. She was concentrating hard on two unknown substances she had just found when the intercom on her desk buzzed and she heard Dr. Ross's strained voice; "Doctor Stewart, could you please come to the lower door, please?"

Eva glanced at the intercom and carefully placed her utensils on the table. Pulling off her gloves, she ran out the door and down the hallways until she came to the door.

"What is it?" she asked, breathless. She had never seen her superior look so agitated.

"It's your Subject," he said tensely. "It's escaped."

"Again?" Eva felt her heart begin to beat faster. "How?"

"We aren't certain, but it's already caused serious damage."

"Where is it? Has it been recaptured?" Eva demanded, pushing loose strands of brown hair away from her face with flustered hands.

"No, we have every available guard searching."

"Is it possible it escaped from Beneath?" Eva kept her voice calm, but even she could hear the strain in it and knew she was fooling no one. *Be professional, Eva.*

"No, it's still down there – the only problem is, there is much more to Beneath than you've seen. The range of Beneath spans a good half-mile all around."

Eva's breath caught uncomfortably in her throat. Of course, she thought to herself, it had to. Storage, extra rooms, probably miles of piping and darkness and difficult-to-search places. "Where did it go the last time it escaped?"

"Some of the guards cornered it before it could get too far," said Dr. Ross, his Adam's apple jerking nervously when he swallowed. "But then they got too close."

Eva's eyes widened. "This isn't good," she murmured, running her hands over the front of her coat.

"No," said Dr. Ross, swiping his card into the slot by the door. It opened. "It isn't good at all."

Eva followed him down the steps, pulling the heavy door closed behind her. A line from Dante's poetry skittered through her head like a rodent – *abandon hope, ye who enter here.* As they reached the bottom of the stairs, four guards ran past in single file. All of them were armed, and their footsteps pounded, echoing through the corridor.

"Where's the warden?" asked Eva.

"Right here," came the gruff reply from the hall to the left. As Brenton came closer, Eva noticed that his ruddy complexion had gone pale. "I'm sure you're aware that we have an emergency."

"Yes, I am," she replied tersely. She took a deep breath and opened her mouth to ask him a question, but the warden interrupted.

"You know you shouldn't be down here, then. As Warden, I'm responsible for your safe— "

"Thirteen is her Subject," interjected Dr. Ross. "She is within her rights to be present."

Brenton barked a laugh. "Your funeral. You can wait in my office."

Eva's eyebrows drew sharply together, but she refrained from snapping her thoughts at the irritating man. She was unarmed and knew she would be no match for Thirteen, should she run into it. "Fine," she said. "But I want your radio."

The warden rolled his eyes, unclipped his walkie-talkie, and handed it to her. "There you go, lady. Just press that button there on the side to scream for help. Maybe somebody'll be listening."

"Why are you still standing here, rather than searching for the missing Subject?" she asked in an inquiring tone.

Brenton looked at Dr. Ross. "We can handle this, Doctor. I'd suggest you go back onto the main floor. There are only so many places to hide, and unless it's wandering around with its eyes closed, its arms folded over its chest and its back to the wall, Thirteen's a walking spotlight."

Dr. Ross hesitated, glanced at Eva, and nodded. "Very well – are you certain you won't come back upstairs?"

Eva nodded. "I want to be here."

Dr. Ross turned back around and walked up the stairs without another word.

"If you're staying, I'm giving you two bruisers." Brenton pushed the door to his office open, waited until Eva stepped inside, and pulled it closed with a slam.

Bruisers. Code-name for standard-issue security guards. Down here, everyone on staff had a moniker according to their job. Eva would certainly have preferred simply to call them what they were, but not everyone looked at things in straight lines as she did.

Eva looked around the dingy room. It was three times smaller than her lab upstairs; a file cabinet in the corner, a desk and chair, and a cot were the only pieces of furniture. A gun rack hung on the far wall, behind the desk, and three weapons – two tranquilizers, one old-fashioned Striker shotgun – hung from it like trophies. A bare light bulb swung gently over the desk. Obviously, Brenton was not the sort to give sway to personal decorating tastes – unless these *were* his personal decorating tastes.

There were two knocks on the door and, before Eva could even say 'come in,' the bruisers entered. They were dressed in black, from the snug-fitting caps on their heads to their trousers and combat boots.

Perfect.

It took Eva only a few seconds to walk out of the room with purposeful strides, tranquilizer in hand. She was not one to sit and wait while incompetents struggled to perform a task which she could better manage herself.

"Doctor, we were given orders to stay with you," objected the first guard, a thick-set man with small eyes.

"Then stay with me," Eva retorted, and continued walking. Subjects who broke out sought freedom first, therefore it would most likely be looking for some sort of door. It would also be trying to avoid capture, and consequently people. The most logical place to look for it would be toward the back of the underground level, in the control and storage rooms.

Guards scurried about like ants whose hill had been stepped on, communicating with radios, shouting, running with heavy, thudding boots. Thirteen's escape was no small matter. In the pandemonium, no one paid attention to Eva as she briskly made her way through Beneath. Guards began to grow scarcer, though she could still hear faint orders shouted behind her.

Eva walked cautiously into one of the rooms at the back. There were no doors – they were only huge, open spaces the size of an ordinary house. Concrete floors, walls, and ceilings meant only to house metal bins, necessary pipes, and supplies.

It was almost pitch black inside. The sputtering florescent lights outside barely shed any illumination into the huge storage room, and Eva found herself squinting so hard her eyes hurt. The tranquilizer gun was cold in her hands, but she held it steady. A faint drip, drip, drip came from somewhere inside.

"Wait here," she ordered the two men behind her. "Tell me if you see anything."

They shifted uneasily. "Yes, ma'am," the younger one said.

Without looking back at them, Eva walked farther into the room, rushing blood filling her ears with white noise as she strained for the smallest sound to alert her of Thirteen's presence.

She stood still and tense, listening, for almost a minute but no longer. There were dozens of other rooms to search as large as this one. "Nothing here," she called to the guards by the door. There was no response. "Guards!"

She turned, and her blood ran cold. The digits 6223-4897 glowed in the air in front of her. A serial number.

She found her gaze travelling upwards to meet a pair of narrowed eyes. All blue was lost in the hatred-filled yellow, and Eva had time only to turn on her walkie-talkie and shout into it before she felt a blow to the side of her head that knocked her to the ground.

She had assumed incorrectly. Thirteen had not gone looking for freedom. It had gone looking for her.

Chapter Four

Eva felt hands encircle her neck, lifting her off the ground into the black air. She tried to draw a breath and when none came, found herself clawing at the hands that were cutting off her air supply.

Dying was quicker than she expected.

A hissing sound snaked through the air and Eva landed heavily on the hard ground again. Her lungs almost burst with relief and she sucked in as much air as she could before scrambling to her feet. *Thirteen – the Subject –*

Flashlights filled the room and illuminated the monster thrashing against a semisteel lasso that had been pulled tight around its arms and chest. Eva shouted as it lunged toward her, lips curled back in a snarl, eyes flaming.

The guards on the other end of the lasso heaved, jerking the Subject backward. Several shots fired in rapid succession and Thirteen staggered like a drunkard for a brief moment before collapsing to the ground, tranquilized.

Eva stared at the gun in her outstretched hand and wondered how she had managed to keep hold of it.

"Are you all right, Doctor?"

A guard stood by her, peering into her face with concern. He shone a flashlight and let out a long, low whistle. "You should get that looked at."

"Yes," she managed. As she walked out of the room, she heard one of the guards mutter "Why don't they just kill it?"

Eva stood looking at her reflection in the fogged-up mirror. A hot shower had done her good, but it had not helped the ring of dark, ugly bruises that encircled her neck like a morbid necklace. Her throat was painfully swollen, but the nurse had given her a drug that eased the discomfort.

Eva drew a comb through her wet hair with long strokes; her hands still trembling from the horror of a near-death experience. Dr. Ross, after expressing his concern for her health and making certain she was not seriously injured, had told her to come back Beneath at noon for Thirteen's punishment.

"Seeing you there will help it understand that you are the reason it is being punished," he explained.

"How did it escape?" Eva had demanded. "Security is too lax down there. That thing is a health hazard for so many reasons I don't care to name them, yet it has escaped four times!"

"According to the guards on duty, Thirteen escaped them while being transported back to its cell from a prepping session."

"Prepping session?" Eva had inquired, but Dr. Ross just waved a dismissive hand and reminded her to go Beneath at twelve o'clock.

"Doctor Stewart, there you are." Dr. Ross smiled and ushered Eva into the room. Unlike most rooms Beneath, it was small and well-lit, no larger than twenty feet on each side. A cylindrical plastiglass tank took over one wall, and various black cords ran through airtight holes in the tank and connected to a series of large dials and switches on the wall to the left.

Curious, Eva was about to ask Dr. Ross what the setup did when four guards walked into the room, surrounding Subject Thirteen. What appeared to be an air mask of sorts covered its mouth and nose. The eyes above the mask had the familiar glassy look of a drugged animal.

Dr. Ross stepped over to the tank and opened a sliding door in the front. The guards pushed Thirteen into the tube and began a process of connecting the cords to various places on its air mask and steel-lined harness.

When they had finished, two guards lowered the door and nodded at Dr. Ross, who turned one of the dials. "Pressurizing and sealing the tank," he said offhandedly to Eva.

She nodded as she began to understand what was happening, and watched in a kind of studious fascination as Dr. Ross turned a large metal wheel on the wall, grunting a little with the effort.

Without warning a rush of water poured down through a ceiling-grate above the tank.

Thirteen shook its head and began to look more alive with desperation. Hundreds of gallons of water rapidly filled the tank until Thirteen was suspended, panicked movements made graceful by the water.

"Start it," said Dr. Ross, motioning to a bearded guard who stood by the red-and-yellow switches. The guard obediently pulled a red switch from its upright position to a horizontal one.

It was as if a miniature lightning storm had begun inside the tank. Electricity coursed through the cords attached to the Subject inside. Thirteen thrashed wildly, slamming against the walls of the tank, but the water slowed it down.

The electricity seemed to feed the phosphorescent eyes. They burned like miniature suns in the Subject's pain-wracked face.

"Won't this kill it?" Eva asked, with the same kind of detached distaste she felt when dissecting a lab rodent.

"No, we regulate it carefully," said Dr. Ross calmly. That was all he said, and Eva watched for ten minutes as Subject Thirteen twisted and convulsed in a tank of electrically-charged water.

"All right, shut it off," said Dr. Ross finally, and the switch was returned to its original upright position.

Another wheel was turned and the bottom of the tank slid aside, allowing the water to drain through a floor-grate. The door opened and two guards unhooked the Subject that could barely stand. The other two guards kept tranquilizer guns leveled at it as the mask was removed from its face.

Its breathing came in shallow, erratic heaves; its broad shoulders shuddered with each desperate gasp for air. Eva followed as the Subject was dragged to its cell and thrown in.

It lay in a heap in the center of the bare room, hardly breathing. "I think you killed it," said Eva flatly.

Dr. Ross, who had come with them, laughed. "Just wait twenty minutes," he said, folding the sleeves of his shirt up to his elbows.

Eva decided to come back in half an hour to see what the doctor meant.

So that's what the doctor was talking about, thought Eva. She stood once again before Thirteen's cell, having just come back from lunch break. The outer door was pulled away and even though the audio was off she could clearly see that her Subject was screaming like a wild animal.

It was up and moving, raking its fingernails across its chest as if trying to rip its own heart out.

Thirteen paced the cell, slamming its fists into the wall and shaking its head as if trying to rid itself of a swarm of bees. It doubled over, gripping the sides of its head, its stomach, tearing at its neck. Black streaks marked its face.

Eva frowned and stepped closer to the glass, trying to get a better look. No, those couldn't be tears. Tears weren't the color of soot. But...

It is *crying,* Eva realized, her eyes widening in astonishment. Black liquid streamed from Thirteen's eyes and streaked its face, dripping down its bloody neck and chest. *Black tears...* another sign of past failed experiments. Eva knew that tears were a physical reaction innate in everyone, even Subjects, but as she watched the raw anguish on the other side of the glass she felt a small prick in the dark recesses of her mind. Thirteen looked almost...

Human.

Eva turned on her heel and walked away.

Chapter Five

Thirteen's tears were not the only thing the color of charcoal – its blood was, as well.

It was the result of a recent experiment with silver oxide in the blood. The Subject's iron content had been reduced to fifty percent, and a solution of silver-oxide base had been introduced to its system.

It was called 'forcible anemia' by the medical staff – there had been high hopes for the treatment. They had believed that by reducing the amount of red blood cells in a body, it would starve the Morbus virus and the body would be left unharmed.

The result had not been completely unsuccessful, but the downsides far outweighed the upsides. The Subject had experienced protein deficiency, extreme fatigue, severe chest pain and shortness of breath.

The trial had nearly killed Thirteen, but – like so many times before – it had clung to life and survived. Eva pondered this in the back of her mind as she scanned notes from her clipboard onto the computer screen in front of her. No other Subject she knew of had ever shown such resilience to testing. It was almost as if it had a will to live.

Smiling a bit at her own nonsense, Eva put aside the clipboard and pressed the keys '5' and '7' on the number pad. So far she had counted fifty-seven traces of foreign element in Thirteen's blood and as she was nearing the end of the testing she could not silence the voice in her mind that wondered how the Subject was still alive. It should be a zombie by now, a vegetable, like the rest of the Subjects Beneath. And yet... she smiled. She was fortunate to have Thirteen as a Subject. Never mind the risks that came with it.

"Warden," Eva called. She stood outside the warden's office, feeling as at home Beneath as she had felt in her office a week ago. She knew several of her colleagues disliked going Beneath; it made them feel claustrophobic. One doctor had even claimed it made her feel filthy simply walking down the stairs. But Eva was very adaptable, and changes never bothered her. It was a test lab, and nothing more.

The door opened and Brenton stepped out, his face folded into a perpetual expression of displeasure.

"I want—"

"Yeah, yeah," Brenton interrupted. He lifted his walkie-talkie. "Two bruisers to cell Thirteen," he grumbled. He clipped the walkie-talkie back onto his belt with a decisive shove and stalked back into his office. The door closed with a resounding *bang*.

Eva strode down the twisted hallways, already adjusted to the confusing pattern of corridors. She knew exactly what she wanted to do today, and her brain was already in the Procedure Room prepping before her body arrived at Thirteen's cell.

"Tiger's getting a lot of attention lately," remarked a guard who stood outside the door with two others.

Eva ignored them and pressed in the number pad by the door to gas the Subject before taking it from the cell. She disliked the fact that the 'bruisers' had given Thirteen a nickname. It was too humanizing. It was, in fact, ridiculous. But there was nothing she could do about it except grind her teeth and sigh, so she did not comment but just stood, waiting for the gas to fill the cell.

I know they're afraid of me. I can smell the air change in my cell, and I know I'm going to fall asleep and wake up somewhere else. Somewhere I hate. And I know I'll see the doctor or bruisers, and I know either way it will hurt. This doctor, the sweet-smelling one, is nice to look at. Her hair is long and smooth and her eyes are green. I hate her.

Eva decided simply to ignore the presence of the guards inside the room. Dr. Ross had ordered her not to let them leave the Procedure Room after Thirteen's last escape. "It's too dangerous," he had said, frowning at her in a way that made him look like a rubber figurine. "The doctor before you met with an *unfortunate* end." He had emphasized the last two words, and Eva remembered what the previous guards had said.

"...*turned inside-out on the floor.*"

So Eva put up with them, and after ten or so minutes they were merely pieces of furniture, albeit armed furniture. They were not her focus, and truthfully, neither was the Subject. It was finding a cure. A cure for the cruelest killer known to man, a killer that wiped out anyone it came across without mercy – men, women, and children died at its touch. It was a horrible death, and it was a death Eva had seen take her mother, father, and twin brother.

A familiar rush of anger and impatience flooded through her veins. She strode over to one of the glass cabinets lining the walls and pulled a sealed vial off a shelf. It had no official name other than J-12. It was a virus that acted much like Morbus, and had proven helpful in testing prototype cures. It was non-contagious and the effects were not as deadly as Morbus, lasting only six hours at the longest.

Eva tore off the seal and filled a syringe with the blue-tinted liquid, her lips pressed tightly together and her eyes narrowed. It could take years – decades, even – to find a cure, and what if Morbus struck again? All it took was for someone to walk through a quarantined area, an area where strains of the virus might still linger, and the globe would suffer years of horror all over again.

Time was of the essence, and it was something none of her colleagues seemed to understand. They labeled her 'determined,' and sometimes even 'obsessed.' She did not care. She would find the cure, and she would find it before Morbus struck again.

She walked over to the operation table with determined steps. Thirteen watched her with wide, hate-filled eyes as she pierced his arm with the needle and noted the dozens upon dozens of tiny scars where needles had pierced him before.

She watched as fifty ccs of a mock-virus entered her Subject's bloodstream and wondered how many more trials, how many more errors would be made before she found success.

Success begins with a first step; she reminded herself as she withdrew the needle and placed the syringe in the sharps container. *And a second, and a third, until you reach your goal.*

She leaned against a worktable a few feet away from Thirteen to watch and wait for the J-12 to take effect. It generally took five minutes, so she estimated three for Thirteen. Eva looked away from the Subject and saw that the guards by the door stood stiffly, their backs ramrod-straight and their weapons raised in anticipation.

They must make themselves sore, if they're that tense all the time, Eva thought to herself with an amused smile. "Gentlemen, there is no need to worry," she said easily. "As you may have noticed when you strapped the Subject in, today and every other day, escape is impossible."

"It's been done before," was the glum response from one of the guards.

"Not since the new precautions were instated," Eva replied, folding her arms. "I doubt anything could escape those confines."

Her only answer was the most unenthusiastic "Yes, ma'am" she had ever heard. What was she to expect? These guards were no more than walking weapons. They had probably never been trained in science, logic, or physics; they had no education above 'head, neck, and chest.' Their minds had not been enlightened with finer education; therefore they were really beneath her notice. *I wonder why I bother;* she mused, and returned her attention to the Subject.

She could already see its muscles straining as the J-12 set in. This was the first of the symptoms. The following would be a raging fever, hallucinations, spasms, difficulty breathing, violent urges and often paralysis. Unfortunately, J-12 mimicked the Morbus so well that the paralysis was often permanent and the Subjects were disposed of, as there was no use in experimenting on the physically dead.

The monitor on the screen began to beep more rapidly as Thirteen's heart rate accelerated from low nineties well into the hundreds, steadily climbing. She watched as its temperature rose from standard Subject-temp 93 to 95, 100, 105 – it balanced out at 107 degrees.

Very high, but still controlled – nothing to worry about yet. Thirteen's eyes grew brighter and brighter until Eva could not look directly at them for fear of retinal damage.

She could see it was straining against the thick straps that held it to the table, but she was not prepared for the scream that erupted from the throat of the tormented Subject. She jumped, knocking the clipboard off the table beside her.

"Don't shoot," she called to the guards, holding a hand out as a warning gesture.

Their faces were as tight as Thirteen's restraints, but they nodded. They gripped their guns so hard their knuckles were white.

Eva wondered if all guards turned this trigger-happy over time. At least they were holding themselves back. She bent down and picked up the fallen clipboard, wishing she had had the forethought to bring earplugs. In the Procedure Room, at least, Thirteen was usually quieter than this.

Veins stood out on the Subject's neck and arms, and it did not sound as if it was going to take a breath before it suffocated. Eva looked over at the monitor again. Its temperature had risen to 108 degrees, and its heart rate pounded at a steadily rapid 98.

She had not given it an overly large dose, especially for this creature's metabolism. She pressed her lips together and fervently wished for the symptoms to die down before Thirteen died of heart failure, exhaustion, or trauma as previous J-12-injected Subjects had.

Finally, after what felt like an hour but was, if the clock was accurate, only seventeen minutes, Thirteen's screaming became gasps so desperate that its chest expanded as far as the straps would let it with every breath.

The monitor showed the Subject's heart rate slowing back down, and the digits showing its temperature went from 108 to 107, then 106.

The monitor stabilized; heart rate 80, temperature 105. It would probably remain this way until tomorrow, which would give Eva a good idea of how this Subject would handle the J-12 – if it was not paralyzed.

"Okay," she said to the guards. "I'm going to leave it here overnight and come back in the morning."

The guards nodded. "Yes, ma'am."

"Don't forget to tell the other guards when you change shifts," she told them as she washed her hands thoroughly in the sink and dried them on a roll of paper towels.

"Yes, ma'am," they chorused again. They followed Eva out of the room and shut the doors. Eva flicked the lights in the room off and strode confidently down the hall, unbuttoning her lab coat as she went.

First step, mom and dad, first step.

Chapter Six

I can see through the darkness. I hear the bruisers talking outside; their voices low, whispering. I burn. I have burned before, but never this hot. I wonder if I will turn to ashes. I would be freed.

No.

When I die, it will be my own choice. Not the choice of a bruiser or a doctor. Especially not the new doctor. She is so small and fragile. I could tear her apart, kill her the same way I killed the male before her.

But I won't.

I will be gentle with the female, so she will know that gentleness does not matter if pain and death are the results. I will take her throat in my hands and I will kill her slowly; softly.

My instincts tell me not to wait, they tell me to escape tonight. I am alone, I can't escape – the burning doesn't stop –

She will be back in the morning.

I have to get free.

Eva slept well that night, her head pressed firmly into her pillow and the blankets drawn up around her shoulders. Though temperatures throughout the compound were well-regulated, they did not change the fact that Northern Alaska was cold at night. Her brain was tired from examining and re-examining Thirteen's data charts.

She had to know what she was working with before she could progress… and she was still years away…

The alarm clock forced her awake at 5:45 am. Used to her schedule, Eva turned the alarm off, yawned, and climbed out from underneath her burial mound of blankets. She woke up quickly, a habit her father had taught her from a young age.

"A morning spent sleeping in is a morning wasted," he would say, and Eva had taken his advice to heart.

These last few mornings, Eva realized her first thoughts were about Thirteen. *I wonder if it will be stabilized,* or *I wonder if I should wait before giving it Sterium,* or *how long has it been since it was given a vitamin injection?* She shook her head and smiled as she pulled jeans and a white button-up shirt from her closet. The life of a doctor... she would probably end up marrying another doctor, and instead of children they would have research projects. The thought almost made her laugh.

The morning-shift guards outside the Procedure Room straightened as Eva approached. "Good morning, doctor," they replied.

"Open the door, please," she said, without bothering to tell them good morning. They were not paid to exchange pleasantries, and neither was she.

The guards nodded and the one on the left quickly pulled the large door open to admit her. "Would you like us to remain outside?"

"That will be fine for now, thank you," said Eva. She doubted the Subject was awake or coherent now, anyway. Even if it was, the paralysis should not have worn off yet. She turned on the light switch by the door and lifted an extra lab coat from the hook on the wall. She glanced over at Thirteen as she buttoned the coat up. It was still unconscious, its eyes closed, its breathing only slightly more rapid than usual. Eva smiled. She had a long list of experimental procedures to go through before her furlough – how much could she cram into two weeks?

She pushed some of Thirteen's hair away from its forehead, her skin protected by a thin layer of latex. *I really ought to do something with this so it won't get in the w* –

Thirteen's eyes flew open, burning coals in a face that held so much hatred it actually frightened Eva. She opened her mouth to scream and realized – she couldn't.

Thirteen's hand was around her throat.

How?

Thirteen sat up, every shifting muscle obvious under his scarred, pale skin. Eva thought wildly, gripping the fingers around her neck and trying to pry them away. "Lis-listen," she choked, the words a hoarse imitation of her normal voice. Her vision began to swim, peppered with black and white spots. "J-just…" she couldn't finish.

The black spots began to grow larger, bleeding around the edges of her vision and inward. Her lungs felt as if they were going to explode; stabbing pains attacked her.

Thirteen dropped her. She banged her side and shoulder on the steel table and rolled when she hit the hard floor. Her vision cleared in a burst of color and she gasped once, twice, three times.

Thirteen had collapsed to the ground and lay still.

"Doctor Stewart!"

It was the guard who had told her 'good morning' only minutes before. Eva let him help her up, a groan hissing through her teeth.

"Thank you," she managed in a strangled voice. Her throat felt as if a match had been dropped down it, and her legs could barely hold her up.

The guard helped her to a table and let her sit down on it. "You should go see the medic," he said in a concerned tone.

Again, thought Eva, but nodded in agreement.

The guard looked over at the limp body of Thirteen on the floor. "I apologize for having to tranq Tiger," he said. "But—"

"You – you saved m-my life," Eva managed to rasp out. "Thank you."

This is the second time Thirteen has escaped, tried to kill me, and been tranquilized, thought Eva, her scattered mind trying to re-collect itself. *I can't believe this. This is unheard of.* At least no one had been killed.

How did it escape its restraints? No Subject should be intelligent enough to do that, let alone have enough strength. Thirteen was no ordinary Subject. It had to have mental power left…

Even as she was escorted into the medic's office and a concerned-looking nurse hurried over, Eva could not wait to test her theory.

Chapter Seven

The doctor is gone. I wonder if I killed her. I don't think I did – the bruisers talk about it when I kill people. Is killing wrong? I feel like I shouldn't do it, but the doctors do it all the time. Is it different when you're killing real people and not non-humans? That's what I am. A non-human. The last doctor told me. He didn't think I was listening. The female doctor was so fragile; more fragile than I thought she would be. I wanted to make her stop hurting me, but then I saw her eyes when I tried to kill her. I smelled her fear – she was as frightened as I was.

Does she hurt, too?

"A fractured rib?" Eva stared at the nurse in front of her. "How? The Subject didn't even – oh." She shook her head and sighed. "It *did* drop me pretty hard, and I hit my shoulder and side on the table."

The nurse gave her a sympathetic smile. "At least it isn't a terribly bad injury," she said, patting Eva's shoulder. "How is your throat doing?"

"Better," said Eva, wincing as she swallowed. Her voice still sounded like it was coming from the mouth of an eighty-year-old, but the swelling had been reduced with an NSAID recently developed by WorldCure. So far, it seemed to be doing its job.

"Good. Now, your fracture is just a small one, but I would still suggest taking it easy for a few days."

Eva nodded and stood up. Come to think of it, her side did hurt a little bit. Hard to believe it was a fracture, though. She took the bottle of anti-inflammatory pills from the nurse and left the office with slow, cautious steps.

Dr. Ross looked surprised when Eva showed him the nurse's report. "I'll write you a three-day leave," he agreed. "I'm sorry this happened," he added, looking grave.

Eva nodded her thanks and had her hand on the door to leave – *I have to get to my office* – when Dr. Ross said, "Doctor Stewart."

She turned to face him expectantly, hoping whatever he had to say was short so she could write a report.

Dr. Ross sighed and pinched the bridge of his nose. "If this happens one more time... Eva, I'll have Thirteen put down."

Eva opened her mouth to protest, but Dr. Ross held up a hand. "It's too dangerous," he said firmly. "You've only been a Handler for five days, and your Subject has already tried to kill you twice. This is my final warning." He held her gaze, as if daring her to object.

Eva took a step forward. "Doctor, Thirteen is too valuable to—"

"Doctor Stewart, I said it was *final*." Dr. Ross glared at her, but the glare melted into an expression of weariness that seemed to draw all the lines on his face downward. "I agree, Thirteen is valuable. That's the only reason we haven't already disposed of it. But surely you of all people understand the damage it could do. *Has* done. No – this is its last chance."

Eva arrived at her quarters in a huff. Of course Thirteen was dangerous and yes, it had killed a few people, but it was the best test Subject the facility had! Couldn't Dr. Ross see that it was worth a few risks?

Eva clenched her hands into fists and gave a faint gasp when her rib reminded her of its delicate condition. "Urrgh!" she gave a half-shriek, half-growl and yanked the elastic from her hair, never minding the sting on her scalp as a few strands of hair came out with it.

Three days of nothing stretched before her. Well, she would put the time to good use – there were files to be read more in-depth, and she could schedule next week's procedures ahead of time. Maybe a fractured rib was not so bad after all.

Eva sat on her bed the next morning, eating a late breakfast of sausage, scrambled egg-replacement, and coffee when her phone rang. She picked it up off the mattress. "Hello, Doctor Eva Stewart," was her automatic greeting.

"Eva, my dear!"

"Professor!" She leaned back on the pillows in a half-reclining position as a wide smile lifted her face. "How are you?"

"Fine, fine, fine, as usual, but I called to ask how *you* were!" Professor Albert Pock had a voice as loud and cheerful as a teakettle's whistle.

"Oh... I'm fine," she said carefully.

"Eva..."

She sighed, but her smile did not leave. Prof always *could* see through her. "I fractured my rib. Nothing serious, just a couple days off work."

"Fractured! How?"

"I wasn't careful enough securing Subject Thirteen's restraints, I guess."

"The Subject attacked you?" Professor Pock's voice was horrified.

"It isn't just me," said Eva hastily, hoping to calm the Professor down before he got too excited. "It doesn't like anyone."

"Ah. Non-discriminating attacks." Professor Pock's voice was dry. "That's infinitely better."

"It wasn't as bad as it sounds," Eva laughed. She took a bite of sausage before it became too cold to be edible. "Technically, the Subject didn't fracture my rib at all; it dropped me and I hit the table too hard."

"I warned you, working for WorldCure was a dangerous business." Eva could hear a faint 'ting-ting-ting' noise in the background, like a tiny silver bell, and knew the professor was stirring a cup of tea.

"I know." She took a sip of her own lukewarm coffee, wishing she could be having a hot cup of Earl Gray at the professor's home.

A blustery sigh came through the speaker. "Eva, I know we have many differences of opinion and viewpoint—"

"Yes, professor," said Eva warmly.

"—and I know you don't hold much with religion—"

"Also correct."

"—but I'm praying for you anyway," the professor finished, "every night before bed, and occasionally over tea and term papers."

Eva was silent for a moment. "Thank you, Pocky," she said finally, using the affectionate nickname she had given her mentor during her freshman year. "I don't mind."

"Good!" exclaimed the professor, "because even if you did mind, I'd do it in spite of you."

Eva laughed. "I know you would."

"Oh, bother, Eva – my doorbell is ringing incessantly. Probably another high-hopes student with another blasted term paper. I ought to go answer it before my ears have a permanent ring."

"All right," said Eva, a little sadly. She missed hearing the professor's British voice every day, but since graduation, she had been so busy with work... "I miss you. Call again soon, all right?"

"Indubitably," was the congenial answer, accompanied by a loud sniff. "Take care of yourself, my girl."

"I will," she promised. "Good-bye."

The call ended.

Professor Albert Pock was considered something of an eccentric radical throughout the nation's academic circles. He had once been well-known and well thought of for his unique approach to biology and psychology. But one day, he had made a shocking statement on world-wide television –

"I believe in the sanctity of human life under God. All of it. I believe the Human Rights

Institution was wrong when they declared those born with strong mental and physical defects 'non-humans.' They are just as human as you or I, and have been since the egg. I will not support the Non-Human Act."

He had been asked to step down from his position the next day. After that, he worked in a pharmaceutical company for years until his retirement, and now spent his time tutoring college students and writing essays for scientific Christian organizations.

Eva knew she was fortunate to have met him and loved him like a grandfather, but they disagreed in more areas than she could count. Professor Pock was religious, she was not. She did not believe in 'God', and would find herself arguing with the professor during nearly every conversation. They disagreed on politics, the morality and ethics of scientific experimentation, and on what kinds of tea should be drunk throughout the day.

Professor Pock even believed that HRI-classified 'non-humans' were still people, not natural biological mistakes accepted by everyone as a part of life. Eva disagreed with that as well.

Still, it had been good to hear a familiar voice, and in spite of their arguments Eva loved the professor dearly. She wished she could drive down to Anchorage and see him, but that would have to wait until her furlough.

Pocky had not liked her decision to work for WorldCure, and did not mind saying so at every possible opportunity. "It's an evil institution, Eva," he had told her on that fateful day eleven months ago, when her application had been accepted.

"Mark my words; you'll see things you wish you could forget. It will change you, Eva. It changed me."

Chapter Eight

The doctor must be dead. She has not experimented on me for days. I am punished for killing her, but I deserve it. I deserve more pain. I killed the green-eyed doctor with the long hair. My eyes leak when I think about it. I wonder if this means I am sad. I feel sad...

"Warden!" Eva knocked rapidly on the office door. She heard a mumbled "Coming" and the door opened to reveal Brenton, his customary bulldog expression the same as it had been three days ago.

"Oh," he said in a voice bereft of any emotion, "it's you."

Eva bristled, but brushed past his unenthusiastic greeting. "I need—"

"Bruisers," Brenton interrupted with a sigh. His walkie-talkie was already halfway to his mouth. "Thirteen'll be in the prepping room; I'll have some boys meet you there."

Eva frowned. Dr. Ross had mentioned the prepping room the first time Thirteen had escaped under her handling. "What is the 'prepping room'?" she asked before the Warden could call the bruisers.

He looked at her as if she was the sole bane of his existence and paged, "Two bruisers to my office; escort *Doctor* Stewart to the prep room."

Eva folded her arms in annoyance and waited for the guards to arrive. They must have been close by, because it was less than a minute before they appeared. They were exceptionally tall and heavy-set. Eva guessed the smaller guards never dealt with Subject Thirteen for practical reasons.

She followed them down the hall until they came to what looked like a doorway without a door. The taller of the guards unclipped his ID card from his thick utility belt and swiped it through a slot in the wall. The air in the doorway shimmered like the horizon on a hot summer day, but only for a moment.

Eva realized that there had been a faint hum in the air before the card-swipe that was now gone. *It must be an electrical barrier,* she thought. These were generally safer than your average door.

She stepped through first and turned on the light switch. The result was one small bulb high in the middle of the ceiling flickering on with a protesting *snap.*

The room was not at all what Eva had expected. It was spacious, with only four cement walls and a concrete floor. A pillar, also cement, rose floor-to-ceiling on one side, and a rack of what appeared to be chicken wire hung from another. It was strung with tools, as if someone had raided a home improvement store.

On its knees, chained by its wrists to the far wall, was Subject Thirteen.

"What… is 'prepping,' exactly?" asked Eva, unmoving. This was *her* Subject. Hers! And they had used it without her permission.

"Prep's just slang," explained the guard who had swiped his card at the door. "The Subjects are kept in line this way. Not that many of them need it anymore."

"Except Tiger," corrected the other.

"Right, 'cept Tiger."

Eva carried herself across the room with brisk strides and stood two yards away from Thirteen. The Subject seemed to be asleep or unconscious, but Eva was not willing to take any chances again.

She sank into a crouched position, looking it over. It was thinner than it had been three days ago, and it looked as if it had been thoroughly roughed up by the guards. Perhaps 'bruisers' was an apt name for them. "Has it been fed?"

"No, ma'am. Doctor Ross stopped its System Treatment as punishment for its attack. Okay by me, though. Tiger doesn't put up much of a fight when he's weak."

Eva looked up sharply at the guard. "*It*, not 'he,'" she corrected icily. *You'd think he was the Professor.* "Wake it up," she added, rising.

Without so much as a breath of hesitation, the guard drove the butt of his tranquilizer into Thirteen's temple.

The Subject's head knocked to the side, then lifted, eyes flickering open. They glared unswervingly at the guard before landing on Eva, and to her surprise they opened wide, staring.

"What, did you think you killed me?" she asked aloud with a faint snort.

The Subject's breath caught in its throat and it glanced, wild and wide-eyed, from Eva, to the guards, to Eva again.

"Tiger probably didn't think you'd show up again," said the guard behind her. "It killed the last one."

"So I was told."

"Bloody mess, that one. Not sure how he did it."

"How *it* did it."

"Yes, ma'am."

Eva straightened. "Tranq it and take it to the Procedure Room," she ordered briskly. *Sorry to disappoint you, Thirteen, but I don't go down so easily.*

The doctor is alive! I didn't kill her! I can see bruises on her neck from my fingers, but she is alive. I feel better. She is going to hurt me again. The bruisers are taking me to the Procedure Room. I won't hurt her again. Somehow, I'll keep myself from hurting her.

Thirteen was strapped to the table with wide eyes, watching Eva's every move. She found it a little bit unnerving, but shrugged it off as she chose the proper procedure tools and pulled on a pair of latex gloves. She was still careful about her rib; the medic said it was healing quickly and the fracture was next-to-nothing, but it was best not to take chances.

"Brenton issued an order to all the guards the day Tiger tried to kill you," said one of the guards suddenly. His loud voice startled Eva and made her whirl around to glare at him.

"What orders?"

"Under no circumstances are we to leave you alone with him – it, I mean." The guard coughed uncomfortably and looked at his partner, who shrugged and cocked his tranquilizer.

Eva opened her mouth, and then shut it with a snap. She understood the warden's reasons and therefore did not blame him, but she knew his decision stemmed from more than the incident. He saw her as someone too young and altogether too inexperienced to conduct this kind of research, especially on the facility's most dangerous Subject. She wondered if Dr. Ross could have the warden replaced.

"Fine," she snipped with a toss of her head. "Stand by the door and don't interfere." She knew she did not need to add the bit about interfering, but it made her feel more in control.

Once again, as was procedure, she pushed the cable into the back of Thirteen's neck and watched as the monitor screen came to life. Apparently, the lack of System Treatments would have to be remedied before she could operate.

All Subjects were 'fed' intravenously on a regular twenty-four-hour cycle with a liquid mixture of proteins, vitamins, and minerals necessary for keeping them alive. It kept them from having too much or too little of any one thing, and the mixture was also safe for working around. It did not get in the way of procedures.

Eva pulled an IV stand over and filled a plastic bag with the Treatment. It was clear and could easily have been mistaken for water at a glance. She pulled one of the straps around

Thirteen's arm down and plugged the IV in, allowing it to drip for five minutes before pulling it back out.

The Subject did not move while she 'fed' it, but continued to watch her with eyes that were not curious or bewildered or angry, but a subtle mixture of all three. It seemed calm – calmer than it had been before. Its heart rate was not elevated high enough to activate the phosphorescence in its system, anyway.

She noticed faint gray smudges down its face – it had been crying again. She had never seen such an emotional Subject before, not even in research documentaries. This made her smile; a thin, pleased sort of smile. *And to think, Doctor Ross wanted to get me another Subject.*

The doctor does not smell like sweet evil today. She smells different – clean. Fresh. I like it. I feel stronger after the System Treatment, and it scares me. What if I lose myself again? Would I be able to escape the Table? I don't think so. I don't want to. I don't want to wake up and find more blood on my hands. I don't want to hear the bruisers talking about me like they do after... it happens. I don't want to be punished. I don't want to deserve it.

Eva did not like Thirteen's face when it held so much expression. It felt wrong, and she was tempted to give it a sedative... but that would interfere with her work. She glanced over at it again and found those penetrating eyes still watching her. Thirteen's jaw shifted to the side a little, as of it was pondering her. A strand of pale hair fell over its forehead, and she marched over and pushed it out of the way with an irritated swipe.

Why is everything getting under my skin today? She clenched her teeth, shut her eyes, and took a deep breath. *One... two... three...* when she reached ten, she opened her eyes again.

Thirteen still watched her, but its lips were pressed together, eyebrows drawn slightly in a faint frown. It probably wondered what she was doing.

Wondered? It shouldn't be smart enough to 'wonder'! Eva picked up a small, sharp silver blade with determination. She was going to stop being ridiculous, and she was going to get this procedure over with.

Chapter Nine

Eva frowned at the monitor screen. She had a needle placed well into the side of Thirteen's head. It had injected a zero-solution that would bond to any foreign element in the Subject's brain and feed its information to the monitor.

"I didn't think I'd have so much to study before I could really go to work," she muttered aloud as the results ran across the screen, one after another. She opened and closed her fist, waiting for the scan to complete itself.

Most of the elements she recognized. Failed NSAID prototypes, stimulators, sedatives – but there was one name that puzzled her. *Cortoxica.* Eva wrote the name down on her clipboard, frowning. She had never heard of 'Cortoxica' before; she would have to search the computers.

She glanced over at the Subject, surprised to see that it was still awake. Most creatures, animal or human, would have passed out by now. Its jaw was clenched and its hands were in fists, eyes focused on the ceiling.

"Stubborn, aren't you?" Eva shook her head. She had never seen such obstinacy in a Subject.

Those eyes, so piercingly, purely blue, looked at her. Eva felt a small prickle on the back of her neck and looked back down at the clipboard. She erased and re-wrote a line for no reason other than she wanted something to focus on besides the Subject. *Why is it making me uncomfortable? It's a Subject, for pity's sake!*

Two guards stood at the far end of the room by the door, guns at the ready. She was perfectly safe...

She wiped tiny bits of eraser off the paper and looked back up. Thirteen's eyes were closed now; black liquid pooled in the corner of its eyes.

Without quite knowing why, Eva walked over the refrigerator and pulled out a bottle of water. Unscrewing the cap, she walked back over to the procedure table, still situated horizontally. She checked to make sure the straps were secure – it had become almost automatic over the past forty-eight hours.

The Subject's eyes were open again and it was looking at her, eyebrows drawn in worry and fear. If it could have spoken, Eva had the feeling it would have asked, "What are you going to do to me?"

Eva raised the table a little higher and poured a thin stream of water into Thirteen's mouth. She felt strange doing it, as if she was caring about a non-human – something strictly against what she believed. However, there was no harm in giving it hydration.

Thirteen drank cautiously at first, like someone who was dying of thirst but thought the water might be poisoned. But after the first hesitant swallow, he drank until Eva pulled the bottle away.

"There," she said aloud. "That should hold you." For a moment she berated herself for addressing the Subject as 'you,' but she conceded that she had even called her dog 'you' in high school.

She walked away from the table and stood in front of the monitor, arms crossed, reading the words that ran down it like a grocery list. *Cortoxica.* What on earth was that?

She left the Procedure Room, giving the guards strict orders to keep an eye on the Subject until she got back. They answered with a loud, robotic "Yes, ma'am" and she left, jogging up the stairs and emerging into the startling white of the main floor.

After being in darkness and dim light for so long, the effect was almost blinding. She hurried to the computer terminal and sat down. It was an irregular time to use a computer; most of the staff at the facility was busy and she was left alone.

She pulled up the system's files and searched for the word 'Cortoxica.' She was surprised to find that it was a level-two file type – if Dr. Ross had not updated her card when she became a Handler, she would not have been able to open the file.

There was only one mention of Cortoxica, and it was in a report from Dr. Ross himself. She felt her eyes growing wide as she read the words on the screen. *"...an experimental drug designed to inhibit neural-pathway and cognitive connections, particularly in the area of thought-to-speech. A safety precaution..."*

She stopped reading and looked at the date on the file. The report had been written sixteen years ago... that meant that Subject Thirteen had been – what, eight at the time? Confused and brimming with questions, Eva turned the computer off and left the room.

Thirteen had been given a drug to prevent it from forming thoughts into speech. Eva knew what this meant, what it *had* to mean.

Sixteen years ago, Thirteen had been capable of speaking.

"Pocky?"

"Eva, duck! How's your rib?"

"It's fine, but—"

"How is Thirteen?"

"Well," said Eva slowly, "that's actually what I wanted to talk to you about."

"Oh?" The professor's voice became cautious. "How so?"

"It's…" Eva took a deep breath. "What do you know about Cortoxica?"

The other end of the phone was so silent that Eva wondered if he was still there. "Professor?"

"Let me turn the question, Eva. What do *you* know about Cortoxica?" The elderly man's voice, ordinarily so jovial and warm, trembled.

"Well, I was running some tests on Thirteen's brain and it showed up on the monitor. I searched the computer files and found only one record of Cortoxica. Doctor Ross used it on Thirteen sixteen years ago."

"And?"

Eva glanced out the office window into the hallway. Something about this call felt clandestine, but she was not sure why. "I know it's an experimental drug Doctor Ross was using to keep Thirteen... from... *talking.*"

The phone was silent again.

"Pocky?"

More silence.

"Pocky, I know you worked here when this report was filed. Did Doctor Ross ever tell you what he was up to? Do you know what this is about?"

"Eva..." the voice on the other end sounded pleading, almost desperate. "Eva, this is... this is bigger than you think. Quite frankly, I doubt you would believe me and even more frankly, I think it would be wise for you to stay out of it."

That was the wrong thing to say, Pocky. "I'm all ears."

A gusty sigh blew into her ear. "I'm warning you."

"I am warned. Now please, Professor, tell me what this is all about!" Eva's voice was high with curiosity, frustration, and worry. If Pocky was this concerned... Then again, he tended to over-react where WorldCure was concerned.

"There's something I want you to do first, Eva, before I tell you anything more. Will you do it?"

Eva rolled her eyes. "Sure, Pocky, what is it?"

"Promise me."

"I promise I'll do it!"

"Eva—"

"I said I'd do it, all right?" Eva screeched as loud as she dared into the phone.

The professor's voice was resigned. "I want you to go to storage unit six—"

"Where is that?" Eva interrupted.

"It's Beneath – when you walk down the stairs, you know how one branch leads straight ahead and one goes to the left?"

"Yes."

"Take the left branch and go down it; you will see doors with the words 'storage unit' and a number on them."

"Right. So I find the sixth one. And then what?"

"Somewhere inside, probably in a cooling unit, will be a drug called X-C. It will probably be in a small box – I doubt anyone has touched it since I was there."

"Why—"

"You'll see, and anything you don't I'll explain after you go through with this." The professor sounded impatient now, like a parent dealing with an obstinate child. "Take the X-C, and give it to Subject Thirteen."

Eva narrowed her eyes in suspicion. "Pocky, I don't know what you're up to, but it doesn't sound healthy for my career."

"Do you want to know what's going on over there or not?" The question exploded in her ear.

Taken aback, Eva stammered "I – I do. Okay. I'll do it. Fine."

"Good," said the professor, sounding more relaxed. "And I apologize for shouting. Now, administer the X-C to Thirteen. Call me later tonight. Can you do it?"

"Yes," sighed Eva. "I can do it."

"Good. Be careful, duck."

"I will," Eva promised, and hung up.

Chapter Ten

Eva walked briskly down the stairs, shivering in the cold. She should have gotten used to the lowered temperature by now, but she hadn't. She had been away from the Procedure Room for almost an hour – she hoped the guards had not taken Thirteen back to its cell without her permission.

She took the left hallway and walked until she found the door labeled 'Storage Room 6.' She swiped her card and walked in, trying desperately not to turn and run back out. She had never done anything quite like this before – it felt dangerous, out-of-bounds.

"Come on, Eva," she said aloud. "Pocky wouldn't have you do anything dangerous." *I hope.* She searched three freezers before finding the X-C. She had almost given up, but there it was – a box in the bottom corner. She pulled it out and opened it. Inside were six vials filled with a pinkish-red liquid the color of a melted cherry popsicle.

She pulled out one of the vials, shoved it into the deep pocket of her lab coat, put the box back, and closed the lid of the cooling unit with trembling hands. The walk back to the Procedure Room seemed to last a lifetime, and she had to keep fighting the urge to break into a sprint.

The guards straightened when they saw her and Eva was relieved to note that Thirteen was right where she had left it. *As if they would dare remove it. What has got you so paranoid, Eva?* She pulled on a pair of gloves and filled a syringe with the X-C, casting nervous glances at the guards.

As nonchalantly as she knew how, Eva walked over to Thirteen. She pushed some of its tousled pale hair from the side of its head and took a deep breath.

She inserted the needle.

Thirteen's eyes widened and a quiet whimper escaped its closed lips.

The monitor began to beep faster as the Subject's heartbeat escalated wildly. Eva could feel her palms dampening beneath her gloves. *Pocky, what did you ask me to do?*

"Take it back to its cell," said Eva, motioning toward the guards. She watched as they slipped thick cords through the buckles on its harness before releasing it from the table restraints. Thirteen did not protest, but stumbled and nearly fell near the door.

The guards jerked the Subject upright and pulled it down the hall. As soon as they were out of sight, Eva pulled her cell phone out and checked to see if there was any reception.

One bar.

Eva closed the door and dialed the professor. It rang twice before it was picked up and she spoke before he could. "I gave it the X-C. Now what?"

"How did it react?"

"The Subject?"

"Yes! Thirteen!"

"Elevated heart rate, some pain. Nothing unusual, really, but I had it taken back to its cell."

"Wait. Wait, observe it. Call me tonight. And Eva?"

"Yes?"

"Don't leave it alone."

"It seems to be acting up a little, ma'am," said one of the guards as Eva approached cell thirteen.

"It's fine," she assured them, even as she wondered if it really *was* fine. "Leave it."

The guards nodded and walked briskly away toward the Warden's office. Eva glanced at the door, wondering whether or not Pocky had been serious when he asked her not to leave the Subject alone.

She glanced down at her watch. She looked back at the closed steel door and chewed on her lower lip for several seconds before turning and walking in the opposite direction. *Sorry, Pocky, but I have a report to turn in.*

It took Eva nearly an hour to finish her report from yesterday and get it turned in to Dr. Ross's office. She was brisk with him, saying no more than was necessary. She felt she was going behind his back, and as a result she was clipped and short with her superior.

"Is anything wrong, Doctor Stewart?" he asked, eyeing her from behind his desk.

She glanced at him briefly before walking out the door. "No, sir." She closed the door before he could ask any more questions and took off down the hall, looking down at her watch again.

A pang of guilt stabbed her and she found herself Beneath a minute later. She felt bad for having disobeyed Pocky. It wasn't as if she had promised she would stay with Thirteen – it felt ridiculous – but she did love the professor.

Her footsteps echoed off the concrete walls as she approached cell thirteen. She typed in the number to open the outer door. It slid with a grating hiss, pulling back inch by inch. Eva cupped her hands around her eyes and peered in, wishing there was more light. "Where are you?" she muttered.

There – she saw a flashing light in the other end of the cell. A serial number – and eyes! Thirteen was going crazy in the back corner, thrashing and slamming against the walls. *Why is it staying back there?* Eva angled her head, trying to see through the thick sheet of plastiglass.

The guards had hooked the cords from Thirteen's harness to thick rings on the back wall. The Subject grabbed at the walls, sliding tense, splayed fingers down the wall as if trying to peel the cement away. Suddenly it jerked to the side, but was snapped back by the three-foot leash.

Eva turned the speaker volume down and switched off the sound barrier. Choking, gasping cries came from inside the cell - Thirteen sounded as if it was being strangled. Eva looked at the number pad by the door.

The Subject was restrained – she had watched it try to tear from its harness, and it had failed. It would be all right to step in for a short moment. Eva turned the sound barrier back on and pressed the numbers on the keypad.

The plastiglass lifted.

Half of her mind told her that this was akin to committing suicide – the Subject had already tried to choke the life out of her twice. But in the other half, Pocky said in a quiet, persuasive voice *"Don't leave it alone."*

I'm shaking, Eva realized as she stepped under the plastiglass and entered the cell. It was colder than the rest of Beneath; she could see her breath fog the air in front of her. Thirteen stood with its forehead resting against the wall, muscles tightened and teeth clenched. Tears like black rain slid down its face, and it did not even seem to realize that someone was in the cell with it. Eva stood, feeling the urge to run out of the cell and close the doors as quickly as possible. *Pocky, I don't know what you were thinking.*

Thirteen yanked its body around and slammed into the wall. Eva winced at the crack as the Subject's head hit the concrete. She took a few tentative steps closer. The Subject appeared dazed; it sank to its knees, arms held to its sides by the harness.

"Hey," said Eva. Her voice sounded as thin as rice paper, so she cleared her throat and spoke louder. "Hey."

Thirteen's head snapped up as if she had fired a gun. It stared at her for a moment; a split second of eye contact. Eva stared back, her breath catching in her throat. Something was on the wall, behind the Subject's head.

As if in a dream, or another reality, she stepped forward without tearing her eyes from the wall. Words. There were words scraped into the wall with – what? Long, white scratches –

Eva's eyes widened. She froze.

"No," she said aloud. Her voice was quiet, but to her it was as loud as cannon fire over a frozen sea. "You couldn't have."

She turned and fled from the cell, her fingers fumbling so badly she could barely type in the code to close the doors.

Eva's head pounded as she staggered up the stairs and made her way to her office. She ran into an orderly but did not even mutter an apology. She hardly noticed. She opened her office door and slammed it shut behind her.

Something had to be wrong – something was wrong with her. She had breathed in a toxic chemical – it wasn't improbable - or – there had to be an explanation.

Because there was no way that she had seen what she thought she had in Thirteen's cell. There was no way words had been written there.

Those words.

It was impossible. No, it was *beyond* impossible.

I've gone insane.

For on the wall of Thirteen's cell, scratched thin and white on the dark concrete, was one phrase.

Just five simple words.

I still have a soul.

Chapter Eleven

"P-Pocky?" Eva gripped her phone with both hands until her palms stung. It had taken her three tries to get the number right.

"Eva?"

"Pocky, what – what is – I don't understand—" The words tumbled out of Eva's mouth as half-formed, incoherent thoughts.

"Eva, what happened?" The professor's voice was urgent and concerned.

"I–I don't know, it..." She hiccupped and found herself laughing and crying at the same time. "I think I'm hysterical."

"There is always a first time," was the grave response.

This somehow had a rationalizing effect on Eva. She took a deep breath and said, "I gave it the X-C."

"...Yes?"

"Like I told you, nothing... that unusual happened."

"Yes. So you said."

"And I left to go file a report." She waited, hoping the professor would not be angry with her. When he did not speak, she continued. "I was gone for a little under an hour. When I came back, I – I went into the cell – it was secured to the wall – the Subject, I mean, and – Pocky, it *wrote!*" Eva felt a fresh supply of tears begin coursing down her face.

"What did it write?" the professor asked, seeming very calm about the whole thing.

"I-It said I still h-have a soul," said Eva, choking back another sob. *Why am I so fractured? It's a non-human! It isn't intelligent enough to write!* "What was the X-C, Pocky? Tell me."

"The X-C was an antidote for the Cortoxica." The professor's words were measured and even.

"But I don't understand why – Pocky, you worked here when Thirteen was brought in, didn't you? What happened?"

"Eva—"

"So help me, if you don't tell me I'm telling Doctor Ross!" Eva shrieked in a burst of emotion. She covered her mouth and looked at the office door. "Please, Prof," she added, softer." I need to know."

"I wish you could come down to Anchorage," said the professor. "It feels so impersonal holding this conversation over the phone."

Eva sniffed and tried to clear her voice. "Yes."

"It's something of a long story. You may want to sit down."

Eva sank into her desk chair. "I'm sitting."

"I'm warning you, Eva. You won't like everything I tell you."

"That's all right..." Eva gave a faint smile. "I already don't like everything you tell me."

"Ahem." Eva heard the familiar delicate ringing of spoon-on-teacup. "Once upon a time – about, oh, twenty-four years ago, a baby was brought in by one of the staff. It was illegitimate, and the biological father did not want to risk a career scandal by exposing the child to the public."

"It was handicapped?" Eva asked, looking out the office windows at the hallway.

"No, Eva. It wasn't."

Eva blinked. "Then how was it labeled a non-human? What was wrong with it?"

"Nothing. It was labeled, just as you said, because the father wanted his affair kept quiet."

Eva's mind spun so fast she felt ill. "You're saying that – that Thirteen was…"

"You can say it, Eva," said the professor gently. "Human. I was there the day it was brought in. I saw the papers and the scans. I held the child."

Eva could not breathe. "What – what about the mother?"

Pocky sighed. "She never knew. She was told the baby died."

"She never – Pocky! How…?"

"The father paid a great deal of money to the HRI to have the newborn labeled a non-human. He brought the baby to WorldCure and it was raised Beneath as a test Subject. All was going smoothly until one day eight years later, when Thirteen tried to ask the guards for help. You see, due to its negligent 'upbringing,' the child's mind developed differently. He was treated like an animal for so long he became one, and never attempted to truly speak until that day.

"That was the day I realized how bad things were, how corrupt WorldCure was, and the HRI. I tried to go public, but the public didn't want to hear it."

"And you were fired, and Thirteen was given Cortoxica to keep it from ever asking for help again," Eva whispered. Suddenly she sat straight up in her chair. "But Doctor Ross is the one who filed the Cortoxica report!"

"That's right," said Pocky, and the weight of his words fell on Eva like a quiet avalanche. "Doctor Ross is Thirteen's father."

Eva thought she might throw up. She felt sick to her stomach. Thirteen was not just an 'it' - Thirteen was a *he*.

"So... the X-C – Thirteen can talk now? Again?" Eva asked, trying to regain some control over the situation.

"If it did its job – which, from what you told me, it appeared to."

"All right." Eva pushed her free hand through her hair, yanking the snags out. "So what do I do now? Does Thirteen know that Doctor Ross is - that he's..."

"He used to know," said Pocky. His tone was sad. "But I don't know how far gone he is now."

He. Not it*. He.* "I can't believe this," Eva moaned, leaning her head on her hand. "You were right."

"I know," said the professor in his dry accent. "Shocking."

"That's not what I meant," said Eva with a distracted laugh that ended abruptly. "Pocky, what about the other Subjects? They're non-humans, aren't they?"

The professor let out a noisy sigh that may have held an exclamation. "Eva, you know I don't believe in the Non-Human Act. They're as human as we are. Most Subjects do have mental or physical handicaps – Thirteen was an illegal case – but I know for a fact that a good deal of those so-called 'non-humans' were born healthy and stable."

"Then how…?"

"WorldCure does not always do things legally, Eva. Money is what they care about, not the good of humanity."

"What should I do?" Eva asked again as desperation rose in her. "Thirteen is my Subject. Should I try talking or reasoning with it – him?"

Silence. Then, "My guess would be that Thirteen is beyond reasoning, at least for the moment. Work with him. Try to gain his trust."

Eva snorted without humor. "He knows me, Pocky. He knows what I've done to him. What can I possibly do to make him trust me? I'm still trying to convince myself this isn't a nightmare!"

"Eva, my girl," said the professor gently, "Thirteen has never even been given a kind look. Love is a word he doesn't even understand. Show it to him, and I guarantee you, he'll react."

Eva stood outside Thirteen's cell again, astounded at how different it felt in the space of an hour. Beyond this door and its plastiglass was a human. How many other Subjects were illegally obtained?

She put the code into the pad and checked to make certain Thirteen was still harnessed to the wall before allowing the plastiglass to rise. She slid her card through a slot on the inside of the cell and it lowered behind her.

She reached back to make sure the tranquilizer was still securely in her waistband. It was. Reassured, she pulled a flashlight from her pocket and turned it on, lighting up the cell with a bluish beam.

It was much like the prepping room, but only a third the size. In the far right corner were a showerhead and a drain on the floor. Bars crossed the ceiling to prevent climbing through the air vent.

Eva took a deep breath and pointed the flashlight toward Thirteen. The Subject slumped against the wall, eyes shut.

"Thirteen?" Eva's voice was quiet and tentative. She may as well have been approaching a wild animal. *I am,* she realized. She took several steps closer, as quiet as she could. "Thirteen? Can you hear me?"

She glanced at the words scored into the wall and shuddered. What if the X-C had been too much for Thirteen? What if he was dead?

She directed the beam back to the Subject and her heart jumped into her throat. His glowing eyes shone brightly in her direction.

"It's me," said Eva carefully. *Of course it's me, and you're probably terrified.*

Thirteen swallowed but did not move.

Deer in the headlights, thought Eva. *A deadly deer.* "Can you understand me?" she asked, pronouncing the words slowly and deliberately.

Thirteen's face was pale in the blue light. The phosphorous in his eyes faded just enough for

Eva to be able to make out his black irises, now cast downward. She noticed the beam from the flashlight was shaking, and gripped it tighter. "Can you…"

"Yes." The voice that answered was hoarse; hesitant and strained, unused for over a decade except to scream. Those eyes, so full of pain – how had she not noticed before? – rose to meet hers. "Please…"

He collapsed to the floor.

Chapter Twelve

I open my eyes and see blue light. My head hurts so much—the doctor gave me something and now I feel ripped apart. I think and the word has a sound, and it's familiar but strange. I'm frightened... someone else is here, behind the blue light. I can smell her. The doctor...

Eva tried to steady her breathing. Thirteen was waking up, struggling to sit upright without the use of its arms. Its – his – breathing was labored; he kept shaking his head violently from side to side as if hearing something strange.

> *Should I speak to him? It looks like he forgot how to really talk – what was he trying to say before? Please what? Maybe I ought to come back later.*

Eva lowered the flashlight and her thumb pressed against the on/off button when Thirteen's head lifted and he looked at her.

Face to face with – Eva's heart skipped a beat. She had never been as frightened as she was right now, not even when Thirteen had tried to kill her before. Because this time, even though he was secured to the wall he was suddenly no longer a Subject – he was the living, breathing contradiction of everything she had been taught.

"Hello," she said softly. Her voice was barely above a whisper. "I'm—"

She broke off as Thirteen's skull cracked against the wall once, twice. A hoarse scream tore from the Subject's throat with so much effort Eva could clearly see the vein on the side of his neck.

"Hey!" she cried, laying the flashlight on the floor. "Stop that! You're going to give yourself a concussion!"

Shaking violently, Thirteen turned his head to look at her again. His lips parted as if he was going to say something, but no words formed.

"Thirteen, I... I don't know if you really understand me or not," said Eva, crouching about two feet away from the other human. "But, um... well." She could feel her articulate speech slipping through her fingers. "Do you remember writing that?" Eva pointed toward the writing on the wall.

Thirteen's eyes followed her finger and took in the phrase with no change in his heavy-eyed, defeated expression.

Eva sat for a moment, taking in the deep frown lines between his eyebrows, the way his also-frowning mouth turned up rather than down at the corners. She let out a loud sigh to cover up what she feared would otherwise be a tearful choke. She looked away and rubbed the back of her neck.

He'll never respond. He's too far gone, and it's partially my fault.

She just sits and watches. She was speaking to me, asking questions. Should I answer? If I do, will they do more tests? I remember now, the last time I spoke. I was just a child, but I never spoke again – now I know I could speak. But what if I do?

Thirteen shut his eyes and pressed his lips together. A pained expression took over his face and he breathed deeply out his nose, as if exhaling her scent. Eva stood up, scooping her flashlight off the floor. Without a word, she walked out of the cell.

"So he didn't respond?"

"Well, he said 'yes' when I asked if he understood me."

"Anything else?" Pocky's voice sounded hopeful. Eva hated to disappoint him.

"He started to say something – please – but passed out. He wouldn't speak at all after that."

Pocky sighed. "His brain is probably under quite a lot of trauma and stress. Give him a bit before going back."

"If I keep trying to make him talk, he's going to think I'm up to something," Eva pointed out.

"An excellent point, but you may have to overlook it. Why don't you talk to him, but don't try to make him talk back. He may get used to it and want to try it for himself."

"Right," said Eva, nodding wearily. "I'll do my best."

As she walked out of her office, tucking her phone back in her pocket, she heard a deep voice behind her.

"Hey."

Startled, she turned and saw a face she had not seen since her second year in college. "Jude," she exclaimed, tucking her hands in her pockets. "What are you doing here?"

He grinned. "Working. Why else would I be here?"

"Well. It's been a long time."

"Three years, thirty-six months, however you want to say it. I prefer 'too long.'" Jude gave her that same wide smile that had melted her heart the first time she saw him. Unfortunately, it had not been enough to keep the relationship glued for long.

She gave him an unenthusiastic smile in return. "What department are you in?"

"Research," he said, rolling his broad shoulders back. "I hear you're a Handler now. Impressive."

"Thank you." She tossed her ponytail over her shoulder. "Good luck."

"Thanks." He winked a gray eye at her and brushed past. "See you around, Eva."

Not if I can help it, she thought sourly.

Perfect. Of all people left on earth who could possibly have joined this *facility of* this *company, it would have to be Jude Harborn. Pocky, if this is God's doing, then He must have a really nasty sense of humor.*

Eva watched as Jude strode away, his tall, broad frame taking up a good deal of the hallway. She did not hate him, per se, but her memories of him weren't pleasant. They had begun dating in her second year of college – he was a year ahead of her, and she had felt flattered that Jude Harborn, the most popular guy on campus, had singled her out to be his girlfriend.

However, it took less than three months for her to realize that a relationship could not survive on charm and good looks. She had confronted him one afternoon. She could still hear their voices, raised in anger.

"Relationship is a two-way street, Jude! You're not holding up your end!"

"You think I'm not trying, Eva? You're the one who's selfish! Why can't you think of anything but your work and that stupid professor?"

"My work is important to me! Unlike you, I plan on graduating with honors!"

"Well, if that's all you care about, then go ahead and graduate! Don't expect me to cheer you on!"

Eva had slapped him.

Jude had shoved her into the wall.

The relationship had ended that day, after three months of a relationship with more lows than highs.

"I can't believe he made it this far," she muttered, glaring faintly as he turned a corner and went out of sight. He had always been intelligent, but during the time she had known him he was more concerned about having fun than seriously studying. Now he was in the Research Department? She allowed herself an ounce of grudging admiration before glancing at her watch. She was going to go to Cell Thirteen one more time before dinner.

Thirteen had to get used to her as much as she had to get used to him.

"Next time I come down here, I'm bringing a sweater," Eva said to herself as she stepped into the cell. She switched her flashlight on, carefully pointing it away from the wall where Thirteen was tied up. *Blinding probably wouldn't do much to further our relationship.* She moved it across the wall, angled downward, to let him know she was coming.

"Thirteen," she called out in a soft voice. She frowned. She saw no glowing eyes, no tattoo. Not even shoulder blade scars. "Thirteen?" She pointed the beam at the wall.

Thirteen was not there.

She spun around and the beam of her flashlight stopped less than two feet away. "There you are," she blurted. "I'm not here to hurt you."

Thirteen looked down at her, the light from her flashlight making his eyes look like a cat in the dark. "You..." his breathing was heavy. Eva realized he was as nervous and frightened as she was, and the thought was oddly comforting.

"What..." he held one hand over his open palm, as if struggling to form a coherent thought. She wondered how it would be to try to speak after sixteen years of nothing. "What... you want?" He dropped his hands with a 'forget that' motion, his eyebrows drawn together.

Eva cleared her throat. "I'm... well, I came down to see you."

His puzzled frown deepened. She saw his jaw clench. "Why?"

"Because... talking would be good for you right now, I think," she said slowly, hoping she would not confuse him further. He looked on the verge of either punching her, or completely ignoring her. "You haven't spoken in so long."

"Spoken." His eyes took on a faraway look as he whispered the word. He was silent for several heartbeats, and then his gaze returned to Eva, sharp and narrow. "Leave."

Take it easy, Eva. Don't try to rush things. "All right." She nodded and backed toward the door, her movements slow so as not to startle him. Thirteen watched her go, and Eva noticed for the first time the dark circles under his eyes.

She dialed the code outside the doors and they slid shut, enclosing the human Subject inside. Eva realized her heart was pounding and she was holding her breath. She regained control of herself and walked to the warden's office.

She walked in without knocking. "Why was Thirteen unhooked from the wall?" she demanded.

Brenton did not even glance up at her. A gun, open and dismantled was spread on the desk in front of him and he was oiling a piece with a rag. "Tiger was prepped a couple hours ago. Don't worry; it'll be fine for your work tomorrow." He wiped studiously, back and forth, until the metal shone.

"Fine," said Eva after a moment, "but when you put it back in its cell, I want your guards to keep the harness on it. They don't always have to chain it to the wall, but the harness must stay on." *If I'm going to be visiting Thirteen regularly, the harness will be a good safety measure.*

"You're the doctor," was the short, snide reply. Brenton glanced up at her with an expression on his face that suggested she was a fly he could not swat away. "Close the door on your way out."

Eva turned on her heel, left the room and pulled the door closed behind her, but paused just before it latched. With a smug smile, she strode down the hallway and back up the stairs.

Chapter Thirteen

Eva hurried Beneath as soon as she finished showering the next morning. She had sped through her commonplace routine, feeling a stomach-fluttering mixture of equal parts trepidation and excitement. Thirteen was speaking – maybe today she could coax him into a conversation!

Whoa, whoa, Eva, hold up, she reminded herself as she reached the bottom of the stairs. *Slow down. Remember what Pocky says. You don't want to scare Thirteen.* She continued walking toward the cell, her steps slowing as she grew nearer. *I wonder if he has a name?* Pocky had not mentioned one – it was very likely that the baby had never been named, seeing as how the mother thought it was dead at birth and Dr. Ross did not seem like the naming sort.

Especially after he lies about the kid, shells out money to have it labeled a non-human, and uses it as a Subject for the next twenty-four years, she added silently, twisting her mouth in distaste. Only a few weeks ago she had known Dr. Ross as an intelligent man and her superior whom she respected. Now, she was almost repulsed by him.

She paused and pretended to look busy as two guards walked past her, laughing so loudly the echo hurt her ears. As soon as they were gone she continued down the hall, fingering the mild painkiller in her pocket. She stood outside Thirteen's cell, wanting to go in but hesitating. Thirteen had only been given a painkiller six times in his entire life. His third Handler had thought it would help him behave; an incentive for good conduct. And it had worked, but not for long – Thirteen had stopped succumbing to the painkiller, to everyone's surprise and nobody's pleasure.

Still, she thought it might make a good peace offering if things turned sour. She slid open the outer door and peered inside to see if it was safe to open the inner door, or if she would have to gas the chamber before entering. She could not see him, so she entered the numbers and waited while gas filled the chamber. She entered thirty seconds later, scanning the cell for Thirteen.

He was in the far corner on the floor, his eyes shut and breathing unusually calm and even. He looked for all the world like he was sleeping peacefully, rather than having been knocked unconscious by a drug.

Eva carefully sat down on the clean concrete floor several feet away and waited for him to wake up. She studied the dark room and felt increasingly disturbed. What would it be like, to grow up in a lightless box of a room with four walls of concrete ringing you in? What would it be like to know that every time the doors slid open, you would be taken for surgery, experimentation, or... *prepping.*

Eva lifted her head, staring at the opposite wall with wide eyes. *Eva, you're so stupid!* She balled her hands into fists and hit the hard floor in frustration. She knew that 'prepping' was the politically correct term for 'beating into submission,' but it had not even entered her mind yesterday. She remembered speaking to Brenton and felt a blush of shame crawl up her neck. *I didn't even consider…*

She heard a faint groan to her left and turned to face Thirteen as he awoke. His eyes, which were looking away from her, seemed to be struggling to stay open. Eva wondered if he did not know she was there – and then Thirteen lifted his head higher, took a deep breath through his nose, and spun to look at her with wide, glowing eyes.

"It's me, Doctor Stewart, and I'm not here to hurt you!" she cried out quickly, scrambling backwards as fast as she could.

Thirteen stared at her as if she was an apparition. He opened his mouth, then shut it. Opened it, and shut it again.

"I just came to talk," said Eva, her tone milder and, she hoped, more controlled. "Please," she added in a whisper as he suddenly came nearer in one swift crawling motion.

He was poised less than two feet away. Eva tried to look him in the eyes, but they were too bright and she had to glance away. "Listen," she said, still looking away, "I… I want to help you. I'm not lying."

"Help."

It was one, simple word, but Eva wondered whether he was trying the word out for size, asking her for it, or mocking her with it.

Or all three.

"Yes." She nodded, swallowing hard. "I – I brought a flashlight, do you mind if I turn it on? I can't see very well in here." She knew that the phosphorous helped Thirteen see in the dark, but after a few minutes in the dim light her eyes were feeling the strain.

Thirteen looked down at her hand, shoved into her pocket. Guessing that he mistrusted her and probably thought she was going to pull out a tranquilizer or something worse, she lifted the flashlight just a few inches to let him see it.

He seemed to relax, just enough for Eva to get the feeling he was allowing her to use it. She turned it on and laid it on the ground so that it illuminated the room with a dim blue light. "Thank you," she breathed.

She looked at Thirteen's face. The glow in his eyes had dimmed, but he wore an expression of confusion she did not blame him for. "Do you have a name?" she asked suddenly. She doubted it, but it was possible–and it was a well-known conversation starter, if slightly rephrased.

Thirteen cocked his head to the side, the corners of his mouth quirking inwards as his eyebrows drew closer together.

"No?" Eva prompted. "You don't have a name?"

Thirteen's eyes widened; and his face took on the expression of a child who had finally grasped a difficult concept. He lifted a hand and pointed it at himself with a surprised-sounding, "Me?"

"Yes, you," said Eva, a bit too loudly. She felt relief release her from a good amount of tension. It did not look as if he was going to attack her–right now, in any case.

The line between his eyebrows deepened again. He frowned, confused. "Me," he said again.

Eva sighed and squinted at him, studying his face. She could hardly keep calling him 'Thirteen' now that she knew his history. It just didn't seem right.

His face was on the thinner side from having been fed intravenously his whole life, but he was muscular from stress tests and a good deal of extra physical exertion. His eyes were narrow, but when he widened them in curiosity or surprise it gave his face a look of childish innocence that she found almost endearing. His mouth was the sort that could spread wide in a smile, but could also pull inward into a model pout. His eyebrows, a few shades darker than his hair, were shaped to seem almost sad or surprised.

It was a detailed minute spent observing him, but she realized not a single name she knew fit him. "You," she said with a sigh, "are difficult to name."

He pointed to himself again with that faint surprised expression. "Me?"

Eva laughed, but the laugh was cut short with a new thought. "Me," she murmured, then said louder, "Mir!"

"Mir?" The confused expression was back.

"It means 'me' in German," Eva explained. "I think it suits you."

"Me... Mir?" he asked, still squinting at her.

She cleared her throat and coughed several times. "Well," she said finally. "If it's all right with you – I mean, I could just call you Thirteen, if you don't want a name. Nobody else will know about it, you know. Only you and me."

The Subject quirked one side of his mouth up, looking incredulous, and pressed his curled fingers to his chest. "Mir...?"

"Yes," said Eva nodding with another quick, slightly embarrassed laugh. "Mir. Mir is your name."

Still moving cautiously, muscles tightened like a coiled spring, the young man moved closer to her, looking at her with a slanted expression. Reaching out with a hand Eva realized was shaking, he touched her shoulder.

Eva blinked at him for a moment. "What?"

He pulled his hand away, fingers clenching into a fist. His lips flattened and he looked frustrated with himself.

"Oh!" Eva exclaimed softly, and smiled. Pressing a hand to her heart, she said clearly "Eva."

"Ee-va," he repeated in a voice deeper than its age.

"Yes." Eva could hardly believe what was happening. She was sitting in the cell of a Subject whom she had just named, and who had just pronounced *her* name. It was absurdly simple, but at the same time it had almost a miraculous feel to it. Slowly so as not to frighten him, she stood, picking up her flashlight.

I don't want to overstay my welcome, she thought. And she wanted to call Pocky and let him know what had happened. She walked slowly to the door, glancing back at him. He did not attempt to go after her; simply remained crouched on the ground with one hand propping him up, the other resting on his knee.

His expression was one of wary fascination.

"I'll see you later," she promised as she stepped through the door. Just before it closed behind her, she added quietly, "Mir."

Chapter Fourteen

She came and spoke to me again today. She did not hurt me, and I am confused. Her name is Eva. She gave me a name. Only humans have names. How can I be a non-human and have a name? I don't care. My name is Mir.

"Hey, gorgeous."

Eva stopped chewing and looked up from her lunch tray. "What do you want?" she asked shortly.

Jude smiled widely and sat down across from her, his long legs stretching under the table. Eva pulled her legs back with a frown. "Come on," said Jude coaxingly, ripping the foil lid off a Styrofoam cup of soup, "can't I talk to my ex without getting a stink eye?"

Eva sighed and looked down at her sandwich. *I suppose I could be more civil.* "All right." She gave him her best imitation of a smile. "How is your day proceeding, thus far?"

He laughed. "That's the spirit. And 'thus far,' my day is smashing." He lifted the cup and took a swallow of the soup without bothering to use a spoon. "Everyone here is very welcoming – or at least, mostly everyone." He gave her a pointed look with raised eyebrows.

"I'm making an effort," said Eva, grinding her back molars.

"I appreciate it." He raised his cup as if toasting her. "I begin work this afternoon."

Eva decided she was not hungry enough to finish her lunch and stood up. "It was nice talking to you," she said, with just enough sarcasm laced in her voice to let him know she thought the opposite. "Don't think that smile will fix our relationship."

His smile only broadened, and he winked at her again. It was the wink that had made all the college girls swoon, but Eva was determined her heart would not flutter in the slightest. "I'll take your warning to heart," he promised, obviously undeterred.

Eva walked away, gripping the sides of her tray so hard her hands stung. *Jerk,* she thought, but she knew even as she dumped her half-eaten lunch into the trash that she would have to watch herself carefully. She was not going to be lured in by Jude's charms again.

She sat, stun gun in hand, on the opposite side of the cell. She wanted to spend as much time with this…man, she supposed, as possible. "So," she said after a moment, more to fill in the silence than to begin a sentence.

The Subject sat across from her, lip curled in what could have been a snarl or an expression of faint disgust. He had made no move toward her when she entered; only backed away and sat down, one leg outstretched and the other drawn up.

Eva ran a finger up and down the line of buttons at her neck. She knew it was only her imagination, making her feel as if it was hard to breathe, but knowing it did not help. "Do you know about the Morbus?" she asked. "Do you know why you're here?"

"Yes," he answered, surprising her.

"Why?"

"I'm supposed to make other people better." His voice was heavy. Hopeless – as if making other people better was a death sentence.

She looked at the stun gun, smooth in her hands. "I know it must be hard," she said haltingly, "but..."

"Hard."

Eva's left hand moved to her braid. She could not just sit there, she had to be doing something or her nervousness would get to her. "I lost my family when I was a little girl."

He tapped his finger on the floor. "Lost?"

"They were killed. By Morbus."

For a moment, the only sound was their mingled breathing. "That's sad."

Those two words would have been sarcastic, hurtful from another mouth. From Mir, they sounded genuine, as if he really was sad for her. She frowned, and the frown melted into a sigh. "Yes, it was."

"What was your family?"

Eva straightened, her shoulder blades pressing against the hard wall. "What was my family? They were...well, I had a mother, and a father. And a twin brother."

"Twin?"

"A brother born right before me, on the same day," she explained, smiling a little. "His name was Luke. We were going to..." She laughed at the childish memory, the good memory. "We were going to change the world."

"But he died."

"Yes."

Mir moved and Eva held the stun gun out, her eyes narrowing. She lowered it a second later, when he only moved into a different position.

"You called them your family."

Eva nodded. "They were." She tilted her head and watched him, but he did not move, and said nothing until she left a few minutes later.

"You named him Mir?"

"That's right." Eva leaned back in her seat, her phone pressed against her ear. "He kept saying 'me' and I thought it fit. What, do you think it's a bad name? He seemed to like it."

"No, it's a fine name!" the professor exclaimed. He added in a quieter voice, "Eva, I'm proud of you."

She gave a flighty laugh and shook her head. "Well, you shouldn't be. I don't know how to process all this. It's so... I'm talking to a Subject, Pocky. I gave it a name, of all things! I gave a labeled non-human a *name*."

"We're all God's children, Eva."

"Pocky, please. I have enough to focus on without you throwing religion into the mix."

The professor grunted. "God, not religion. And it's in the mix even if you refuse to acknowledge it – but I digress."

"Thank you. Oh, by the way, did I tell you Jude Harborn is working here now?" she asked, switching the subject.

"Your former boyfriend? That Jude Harborn?"

"The one and - thankfully – only."

"What is he doing there?" exclaimed the professor.

Eva traced circles on a sheet of paper with her pen. "He was hired as a research scientist."

"Well, he always was a bright student, if lazy."

"He talks to me every time he sees me. I think he may want to pick our relationship back up where it left off," Eva confessed.

"Hmm." The professor was silent for a moment before asking "And how do you feel about his being there?"

"Oh, he could charm a snake up a tree, but I don't want anything to do with him. As a scientist, his work is intelligent and respectable. But as a boyfriend, his performance is less-than-stellar."

"So tell him to bugger off! Or is he the difficult sort? I seem to remember he was somewhat persistent when it came to the female sex."

"He wants what he wants," said Eva, absently inking the numbers 1 and 3 onto the paper. "And he usually gets it."

"Your stubbornness is enough to send any man running."

"Thanks, Professor, that's the nicest thing I've been told all day," said Eva, laughing in spite of her sarcasm.

"You know what I meant," Pocky chuckled. "If Jude starts giving you any unwanted attention, you could always file a complaint."

"I know, but I can't very well file a complaint because he speaks to me. That would have to be harassment or something equally worthy." She dropped the pen and spun the chair in an absent half-circle. "He's annoying, but nothing I can't handle. I'm just complaining."

"We all complain sometimes. Best to do it to a friend," was the kind answer. "Keep me informed about your progress with Mir. Oh, and Eva, before I go, there was something I wanted to point out to you if you hadn't already thought of it."

"What is it?"

"Doctor Ross cannot suspect you are communicating with Mir on a personal level. He will have Mir terminated."

"I have thought about that." Eva curled her hand into a fist and hit the top of the table just hard enough to make the pen roll. "But how can I go on experimenting on a Subject I know to be fully human? I can't even ask them to stop the so-called 'prepping sessions' without arousing Ross's suspicions!"

"Just... be gentle, I suppose," was the doubtful answer. "As gentle as you can be. Providence, my girl, Providence."

"I wish I could be as optimistic as you," said Eva, twisting her mouth to the side. "I also wish you were here to give me some backup."

"I would love to be, but you know you work in a restricted facility. Your furlough is coming up soon though, is it not? You must come see me then."

"I'll be there on Monday."

"I look forward to it, my girl."

Chapter Fifteen

Eva was called to a progress meeting that evening and was not able to see Mir. She had hoped to leave early, but the board members were particularly interested in her progress with Subject Thirteen and she had to stay and give them detailed reports.

Also, Dr. Ross pointed out during the meeting that she had not taken Thirteen to the procedure room in two days, and he had wondered why.

Thinking quickly, Eva replied in a voice as calm as she could force it to be "Thirteen's vital signs were a little weak. I was allowing it to recuperate before I operated again."

Her answer, undeniably smooth and believable, was accepted by the board members. Dr. Ross, however, had told her on no uncertain terms that he expected to continue receiving frequent progress reports as soon as she came back from her furlough.

My furlough! Eva sat up in bed and looked at her clock. The digital numbers blazed 2: 37 in the dark. Every WorldCure staff member was required to take a one-week furlough every six months, to prevent exhaustion or 'cabin fever.' She could not decline she would have to go, and leave Mir for seven whole days.

What if she lost all the progress she had made by being absent that long? She slammed her hand, palm-down, into her pillow. "I don't believe this." She picked up her cell phone and sent a text message.

To: Pocky
FURLOUGH???
From: Eva

She laid her head down on her pillow and closed her eyes. She had just drifted back to sleep when her phone buzzed. She picked it up and read

To: Eva
Indeed.
From: Pocky

"Thanks for the help, professor," she sighed. Pressing buttons and deleting them when her sleep-numbed fingers mistyped, she responded –

To: Pocky
I have 2 leave Mir!
From: Eva

The reply came quickly.

To: Eva
Not good. Praying.
From: Pocky

Eva sighed and hoped prayer helped.

"Good morning, sunshine," sang a familiar voice.

"Go away, Jude." Eva took a sip of her coffee without lifting her eyes from the papers scattered over her desk.

"Go away? Is that any way to speak to a well-wisher?"

"You didn't knock."

"The door was open."

"It's an office. You knock before entering."

"I'm afraid I'm behind on customs of ex-girlfriends these days." Jude let out a deep sigh.

"Work going well?" he inquired after a brief minute.

Eva looked up and scowled at him. "It was, until I was interrupted. I'm afraid I'm not getting any work done at the moment."

"Listen, Eva..." Jude ran a hand through his straight blond hair. "I just want to be friends. Now, I don't feel like that's asking for the world on a silver platter."

Eva clenched her jaw and stared hard at him for a moment across the desk. *He's not worth the trouble it would take to fight him,* she thought wearily. Straightening, she held a hand out to him. "All right," she said finally, exhaling. "Truce."

Jude grinned and shook her hand once, twice, three times, and then stuck his hand back in his pocket. "Good," he said. "Glad to know. Now, you're wanted in the third lab – Ross thinks you can give them a hand with trial six."

The Morbus trial took all day.

Worn to a thread, irritated, and upset, Eva was not able to escape the lab's demands until it was after seven-thirty and she was not allowed to go Beneath.

"I can't believe this," she wailed to Pocky over the phone. She had once again closed herself in her office and locked the door. She only hoped nobody heard her ranting and tried to listen in. "My last day before furlough, and I wasn't able to see him. Pocky! What am I supposed to do?"

"Well, considering this is the closest thing you have had to a meltdown in... oh, three or four days, I would suggest taking a sedative," was the dry answer.

"Pocky."

"You could come down and see me tomorrow," was the next suggestion. "After you take the sedative, of course."

"You know I'm going to, Pocky, but I'm serious!" Eva tugged at her hair in frustration, wincing as a few strands came out. "I'm going to lose all the progress I've made with Mir over the past few days. He was actually talking to me! He's probably going to try and kill me again when I get back."

"I highly doubt it. He's not an animal, Eva; he's reasonably intelligent."

"Oh, I think he's more than 'reasonably' intelligent," Eva agreed. "It's just... well, like you said. He was treated like an animal and expected to behave like one for so long that I never know what he's going to do next."

"I'm sorry, my girl, I really don't know what to tell you," said the professor. "It seems a hopeless business."

"But you believe in that 'all things work out for good' nonsense, Pocky, and I don't. I'm a realist."

"I think I ought to be offended."

"Well, don't bother," Eva sighed. "I'm sorry. I'm just so...so frustrated. This situation is impossible. I wish I could erase this past week."

"You don't really mean that," said the professor in a soothing voice.

"Yes, I..." Eva faltered and fell silent for a moment. "No, I don't. Though it was far more comfortable."

"The truth is a very uncomfortable thing."

"That ought to be a campaign slogan for something," said Eva. "I have to go, but I'll see you tomorrow."

"Good! I have the spare bedroom all made up for you. I hope you don't mind stacks of books everywhere; I did my best to tidy them up but they simply won't be told."

"Pock, it wouldn't be your house if I didn't trip and fall over a stack of books at least once during a visit. I have insurance. I'll be fine." Eva smiled and hung up. She slowly put the phone in her pocket, chewing on her lower lip. *I can't just run off...*

She unlocked her office door and hurried out to find Dr. Ross. "Doctor?" She knocked on his door.

The door opened and Dr. Ross stood there, a file full of papers tucked under his arm. "Doctor Stewart."

"I was wondering..." Eva tried to pull her thoughts together into a reasonable excuse for her question. "I would like to have the Warden's walkie-talkie number so that I can contact him in case of emergencies."

"Ah, yes. His is number seventeen." Dr. Ross smiled and walked past her, his long legs moving him at a brisk clip.

That was much easier than I thought. Eva watched him go, bewildered. *Something must be weighing on his mind.* She borrowed a walkie-talkie from a security guard and called number seventeen.

"Warden, this is Doctor Stewart."

"Yes, Doctor Stewart, what can I do for you?" he asked, sounding depressed.

"I'm leaving on furlough. I will be gone until Sunday."

"Right. Is that all?"

"I would like it made known to Subject Thirteen."

There was silence for a moment. When Brenton finally spoke again, he asked "Why would I bother telling a Subject that its Handler is leaving?"

Brilliant, Eva. Think up another excuse, quick! "I... Thirteen is mentally very unstable, and having its Handler leave without warning could add to the unbalance."

"...Right. Have a good furlough, Doctor Stewart."

The walkie-talkie went dead. Eva almost tried again, but thought better of it. She handed the walkie-talkie back to the guard, who secured it onto his belt while Eva walked down the hall.

She had packing to do.

Chapter Sixteen

Eva left early the next morning and arrived at Pocky's home at midnight. His house was large and welcoming, and it was very easy to believe that it was in the middle of nowhere rather than a few miles away from the heart of Anchorage. She turned up the long driveway, honking her horn several times.

The porch light turned on and the door opened to reveal the stocky figure of Professor Pock. Eva climbed out of car, waving and calling "Pocky, I'm home!"

"Eva, my girl!" He jogged down the driveway to meet her. "Come on inside, it's cold out! But first, the bags!"

"I only have two," Eva laughed, shouldering one while Pocky took the other. They walked inside, talking over each other in loud, exuberant voices. Pocky put the bags into the spacious guest bedroom and met her in the kitchen. He turned on the teakettle, hopped up onto the kitchen counter to sit, and demanded, "No work. Tell me about yourself. I may speak to you over the phone frequently enough, but I haven't laid eyes on you in six months!"

"Six months and one day," Eva corrected with a smile. She leaned against the counter, listening to the hissing sound of the water boiling in the kettle.

"Well, it feels closer to a year any way you look at it," said Pocky, swinging his legs like a schoolboy. He wore a knitted sweater, slacks, and green socks with a pattern of red reindeer running around the ankles. He had been bald on the top of his head ever since Eva had known him, but his graying hair stuck out from the sides like a halo.

"I know." She walked over and hugged him again, inhaling the smell of books and Earl Grey. "I miss you so much, every day."

"I miss you too, duck." The teakettle began to shriek as steam billowed from its mouth. "Would you mind grabbing the kettle before it explodes?"

Eva grinned and poured boiling water into the two prepared cups, carefully holding the tags at the ends of the teabags so they would not sink. "Pocky, why on earth do you think this all had to happen to me?" she asked, stirring absently as the hot liquid darkened.

"What is the 'this all' you speak of?"

"You know what it is," said Eva, sighing in spite of her smile. "WorldCure, Mir, and now Jude – it feels like it's all some sort of conspiracy."

"Not conspiracy, dear. Providence."

"You sound awfully certain," said Eva, turning and leaning back against the counter on her elbows. "I just don't believe that life has an easy way out."

"'Easy way out'?" The professor raised his eyebrows. "As much as you might not like to hear this, Eva my girl, God is not an 'easy way out.' He created the way out, and He leads us *to* the way out, but it certainly is not easy."

Eva chewed on her lip and looked back at his teddy-bear face. "I've never really been one for fairytales, Pocky."

The professor rubbed a hand over his face, then made a motion with it as if he was shooing a fly away. "It's too late to argue. Come on, let's get you unpacked!"

The week went by far too quickly for Eva. It was a comfortable routine of long discussions, late-night reading, and earl grey tea, and the seven days flew by like they were determined to usher Eva back to the lab.

She stood outside, the cold wind blowing her hair around her face, waiting for Pocky to come back outside. He had run into the house saying he had something for her, and she was curious to know what it was. She pulled her scarf tighter and turned the heater on inside the car so it would be warm when she got in.

The front door opened and Pocky came running out, holding a basket covered by a red blanket. "Sorry, sorry, sorry," he huffed, coming to a halt in front of here. "Here are some things you might like – cookies and books and such. Since I know you don't get many new things at the facility." He winked.

Eva took the basket and hugged him, smiling. "Thanks, Pocky. Thanks a lot."

Eva did not arrive back at the lab until four o'clock in the morning, and when she had checked in she went straight to her room and collapsed on the bed until her alarm went off.

She hurriedly showered, dressed, and strode to the working quarters of the facility. Several of her coworkers greeted her with friendly but offhanded 'good mornings' and 'hey, Eva's' but barely heard them as she hurried Beneath to see Mir.

She swiped her card at the door and jogged down the stairs, her shoes scuffling against the concrete. She hurried past the Warden's office and down the hall to Cell Thirteen.

She waited impatiently for the outer door to open and peered in through the transparent plastiglass. She craned her neck, looking in every direction, trying to see a glimpse of the Subject.

Mir?

"Are you looking for something?"

Eva turned at the Warden's voice. "Where is my Subject?" she asked, carefully keeping her question sharp and professional.

"Tiger's in the Procedure Room," said Brenton, tilting his head and giving her a smile she thoroughly disliked.

"The Procedure Room? But – how? Who's using it?" She took a step closer, her hands tightening into fists.

"Some research scientist named Harborn." Brenton slung his gun over his other shoulder as if it had gotten too heavy for him. "Oh, don't worry," he added. "He had permission. Doctor Ross brought him down here himself."

Eva could hardly contain her anger. It was all she could do to grind out the words "Thank you" before turning on her heel and rushing to the Procedure Room.

Two guards stood outside, but they recognized her and let her burst into the room. She opened her mouth to yell for Jude, but froze.

Unable to move, Eva beheld the scene in front of her with horror.

Mir was held to the operation table by straps that covered almost every inch of him except his beltline to his chest. The entire length of his exposed body had been cut open in an x-pattern, exposing the delicate network of entrails and muscles inside.

Mir's hair clung to his forehead above wide eyes. A strap around his mouth did nothing to stop the heavy whimpers from escaping beneath it. Black tears streaked down the sides of his face, mingling with the sheen of sweat that covered him, and Jude leaned down over Mir, probing him with a six-inch director.

"Stop it! Stop right now!" Jerked from immobility, Eva strode forward.

Jude's hands jerked away from the Subject, and Mir gave a muffled cry of pain that Jude did not even seem to notice. "Eva, I'm a *little* busy!" Jude wiped his hands on a towel and gave her a disapproving look. "You should know better than to just walk into a surgical—"

"What are you doing?" Eva demanded, hardly able to draw breath enough to speak.

Jude spread his hands, eyebrows raised in exasperation. "We needed a Subject in order to—"

"Not *my* Subject!" Eva glanced at Mir – *why isn't he unconscious?* – and grabbed hold of Jude's arm. "I'm going to be doing Morbus antidote tests on it soon, and I can't have any 'research' messing it up!"

"Hey now," Jude protested, "I was given permission by Doctor Ross! Thirteen is the only Subject in good enough condition to do this sort of work on right now."

Eva paused and looked at Jude for a long moment, then at Mir. Mir's eyes were closed, as if he were wishing himself unconscious but could not make it happen. *I can't stop him in the middle of a procedure. Mir has to be repaired before he can be taken back to his cell... oh, Eva, what have you done?* "Finish up, and be quick about it," she snapped. "And give it a sedative!"

"I was going to, to prevent struggling," Jude explained, shrugging his arm away from her in annoyance, "but its metabolism is too fast. Sedatives just wear off."

Eva shut her eyes briefly. Mir's pain was so overpowering it was almost tangible. "Then just... hurry up, all right?"

"Yes, *ma'am*," Jude retorted with a frown. "Now if you don't mind, please leave the room. I can't have distractions."

I can't leave! You have a human on that table, a suffering human, and you're torturing him! You expect me to leave?

Eva turned slowly, reluctantly, and left the room, knowing she could not stay or protest any further without arousing suspicion. What horrified her was that, standing there and watching Jude torture Mir, she had come to a realization.

She was looking at herself.

Chapter Seventeen

Eva could not keep her mind focused on her work – it kept replaying Mir. Flashes would come to her no matter how hard she tried to concentrate on the task at hand; a glimpse of blue eyes blackened by tears, a muscle taut, straining with agony, the whimper that had driven a nail into her heart.

How long had he screamed, to have his pain manifested in a whimper? How long had Jude ignored the Subject's suffering?

Mir was a man only a few years younger than Jude himself – their places could have been reversed if not for chance. Or, as Pocky called it, 'Providence.' *Like God would ever let something this unjust happen to someone as innocent as Mir.* Eva heard a snapping noise and looked down to see her pencil broken in half between her fingers. For some reason, it infuriated her. She picked up both halves and threw them across the room, where they hit the wall and clattered to the floor in a very unsatisfying way.

The clock said it had only been an hour since she came upstairs. It felt more like an eternity, stretching endlessly and mocking her when she checked to see that it had been just seconds since she last looked.

She managed to go another half hour, and that was all she could take. She left her office and ran Beneath to the Procedure Room. There were no guards outside – that meant the surgery was over. She turned and ran, her strides as long as she could make them, to Cell 13.

"Thanks for telling me you were done, Jude," she muttered, punching numbers into the keypad and waiting anxiously for the doors to open. She ducked inside before the plastiglass had completely lifted and gave it the order to close immediately.

"Mir?" She shone her flashlight around the cell until the beam found him. He was lying on his back, one hand flung into a puddle of water from the dripping showerhead, the other hand slid underneath one of the straps of his harness. His eyes were shut, and the flashlight could not make out any breathing.

They put his harness back on? Horrified, Eva knelt next to Mir and unbuckled the various straps on the harness, mentally cursing Jude with every word she knew would have shocked Pocky if she said them in his presence.

"Mir?" She put one hand on the side of his neck, feeling for a pulse. For an agonized moment she felt nothing, but then – there it was; a fluttering, whisper-soft, under her fingertips. "Mir? Come on, baby, wake up." She paused. *Did I just call him baby?* That was an inordinate amount of affection, even for her. She meant it in no romantic way - something about Mir brought out every caring female instinct she had.

She shrugged it off and shone the flashlight onto his stomach. It had been sewn well, no doubt because she had insisted she needed the Subject healthy for her next experiment. The black thread was a stark contrast to Mir's pale skin. Rows of small X's joined to create one large X, each stitch a mark against Jude.

No. She forced herself to breathe deeply and think rationally. *A few weeks ago, Eva, you would have done exactly the same thing and been just as cold about it.* She did not want to be fair, but logically, she knew she must.

"Mir, wake up. Please, wake up, wake up," she urged, brushing his hair away from his face and patting his cheek lightly. She leaned down with her ear above his lips. *Let me feel some breathing, Mir. Come on...*

She lifted her head and balled her hands into fists. He was alive – barely, but he was alive. Perhaps it was better that he was unconscious – waking up would only mean more pain for him. Fighting her own impatience, Eva drew up her knees, clasped her hands around them, and decided to wait.

Eva was pulled from her doze by... something. It took her nearly half a minute to realize what it was – Mir's breathing had changed and her subconscious must have noticed.

His eyes were watching her, their eerie glow familiar by now. He rested most of his weight on one hand, half-reclining. At least he looked alive.

Eva reached out to touch his arm. "Mir—"

It was as if her touch burned his skin. He flinched and pulled away, and Eva realized that the expression he was giving her was not a welcoming one.

"What's wrong?" she asked, trying to convince herself not to be alarmed.

"Eva left." The words were almost angry, but not quite; filled with resentment and bitter disappointment.

Eva's heart sank farther than she had thought it would. From her perspective, she had gone on a short vacation to see a beloved mentor. From Mir's perspective, she had offered him a glimpse of kindness and then abandoned him to Jude for a week that must have seemed like an eternity.

She could see it in his eyes – she had failed him. Brenton had not told Mir she was leaving, and if he had would Mir have even understood? *Eva, you're a Doctor. You graduated with honors. You work at the biggest medical company in the world. How can you be so stupid?* "Mir, I–I didn't... leave you." Her voice shook. How could she make him understand?

"Why?"

Eva blinked. "What?"

"Why you leave?" Mir's English was not as broken as his voice.

"I – I was visiting a friend," she faltered.

"Friend?"

Eva's breath caught in her throat. He did not even understand the meaning of *friends*. "A friend is someone – a person you love and want to be with."

Only breathing interrupted the silence for a long moment.

"What is...*love*?"

In that moment, the carefully held-together pieces of Eva's heart broke. "Love is..." her voice faded. How was she to explain something as complicated and foreign as love to this creature before her – a product of darkness and fear and abandonment, everything love was not? But Thirteen's luminescent eyes watched her unblinkingly, waiting for an answer. She began again. "Love is when... when you feel strongly for someone in a good way. You want what's best for someone else because their happiness is more important than yours." She took a deep breath and rubbed her shaking hands together. "Love is when you'd give up everything you value if it would help the other person. You would die so they could live."

Thirteen curled his left arm around his stomach and Eva paused, waiting for him to speak. After several heartbeats, she asked flatly, "You don't understand anything I'm saying, do you?"

When Mir spoke, his voice was thick and hard to make out. "You would die?"

"Yes," said Eva, swallowing past a lump in her throat, "if I loved them enough."

More silence, while Eva, growing uncomfortable on the hard, cold ground, shifted into a more comfortable position. She waited, and finally in a quiet, husky voice that Eva had to lean forward to catch it all, he asked, "You would live, too?"

"Live?" Eva could feel her composure cracking. "Well, of course I'd live. Everybody wants to live."

Mir lowered his head and looked away, ghostly in the blue glow of her flashlight. "Not everyone."

Chapter Eighteen

Eva was speechless. She had nothing to say; no thoughts that would make sense, even to her. The thought that a life could be so hopeless... but Mir wasn't hopeless. Mir had a will to live, an instinct for survival that she had never seen in another Subject.

She scooted closer and put one hand on the far side of his face, forcing him to look at her. The light in his eyes was dim; she could see blue irises, half-covered by heavy lids, looking back at her. "Listen to me." Her voice held a firmness that surprised her. "I... you – look." *Deep breath, Eva.* "A life – *any* life – is better than dying."

His eyes did not leave her face. "I have died," he whispered.

"What?" Eva tilted her head, gazing earnestly at him. "No, no, no, you haven't, Mir. You haven't. You can't die."

"I have," he answered again, never looking away.

"No!" Eva's voice snapped in the quiet room, her breath mingling white with the cold air. Mir flinched and Eva took her hand away from his face. "You haven't died, Mir," she said, standing slowly. "You're still alive, and you're going to stay that way."

"Hey, lady."

Eva did not acknowledge Jude as she sat down at the computer terminal. She opened the documents and searched for Mir's records.

"How was your vacation?"

Eva's left hand curled into a fist while her right hand clutched the mouse so hard she thought she might break it. "Fine."

Jude turned to face her more fully, one blond eyebrow raised, the corner of his mouth quirked in that smug grin he wore whenever he had the upper hand. "Did you miss me?"

"No," Eva snapped, looking at him only long enough to glare before facing the computer screen again. "Leave me alone, Jude."

"Hey." Jude sounded surprised, maybe even angry. "What's your problem?"

YOU! You're my problem, jerk! Stop talking to me! "Nothing. I'm just... I'm not in the mood. Please, Jude, go away."

"It's not a private room, there's more than one computer," he retorted, and turned his chair back to face his own computer.

Irritated but relieved, Eva skimmed over the titles of each sub-folder in Mir's file. There were records of every action ever taken with him from infancy to now. She scrolled endlessly down the page until the title of one of the folders caught her eye.

/053/Sub/13/Death/Final

Almost afraid to open it, she pressed her finger down and double-clicked. Her eyes widened at the text in front of her. "This is impossible," she breathed.

"What?"

She jumped and looked over at Jude. He was giving her a quizzical expression. "Nothing," she said flippantly. He huffed and turned back to his work, and Eva kept reading.

...Subject Thirteen's heart cannot endure another system failure without permanent results.

System failure.

Permanent results.

They were talking about a human, not a computer. System failure was code for what happened when a heart had stopped beating for more than five minutes. In other words, the heart's owner was technically dead.

Her eyes flew over the words, the descriptions of the events – there were even video feeds taken from the security cameras.

She looked on, one hand pressed over her mouth, as doctors ran around the unconscious Subject, shouting over one another to make themselves heard. The only thing she could make out were the words "Hurry! It's almost gone!"

Eva watched as a doctor she did not recognize appeared with defibrillators set on high and placed the instruments on Mir's chest, jolting him again and again, trying to bring him back to life.

This had not only happened once or twice.

Mir had been telling the truth. He *had* died.

He had died twelve times.

And the next time would be his last.

Eva went Beneath again several hours later, after she had finished enough work that she could file a report at the end of the day. *You're going to have to spend less time down here, Eva,* she told herself as she went down the steps once again. *People are going to start getting suspicious.* She paused as she realized the irony of the situation. Those who had been her colleagues and respected coworkers less than two weeks ago were now people around whom she had to watch her every move.

Fingering the syringe in her pocket, she allowed the outer door to lift and knocked quietly on the plastiglass. "Mir?" she mouthed, even though she knew he could not hear her. She took in a deep breath. Mir was intelligent enough that he would not try to escape or attack in his condition... she opened the plastiglass and stepped inside.

I'm going to install some sort of light in here, she promised herself as she swept the darkness with the flashlight beam. The blue light caught Mir, lying on his back at the far end of the room. *What other position is there that won't hurt him more?*

She could tell he knew she was there, but he did not move until she had narrowed the distance between them to nothing and was kneeling beside him. She wiped his arm with a disinfectant wipe and pulled the syringe from her pocket. Then his eyes opened and he slid away without looking at her, intentionally avoiding her.

"Hey, Mir, I'm trying to help you," Eva said firmly, grabbing his arm. He jerked it away, but the movement was so feeble she was able to keep hold of it. "I'm sorry I yelled at you," she added softly, loosening her grip. "I really am. I looked up your file, and... I should have believed you. I thought you were just being obtuse."

He looked sideways at her.

"I mean, I thought you were... being... I don't know." She let out a sound somewhere between a laugh and a moan, rubbing her hand over her face. "I'm sorry," she said again. Then, leaning forward to look him in the eye as well as she could, Eva asked "Will you forgive me?"

Mir swallowed, and Eva absently watched the swallow travel down his throat. Finally, he nodded once, and Eva leaned back. "Thank you. Hey," she tilted the flashlight beam to highlight his face, "You don't look that good."

He blinked rapidly in the light and she noted that his skin was almost gray. Slowly, so as not to startle him, she rested the back of her hand against his forehead. It was clammy and hot; raging compared to his usual temperature.

She picked up the syringe again and lifted it to his arm, but once again he slid away. "W-w-what—" he stuttered, a look of panic flaring in his face, "-is th - that?"

Eva stared at him for a moment. *He's stuttering? Mir stutters when he's nervous?* Finding this strangely endearing, she cleared her throat and said in a calming voice "It's a painkiller, Mir. It will help make you feel a little better."

She knew Mir was at least vaguely familiar with painkillers, so she settled back and waited for him to make his decision. After almost a full minute, he extended his muscled arm toward her.

Eva knew this was a large step for him, a small sign that he was, perhaps, starting to trust her. She put the needle in his arm and watched as the liquid from the syringe entered Mir's bloodstream.

"It should start working any minute," she promised him, taking the needle out and putting it back in her pocket. He was breathing heavily, and though he had accepted the medicine every line on his face told her that his instincts believed this would hurt, not help.

Eva sighed and bent down to inspect Mir's stitches. *That looks like it hurts,* she thought to herself, *but not nearly as much as what's underneath.*

Something like a quiet sigh escaped Mir's lips and she looked up. His face wore an expression that was equal parts drowsy, confused, and surprised. She smiled. "Feel better?"

He did not answer; his eyelids drooped closed and his breathing became slow and even, his chest rising and falling without difficulty. Eva stayed there for several minutes, a smile curving the corners of her mouth as she watched him sleep in what was probably his first natural, peaceful sleep in years.

"I'll see you tomorrow, Mir," she said in a low voice, and left the cell.

Chapter Nineteen

"Doctor Ross!" Her voice came out as a squeak.

The doctor stood there, his thin lips pressed together and his eyebrows drawn. "Doctor Stewart."

"What are you doing here?" She wanted to bite her tongue as soon as she asked. *Asking the most obvious cover-up question in the history of cover-up questions, Eva?*

"Doctor Harborn told me you were unhappy with his procedure earlier today." Dr. Ross raised his chin and looked at her with an expression that was anything but pleasant. "I know I appointed you Thirteen's Handler, so you are not entirely out of bounds to request notification before someone else uses the Subject, but you *are* out of bounds if you think you can pull a full-stop on a second-level procedure."

Eva cleared her throat and dug her hands into her pockets. "I was...taken by surprise, that's all." She shrugged. "I had been planning on running another test on the Subject later this week, so naturally I wasn't happy with a delay."

Dr. Ross nodded. "I can understand that." He looked at the door behind her. "But remember, you are not the only person with access to Thirteen. It is a test Subject, an experimental lab rat, if you will, and unless I say so, those with authority can and *will* use it at any time."

Eva felt her heart sink, but nodded. "Yes, sir. I understand."

Dr. Ross grunted. "What were you doing in there?"

"Oh – in there?" Eva glanced behind her. "I was… checking the layout. I need to have a light installed, I can hardly see a thing. I have to bring a flashlight for checkups." She laughed even though she had not made a joke, but cut it short before it sounded too nervous.

"It would be safer if you allowed the guards to take the Subject to the prepping room before you examined it." Dr. Ross looked at her with narrowed eyes.

A smile flittered across Eva's face. "I prefer it this way. It's perfectly safe; I gas it before I go in and make certain it is harnessed to the wall." *Except for when I take it off,* she mentally added.

Dr. Ross sighed. "I know every doctor who joins these out-of-the-way WorldCure facilities has to sign a waiver, but I hate to see them put themselves in open danger."

"But it isn't dangerous," Eva protested. She gave him her prettiest smile, hoping it was persuasive enough. "I know what I'm doing."

He grunted again. "Very well," he said after a moment. "In any case, we won't have to worry about the Subject again soon anyway." He moved to walk past her, but she grabbed his arm.

"I beg your pardon?" she asked, trying to keep the nervous pitch from her voice. "What do you mean 'we won't have to worry about it'?"

He looked over his shoulder at her. "I've hired a specialist to take care of it; keep it under control. He'll be arriving here next week."

"A...specialist? What–what kind of specialist?" Eva stammered.

He gave her a smile and patted her hand before prying it from his arm. "Don't worry; he won't interfere with your procedures. He's going to keep the Subject in line since no one else seems to be able to."

"But who is he?"

"His name is Fyodor Igorov, a retired Russian Special Forces operative. You will meet him when he arrives – and no doubt you'll become well-acquainted." Dr. Ross gave her a cold smile that made her think of a snake she had seen once, frozen underneath a glass cover. "Have a nice day, Doctor Stewart," he said, and strode away from her, down the hall.

"What am I going to do?"

Pocky's voice was highly indignant. "Well, I'll tell you what I'm going to do – I'm going to march over there, roll up my sleeves, and punch Harborn in the nose. No – I won't bother rolling my sleeves up first."

"Well, you'll have to get in line," sighed Eva, leaning her head against the cool wall. "I'm punching him before you, and I'm punching Doctor Ross, and... well, I'm not so sure about this new SPETSNAZ guy. He sounds like trouble."

"Hmm." Pocky was silent for a moment. "Russian Special Forces, eh? I agree. Trouble."

"Any advice for me, Prof?" Eva fiddled with a pen between her fingers.

"Yes. Have you gone through that basket I gave you?"

"I ate half the cookies you packed, if that's what you're asking. They're delicious; you have to make more when I come down again."

"I will," Pocky chuckled. "There's a notebook, one of those flip-through kind. Take a look at it – it's all the advice I can think to give you. I thought it might help since I can't really be there when I want to be."

"Aw." Eva smiled, envisioning the professor sitting at the table with a cup of tea and a melancholy expression. "Thank you. I'll go do that as soon as I'm off."

Eva did not see Mir again that day. She did not want to risk waking him from his sleep, and she did not want to arouse any further suspicion in Dr. Ross. She took a shower and sat on her bed, wrapped in her favorite pale pink sweater, and dug through the basket Pocky had given her in Anchorage.

She opened a package of homemade butter cookies and took a bite, pulling books out of the basket in search of the notebook. There it was – she smiled at the owl on the cover.

She flipped the cover open with her thumb and read the first phrase, in the professor's neat, precise handwriting.

I know the plans that I have for you, plans of good and not evil, to give you a future and a hope.

She smiled, but it was a faintly confused one. She felt as if she had heard that phrase somewhere before, but could not quite place it.

"Thanks, Pocky," she said quietly. Curious, she flipped to the next page.

Do not be afraid, do not keep silent.

"That's easier said than done," she sighed aloud, finishing the butter cookie. She set the basket on the floor, turned off the light, and shut her eyes.

Eva sat up with a feeling in her stomach like a coiled snake. Something was wrong, she could feel it. She looked around her room. Cold shadows rimmed with moonlight enveloped everything. She tossed the covers aside and stood up.

She looked down at herself – yoga pants and her oversized sweater would be all right for sneaking Beneath. She grabbed her ID card and left her room. The halls in the living quarters were dark; only dim nightlights lit her way through to the working facilities.

She rounded a corner and her heart jumped into her throat. A security guard stood there, arms crossed, leaning against the wall. *Think reasonably, Eva. You aren't a thief, you're an employee. You don't have to skulk.*

She straightened and walked past him with as much confidence in her step as she could manage. She was almost around the next corner when she heard, "Hey! Ma'am?"

She paused, took a deep breath, and turned around with a smile. "Yes?"

"Is anything wrong?" He walked toward her, his large frame taking up a good deal of the hall.

"No, nothing," she assured him. "I'm a Doctor." She held up her card. "Doctor Stewart."

The night guard shone his flashlight onto the card. "Mm-hmm," he said, and nodded. "Thanks."

Without bothering to reply, Eva hurried around the corner and swiped her card through the slot by the door. She pushed it closed behind her and shuffled down the stairs. She immediately wished she had put on warmer pants as cold air sent shivers over her skin.

"Oh, please be okay, please be okay, please be okay," she whispered, licking her lips. She swiped the card and clenched her hands into fists. The doors slid open and she hurried in, turning her flashlight on and setting it on the ground at an angle where it dimly lit up the whole cell.

She thought Mir was asleep at first. He had moved onto his side and was curled inward, his hands clenched into fists. She opened her mouth to say his name, but was interrupted by a soft noise.

She froze, wondering whether that had come from her, or...

It was Mir.

She walked over slowly, wondering what in the world she was supposed to do. Mir was crying. Not agonized screaming like before, when she had first seen his black tears, but quiet sobbing.

She bent down and put a hand on his shoulder. "Mir?"

He rolled onto his back, away from her. It was as if he did not care that she was there. Eva was not used to seeing men cry, even young men. She wasn't used to crying herself – her life was a straight progression of logic and practicality, with no time for excess emotion.

"Come on, Mir!" She kept her voice soft and persuasive, but was at a loss how to react. *Come on, Eva, you're a woman! You're supposed to know what to do in this sort of situation! Think! What would your mother have done?*

She hesitated, but all she had to do was look down at Mir to know she had to do something. Recalling what her mother used to do when Eva was sick or crying, she eased herself down so she was lying on her side about a foot away.

She cleared her throat and began to sing softly "You are my sunshine, my only sunshine..." she broke off for a moment. *Eva, this is ridiculous.* But something inside her refused to let her stop. She took another breath and continued, "You make me happy when skies are gray, you'll never know, dear, how much I love you, please don't take my sunshine away."

Mir was looking at the ceiling. He looked as if he was trying not to cry, but faint sobs continued to choke him.

Eva quickly thought of another lullaby she knew and began to sing it. "Golden slumber kiss your eyes, smiles await you when you rise. Sleep, pretty baby, do not cry, and I'll sing you a lullaby."

Mir turned so he could look at her. Eva found herself shocked by the blue in his eyes. They were glowing just brightly enough to make her feel like she was staring at twin stars.

Remembering what her mother would always do, she reached up and began to smooth Mir's hair in slow strokes, from the corner of his eyebrow and back. "Care you know not, therefore sleep, while I over you watch do keep. Sleep, pretty darling, do not cry, and I will sing a lullaby."

Mir's eyes were half-closed, but he was still watching her. Feeling calmer and more assured of herself, Eva re-sang the lullaby twice, her voice growing stronger and smoother with each verse.

She sang every lullaby she knew. How long she lay there on the cold floor, with her fingers brushing across the side of Mir's face, she had no idea. She only knew that she must have fallen asleep, because when she awoke, she was half a foot away from Mir. His eyes were closed, her hand was still on his face, and he wore the shadow of a smile.

Chapter Twenty

Eva knew she could not move without waking Mir. She also knew that she was freezing. She could see the tiny bumps on her arms and even her face felt numb. "How do you stand it, Mir?" she asked in a quiet voice so as not to wake him. She knew his body had probably adjusted to the temperature years ago, when he was just a baby, but did he ever feel the cold like she did?

She lay there, wishing she could move if only so she could get into a more comfortable position. She carefully pulled the folds of her sweater farther down over her waist and wrists, trying to warm as much of herself as possible. She craned her neck to get a good look at Mir's stitches. They weren't exactly being taken care of, but they seemed all right.

"You know, a few weeks ago, if I had looked into the future and seen myself now," she whispered, stroking Mir's face. "I think I would have put myself on sick leave." She gave a quiet laugh and watched the sleeping face opposite her.

For the first time, her heart truly hurt for him. Him – he wasn't even considered a 'him' by the rest of the world, only an 'it.' He looked younger than his twenty-four years... younger and, in some ways, much older. Eva shuddered as the times Mir had tried to strangle the life out of her came to mind.

And now I'm in the same cell with him? Singing songs to him? My life has taken a turn for the insane, she decided. She wondered what time it was, and fervently hoped it had not been too long. *It's not that I want you to wake up, Mir, but… I'm going to have to leave pretty soon before I'm caught and fired and possibly imprisoned.*

Without warning Mir's eyes were open, and the light in them almost blinded Eva. His breathing began to speed up and went from gasps to heaves.

"Mir?" Eva cried, moving so she was half-sitting. "Mir? Mir, what's wrong?"

He was not crying, but he was sweating as if the temperature had suddenly gone up eighty degrees.

A pang of fear slithered through Eva – what if this was one of Mir's attacks? What if he didn't recognize her – what if he attacked her again, while she was alone and had no defense?

"Mir, listen to me," said Eva, carefully keeping her voice as calm and controlled as she could. "You have to calm down; tell me what's wrong. I can help you."

He did not seem to hear her; his eyes did not move from the spot they had locked on before. "Mir!" Eva reached forward and tentatively touched his shoulder, hoping at least to turn his attention to her. "Hey!"

He was trying to say something, his face frozen while strangled sounds caught in his throat. Frightened – for him and herself – Eva reached over and grabbed his face with both hands. "Mir, stop it!"

She squinted, blinking furiously as his eyes shone into hers, and she realized that Mir was not even awake – he was asleep, and he was having a nightmare. She pushed his hair away from his forehead, hoping to soothe him after trying to shock him out of his fit.

"It's okay," she crooned, stroking his head as if he were a puppy. "It's okay. Shhh, it's all right. You're fine." *No, you're not.* "Everything is fine; everything is going to be all right." *Please, let it be all right.*

"Doctor Ross, Mi–my Subject is sick." Eva stood in her superior's office with her hands on her hips. She had left Mir once he went back to sleep, which took a good deal of humming on her part. She had come out of the cell and discovered she had been there for three hours, and no one had seen her.

"Sick?" He looked up at her, fingers poised above his keyboard as if she was only a temporary annoyance and would leave soon. "How so?"

"I think it was Doctor Harborn's 'research,' Thirteen got an infection." She fought the urge to punch the wall at the thought of Jude.

Dr. Ross sighed. "Is it serious?"

"Mild. I… couldn't sleep last night, so I was going to study Thirteen a bit more…" she floundered for a moment, trying to come up with a plausible reason for her knowing Mir was ill. "It seemed to be… acting up in its sleep, and it had a fever."

"Was it harnessed? You know I don't approve of you going into the cell without taking cautionary measures. If it escaped it would not only kill you, it would kill anything else in its way until someone was able to take it down. This won't be as big of a problem once our specialist arrives, but for now, I would like you only to visit the Subject with proper precautionary measures."

Eva bit back a loud sigh and nodded as respectfully as she could make herself. "Yes, sir."

"Give it some antibiotics. It will be fine. If it isn't, it's replaceable. Ah—" he held up a finger before Eva could protest, "I know the Subject is 'special,' but we *can* afford to replace it."

Eva nodded and stretched a smile across her face. *It's your* son, she wanted to scream. *He can't be 'replaced!'* "Yes, sir," was what she said instead. "Oh, and it would be very helpful if we could install some sort of faint light in Thirteen's cell."

"Ah, yes," he agreed. "I'll have that put in this evening if the electricians can manage it."

"Thank you," she said, and left the office.

Work detained her for the rest of the day, but she returned to Thirteen's cell the next morning. When she walked in the first thing she noticed was that Dr. Ross had been true to his word and the electricians had done a quick job in mounting a faint blue light on the wall nearest the doors.

The next thing she saw was Mir. He stood under the showerhead, water soaking his hair. He cupped the water in his hands and splashed it over his shoulders, carefully avoiding touching his stitches.

And Eva was struck with the realization like a blow to the head, that Mir was beautiful. In that moment, she knew she was seeing him not just as a damaged Subject who needed her, but as a man. Naïve, young, hurt – but a man nonetheless. And he barely realized it. He was like an abandoned boy in the body of a twenty-four year old; innocent where he should be experienced and experienced where he should be innocent.

Girl meets guy, guy is a non-human, girl falls for guy... I have no idea, she thought. But then and there she felt very much like what she was – a twenty-three year old girl looking at the most important male in her life. *Come on, Eva, don't lose your head.*

"Coming in?"

Mir's puzzled question shattered Eva's mental state. She walked closer, experiencing a sensation she never thought she would with Mir – butterflies in her stomach. They were small, but they were there.

"I brought you something to help your infect—isn't that water *cold*?" She broke off her original thought and allowed a few drops of water to splash her outstretched hand. "Well," she said, more to herself than to Mir, "lukewarm, anyway."

Mimicking her movements, a confused frown drawing his eyebrows together, Mir watched the water trickle through his fingers and looked at Eva. "Luke...warm?"

"It's the temperature of the water," she explained, drying her hand on her lab coat. "It means it isn't cold, but it isn't really warm, either."

And then she laughed, because Mir's expression took on such a typical 'well, whatever' expression, as if he thought she was silly and did not really care. It was one of the few normal expressions she had seen on him, and it had taken her aback.

"Here." She suppressed small outbursts of giggling and held up the antibiotic pills. "Put these under your tongue and wait until you can't feel them anymore before swallowing."

Mir looked down at the pills and raised his eyes to hers, that near-permanent mixture of confusion and mistrust on his face. The horror of his life was stamped on his face like words on the cover of a book, even during ordinary situations.

"W-What are they?"

"They will help you," Eva assured him, "they're for your infection. And you really should keep your stitches dry," she added.

Mir stepped back immediately, out of the stream of water. "Okay?"

Eva smiled. "Yes. But you should dry it." She glanced around. There was nothing to dry it *with*. She looked down at herself. *Aha, over shirt.* She took off her coat and unbuttoned her outside shirt, shivering as the cold air enveloped her bare arms. *Remember to never come Beneath in a camisole. Ever. Bring a towel for Mir.*

She ignored Mir's intense look of concentration and bewilderment and folded the shirt into a square, tucking collar, cuffs, and buttons inside. "Here," she said, moving closer to him. Slowly, careful not to apply too much pressure against the stiff black stitches, she pressed the shirt against his stomach.

He bit his lip but did not pull away. "Your infection will get worse if your stitches get wet," Eva explained as she dried Mir's X-shaped wound.

He nodded and stood patiently while Eva finished. *Doctor Ross,* she thought venomously, *if you only knew what you could have had. Mir would have been an amazing son, but you had to go and have him labeled a non-human – I ought to turn you in, you pathetic, insufferable, unfeeling –*

Mir suddenly brought his hands up around hers and pushed them away from himself. Eva realized that during her brief mental tirade she had forgotten to be gentle; she must have applied too much pressure.

"I'm sorry," she said quickly, but her voice came out a whisper. She coughed and repeated herself, louder. "I'm sorry."

Then she stiffened.

Mir had leaned his head down and was inhaling the scent of her... hair? "Mir?" she asked, doing her best to keep her voice from squeaking. His face was entirely too close to hers for comfort; she could feel his breath on her temple, her ear. "Hey, what are you doing?" she demanded. She had to regain control over the situation before it grew any stranger.

"Eva smells good," said Mir quietly.

She felt that unexpected flutter in her stomach again. "It's cotton-scented shampoo, so I suppose my hair smells like cotton."

"Cotton," he repeated the word, his voice soft.

Eva allowed him to breathe in one more time and then ducked her head and took a step back. "Take the pills," she said, placing them in his hand. She clutched her wadded outer shirt and draped her coat over her arm. "I'll... I'll see you tomorrow."

She turned and crossed the cell with quick steps. As the doors closed behind her, she let out a deep breath and leaned against the wall. Something had changed, and she knew what it was.

In the course of ten minutes, Mir had become very, very human.

Chapter Twenty-One

Eva saw Mir once the next day but it was a brief visit. She checked his stitches and made certain his fever had gone down, but she left as soon as possible. She wanted to stop her developing feelings for him before they progressed too far. It was unwise, it was dangerous, and it was really quite impossible.

She wanted to call Pocky, but every time she reached for the phone she hesitated. *What would I say?* Eva hardly slept; two of her usual dreamless, peaceful nights were spent tossing under the sheets. On Thursday, she decided as she ate lunch that she was going to continue her visits to Mir, but she was going to keep them short and professional.

After all, she told herself while chewing a sandwich that seemed unusually dry and tasteless; *I'm still a doctor with a job to do. I can't slip up. There has to be some sort of Subject-Doctor boundary...*

She did not even convince herself.

Unable to finish her meal, she threw the remains into the trash and went Beneath. Four guards walked past her, talking in loud, rough voices. She gave them a brief glance but thought nothing of it until she saw three more guards headed in the same direction.

With a growing sense of foreboding, Eva quickened her steps to Cell Thirteen. The doors opened, but the steady glow from the light told her what she had been afraid of. Mir was gone. Instinct told her where to go; she left the cell without closing the doors and ran to the Prepping Room.

At least twenty guards crowded around the door when they could not fit inside. Eva shoved her way past them into the room, her ears nearly deafened with shouts and whistles from the men around her.

She reached the front of the small throng and stared, her face flushing so hot she could feel it.

Mir's wrists were chained to the wall with two feet of slack. Two guards, their sleeves rolled up and hats discarded, circled in front of him, taunting him with calls of "Come on, Tiger, fight back!" and "Here, kitty, kitty!"

The heftier of the guards struck Mir with something like a cattle prod and Mir jerked back with a hiss.

"Aww, did that hurt?" Another swipe of the cattle prod struck Mir's cheek. He hissed louder and pulled at the chains; eyes, tattoo, and scars blazing dangerously. When the other guard closed in, Mir turned his attention on him and bared his teeth, a growl rumbling from his throat.

"Ooh, good boy," cheered someone behind Eva.

The second guard up front laughed and mimicked Mir's ferocious expression, circling like a boxer. Mir lunged as far as he could, his arm jerking painfully in its socket. His tormentor dodged out of the way, whistling sharply.

"Hey, Tiger, over here!"

Mir's head turned to look at the other guard and the second man struck out, a low blow that doubled Mir over with a cry of pain and rage.

"What is going on here?" The shriek tore itself from Eva. She walked into the center of the room, all eyes instantly on her.

The guard with the cattle prod gave Eva a sneer that only served to make his twisted face even uglier. "Orders, Doc." He twirled the prod like a baton. "We're prepping him for the Russian Specialist who's coming tomorrow."

Tomorrow. "Did Doctor Ross tell you to do this?" she demanded, giving him a superior, angry expression in spite of the fact he had a good five inches on her.

"Yeah, that's right." His partner nodded. "He said he wants him good and riled up for the test round."

"Test round?" Eva's eyes widened. "This is not the Roman arena, this is a *testing facility*! And Thirteen is not a lion, he's a Subject!"

"Is there a problem here, Doctor Stewart?"

Eva turned at the cold sound of Dr. Ross's voice. "Sir, with all due respect, this is pure abuse. How are we supposed to keep Thirteen in experiment-ready condition if—"

"This is a rare occasion, Doctor, and a battle-ready Subject is what Mr. Igorov requested." Dr. Ross's pale eyes viewed her with narrow disapproval. "I must ask you not to interfere. You may watch if you can keep silent, but if you cannot then I must ask you to go elsewhere."

Humiliated and enraged, Eva barely managed a civil nod. "Yes, sir," she spat.

Dr. Ross's expression did not change, but Eva knew he was not pleased with her behavior as he turned and left the room.

Eva turned to look at Mir, but his gaze was already on her. His mouth was swollen and bloody, his face bruised and burned from the cattle prod. His hair hung over one eye, but the other pierced her heart with a pang of regret.

He was less than ten feet away and she, his Handler, was helpless to save him.

They looked at each other eye to eye for a moment longer, and Eva knew that he was telling her he understood.

Swallowing a lump of tears, Eva hurried and left the room, pushing past rows of silent guards. She tried to block out the cheers and shouts that resumed as she strode down the hall.

To Eva's further fury, she was not allowed to see Mir until the next day at noon, when everyone would finally see the Russian Specialist for the first time.

Her protests only earned her the frigid remark from Dr. Ross, "Youth does not equal wisdom, Doctor Stewart; you have one but not the other."

When she reached her room, the first thing she did was open Pocky's owl-covered notebook and turn to the third page.

Wisdom will save you from the way of evil.

She paused, then turned to the next page, and the next.

Do not withhold good from people when it is in your power to give it.

Hate starts quarrels, but love covers every wrong.

A merciful person helps himself, but a cruel person hurts himself.

She scratched her head and sighed. The advice was thought-provoking and wise, but also vaguely familiar in a way she could not place. Had Pocky said these things to her before?

She reread the phrases. "All right, so: giving, loving, and merciful." She wanted to be these for Mir, but... "No," she said firmly. "I will be these for him, if this is what he needs, regardless of what my feelings might be."

She dreaded tomorrow.

Noon came too quickly the next day, and when Eva went Beneath she saw that the entire security staff seemed to have come out in full force – even the off-duty guards stood around in the hallways, waiting for the demonstration.

Eva felt awkward among them, but she was determined to be present. "Excuse me," she grabbed a hold of Brenton's arm as he stepped out of his office. He slammed his hand into the door and cursed loudly before turning his ever-deepening scowl in her direction.

"What?"

"Where will the...'demonstration' be held?" Eva asked stiffly.

He jerked his head to the right. "It'll be in the observation room, at the end of the second hall on the right."

Eva did not thank him; she turned and hurried down the hallway searching for a room she had never seen. She found it easily enough. It was very distinctive; the entire wall facing outward was made of the same plastiglass as the inner cell doors. It was a large concrete room with nothing inside - the architect had designed the facility for practicality and not taste.

She glanced behind her and saw that the guards had been told where to go. They were streaming toward her with heavy footfalls and raucous talk. She sighed and folded her arms. She would ignore them and worry.

It felt like an eternity waiting for Dr. Ross and the Specialist to show up. That word almost frightened Eva. 'Specialist.' It was just vague enough to mean many things and none of them promised anything pleasant.

Eva pulled out her phone to check the time. It had been forty-three minutes... She straightened. She could see Dr. Ross now; coming down the hall toward them, and behind him stalked the biggest man Eva had ever seen.

He was six foot five if he was an inch, and he had to weigh at least 250 pounds – all muscle. He wore fatigues that looked as if they had been used for many years and were now so much a part of him he would not wear anything else. A thick black vest made of something that looked like canvas, heavy combat boots and tough half-fingered gloves were his only accessories.

His head was close-shaven, revealing tiny shrapnel-sized scars. His nose was large and bent, his eyebrows thick, and his mouth devoid of any expression whatsoever. He looked to be in his early fifties; not exactly ugly, but hardened and used to violence. Perhaps *too* used to it.

Behind him and Dr. Ross were six guards. One held a large box from which hung two straps and two long cords, but it was not this contraption that held Eva's attention, it was the one behind it: a long iron rod draped with chains. Mir's arms were chained behind him, wrapped around the rod, and a manacle around his neck held his head back with another foot of chain. Five guards held the rod, chains, and Mir's arms. Their faces were pale in spite of their stoic expressions.

Eva reached out and touched Mir as he was forced past, but even as her fingers brushed his skin she knew he would not respond. He had been sedated for transportation.

She looked on as Igorov, Mir, and the six guards entered the Observation Room as if they were going to a business meeting. Since she had gotten there first, she had a view next to the window.

Igorov caught her eye through the plastiglass, but his expression did not change. He motioned to the guard with the silver box and stood with his arms out while the younger man looped the thick straps around his arms and the Russian buckled them around his broad chest. Waving the guard away, he pulled the two cords from the box down his sleeves until the tips reached his hands. He reached into his jacket pocket and withdrew two gold objects.

Eva watched with increasing horror as Igorov slid his fingers through the holes and flexed them.

Brass knuckles.

The Specialist calmly twisted the tips of the cords into small holes in the knuckles. He rotated his neck and shoulders, limbering up, and Eva felt the bottom fall out of her stomach. Igorov exuded strength and power, with no sign of mercy or even care on his scarred face.

The sound barrier was off, so everyone outside could hear what happened inside the room. Igorov spoke to the guard. "Turn it on."

Eva looked on as the box-shaped object on the Russian's back began to hiss, sending faint flashes of light down the cords on his arms and finally surging around the brass knuckles; an electric storm in miniature.

No.

Eva swallowed hard.

The guards unhanded Mir, but left the manacles around his throat and wrists. They pulled the rod from his arms and left, but not before one of them handed Igorov a syringe.

The Russian nodded and waited as the room was cleared, leaving only him and the Subject. Mir stood, his eyes vacant and head lowered. Igorov confidently closed the space between them with three long strides and jammed the needle into Mir's arm.

Mir barely seemed to notice, but one of the guards outside immediately deadlocked and bolted the door at some sort of unspoken signal.

Eva's heart pounded. She could not drag her eyes away from Mir – she did not want to. For an agonizing moment, he did nothing.

Nothing.

Nothing.

Nothing.

And it was as if something inside him exploded. His back stiffened, his fingers spread like claws and his battered face darkened into such an expression of animalistic fury that Eva took a partial step back from the window.

"Whoo, look at him light up!"

"I'm betting on Igorov."

"No way, Tiger'll take him out."

"You kidding? Igororov's SPETSNAZ; he's not going down just cuz Tiger glares at him."

The chaos around Eva sounded muffled to her ears, as if she was sinking underwater. Mir looked truly non-human inside the concrete cage.

Igorov was neither frowning nor smiling; his face wore an expression of total indifference. He stood, legs spread in a ready stance, waiting.

For another moment there was nothing, not even breathing.

Igorov's knuckles sparked.

Mir jumped.

His strength and agility carried him across the room, but his opponent twisted and caught him with a punch that slammed Mir sideways into the wall. He recovered quickly, crouching like a panther ready to attack. Standing easily, almost carelessly, Igorov turned and exposed a good portion of his back.

No, Mir, don't take the –

But Mir had been abused, drugged into a frenzy. He sprang again, twisting with a snarl as Igorov turned and swung out again, narrowly missing his attacker. Mir did not falter. He grabbed Igorov's legs, catching him off-balance.

Igorov fell heavily and Mir was on top of him, teeth bared and hands digging into his throat. Igorov grunted, but was not helpless. He brought his knee up into Mir's stomach, eliciting a sharp howl from the Subject as he rolled away, blood dripping from several broken stitches.

Eva stepped forward again, as close to the glass as she could get without fogging it up with her breath. Igorov got to his feet and aimed a kick at Mir, but Mir rolled to the side and scrambled to his own feet.

His eyes shone as brightly as the charged sparks that sizzled over Igorov's hands. They circled each other, each tense and waiting. Igorov faked a lunge to the right, but Mir seemed to sense it. His fist collided with Igorov's throat and the Russian staggered for brief second, coughing.

Then without warning he spun, his fist slamming into the side of Mir's face. Mir's head jerked to the side; Eva could hear the static hiss of electricity in the room through the speakers on the wall.

Mir appeared dazed; he took a step but fell to his knees, shaking his head. Igorov was not about to wait for him to recover. He moved forward with speed surprising for someone so large and drove another punch into Mir's face flat-on. Mir's head snapped back hard. Eva found her hands clenched into fists with fear, her fingernails cutting into her skin.

"Come on, Mir. Please, get up," she whispered. The shouts around her drowned out her whisper, but she willed it somehow to reach the injured man inside.

Igorov brought his fist down again but Mir turned and Igorov barely kept himself from punching the ground with a blow that would have broken his hand. He reached for Mir and grabbed his arm, but Mir stretched and sank his teeth into the side of Igorov's neck.

Igorov bellowed and drove his fist again into Mir's side once, twice, three times until Mir let go. Igorov grappled his opponent to the ground, using brute force against Mir's slightly smaller frame. Mir wrapped his arms around the Russian's head, twisting it almost to the breaking point, but Igorov allowed himself to roll with the movement and broke free.

Mir clawed at Igorov's face, his fingernails tearing at his skin. Igorov pressed his elbow into Mir's throat, making it impossible for him to breathe.

He brought his right fist down on Mir's face; Eva wanted to cover her ears to block out the sounds coming from inside the room, but she was held there, captivated with horror as Igorov punched Mir's face again and again and again, beating him senseless.

Finally Mir's head fell back onto the concrete and he lay there, unmoving and barely conscious. Igorov un-straddled him and stood up. Eva thought he was going to leave, but instead he bent his hands inward, tapped the brass knuckles together, and held them down over Mir's chest.

Eva's cry was lost amid the roaring of the guards as she watched Mir electrocuted into unconsciousness, the light gone from his half-open eyes.

Igorov turned and knocked on the door, the signal for it to open. The guard who had locked the door previously now unlocked it and let the Russian out. Igorov closed the door behind him and untwisted the cords from his bloody brass knuckles.

He looked at Dr. Ross and said in his thick, heavy accent, "I can handle him."

Dr. Ross nodded, a thin smile stretching across his face. "So I see." He looked at the guard next to him. "Take Thirteen back to its cell. Igorov, if you'll follow me to my office?"

And they left, leaving Eva to watch through tear-blurred eyes as Mir's limp body was picked up and carried down the hall to his cell.

Chapter Twenty-Two

Eva knew she could not risk going to Mir's cell until the guards who had gathered for the demonstration left. They hung around talking and exchanging money lost and won on bets.

She went above and tried to busy herself in her office, but her mind wandered with everything she did. Even straightening papers was impossible. She could only think of Mir. Even the thought of calling Pocky never entered her mind. She had no idea when the guards would go back to their places – the fight Beneath had been the most exciting thing to happen in years.

She did not want to leave Mir alone, but there was no way she could get to Cell Thirteen without being seen and questioned.

Her intercom buzzed and she jumped, answering as quickly as she could reach it. "Hello?"

"Doctor Stewart," said Dr. Ross, "Would you come to my office for a moment?"

"Yes, sir." She switched the comm off, walked to Dr. Ross's office and knocked on the door.

"Come."

She opened it and saw Dr. Ross sitting behind his desk and Igorov, metal-toed combat boots stretched well in front of him, sitting in a chair.

"You asked for me, doctor?" She glanced at Igorov with a polite smile on her lips. He nodded his head in return, but seemed more interested in what Dr. Ross had to say. She saw an angry, red bite mark on his neck and bit back a triumphant sound.

"Yes, I did." The doctor steepled his fingers and looked at Eva above the tips. "I wanted to know what you thought of the little demonstration downstairs."

"I... uh... it – Mr. Igorov seems very efficient." Eva twisted her fingers inside her coat pockets. She tried to look as indifferent as possible, but it was more difficult than she thought. The effort of contorting her expression into something that revolted against her real feelings nearly made her sick.

"Yes, I think he's perfectly capable of handling Thirteen," Dr. Ross agreed. His cold eyes seemed to be challenging her, daring her to disagree with him.

He knows. A sudden, hollow fear took root in the pit of her stomach. She fervently hoped she was wrong. "Yes," she said with a fresh, forced smile. "I'm relieved that Mr. Igorov is here."

"Fyodor will oversee all procedures and prepping sessions with the Subject from this moment forward." Dr. Ross gestured toward the Russian with one hand.

Igorov eased his large body out of the chair and stood, towering over Eva. "I will leave first," he said, his accent twisting around his words like a snake. He left the room and pulled the door closed behind him, leaving the two doctors looking at each other with unreadable expressions.

"I assume you know why I hired Fyodor."

"Sir?"

"I hired him to protect you." He leaned back in his chair, and it squeaked faintly. "You have potential, Doctor Stewart, but you lack caution. I have already warned you that if Thirteen escapes again, I will have it put down."

Eva took a deep breath. "But sir, if you—"

"It is final." His eyes seemed to drill into the very core of her being with a very different effect than when Mir did it. "Research is not worth another human life."

Eva stared. She wanted to throw something at him, to scream, *He's your son! He is another human life! You want to save my life by killing him? You know he's a human! You know it!*

"Am I dismissed, sir?" Eva asked finally.

He stared at her, long and hard, before giving her an abrupt "Dismissed" and returning his gaze to his computer.

Eva left the room with an overwhelming feeling of simultaneous relief and panic. He had let her go, but did he suspect her? If she had her Handler's license revoked, or if she was transferred or even fired... what would that mean for Mir?

She clutched her head and walked down the hall, telling herself, "You can't get caught, Eva. If you do, everything will be ruined. You can't pull a full-stop on your work – it's been almost two weeks without a procedure! How can you expect him *not* to be suspicious?"

"Everything okay, Eva?"

Eva turned. "Shut up, Jude, and leave me alone," she snapped.

He stared. "Fine!" he exclaimed. "What's the matter with you, anyway?"

"Nothing that concerns you!" She turned on her heel and quickened her steps, away from Dr. Ross, away from Jude. She wished she could keep walking, out into the frozen, barren surroundings, away from the facility. Away from WorldCure.

But she could not leave Mir.

She slammed her office door and sank into her chair. Tears threatened to spill over her lower lids, but she refused to let them. She was stronger than this; she would not cry. She never cried.

"Aaiiaaah!" She slammed her fist down onto the desk with an angry shriek. It helped a little, but not enough. With a moan she folded her arms onto the table and buried her head in them.

For the fourth time that day, she went Beneath. It had been five and a half hours since the so-called 'demonstration,' but the guards were reluctant to disperse.

"They're gone," she whispered to herself. *Finally.* Moving as quickly and quietly as her business heels would let her, she moved down the network of halls to Cell Thirteen. Biting her lip so hard it almost bled, she waited for the doors to open.

Why did they always seem slower when she was impatient?

She squeezed inside before they fully opened and closed them again behind her, hoping nobody came looking for her. She screeched as her foot caught on something and she tripped, barely catching herself. Mir lay on the floor near the door, looking as if he had been thrown there and did not have the strength to move.

She moved around to his other side and knelt down, tucking her hair behind her ear. "Mir?"

She leaned down closer... yes, he was breathing, but it was stinted, erratic. "Oh, Mir, I'm so sorry." She sniffed, trying to hold back insistent tears. "Come on, wake up. Open your eyes; come on."

His eyes opened after several tries and he uttered a groan that sounded as if it came from somewhere deep inside him. When he saw Eva, his face took on an expression that was not quite a smile, but looked pleased. "Eva," he murmured.

"I'm here." She forced a smile and pushed his hair away from his forehead. He looked terrible, even in the faint blue light. Blood and bruises coated his face and torso where he had been kicked and the stitches had broken. Her breath caught in her throat. "Oh, no," she muttered, squinting closer. She carefully felt his side and pressed as gently as she could.

Mir made a choking noise and tensed in pain. "Your rib is cracked," Eva told him, immediately taking her hands away. The mental image of Igorov's metal-toed combat boot hitting Mir made her face hot with anger.

Mir said nothing; his eyelids were nearly closed, his pain etched on every line of his face. "I brought a towel this time," said Eva suddenly, pulling it from her pocket. She looked at it and gave a brief laugh. "Well, more like a washcloth." She soaked it in the dripping showerhead and brought it back.

Settling down, she wiped it carefully across Mir's face, clearing away the dried blood. He said nothing, only his breathing would shift a little if she pressed too hard or wiped over one of the larger cuts. It looked like a glass window had exploded in his face, and Eva found herself mentally calling Igorov every ugly name that came to mind.

"Mir, I'm sorry this happened. I really am. I… I didn't want to…" she stopped and shook her head. "I'm sorry," she whispered.

Mir's eyes opened further and he struggled to sit up, pushing himself with right arm. "Hey," said Eva, alarmed. She reached out and helped him sit up even as she scolded him. "You really should lie down."

His head was lowered, his breathing heavy with the effort of sitting.

"Mir…" Eva's voice betrayed her worry.

He looked up. Eva gently wiped the swollen side of his mouth with the washcloth, clearing it of blood from his split lip. "I never wanted this to happen," she said absently, her heart doing strange things in her chest. "This all… I never even… you know, this is all your fault," she huffed, her voice rising. "If you hadn't written on the stupid wall, I wouldn't have all this conflict and you wouldn't be beat up this badly and Igorov wouldn't even be here because I wouldn't have done anything stupid and… and – Mir, why – stop looking at me like that!"

She pulled the cloth away, wide-eyed. Mir was looking at her with an intensity that made her heart do a complete series of acrobatic feats. "Mir," she said again, and leaned closer.

And closer.

She kissed him. His lips were parted in surprise, as if he had no idea what she was doing. He had probably never seen a kiss before in his life, Eva knew. She lifted her hands to his face, stroking his jaw with her thumbs. She felt him move his lips slowly, hesitantly, against hers.

She pulled back for a moment, smoothing the hair across his forehead with the tips of her fingers. "Are you all right?" she asked.

He nodded, his brilliant blue eyes focused on her mouth, fascinated. She remained still while he tilted his head, hesitantly, and then pressed his lips against hers. She closed her eyes as Mir's innocent kiss remained against her mouth for several seconds, and then his jaw moved, deepening the kiss. *He's experimenting,* she realized. He had never done anything like this before, and he was only going where it was natural for him to go.

They kissed for several moments. Eva felt herself slipping away, going under. Her mind was shutting down, filling only with Mir and emotions and hormones and —

And it felt wonderful.

Eva! her brain screamed.

Suddenly she placed a hand on his chest and pulled back, staring. He did not say anything, only looked at her with a mixture of confusion and reproach.

Eva, you're an idiot. How could you do that to him? He has no idea of boundaries, he's never been told – foolish, Eva, foolish. "I'm sorry," she gasped. She scrambled to her feet, her heart pounding heavily. "I'll be back later. I'm sorry, Mir." She hurried from the cell and almost ran down the hall and up the stairs.

She closed the door to Beneath behind her with a solid slam, her hands shaking. She pushed her hands into her hair and tried to straighten her thoughts, but the only one that would return to her was –

She had just kissed Mir.

Mir had kissed her back.

And then she had pushed him away.

"Oh, Pocky," she choked, fishing her phone out of her pocket. "Please say you know what to do."

Chapter Twenty-Three

Eva did not call Pocky. She couldn't bring herself to tell him, to make a complete fool of herself again. Instead she searched for the book he had given her, hoping to find a phrase that would tell her what to do or at least comfort her a little.

She did not get past the first few pages she had already read because her eyes landed on the words 'Do not withhold good…'

"When you have the power to give it," she finished aloud. She squeezed her eyes shut and sat, still and alone and wishing she had the power to change everything.

Her phone rang just as she was putting the booklet back on her bedside table. She looked at the caller and saw it was Dr. Ross.

"Hello, this is Doctor Stewart," she answered.

"Doctor Stewart, your work on Thirteen has been lagging."

Eva swallowed but said nothing. She had known this moment would come sooner or later; it just came sooner than she had expected. "I know. I've prepared a procedure experimenting with the effects of a counter-hallucinogen. I'm going to begin in just a few moments."

He sounded pleased. "Good. I'll tell Igorov."

Eva shut her eyes and suppressed a *no!* "Thank you."

"Not at all."

Eva lowered the phone after hanging up and sighed at the wall. She stood up and left her room; she had to go to the working half of the facility. She hardly ever left and went to her private quarters during work hours, and the one time she did she was called back to work immediately.

She sighed as she swiped her card at the door to Beneath. *My life is one stroke of bad luck after another,* she thought bitterly. Then a small smile tugged at her mouth. *Well... except Mir.*

Igorov was already outside Cell Thirteen when Eva got there. She greeted him with a 'hello' and he nodded in response. *A man of few words,* Eva thought dryly and reluctantly pressed the keys to gas the cell.

Igorov dragged Mir to the Procedure Room and laid him on the table none-too-gently. Eva wanted to tell him to be gentle or to let her take over, but she could only prepare her serums and watch from the corner of her eye as Igorov strapped Mir down.

Eva lifted the vial and studied the hallucinogen inside the slender glass tube. She would give it to Mir, wait for hallucinations to manifest themselves, and then inject him with a trial drug it was hoped would stop them. It was one possible step in the treatment of Morbus symptoms.

"Ready," Igorov grunted, pulling up a metal chair and straddling it backwards without taking his eagle-eyes off Mir.

A couple of weeks ago I would have been glad he was there, Eva thought to herself. She felt a sudden rush of anger at herself, at Dr. Ross, at Jude. She turned so abruptly that she knocked over a tall glass jar. She caught it quickly and put it back with shaking hands. *Get a grip, Eva.*

She walked over with the syringe, plugged the neural-needles into the back of his cerebral cortex - but just as she bent down to put the needle in Mir's arm, her breath caught in her throat. He was awake.

Cursing his metabolism for possibly the two hundredth time since she became his Handler, she hesitated. Wishing Igorov weren't there so she could say something to Mir, or at least tell him what she was doing so that he would understand; she took a deep breath and put the hallucinogen into his arm, her expression fiercely determined.

Eva is angry with me. I shouldn't have put my mouth against hers. I think I frightened her. I can smell the cotton in her hair, but there is another smell. I know the man is here, where I can't see him. He smells like blood. They brought him here because I'm a monster. They need another one to keep me from killing. I would never hurt Eva. The liquid in the needle hurts my head, but Eva's cold eyes hurt more. In front of her I feel smaller.

Eva did not look at Mir. It was taking all her concentration to keep an indifferent expression on her face for Igorov's benefit. He could not know that she had become attached to her Subject, he could not know that she was repulsed by what she did even now.

And it's far milder than other things I've done to him. She turned her back on Mir and busied herself at the counter at the far end of the room. It took the hallucinogen three to four minutes to kick into Mir's system, and during that time she did meaningless organizing. She could not look into his eyes. She felt as if she had betrayed him, but it was a necessary betrayal – if she did nothing, Dr. Ross would choose another Handler. Another Handler who would probably kill Mir.

...cannot sustain another system failure...

She heard the monitor begin to beep and inhaled deeply. *I can put up with this. Please, please, just let Mir understand.*

It was everything she could do not to cover her ears when the screaming began. She hurried to pick up the vial of anti-hallucinogen, but the ear-shattering, frightened noise jarred her nerves so badly that she missed the correct vein twice.

Please let it work.

She couldn't help but wonder what Mir was seeing. Whatever it was, she was glad she wasn't the one seeing it – Mir sounded as if his heart was being torn apart inside him.

It took three minutes for the anti-hallucinogen to kick in. Igorov had not moved, and he never took his gaze off Mir. He seemed undisturbed by the proceedings, and Eva found his presence both strangely calming and extremely inconvenient.

Mir finally calmed, swallowing huge gasps of air like a drowning person who had finally broken the surface. He looked at her, and even though Eva had promised herself she would not meet his eyes for the entirety of the procedure, she found herself unable to look away.

He looked stricken. She could see the question on his face, written in every pain-etched line. *What did I do?*

Nothing, Mir, she wanted to tell him. She wanted to tell him so badly. But all she could do was turn to Igorov and give the orders for Mir to be tranquilized and taken back to his cell.

Eva did not go back beneath until one o'clock that night. Igorov seemed to have been ordered to keep an eye on her, but she had not been able to speak to Dr. Ross about it.

She almost did not go inside the cell. For the first time in over a week, she felt hesitant to be near Mir. She turned and walked away, but came back before she had gotten ten feet.

She had to explain things.

She had her hand on the tranquilizer in her pocket as she walked in, letting the doors quickly slide closed behind her. "Mir? I know you're in here." She scanned the corners of the room and felt a familiar quickening of her pulse.

She heard a noise behind her and turned. "Where were you?" she yelped.

His eyes flickered up at the bars above. Eva had never thought that a person could fit up there between the bars and the ceiling. *Hmm.* "Well, look." She stepped toward him and he flinched, backing up until he hit the wall.

He doesn't trust me.

Again.

Eva stood still for a moment, barely breathing. "Mir," she said in a feather-soft voice, "It wasn't your fault."

His eyes glowed dimly, like fading electricity. He whispered hoarsely "Did I frighten Eva?"

"No," she said, feeling as if molten lava had settled somewhere in her chest.

"Did I hurt Eva?"

"No. You didn't hurt me."

He took a step closer. He swallowed, tears muddying his eyes. "I'm sorry."

Eva blinked, taken aback. "Sorry for what, Mir?" she asked gently.

He reached up and pressed two fingers against his lips.

"Oh," she said, realizing. "Kissing me."

He tilted his head, one hand running nervously back and forth across the wall even though his attention was focused on her. "Kissing?"

"Yes. That's what you did. You kissed me." Once again, Eva's heart hurt to think of how little he knew. He didn't even know what a kiss was called. "One is called a kiss. Kisses is plural, kissing is the verb."

Mir stared at her. "I'm sorry about... I'm sorry I had to – look." She took a deep breath. "There's a problem. If I don't.... work on you, then Doctor Ross gets suspicious. He can't know that – that we're – well, I could get fired and you'd get a new Handler who will..." She clenched her hands into frustrated fists and sighed.

Mir's hand stopped moving across the wall. He looked at her, long and hard. Eva knew he was searching her face, looking for something deeper. He wanted to believe her. She would not blame him if he could not.

There was silence, and it seemed to stretch forever.

"Please understand," she said, tears threatening to push her over the edge. She had never been so close to crying this many times in a week before. "I don't want to hurt you – but I have to."

His eyes did not leave hers. She wanted to look away but found that she couldn't. His expression seemed tired, defeated almost.

"It's all right," he said after a moment. His voice, so much gentler than his expression, surprised Eva. "Don't worry about me."

"But I *do* worry about you," she burst out, more vehemently than she intended. She felt her face blush warmly and cleared her throat.

Mir's face softened, his eyebrows curving upwards. "Why?" He sounded surprised; not as if he was coyly coaxing information from her, but as if he was genuinely surprised and wanted to know.

"Because you... you're... because I want to," she said, crossing her arms. "I like you."

He made a little sound, a gasp of surprise. Then he said, carefully, as though he expected to have to apologize afterwards, "I like Eva, too."

Unable to give words to the sudden swell of emotions inside her, Eva hugged Mir in an uncharacteristic gesture. She had not quite realized before how petite she was; her head fit under his chin with several inches to spare. His arms lifted, awkwardly and unsure, and he patted her back.

"Thanks," she said shakily after a moment, pulling away. She laughed tearfully and wiped her eyes before they could betray her. "I've got to go now. I'll see you tomorrow, all right?"

He nodded and watched as she left the cell.

Eva had never felt so conflicted before in her life.

Chapter Twenty-Four

"My dear girl, I don't suppose I ought to ask you why you have rung me up in the middle of the night?"

"I'm confused and I need to talk to you."

"Very well, then." She heard shuffling and rustling of sheets. "I wanted a cup of tea anyway."

"Mmh." Eva smiled and looked at herself in the mirror. Faint dark circles smudged under her eyes and her complexion was paying for her recent stress. She groaned and walked across her room to fall onto her mattress.

"Are you all right? I thought I heard something fall."

"That was me."

"Any particular reason, or did you just feel like it?"

"I just felt like it. Pocky, I don't know what to do."

"Oh dear."

"I hate not knowing what to do!" she exclaimed with honest feeling as she sat up.

"This I know. What exactly is your dilemma?"

"It's Mir."

"What about him?" asked Pocky in a voice that said he was not surprised.

"I like him," Eva confessed after a moment of silence.

"I wouldn't exactly call that a problem."

"No, it's – I like him… as a man, Pocky. Not just as a – *a project*."

"…Or a Subject?"

"Certainly not. Not anymore, even if I have to treat him like one."

"I see." The last word was drawn out in a thoughtful manner that suggested he really did see and was turning the issue over thoroughly in his mind.

"Help me, Pocky." Eva was on the verge of pleading. "What should I do? Oh, and on top of this new development, Doctor Ross has noticed that I haven't been operating on Mir. I have to continue with the procedures or he'll know something's wrong, and I think he suspects already."

"Duckie! And you have to go through all this by yourself!"

"Not quite; I can call you." Eva smiled at the concern in his voice. "And I have your book of advice. It's very good, you should publish it."

"I'm glad you think so, its advice has helped me for many years. Though I highly doubt I'll try and publish it."

"You've always been so good to me." Eva drew her knees up and listened to the sounds of tea-making on the other end of the phone.

"Well, you put up with my oddities marvelously, my girl. Let's not forget that. And as for your situation with Mir…" He was silent for so long that Eva wondered if the connection had died – until the kettle whistled like a freight train.

"Prof?"

"I'm still here, just thinking."

"Think as long as you like," Eva sighed. "The more thought the better."

"I have no doubt of it. Eva, has... has Mir approached you in any way?"

She had to smile at his attempt at subtle wording. "He... well, he... I... that is, we..."

"We *what*?"

"Kissed," she said quickly.

The gusty sigh of relief from the professor nearly blew her over. "Did he instigate it?"

"Not exactly. I—" she coughed. "He went along. For a minute. But then I had to cut it short."

"Why?" Pocky asked in a cautious voice.

"He was getting a bit too..."

"Intimate? Passionate?"

She laughed quietly. "Both, I suppose. I felt like such an idiot for letting it get even that far without explaining boundaries to him."

"Yes, he's not entirely to blame," the professor agreed.

"I actually still feel bad about it. I doubt highly he'd ever kissed anyone before, and I pushed him away."

"I'm assuming you're on relatively friendly terms now," he said dryly.

"Yes," Eva agreed after a moment's deliberation. She explained the day's events to him and finished with "I don't see how he can still be so... willing. He's afraid, but wants to trust me." She stood up and looked out the window at the cold night sky scattered with stars. "It's as if his lifetime of pain and torment... all it did was make him a better person."

"When he isn't trying to kill you in a fit of insanity," Pocky added, dragging her back to reality.

"He hasn't done that in a while," said Eva.

"One week? Two?"

She rubbed her temples. She understood his concern and could not be truly upset with him, but distress pounded in her head. "He's responding to me very well."

"Obviously, if he kissed you."

"You can't get over that, can you?" asked Eva, wavering between exasperation and amusement.

"Cannot. But I can put it aside for a moment to give you some words of wisdom, if you'd like," he said in a bright voice punctuated by a heavy yawn.

"I'd love it."

"Your attraction to Mir is understandable, especially if he is physically attractive. I wouldn't know, I haven't seen him since he was an infant. You have to remember that mentally, he is unstable and has no concept of normal human realities. Be humane, be kind, but remain cautious. It isn't very long ago he nearly choked you to death."

"I remember," she sighed.

"Good. Use your head, not your heart. As much as we like to follow that, it too often leads us in the wrong direction. Be sure your head is in control before following your heart anywhere."

Eva nodded slowly. "I will. I promise."

"Good tea."

"What?" she asked, startled.

"I made an excellent cup of tea. And yes, listen to what I said. I worry about you over there, duck."

I'm not alone, she thought with faint surprise at her own thoughts. I have Mir. "I wish you could be here. Look, I have to get some sleep before my alarm goes off at five forty-five."

"Sleep, what a brilliant idea! Wish I'd thought of it myself," said Pocky with enough sarcasm to fill a small lake. "Keep me updated, dear."

"I will. Thank you," she agreed, and hung up.

When Eva went Beneath the next day, she found Dr. Ross and Jude already in the procedure room with Mir on the table. Igorov leaned against the wall in the far corner of the room, arms crossed.

Mir's eyes were closed, and something like a restraining device from which ran wires and tubes surrounded his head. The tubs were clear and thick, and they were attached to two bags of blue liquid that hung from a rack a few feet from the table.

The wires ran through what looked to be some sort of computer setup in the middle of the room, and came out the other end – attached to another Subject's head.

She looked to be in her mid-thirties. Eva had never seen her before.

"Ah, there you are. I'm sorry you weren't notified sooner."

Eva's eyes snapped over to Dr. Ross, who was watching her as he stood at the computer set.

"What are you doing?" She transferred her gaze to Jude, who was peering into the woman's eyes with an optical light.

"If it works, it's going to be one of the biggest scientific breakthroughs in history." Jude walked over to Mir and repeated the eye-inspection, the light glaring off the Subject's blue irises.

"What breakthrough?" Eva did her best not to sound too upset.

Jude's hard blue eyes smiled at her. "Memory transference."

Eva knew her mouth had fallen open. She knew it sounded like science fiction, but it had become near-possible over recent years. She just had not realized *how* possible.

"One of our scientists in Washington has a theory that brain cells can be isolated, rearranged and even transferred using electrical currents." Dr. Ross positioned the screen and sat down in the chair in front of him. "You are invited to watch, of course."

It suddenly felt as if the temperature had dropped significantly in the room. "What percent chance of success do we have?" Eva asked, worry competing with her interest. She and Jude both moved to watch the screen over Dr. Ross's shoulders, while Igorov remained where he was.

"It's unclear, but the estimate is a forty-seven percent chance for Thirteen and eighteen percent for Eleven."

Eva looked again at the female Subject stretched out on the second table. Her skin was a pale gray color, covered in faded scars and sores. She looked on the verge of death already.

Fighting the sick feeling in her stomach, Eva focused on Mir. Forty-seven percent chance to live. That was less than a half-probability. If he died now...

"Let it begin," said Dr. Ross with a grim smile, and pressed 'Enter.'

The screen was split into two views of the Subject's brains; a collection of blue computerized cells.

As she watched, several of the cells in Eleven's brain were highlighted with yellow, a computerized way of showing the experiment's progress.

. Dr. Ross's fingers hit the keys in a flurry of clicks, directing the electrical waves. The cells grew brighter for a split second –

And vanished.

Eva immediately looked at Mir's side of the screen.

Nothing.

Eleven still had the appearance of a corpse. Mir's eyes were moving under his closed lids, but that was the only indication that he was still functioning.

Jude let out a disappointed curse. "Well, that was disappointing," he said, straightening.

Dr. Ross slammed his fist down onto the platform, his expression twisted into something completely unlike his usual calm exterior. He said nothing, and Eva was glad of it.

"Look!"

She pointed at the screen that had suddenly grabbed her attention. Connecting the Subject's minds was a red, flickering line.

"It's an electrical current," exclaimed Jude, leaning forward again. "It's doing something there!" He tilted the screen. Small, faint blips had appeared in Mir's brain, and they were growing steadily.

"It's them," said Dr. Ross in a voice so tight and high-pitched that Eva half-expected him to break into maniacal laughter.

"It worked," said Jude in an awe-filled voice. "It actually worked."

Eva asked, "What memories will Thirteen have?"

Jude and Dr. Ross exchanged glances before Dr. Ross replied "We have no way of knowing as of yet. Our technology is not that advanced. In time, we may be able to isolate whatever memories we like, but for the moment we can only know that *something* was transferred."

Eva nodded and pressed her lips together. She wondered what sorts of stolen memories now resided inside Mir's traumatized mind – and what he would do with them.

"Eleven's heart rate flattened," said Jude suddenly, looking at the monitor across the room.

Dr. Ross sighed. "I'll have it taken care of."

Jude nodded and said, "I'm going out for a smoke."

As he left the room, Eva could only stare at the female Subject on the table. She hadn't known her, she did not even know if there was anything of a personality left inside before that moment.

But Mir was alive. For Eva, right now, that was all that mattered.

Chapter Twenty-Five

Eva quickly discovered that seeing Mir during the day was next to impossible. Igorov's eyes seemed to follow her no matter where she went, and though he said nothing, she knew in her gut that he would report anything suspicious he saw to Dr. Ross.

She drank four cups of highly caffeinated coffee from the cafeteria that afternoon so she could be certain she would be awake at midnight when she went Beneath. She knew that keeping this habit up for an extended period of time would definitely deteriorate her health, but she had no other option. It was either have trouble staying awake during the day, or forfeit seeing Mir in the evening. She would not forfeit.

"I can't fall behind," she muttered to herself, typing furiously on her computer at a top speed of ninety-eight words per minute. She leaned back in her chair and rubbed her eyes. Her late night the evening before was already wearing on her. She picked up her Styrofoam cup of coffee and finished it off.

She went to bed early that night and slept until her alarm rang at 12:30 a.m. She pulled on a sweatshirt and a pair of sneakers, and walked through the living quarters to the working facility. She smiled at the night guard, who nodded in her direction. He had seen her a few times before this late, and she wondered with a sudden pang of worry, if he would end up becoming a problem.

She pushed the thought from her mind and went Beneath, her steps as light and noiseless as she could make them. She hid in the shadows when she heard a guard passing by and cursed the night patrol under her breath. Once the footsteps had faded she jogged to Cell Thirteen and hurried inside. She knew that Igorov always harnessed Mir when he put him back after he was used, so she knew she did not need to gas him.

Mir was on the floor across the room, facing the far corner. Eva wondered if he was asleep. "Hey," she called softly.

He did not move. Curious and slightly worried, Eva knelt down next to him and turned him over. His eyes were open, wide and staring.

They were not glowing.

"Mir?" Eva put her hands on his shoulders and shook him, just hard enough that she hoped it would snap him out of whatever state he was in. "Mir, come on! Come on, come *on!*"

He gasped and jerked away like a coma patient suddenly awakened. Eva did not move, waiting for him to see her.

Waiting for his reaction.

What memories did they give you?

"Mir, if I take the harness off, will you be all right?" She turned slowly, positioning her body so she could see him better, careful not to move to suddenly. He was still on his side, gasping.

Eva wondered if he was in shock, until he began to speak.

"No," he panted, his eyes wide and staring at nothing. "Please don't take me! Please! What will he say? You can't, I haven't done anything!"

"Mir?" Eva took his head in her hands and forced him to look at her. "Mir, what are you doing?"

"You don't understand!" His voice was higher; he was looking at her with a look of intense panic on his face – but his eyes still seemed to be looking through her rather than at her. "I have to get back to them. You can't take me away!"

"Mir, I'm not taking you away! What—" She cut herself short and looked back at him with wide eyes. He wasn't speaking for himself – these were Eleven's words. He was quoting her memories, her voice inside his mind. Eva's hands fell away from his head and he let it fall back onto the cement, crying out until his voice was raw.

"You can't! I have to go back to them! They won't understand – I can't leave them like this! Please, you have to let me—"

His voice was cut off and he fell abruptly silent, his eyes staring, wide and frozen at the ceiling.

Eva's heart was in her throat as she grabbed two of the front straps on the harness and shook him as hard as she could without injuring him. When that did not work, she hurried over to the dripping showerhead and filled her cupped hands with water, which she splashed over Mir's face.

He blinked, and his chest rose and fell again. Eva let out a sigh of relief and pulled him up into a sitting position.

"Mir," she said in a soft, careful voice, "I can't take the harness off until I know you'll be... all right. I have to keep us both safe. Mir, do..." Her voice trailed off with a sudden, agonizing thought. She swallowed hard and finished "Do you remember who I am?"

"Eva." His voice was heavy, as if saying her name took all the energy he had.

Eva was so relieved she let out something between a sob and a laugh. "That's right, that's who I am. Who are you?" She looked carefully into his eyes.

"Mir."

Eva smiled and leaned her forehead against his, a drop of water rolling down her face from his hair. "Good. Very good." She pulled away, still holding the straps of his harness. "Mir, I know you remember some things that aren't really you."

He nodded, his eyes locked on her face. "Yes," he whispered.

Now came the dangerous part. "*What* do you remember?"

He caught his lower lip with his teeth and stared thoughtfully at her. "I – she...they took her away." The intensity of his gaze hardened, and she could see the small beads of light in his eyes begin to pool together, to brighten. "She had a husband. There were children – she was sick, and they took her away. She loved them." His voice broke and he began to cry, a heaving cry without tears; as if there was too much grief to fully let out.

Eva stared and lifted her hands, dropped them, and lifted them again. She pulled Mir to her, so his head rested against her shoulder, and lightly rubbed the back of his neck. *Without Mom, I would have no idea of how to deal with situations like these,* she realized, with the certain, uncomfortable feeling that she was more machine than woman these days.

But as she looked at herself, holding a traumatized, even dangerous, young man only a year older than herself, in a cell, inside a WorldCure facility, she knew that he was teaching her more about what it meant to be human than she could ever have learned on her own.

She held him until he quieted, then asked him again if he would be all right if she took his harness off. He nodded mutely, watching her with red-rimmed eyes as she undid the buckles.

She pulled it off and shoved it a few feet away, scraping it across the concrete floor. She was quickly growing to hate that device; it looked more reminiscent of an Inquisition than anything else.

"So." She folded her hands in her lap and looked across at Mir, who watched her with half-squinted eyes and a mildly curious expression. "You seem all right," she said aloud, more to reassure herself than to him.

He blinked. "Should I be?"

"Yes," Eva laughed. She pulled her sweatshirt down farther. It was long, and she hoped it would cover some more of her legs. They were prickling with the cold, and she made a bold mental note to wear long, warm pants tomorrow night.

"Is Eva – are *you* all right?" He leaned closer, his blue eyes searching her face.

Eva wondered if the feeling she felt now was the same one a mother felt when her child used the right word for the first time. "I'm fine," she assured him with a faint smile. "I worry about you, is all."

"I told you not to worry."

Eva's mouth opened in surprise; she had never heard him sound at all commanding before, even faintly...and for once, she had nothing to say. Instead, she raised her arms in a gesture of exasperated defeat before lowering them back to her knees.

Then something happened that shocked Eva.

Mir smiled.

And it struck her as the warmest, most perfect, most beautiful thing she had ever seen. She could not help but smile back at him; she knew she was smiling for more than one reason. She was smiling for the sheer joy of it, she was smiling because his smile demanded one in return, and she was smiling out of relief because she had truly thought she would never see him give her a real, genuine smile.

She felt wonderfully unprofessional.

She almost told him he had a nice smile, but she knew it was probably the most clichéd thing she could have said. So instead she simply took his hand in hers, felt her own lips curving up at the corners, and stayed that way for a long time.

Chapter Twenty-Six

Eva racked her brains all morning trying to find real experiments and tests she could run on Mir without hurting or damaging him any further. It was more difficult than she had expected, and she began to grow disgusted with herself as she realized that just weeks ago she had no qualms about this sort of thing.

She looked down at her clipboard, then up at her computer screen. It was a detailed list of all experiments and tests run on Subjects since the facility opened. Just glancing through them placed her stomach on a precipice, over which it threatened to topple.

The thought of doing even one of these procedures on Mir... she shook her head and shut her computer off. She shuffled a few papers on her desk in an attempt to look busy, even though she was alone in her office.

She stopped and looked at the clock. She could not carry this on forever; she could barely manage it a week.

"I have to get him out."

I am being taken back to my cell. I ache all over, but I always hurt after Prepping. It isn't so bad when I know Eva will come tonight.

"Haven't seen Doctor Stewart down here in a while."

I listen as the guards talk. They talk a lot, but not about Eva.

"She still works, we just don't see her. She's all wrapped up in Tiger here."

My leash is suddenly jerked forward, but I catch myself before I fall.

"Girls can be like that; they think it's a fairy-tale, like beauty and the beast or something."

"Doctor Stewart's pretty dedicated. I can't see her being the fairy-tale type."

The second guard laughs. "All I know is she was spendin' an awful lot of time in Tiger's cell a while back, if you get what I mean."

Another laugh comes from the other guard. "Wonder what Tiger'd tell us about her, if he could talk." A rifle is jammed into my back and this time I do fall, to my knees. "How is she, Tiger? Is she good, a pretty little thing like that?"

He looks down at me. The leash is around my neck, choking me, but I look at him with all the disgust I feel.

"Hey." The guard backs up a step. I am frightening him. Good. "You know, he almost looks like he understands what I'm saying?"

"Naw, he doesn't." My head is slapped to the side by the guard behind me. I feel my heart begin to burn. My hands tighten. "Non-human, remember? Dumb as your mother."

I stiffen as laughter, hard inside my head, pounds the air around me.

"I'd like to have a go at the sweet doctor myself."

"Who knows, maybe she likes the soldier-type. Can I have her when you're through with her?"

191

I know the tones of their voices. I know what they would do to Eva. I lean against the wall and stand up, my blood hot with anger.

"Easy, keep him down," says one of the guards. I can smell his fear, too. "What'd you do?"

"I didn't do anything! What's got him so riled up all of a sudden?"

I run forward and slam him into the opposite wall with my body. "Stay away from Eva." I feel the words growl from inside me. I see the guard's eyes widen.

I turn quickly, knowing the other one is right behind me. The harness holds my arms down, so I lunge forward and snap my head into his. He staggers and falls, groaning.

"Get security!" he screams.

"No! This is a Red, get Doctor Ross!"

Eva was sitting in her office when the walkie-talkie, balanced carefully on the edge of the desk, crackled and spoke.

"Doctor Stewart, come to storage block C."

Eva recognized the heavy Russian accent in spite of the bad connection. She snatched the walkie-talkie up and hurried out of her office. "I'm coming right down."

She ran down the stairs Beneath, not caring that her arms were freezing because she had forgotten her coat. She went out of her way to avoid Igorov; they had barely spoken more than ten words in exchange. So why was he calling her to a storage block?

She ran down a hall, her eyes grazing over A, B – there was C. She felt a fresh wave of fear entangle in her stomach. She knew this block.

A flash of memory jolted her mind.

Mir, trapped in water, thrashing against the glass –

She pushed open the door and ran inside, water splashing at her feet. Igorov stood at one of the wheels on the wall, opening the door of the water tank. It was halfway open; gallons of water poured onto the concrete floor and began to swirl down the drain in the center of the room.

Mir was in the tank.

With an outcry she could not keep silent, Eva ran to the tank and pounded on the glass, shouting, "Get it open!" She felt as if every nerve in her body were straining along with Igorov's muscles as he pulled the rusty wheel in a circle.

The door pulled open the rest of the way and Mir collapsed, held half-up by the wires screwed into his harness. Igorov walked over with long, heavy strides and quickly unstrapped the harness rather than taking the time to undo all the wires.

Shaking in panic for Mir and confused why Igorov was helping, Eva hardly knew what to do with herself. "What happened?" she demanded, her voice strained and several octaves higher than usual.

"I walked past and the door was open," said Igorov, his 'w's sounding like 'v's in his mouth. "Someone had put it in the tank and left the electricity going. It's my job to keep it from killing anyone, but I can't do that if it's dead."

"For how long? How long was it in there?" Eva could hardly breathe. An iron fist squeezed her lungs.

He shook his head. "I don't know."

Eva's fingers raced from Mir's wrist to his neck, trying desperately to find a pulse. "He's not breathing!"

She was pushed out of the way by Igorov, who straddled Mir and pressed the heels of his gloved hands down firmly on his abdomen once, twice, three times.

There was no response from Mir.

"No!" Eva leaned down, her ear pressed against his heart. She could hear nothing. She looked up at Igorov. "Get the defibrillators from the procedure room!"

He hesitated, but Eva cut him off before he could speak. "He isn't even breathing, he can't hurt me! Hurry up!"

He nodded and left, his footsteps fading quickly down the hall. Eva immediately took Mir's face in her hands. "Mir, come on, wake up! Wake up, please, come on."

His eyes remained shut, his chest still.

A cold feeling crept inside of her as she remembered what she had read in his file.

System failure...

Final death.

"No," she whispered, and the tears came, spilling over her cheeks and stinging her chapped lips with salt. "No, Mir, please don't." Her words were quiet. Empty. The door opened and Igorov came in with the defibrillators. "Give them to me!"

cried Eva, taking them when he handed them to her. She turned them on and did not bother to call 'clear' before putting them against Mir's soaked, pale skin and shocking him.

His body jerked from the shock.

He did not breathe.

Tears would not stop blurring Eva's vision as she shocked Mir again and again until she knew she had to stop. She heard the defibrillators turn off and knew Igorov had flipped the switch, but she could only sit in silent agony, feeling as if her heart had been ripped from her chest and left behind an empty black hole.

Mir was dead.

Chapter Twenty-Seven

"I get Doctor Ross," said Igorov, standing up.

"No!" Eva stopped herself before reaching out and grabbing him. "I'll tell him. Just give me a minute."

He nodded and left the room, pulling the door closed behind him.

Eva let out the sob that had been strangling her, and it led to another, and another. Every breath was a tear in her lungs. After all Mir had been through, after all *she* had suffered with him, this ending... it wasn't right. He deserved more. Better.

She stretched out beside him, not caring that cold water from the tank soaked her. She laid her head on Mir's chest, longing for a heartbeat, *praying* for one without a single idea what to say.

Eva could not even form words into a prayer; but her soul screamed to heaven or anyone as tears streaked across her face and trickled down Mir's skin. She could only cry. There was nothing else.

And then.

She felt it. A faint breath on her ear, so light she thought it only her imagination, overreacting out of longing.

And then her head lifted a fraction of an inch.

She sat up, looking at Mir with wide eyes. For a brief instant she thought she was hallucinating.

Mir was breathing.

"Mir!" she screamed, lifting his head onto her lap. "Mir, open your eyes, come on!" *Oh, God, if you're there, then make him open his eyes!*

She reached down to feel his wrist. At first she could feel nothing, but then a faint, fluttering pulse; slow but perceivable, throbbed under her index finger.

Mir's hand moved, sending small ripples through the thin puddle spread across the floor. Most of the water had drained, but some swirled behind.

Eva pulled her walkie-talkie off her belt and requested Igorov to come back to the block. He arrived a moment later, and Eva was standing – albeit soaked – and trying to look as unassuming as possible.

"The Subject has resumed breathing," she said, wondering who the Subject was; her or Mir. "Please take it to the procedure room so I can give it some oxygen."

Igorov nodded and followed Eva to the procedure room. It was all Eva could do not to burst into a run, to let off her excited, panicked, hysterical energy into a wild yell that would echo off the walls and down the furthest corridor. Instead she maintained a steady pace and opened the doors to the procedure room, waving at Igorov to put Mir on the table.

She brought an oxygen tank over to the table and placed an oxygen mask over Mir's face, then turned the air on. She looked down and saw that her hands were shaking. She hoped Igorov did not notice, and if he did, she hoped he thought nothing of it.

It took several minutes for Mir's breathing to become regular and deep enough that Eva was no longer fractious. When she felt that he was out of danger, she told Igorov to take Mir back to his cell. Without a word, Igorov obeyed.

Eva slid down the wall, collapsing in a heap of relieved, choked sobs. She would be in Cell Thirteen at midnight, not a second later. She had to see Mir. She had to get him out of this place – and she had to find out who had tried to kill him.

Eva walked into Dr. Ross's office without bothering to knock. He was studying a chart on the wall and spun abruptly as she entered, her jeans and coat still damp and her face flushed.

"Doctor Stewart," he said, measuring his words and tone as a spendthrift would nickels and dimes. "Can I help you?"

"I want to know who tried to kill my Subject." Eva hurled the words across the room with as much force as she could gather.

"Kill? Aren't you being a bit melodramatic, Doctor?"

"*Dramatic?*" Eva strode forward until she was a foot away from Dr. Ross. "Somebody locked my Subject in the tank and electrocuted it to death."

A faint gleam, something she couldn't place and certainly did not like came into his eyes. "The Subject is dead?"

"Not anymore, it isn't. I got its heart working again."

198

A sickly, spiteful expression cut across Dr. Ross's face and was gone, but not before Eva saw it. "Do you know who was responsible for the incident?" he asked. His voice was once again even and controlled.

"No, I don't. That's why I came to ask you. I want them found out and I want them punished. Surely you of all people, Doctor Ross, know how valuable Thirteen is. I feel as if I'm repeating myself, but it's true." Eva knew she sounded irritated, angry even. There was no way she could not.

"I will investigate the matter, and you can be sure justice will be dealt," was her superior's smooth reply. "Now, if you'll excuse me, I'm in the middle of something."

Eva pinched her lips together and left the room with brisk steps, slamming the door closed behind her. The office windows rattled in their places.

Eva sat in her office, staring at the top of her desk. She had so many thoughts, swirling just out of her grasp. No ideas, no plan, no nothing...except one.

One option, the only option she could think of that made any sense. She pulled her cell phone from her pocket. Her hands had started shaking again, at the very thought of what she was about to do.

It would be simple. It would be easy.

It might not even be traced back to her.

She took a shaky breath that was not as deep as she would have liked and dialed a number. It rang twice and a young woman answered who sounded as if she tried very hard to be cheerful and perky.

"Hello, this is Humanity International, how can I help you?"

"Yes, I – I'd like to speak to the person in charge."

"Who is this, please?"

"I... I would like to remain anonymous," said Eva hesitantly, curling her fingers tightly around her pen.

"One moment."

The 'moment' stretched into several minutes, and seemed more like an hour to nerve-wracked Eva. Finally, another woman's voice, deeper and steadier, picked up the phone.

"This is Katherine Diaz with Humanity International. How can I help you?"

You can hang up, Eva. You can hang up now.

Hang up.

Hang up!

"I have some information about WorldCure. It's urgent, and it involves false labeling of non-humans."

There was dead silence that lasted only a few seconds. "Go ahead."

Chapter Twenty-Eight

Eva remembered to wear long, warm pants when she went Beneath that night. She ran, bouncing her steps slightly so she would make as little noise as possible. She ducked under the cell door as it opened and walked over to Mir, who leaned against the wall with his back slightly arched.

"Are you having trouble breathing?" asked Eva, alarmed. She crouched next to him.

His eyes opened but it took a moment for him to say anything. Eva could hear his breath; it was erratic, shallow. She swallowed and leaned forward to look him over. Deep blue-and-green bruises clearly showed where she had shocked him with defibrillators earlier.

"Oh, Mir." The words were something between a groan and a whisper. "I'm so sorry."

He finally spoke, but the words were paid for with effort. "Your eyes are l-leaking," he managed. Eva shivered as his thumb wiped away a tear that had tracked down her cheek.

She smiled and wiped her sleeve across her face just in case. "That's called crying. When a person's eyes... leak," she smiled to herself, "they're crying."

"Why is Eva crying?"

She laughed through a lump of tears in her throat. "Because. I – I don't like to see you hurt." *Stop blubbering, Eva. You've never cried as much in your life as you have during the past week!*

"I don't like to see you cry." Mir gave her a smile that shone through the pain that etched between his eyes, the pain that deepened the corners of his mouth.

"All right, then. I won't," she promised, mentally making it an order to herself. She smiled back at him. She loved to see him smile, even if it could not be an unshadowed smile. "I won't, if you promise to stop getting hurt."

She wished she could take it back instantly.

The bewildered, hurt look on his face cut her to the core. She was turned to stone for several heartbeats until he said softly, with several strained breaths between words, "I don't like to hurt."

"I know you don't, Mir." She brushed the hair away from the side of his face. "I didn't mean it that way. I just don't like it when you *do* hurt."

He smiled; she felt his cheekbone lift in the curve of her palm. "Could you c-come here?" he asked, looking into her eyes. His were not glowing brightly, but they reflected the blue light enough to make him resemble a cat.

"Here? You mean like this?" Eva leaned a bit closer, wary. She could not let him kiss her again, not yet. Then she realized what he was doing. He was smelling her hair.

"Cotton?"

"Cotton," she affirmed, unable to stop the light laugh that left her. There was something so innocent about Mir, in spite of everything he had been through... something childlike remained underneath the darkness he carried.

She let him play with her hair for several minutes. It seemed to relax him; she heard his breathing become a bit more even as he focused on something else. Mir was very gentle and Eva discovered that it actually felt very nice. She cut her own hair here at the facility, and so had not been in a salon to have her hair professionally played with in years.

"All right," she said finally, pulling away and smiling at him. "That's enough." They were silent as Mir's fingers reluctantly left her hair. "There... there's something I have to tell you," said Eva hesitantly.

Mir tilted his head and waited.

"I'm – I'm going to try and get you out of here." Eva could feel her heart beating in both her wrists, as if her heart was pumping overtime, trying to explode her veins. "I'm going to try and get you out of WorldCure."

Mir's expression did not change, but his eyes went wide. "Out? W-where?"

"Probably Anchorage. I have a friend who lives there, and we can trust him." Eva knew she would be making another early-morning phone call to Pocky when she went above.

"Anchorage?"

"It's a place away from here."

"Out... out will be dangerous. You could be hurt!" Mir leaned forward, his expression bordering on panic.

"I'll be careful," Eva promised, taking his larger hand in hers and linking her fingers through his. "All right?"

He looked tense, but nodded. "When?" he asked, his hand closing tighter around Eva's.

"I don't know exactly." Eva chewed on her lower lip for a thoughtful moment. "Soon, I know that. I told some people about what's going on here, and they're coming to look at it."

"When?"

"They said some time next week. So it could be either three days or seven. I don't know." She realized as she told Mir that she was afraid. This was more dangerous than anything she had ever thought she would do, and the thought that something could happen to her or Mir... "I don't know what's going to happen." She looked into his eyes and rubbed his cool cheek with her palm. "But... I..."

He reached up and covered her hand with his free one. "I know. I love Eva, too."

Chapter Twenty-Nine

"Pocky?"

There was a loud yawn. "This can only be Eva. Why, you ask? Because only Eva is cruel enough to awaken me in the middle of the night *twice*."

Eva laughed, but it was a short laugh. She had too many things on her mind to allow her to laugh for long. "I called Humanity International."

"Humanity Inter – *the* Humanity International?"

"That's the one."

"Did you tell them about WorldCure?"

"Yes, I did. I know they're in bed with the Non-Human act, but they're also very strict about obeying the law. They weren't happy about the way WorldCure is labeling healthy people non-humans."

"It was a wise move, Eva. I'm glad you made it."

"So am I, Pocky, but I can't help but wonder – why didn't you? When you found out about WorldCure, what kept you from calling them? Wouldn't they have done something then?" Eva positioned herself more comfortably on her pillows and looked up at her ceiling.

"That... it was complicated. Then, Humanity International was all for the HRI's Non-Human Act because they were so concerned about 'over-population' and such nonsense."

"Right, but..."

Another yawn – no, it was a sigh; a heavy one. "I…"

He was silent for so long that Eva sat up and asked in a soft voice "What was it, Pocky?"

When he spoke again, it was as near to breaking down as she had ever heard from him. "My wife was still alive then, as you know."

"Yes," said Eva slowly, nodding. "She died just a few years ago, didn't she?"

"She did."

Eva felt as if a heavy blanket had suddenly been pulled over her head and was smothering her. "Pocky, WorldCure didn't…. threaten you. Did they?"

"Only by proxy." Another stretch of silence, then, "They threatened Margaret. Threatened to give her a non-human label and take her to one of their facilities."

Horror turned Eva's stomach and she laid back down, her head swimming. "They did that to keep you silent?"

"Yes." She could envision him sitting upright in bed, his head bowed. His voice was full of regret, obvious through his cultured British accent. "I am ashamed to say I let them cow me into submission. I didn't want anything to happen to Margaret."

"I don't blame you, Pocky," said Eva, her voice full of the sympathy she felt. She carefully kept the disgust she felt toward WorldCure out of her tone. "I probably would have done the same thing, if they threatened someone I loved." As the words left her mouth, a realization spread over her like a high tide.

WorldCure had done worse to someone she loved.

I do *love him,* she realized with a gasp.

"Eva, my girl, are you all right?"

"Y-yes," she stammered, clutching at her composure. "I'm fine. It's just – WorldCure, that's all."

"They are evil, Eva. And now that you have called Humanity International…"

"They're coming to inspect us sometime in the next seven days." Eva ran her hand over the comforter, twisting her fingers into the soft folds.

"Don't relax even for a moment. WorldCure is not to be trusted, and I wouldn't put it past them to do… anything."

"I know. I'm worried. I feel like something bad is going to happen, but I don't know what."

"Does WorldCure know that Humanity International is coming?"

"I don't think so. I don't see how they could."

"Good." Pocky's voice held all the foreboding she felt. "Because if they do find out, you will be sitting in a crucible."

"I think I already am," murmured Eva.

Nothing suspicious happened the next day. True to her word and Pocky's warning, she did not let her guard down even for a moment. She felt like a criminal, except she was doing the right thing.

Since when did I become a vigilante? she wondered the day afterwards as she studied Mir's blood in her office. It had taken her a ridiculous amount of time to isolate a single component of his actual blood, pulling it away from the other pollutants so that she could study it separately.

She turned the microscope, zooming in closer to the small drop of blackened liquid on the glass. She glanced up at the screen in front of her; one half showed the composition of blood cells while the other side analyzed the elements.

Mir had an unusually high amount of white blood cells, Eva noted. This would account for his improbable recoveries from virus strains and other infections.

She leaned over and picked up one of his medical charts from the desk. She scanned it, comparing other physical results to the crude blood test in front of her.

How long she stood there, staring at the results that sent a cold chill inside her, she did not know. She lost track of the time. She wanted to disbelieve what she saw; she wanted to look away. She wanted to take the tests again, to prove that they were wrong and change them somehow.

"Oh, Mir," she breathed, a strange lump squeezing her lungs and making it difficult to breathe.

A loud knock pounded on the door and she dropped her clipboard, startled. "C-come in," she called hastily, picking up the pieces of paper that told her what she would have given anything to change.

The door opened, and Igorov's bulky frame stood there. His face was set in stone, but there was an air about him that seemed... different.

"You have to come Beneath," he ordered.

Eva felt her blood freeze. "Why?"

"Humanity International is coming. Doctor Ross has ordered the extermination of all the Subjects."

Chapter Thirty

"Tell me quickly," Eva demanded as she hurried down the hall, almost running to keep up with Igorov's long strides. "What happened?"

He spoke without looking at her, his eyes set ahead. "Someone from HRI told Doctor Ross that Humanity was coming. Then Ross is ordering me to assist the guards Beneath in killing the Subjects. 'Destroying the evidence,' he said."

Eva's nerves had no idea what to do. She wanted to scream, break into a run, and punch someone, but most of all she wanted to get to Mir. "Have they started yet?"

"Yes, that is why I came to warn you. I know you are attached to Thirteen."

Eva's eyes locked on his face, but it was as expressionless as a wall. She grabbed his fatigue-covered arm. "Are you going to help me?" she asked, her voice tense. She had only minutes – she couldn't tell Pocky, how was she going to get Mir out? What about the other Subjects? "I have to know."

He finally looked down at her, his pale eyes unblinking. "I did not get paid to see Subjects get killed," he said clearly, making every word perfectly enunciated for her. "That was not my job."

"So you'll help?" She searched his gaze, hoping she did not have to do it alone.

He nodded sharply and began walking again. With a small rush of hope, Eva and he fairly ran Beneath.

It was chaos.

Guards were everywhere, running like military ants in a frenzy. Somewhere in the distance, an explosion of noise that she knew to be bullets pounded the air. Eva pushed past them, nearly trampled in her effort to get to Cell Thirteen. She did not stop to check if Igorov was behind her, her mind was focused on Mir. She had to get to him before they did. She *had to.*

Thirteen's cell was open. Eva turned. "Where is he?" she screamed at Igorov as three guards ran past, shouting to several more down the hall. Everywhere there was noise, but she could not hear Mir.

"Follow me," Igorov instructed as he hurried down the hall and to the left. He shoved guards out of his way, making a path for Eva. The guards were ignoring her; they were focused on exchanging orders. Eva saw a black-clad man open a cell and aim a round of machine-gun spray into the room – her heart twisted into a knot.

That couldn't have happened to Mir.

She grabbed the man's arm. "Where are the other Subjects being taken?" He turned, and she did not look into the cell. She could not bring herself to. "Where?" she demanded again, pulling as hard as she could on his arm.

"They're being rounded up," he scowled, jerking his sleeve from her grip. "Some are being taken to the gas chambers, the rest are being shot. This is orders, you know, doctor."

"Doctor Stewart!"

Eva turned and saw Igorov motioning for her to catch up. She sprinted back to him, her shoulder running into the butt of a guard's rifle. She felt trapped in a nightmare. "They said they're taking them to gas chambers," she called as soon as she was behind Igorov again.

"They are at the end of this corridor."

There were six doors, all of them labeled with 'Keep Out.' One door was open, and Eva pushed it open the rest of the way to look in, her hands shaking.

She pulled the door closed behind her as nausea threatened to overwhelm her. "Next one!" she cried frantically.

Igorov forced his way into the next room. Eva gripped the doorway at the horror of what she saw. She had no idea how many Subjects there were, but they were dead; tossed over one another in the middle of the floor like a rubbish heap.

"Hurry!" The word was almost a scream. "We have to find Mir!" She did not care that she used his real name. It was too late now; she had to get to him.

And then she heard something that seemed to send electricity through every vein in her body.

"Eva!"

"Mir!" the word ripped from her throat. She turned in a circle, trying to judge where his voice was coming from; but her mind spun. She had no idea which direction he was. "Mir, where are you?"

She whirled around as four men rushed out of the farthest room, pulled the door shut, and ran in single file down the other direction.

Igorov leaped into action before she did. He sprinted down the length of the corridor and unslung the AK574U from his shoulder. Propping it up, he fired a round of bullets at the electronic lock on the door.

He turned and threw something to Eva, which she barely caught. An oxygen mask. He must have been prepared for this. She strapped it around her head and positioned it over her face while Igorov did the same.

He shoved the door inwards with the side of his body, and a cloud of thick, suffocating air enveloped them. Her brain finally kicking into high gear, Eva dropped to the ground and crawled forward, where the air was thinner.

"Mir!"

Her voice was muffled through the mask. He had fallen amid half a dozen other Subjects, and one thought settled over her mind, strangling her. *Mir is dead.*

And then she heard another sound; a faint, high wail. Igorov bent down and lifted Mir by his arms. Underneath Mir's body were three small bodies.

Eva ripped her coat off and placed it over the infants' faces, picking them up in a hurried bundle. She screamed "Get him out!" to Igorov, who was already dragging Mir from the room as Eva fled, getting the babies away from the poisonous air.

She knelt in the hall and put the babies on the ground. They were alive. She blinked away tears that blurred her sight and looked up at Igorov, her heart threatening to rip in half. *Please say he's alive,* everything in her begged, but no words would come.

Igorov pulled his oxygen mask off and placed it over Mir's face before pounding on Mir's chest with his glove-clad fists. Eva watched; hugging the infants and trying to breathe as the Russian tried to force air into Mir's lungs.

Again.

Again.

Again.

Igorov raised his arms for the last try – and Mir rolled onto his side, knocking the oxygen mask off with a fit of violent coughing. Eva looked down at the babies and felt herself choking on a tearful mixture of soul-deep relief and hysteria.

Mir saw her and smiled as Igorov went back to the gas chamber. His skin was gray, but he was alive and breathing. "Eva." His joy in seeing her was unmistakable in spite of the weakness of his voice.

"You – you did a good thing, saving these babies," she said by way of response, afraid that if she tried to say anything else, it would unleash a flood of emotion and tears that she did not have time for.

He smiled exhaustedly again and looked at the tiny human beings, their eyes tightly closed and mouths open to unleash tiny, hiccupping cries. "Igorov," Eva called, standing. Mir got to his feet and, knowing she could not carry all of them, she handed one of the babies to him. The pink identification tag on her wrist told them it was a girl, and Mir held her as carefully as if she were made of glass.

Igorov came back, shaking his head. "All dead. Come, we must get you out." He made herding motions with his arms at them.

"Where do we go?" asked Eva, fighting another surge of panic.

"This way. There is an exit from a storage block." They ran as fast as they could, keeping as clear of guards as was possible. Eva felt her throat tighten every time she heard a burst of machine-gun fire.

The storage block was near and mostly empty. Not one to waste time, Igorov slammed the butt of his gun into the lock four times until it finally gave way. He pushed the metal door open and they were greeted by a rush of freezing air and the blinding white of snow.

Mir took a step back, clutching the infant tightly in his arms as he gazed, wide-eyed, at the frozen expanse beyond the door.

"Where do you think you're going?"

Dr. Ross stood behind them, a pistol clutched in his hand. Eva froze. They were so close to finally escaping…

She turned and felt the Alaskan wind on her back. Dr. Ross was looking at Mir. Eva saw his eyes flicker to the child in his son's arms, then back to his face.

"So." His thumb twitched on the gun. It was now set on a hair-trigger. "You almost made it."

Eva held the babies closer. She knew Dr. Ross would shoot them, all of them, where they stood. She had no doubt. If he would slaughter dozens of Subjects, what was to separate them?

"Nyet." Igorov took one, two, three slow, careful steps in front of Eva and Mir. "Do not shoot."

"Why not?" Dr. Ross's hand moved, pointing the gun at the Russian. "I hired you to keep Thirteen in line. It looks like you went astray, the same as Doctor Stewart."

"He's not Thirteen, he's your son." Eva was surprised at how confident she sounded when she felt anything but. She had wanted to say this for weeks, and now that she could, it was impossible to stop. "He's your son, and you told his mother he was dead just so you could cover up your affair."

Igorov's expression registered surprise, but he did not waver from his position. Mir stood looking at his father with a determined expression. Watching him Eva could see from the way he held his mouth, the wideness of his eyes –

"Mir, no." She spoke quietly, but firmly.

He was tense, but he still held the tiny girl protectively in his arms. He glanced at her out of the corner of his eye; she caught his expression and shook her head slightly.

"You are not my son."

Dr. Ross's words, aimed at Mir, inflamed Eva. She opened her mouth to say something, anything in Mir's defense, but a shot rang out before she could.

"GO!" Igorov bellowed, lunging toward Dr. Ross.

Eva grabbed Mir's arm and they fled out the door, stumbling into the knee-deep snow. Eva heard two more shots and a strangled cry from Dr. Ross.

Igorov did not follow.

Chapter Thirty-One

Running over the snow, Eva led Mir to the back of the facility. The bitter wind blew through Eva's thin shirt; she had her coat wrapped around the baby boys in her arms. She knew Mir, although used to lower temperatures, was even colder than she was; he didn't even have a shirt. "We're almost there," she called over her shoulder.

"Good," said Mir. His voice sounded faint.

Eva knew that most of the guards were busy 'exterminating' inside, and the only silver lining was that they would not all be out looking for her and Mir. Her car was parked outside; it wasn't far now…

She fumbled for her keys with numb fingers. A faint tremor shook the ground and she froze, looking in all directions before realizing with a sickening lump in her stomach that they were still destroying evidence.

People.

She unlocked the car and yanked the door open, shouting "Get in." She tucked the wailing babies in the back and added "Could you sit in the back and be with the children?"

She turned and noticed Mir's face was pale, as he stared at the car. "It's fine," she assured him, trying to keep the panic from her voice. "Please, Mir, just get in. I drive these all the time. They're perfectly safe."

She waited until he pulled the door open and then turned the keys in the ignition, switching the heater on as high as it would go. She gunned the engine and plowed the car backwards, spun it to the right, and pushed down on the accelerator.

Eva's mind spun as fast as the tires below her. Was Dr. Ross dead? Fyodor must be, or he would have followed them. She felt an unexpected urge to scream and mourn for Fyodor – she had despised him until half an hour ago.

She had judged him too quickly.

Eva replayed the scene at the exit door in her mind. She could see every line on Dr. Ross's cruel face, the determined way Igorov held himself, the way Mir curled protectively around the tiny girl in his arms, the gunshot...

"Mir?" She looked into the rear-view mirror.

Mir's skin was the color of ash. He stared ahead as if he were frozen in position, his lips slightly parted as he sucked in difficult breaths. "Eva..."

"Mir, what is it?" Eva's voice was hard with panic. She had never seen the stray bullet hit anything. Flying down the desolate stretch of barely-paved road, she twisted in her seat to look at him. His left arm was braced protectively over the three infants wrapped in Eva's coat. Black blood ran from a hole on his upper arm, surrounded by a mass of rapidly spreading bruises.

"Mir, you need to stop the bleeding," she instructed, trying to stay calm. She looked back at the road and took a deep breath. "You need to press something against it."

"I can't," he rasped, pressing himself against the back of the seat.

"What do you mean, you can't?" she cried, veering sharply to avoid a stretch of ice. She craned her neck to look and realized he was right. There was nothing keeping the squirming babies from falling off the seat except his arm.

"Mir, hang on, all right? I can't stop here. I don't know if we're being followed – uh, you – just breathe deeply and focus, okay? Don't pass out. Stay with me."

"I will," was the whisper-faint reply.

Please, Eva pleaded to nothing. *Please, let us make it.*

Eva's eyes constantly looked back and forth between the road in front of her, the road behind her, and Mir. There was nowhere to pull over where they would not be seen if they were being followed.

For the first time in her life, Eva wished she believed in Pocky's God. She glanced at the digital clock display on the dashboard. She had been driving for almost twenty minutes.

It felt twice that long.

A heavy thud came from the back seat. "Mir?" Eva twisted to look. Mir had collapsed on the floor of the car, his eyes shut and his skin the pale gray of the sky outside.

Eva hauled the steering wheel to the side, driving the car off the road and up onto the frostbitten weeds. Almost before the vehicle had come to a full stop, she climbed out of the car and ran around to yank open Mir's door.

Two of the babies who had fallen asleep were still curled on the seat where Mir had put them, but one of them – the girl Mir had been shot protecting – was awake, her large blue eyes blinking widely up at Eva.

Eva stretched over and pulled Mir up by his arm, careful not to pull his injury any more than she had to. She knew she could only stop for a moment – everyone at the facility would be busy, but she could not be sure they were not being tailed.

She slapped Mir's face. "Wake up, Mir! Come on, honey, please wake up!" She looked down the road; she could only see a small stretch of it from her position, but thankfully, it was empty.

She reached under the back seat and pulled out a stray scarf she had shoved there weeks ago. Tying as well as she could under pressure and with only a few moments at her disposal, she created a makeshift bandage around the bullet wound and carefully laid Mir back on the floor. She realized her mind was automatically scribbling out strange, erratic prayers – *please, let him be okay – we have to make it – it's going to be all right – let this work out.*

She leaned over to put the baby girl in a position where she could cross the other seat belt across the girl and the two boys, but froze when something caught her eye. All the infants wore an identification tag around their wrists; pink for girls, blue for boys.

But the lettering on this one took her heart and electrified it.

In tiny, black lettering, it read –
ID: 29629F – M: S23/F: S13

It was coded, of course, for efficiency, but Eva knew what it meant.

The child's identification was 29629. It was a female. Its mother was Subject Twenty-Three.

Its father was Subject Thirteen.

Eva situated Mir and the babies as well as she could, trying to rationalize the fact that there was a tiny infant girl in the back seat who had been fathered by the man she was in love with.

She drove for what felt like days, constantly looking back to see if Mir had woken up. He remained unconscious, and Eva did not know whether she was grateful or not. The babies in the back seat slept for hours, but woke up and began to cry with surprisingly loud voices coming from such small bodies.

Eva was driving as fast as she dared on the icy road. There had been no sign of anyone following her, and at this illegal speed she was only half an hour away from Pocky's.

Then she saw what she had been dreading, coming toward her in the rearview mirror.

Headlights.

She tightened her grip on the steering wheel, praying it was no one. Praying they would not look in the back seat. Praying...

The headlights honked and passed her on the right. For a moment, Eva was stunned, disbelieving. It was just a car, being driven by no one from the facility

She pressed down on the accelerator, the pounding of her heart still uncomfortably hard and

222

fast. What if Mir had lost too much blood already? What if he was—

No.

She would get to Pocky's, and Mir would be fine.

She pulled into Pocky's long, winding driveway, the tires screeching in protest at her sharp turns. She honked the horn, knowing there was nobody around to hear her except the professor.

The porch light turned on and Pocky looked out door, dressed in flannels and holding a shotgun. "Eva!" he called as she shoved her car door open.

"Pocky!" Eva gasped, "Hurry! Mir is in the back – in the back - one of them is his! Hurry, we have to get them inside! Mir was shot!"

Pocky looked bewildered, but was at the car and pulling the other door open before Eva could finish her jumbled, panicked sentence. "Children?" he exclaimed. "How in heaven's name did you acquire children?"

"I'll explain when we get inside! I'll get the babies, you get Mir!" Eva gingerly picked up the wailing infants and rushed them inside, embraced by the warmth inside the house. *What do I do with them?* Her brain asked, looking down at the babies in her arms.

She had never really dealt with a child, especially a child obviously under a year old – what was she supposed to do with it? At a loss, and in a hurry to get back to Mir and explain things to Pocky, she set the babies on the rug in the living room.

She ran back outside to where Pocky was trying to help the much larger Mir reach the door. She picked up Mir's other arm, pulling it gently around her shoulders and together they got him into the living room with the three miniature Subjects.

"The first aid kit is underneath the kitchen sink," Pocky told Eva as he carefully unwrapped the scarf that bound Mir's bullet wound.

"Okay." Eva retrieved the kit and handed it to Pocky. She bent over and tucked the hair that had fallen from her ponytail behind her ear. "What can I do? Can I help?"

"Just keep him quiet. He's waking up, and this isn't going to feel good." Pocky opened the first aid kit and pulled out a long pair of tweezers and a sanitary towel. "Can you tell me what kind of gun caused this?"

Eva shook her head. "No, I didn't pay attention. It was a handgun, a – a nine millimeter, I think."

"Ah." Pocky adjusted the glasses on his nose and peered closely at the wound. He gently pushed the skin around the bullet wound aside for a better look. "I beg your pardon, Mir."

Mir's eyes were open halfway, glazed and flickering from the ceiling to Eva and Pocky's faces. His skin was sickly-looking and when Eva took his good arm, she could feel that it was clammy, but strangely warm.

"Pocky, how will his body adjust to the temperature in here?" she asked suddenly, her eyes gazing widely at the professor.

He glanced up at her without moving his hands away from Mir's swollen arm. "Ah," he said slowly, "I'd forgotten about the temperatures Beneath. Turn the thermostat down a few degrees, but not too many – we have the infants to worry about. Mir will adjust, I should think, but it may take a little time."

Eva obediently turned the thermostat down to seventy degrees and crouched down beside Mir again. She wanted desperately to gather him in her arms and tell him it was fine, to explain where he was, and to tell him he was safe – even if only for a short time.

"Hold him still," said Pocky in a quiet voice, inserting the tweezers.

Mir shuddered and grabbed Eva's hand tightly when she slipped it into his. His mouth opened as if to groan, but no sound came out except something like a sigh. He was too exhausted, he had lost too much blood.

Doing her best to keep the worry she felt off her face, Eva looked at Pocky. His own round, grandfatherly face was bunched up into a squinting frown as he dug the bullet out of Mir's shoulder.

"I'm assuming it was shot at close range," he said without taking his eyes off his patient.

Eva nodded. "About ten feet."

"How much blood did he lose?"

Eva looked over at the scarf. Black soaked it in patches where it had been wound around Mir's shoulder. "A lot. I haven't checked the car floor, and I didn't even know he was shot for about ten minutes afterwards."

Then Eva remembered. The baby. The little girl.

Mir's daughter.

"Pocky, when you're done with this, I really have to talk to you." She knew her tone was urgent, but she felt urgent. Her mind was still trying to process everything that had happened, everything that *was* happening and could possibly happen within the next twenty-four hours.

"All right, dear, patience is a virtue, you know," was Pocky's gentle answer, quickly followed with "Ah-ha!" as he pulled the bullet out, slick and black with blood – but free from Mir's arm. He wiped the wound clean with an antibacterial cloth and wrapped it, firmly but gently, with a thick strip of bandage.

Mir's fingers wrapped around Eva's like iron clamps, but Eva hardly noticed. "Pocky, do you have anything you could give him to help him sleep for a while?" she asked in a low voice.

He looked at her for a moment before nodding. He pulled a syringe from the first aid kit and filled it with clear liquid from a small bottle. "This is only a mild tranquilizer, which I am going to go out on a limb and assume he has had before?"

Eva nodded and watched as Pocky found the vein in Mir's arm and injected the sedative. It worked almost instantly; Mir released his grip from Eva's hand and his eyes closed.

"Now, would you mind telling me why there are three squalling infants on my living room rug?" Pocky asked as he stood up, taking the first aid kit with him.

Eva rose too, suddenly bone-tired. "Mir rescued them from WorldCure. Somehow, Doctor Ross found out that Humanity International was coming. They tried to…" Images of dead Subjects flashed through her mind in a horrific slideshow. "They were killing them, Pocky." She sank down onto the couch and looked down at the three babies, wrapped in her coat, so small and innocent. "They killed all the Subjects except Mir and these babies."

"How did you manage to get out?" Pocky sank down onto his knees and peered closely at the colors of the tags on the infants' wrists.

"Fyodor helped us." She covered her face with her hands, grateful when she felt Pocky's arm go around her shoulders. "H–he – Doctor Ross shot him," she managed after a moment.

"There, there." Pocky pulled her into a hug and she leaned on his shoulder, feeling as if all the strength in her had been drained away. "It's going to be all right. You can explain it more fully to me in the morning, after a good night's sleep."

"I may need some of that sedative," she said weakly, a forced smile pressing into the professor's cardigan.

"I have something better than that for you, my dear. Come to the kitchen when you're ready." He patted her head and stood up, walking out of the living room.

It took Eva a moment of sitting until she gathered the strength to stand. From the kitchen she heard Pocky call "I have fresh milk, can the babies have that?"

"I don't know!" she called back, feeling as if another rock had settled onto her shoulders. "They're too small to be fed intravenously, but I don't know what sort of formula they were on."

"I'll pray hard and give them milk," was the response. Eva nodded, but was too tired to shout a reply. She crossed the room and knelt once more next to Mir. He was the only person she had ever seen who did not look peaceful even in his sleep. A deep line cut between his eyebrows and the corners of his mouth deepened, like he was fighting pain in his dreams. The only time he had ever looked completely peaceful, she realized, was the night she sang him to sleep in his cell.

As was her habit now, she brushed the tousled, pale hair away from his face with her fingertips. "You have a daughter, Mir," she whispered. She licked a salty tear from her lips. "She's beautiful, just like you. You saved her life today, you know."

"He has a what?"

Eva turned and saw Pocky standing there, holding an old plastic bottle of warm milk and looking at her with a raised eyebrow. "The little girl is his daughter," she said faintly. "He was bred a little over a year ago. I'm not exactly sure how old she is, but... she's his."

Pocky opened his mouth, closed it, opened it again, closed it, and handed Eva the bottle. "You ought to feed the babies." He stood by and scratched his head thoughtfully as Eva awkwardly lifted Mir's baby girl and coaxed her to drink the milk.

"I think she likes it," said Eva after a moment as the tiny baby's fists curled and her face scrunched, sucking vigorously at the bottle.

"She ought to," said Pocky. "The poor tot has probably only ever been fed manufactured chemicals."

They fed the other two babies after Mir's daughter and laid them back on the living room rug. Pocky fetched a flannel blanket and spread it over them.

"You can sleep down here, if you'd like," said Pocky. "The couch is unoccupied." Eva usually slept in the guest bedroom, but she knew that Pocky was guessing she would want to stay near Mir and the babies.

"Thank you," she said tiredly, smiling. "I'd like that." She knew she would have to go shopping tomorrow – she had to buy herself and Mir proper clothes, she had to buy things for the babies... overwhelmed, she walked over to the couch, pulled the heavy blanket off it, and collapsed.

She was already almost asleep when Pocky whispered "Good night, my girl," and turned off the light.

Chapter Thirty-Two

Eva awoke to screaming.

She threw off her blanket and stood up so fast that she got dizzy. A light turned on and Pocky ran in, looking as wild-eyed and surprised as she did. They glanced at each other and realized in the same split second that the screaming came from the three babies on the floor.

"I'll go heat up some more milk," Pocky mumbled, looking relieved as he fled to the kitchen.

Eva tried to quiet the babies by shushing them, humming to them, and taking turns holding them, but it hardly helped. She knew they were hungry – she had forgotten about pre-dawn feedings.

She leaned over to pick up the baby girl and realized with a start that what she had thought was the moon's reflection through the window, reflecting off her eyes, was not moonlight.

It was phosphorous.

"Eva?"

She saw Mir, covered in shadows and light from the foyer, crouched as if to spring. She was going to tell him everything was fine, but his question stopped her – "Why are they crying?"

"They're hungry," she explained, keeping her voice calm and soothing so as not to further excite the infants. "Pocky is getting milk for them. They're fine, don't worry."

Mir crawled closer and sat in a position that vaguely reminded Eva of a sphinx. "Be careful of your arm," she warned him.

He looked down and saw the bandage. He looked for all the world as if he had forgotten he was shot. "Oh," he said. He looked at the room around them and Eva watched as he took in the wooden paneling, the leather furniture, the enormous fireplace, the wide-spanning windows.

Eva thought he was going to panic, but he looked at her and a smile – that sweet, miraculous smile, curved his lips. "Can I help?" he asked, and looked at the baby girl in Eva's arms.

Her heart pounded quickly several times. "Of course." She held the baby out to him. "Just be careful."

He's holding his daughter. Mir is holding his daughter, and he doesn't know it.

Mir held the tiny human being carefully in his good arm, touching the round cheek softly with his finger. The baby's crying quieted and soon became a yawn, and then silence. Her eyes no longer glowed, but stared, large and blue, up at Mir's face.

"Mir, there's…" Eva hesitated. No, she had no right to keep it from him. No right. "Mir, she's…" He looked at her with that face, so full of innocence for someone of his age. *Just say it. Tell him.* "She's your daughter."

His lips parted as if he was going to respond, but he only stared at her in silence until Eva thought she would go crazy if he did not say something. His breathing grew heavier and he looked down at the child in his arms, so small compared to him.

She was so innocent. Like her father.

Mir leaned his head down, his hair brushing his daughter's face; with an expression of such profound and quiet amazement that Eva knew she was going to cry again.

"I didn't know." Eva saw a thin streak of black roll from his eye and trail down his face. He looked up and his eyes met hers. "I... I remember, but I didn't know."

Eva leaned her forehead against his and listened as he was shaken by deep, gasping sobs. "It's all right, Mir," she said, taking his head in her hands. "It's all right."

"She could have died." There were so many emotions in his voice it was difficult for Eva to sort them out: awe, shock, guilt, tenderness. "I didn't protect her," he said, anger in his voice – anger at himself for not even knowing the existence of the tiny girl in his arms.

Eva realized that she knew him almost better than she knew herself. "You saved her life, Mir," she said gently. "Not only that, you *gave* her life. You know that, right?"

Mir nodded and leaned down, pressed his lips against his daughter's cheek. "She won't live like me," he said suddenly, panic filling his voice as he looked up at Eva, her face only inches away. "Will she?"

"No!" Eva said the word louder, harsher than she had meant to. "She won't." She wrapped an arm around Mir's neck and hugged him, carefully, like he was a fragile thing. She knew he was not, not really. His spirit was stronger than anyone's she had ever met, and yet it was more sensitive. He was a living, breathing contradiction.

How could she tell him what else she knew about him? How could she tell him something she struggled to admit herself? *Not now,* she thought, as her face pressed into his hair. *Not now. Let him be happy, at least for a little while. Let him be a father.*

Pocky came back out holding the bottle, and Eva pulled away from Mir to take it. "We need to get two more of these tomorrow."

"Indeed," said Pocky. "It makes it rather difficult not to show favoritism, having only one bottle."

Eva smiled a little and held the bottle out to Mir. "Would you like to feed her?"

He looked quietly at her, his sinewy arm wrapped around his child; her head nestled in the scar-marked crook of his elbow. "How?"

"Keep holding her like that," Eva instructed. At least she knew how to feed a baby. She put the bottle of milk in his other hand. "And just... that's right." She watched with an inexplicable feeling of pride as Mir coaxed the bottle into his daughter's mouth. "Good job."

She felt a tap on her shoulder and looked up. A large teacup was poised in the air above her head. "To make up for the cup you were too tired to drink last night," said Pocky with a smile.

"Oh," said Eva, touched. "Thank you." She took the steaming cup carefully in her hands and sipped the hot liquid. Pocky sat down on the floor next to her and they watched as Mir fed the baby as carefully as if it were a fledgling bird.

"She has to have a name," said Eva, picking up one of the male babies and bouncing it gently in her arms.

Mir looked up at her and tilted his head. "A name? Like Eva? Mir?"

"Exactly." Eva smiled. "Names are important."

"I don't know names," said Mir, the corners of his mouth deepening in concern.

Eva looked at Pocky, who scratched his head and took a sip of his own tea. "I think it had better be a short one," he said after a moment. "Like her father."

Eva was about to ask why, but the more she thought about it, the more she liked the idea. Mir's name suited him, and really a long name – Veronica or Marguerite or any other name over three syllables she could think of – simply did not sound right. "How about..." No ideas came to her. The name would have to symbolize something special, something that was fit for someone with her origin.

"We could name her after a month," suggested Pocky, looking from Eva to Mir. "They tend to be short, as long as you don't choose December or October or any other autumnal or winter season."

Eva pursed her lips. "That might work," she said after a moment. She met Mir's watchful eyes and smiled. "April, May, June—"

"What is 'June'?" Mir asked, interrupting her with a hint of eagerness in his voice.

"It's a summer month," said Pocky. "The sixth month of the year and lasting thirty days, according to the Gregorian calendar."

Eva looked sideways at him. "It's warm," she said after a short moment, returning her attention back to Mir and his daughter. "The sun shines a lot in June, and people spend lots of time outside – at least, they usually do. Not so much in Alaska. But it *is* warmer," she amended.

Mir looked at the sky past the glass windows that spanned almost the entire front side of the house. "There is no sun," he said softly.

"It isn't morning yet," said Eva, with a pang in her heart she had not expected. "You'll see the sun. I promise."

He looked at her and smiled quietly. "June," he said, leaning down and kissing his daughter on her forehead. "It's…"

"Perfect." Eva moved over and sat down beside Mir, putting her arm around his back. She smiled down at the tiny girl. "It's perfect."

"I think I may tear up," said Pocky, his eyes red-rimmed. He sniffed and took another drink of his tea. "However," he added a second later, "I think some shopping is in order. We need to drive to the city and get you some things."

Mir passed the empty milk bottle to Eva, who handed it to Pocky. "But how can we do that with the babies? We don't even have a car seat!"

Pocky stared at the ceiling. "You have a very valid point there, my dear."

"I have to take Mir," said Eva. "We have to get him some clothes."

"Agreed," said Pocky. "He can't very well walk around wearing only pants."

Mir looked back and forth from the professor to Eva. He leaned over and whispered in Eva's ear, "Why not?"

"I'll explain later," she responded quietly. "Pocky, can I take your car? Mine's just about out of gas."

"Of course. But," he looked at the babies Mir and Eva were holding and picked up the remaining boy, "we still have the dilemma of the two extra infants."

"We could put them in an orphanage," Eva suggested.

Pocky's expression clearly read while it may work, he would rather not choose such an option. "I believe I know a couple who would like to take at least one of them," he said, standing up with the baby in one arm and the bottle in his free hand. "I'll go get some more milk and make a phone call."

Eva watched as Pocky left the room and looked at Mir. "How does your arm feel?" she asked quietly.

"It hurts, but it isn't bad," he said with one of those unassuming smiles. "How do you feel?"

She laughed a little at the absurdity of Mir asking her how she was. "I'm fine," she assured him. She leaned her head against the side of his broad shoulder, surprised by how comfortable she felt doing it. "Are you... all right, Mir? With all of this?"

She felt him take a deep breath. "I'm scared," he admitted, biting his lower lip. "I don't know what to do. But," he looked at her and, though his mouth remained serious, his eyes lit with a smile, "I have Eva."

Chapter Thirty-Three

Eva leaned over the kitchen island, writing down everything she could think of that they would need to buy. Definitely clothes for Mir, things for the babies... *Oh, hair dye.* Mir's hair was too noticeable, and could not even be mistaken for a towhead. It was simply devoid of color. "Hey, Pocky?"

"Yes, Eva?" came the professor's voice from the living room, where he was feeding the other two babies.

"Do you have boots and a hat that Mir could borrow while we go shopping?"

"Believe it or not, I *do* have some boots under the bench in the foyer. They aren't mine, they belong to Andrew Kreg, but I'm certain he would have no qualms about Mir borrowing them."

Eva's eyebrow quirked in confusion and she frowned. "Who is Andrew Kreg?"

"You know, the nice young couple that lives a mile down the road!"

"Oh, *that* Andrew Kreg. Right." Eva looked down, then remembered the hat. "What about a hat, Pocky? Do you have a ball cap or anything?"

"Ah - I have a jacket with a hood?"

"That should work." Eva folded the list and put it in her pocket before walking out into the living room. "Pocky, are you sure you can handle three babies by yourself?" she asked for the third time in the past fifteen minutes.

Pocky sighed and looked up at her with the condescending, patient expression she had long ago dubbed 'the grandfather.' "Yes, my dear, I am quite certain. Thank you for your concern, however."

Eva sighed and twisted her hair back into a ponytail. "What if something happens while we're gone?"

"I'm going to keep the news going at all times. I should know if the world explodes, or another plague goes viral. And I will certainly hear anyone who knocks on the front door." Pocky got to his feet and put both hands on Eva's shoulders. "Dear. Everything will be fine. You will be gone a few hours at most."

"All right," said Eva, unable to shake the feeling that if she left, something catastrophic would happen. She smiled as Pocky planted a solid kiss on her forehead, patted her arm, and said "Now go. Just because I *can* handle three infants for a few hours does not mean you may extend your outing."

"Right. Come on, Mir," she called, pulling on her jacket from the coat closet. She could not help but smile wryly at the fact that, with everything that was happening – Mir, the babies, WorldCure, the possibility that they had been followed or the law would come down on them – she could not shake the fact that she was in desperate want of a shower and a change of clothes.

She glanced out into the living room and smothered a laugh – Pocky was giving Mir the same talk he had just given her. Mir looked reluctant to hand June away to someone else. His face was drawn and uncertain, and he caught Eva's eye as Pocky took the baby. At the same time, Pocky gave her an exasperated expression behind the younger man's back.

"It will be fine, Mir," Eva assured him, even as Pocky mouthed 'he's worse than you!'

Eva showed Mir the boots and he got the hang of them quickly, pulling them on and taking the fleece-lined jacket she offered him. It was a little tight, but it was warm, it covered him, and it had a hood.

"It will work until we get you something better," she said, zipping up the front and pulling the hood over his head. Mir seemed stiff in the jacket, and Eva had to remind herself that the only covering he had ever really worn was a harness.

"It's to keep you warm and cover you up," she said, looking him affectionately in the eyes as she smoothed his hair under the brim of the hood. She adjusted the sleeve over the bullet wound on his arm, making sure the bandage had not come loose. "Okay?"

He nodded, the corners of his mouth still pulled in deep. "Okay."

Eva opened her mouth to respond with – something – but was so suddenly overwhelmed with the urge to kiss the frown off his face that she instead turned around and grabbed the wallet and keys Pocky had set on the front bench. "Let's go."

They walked outside and Eva led Mir around to Pocky's truck and unlocked the doors. Mir opened the passenger side and sat down, watching as Eva climbed into the driver's seat and pulled the seatbelt across her.

Mimicking her movements with a faintly bewildered expression, Mir pulled his own seat belt over and buckled it. "What is this?" he asked finally, giving the strap a tug.

"It's in case – um, it's to…" Eva had been about to say 'it's in case we crash,' but thought better of it. "It's the law," she said finally, shrugging. "Do you want some music?"

He looked surprised and eager, like a little boy who had just been offered tickets to his favorite sport. "Like… your songs?"

"Well, sort of," Eva laughed. "They're on the radio." She leaned forward and turned the radio on. It was still on the station she had put it to the last time she rode in Pocky's truck. "The radio," she explained as she juggled the volume, "is… well, you hear what's going on. People talk through it and tell you the news and they play music." She looked at him and the realization of everything he would have to learn – everything she would have to teach him – hit her like a category five.

And the funny thing was, she decided, as hard as it sounded… she did not mind. She smiled at him and started the car as one of her favorite songs began. It was a classic called "Catching the Stars" by 3AM, and she had memorized the lyrics by the time she was five years old.

"Look in my eyes, love," she sang as Mir looked out the windshield at the gray-and-white landscape. "Look in my eyes and see yourself, take my hand and hold it tight. The world is a mirror, love, you're everything I see; I know I'll make you happy if you'll just be with me."

Out of the corner of her eye she saw Mir turn to watch her as she sang. She almost stopped, self-conscious, but no. He liked her singing. She continued on to the chorus. "I'll take your hand, love, and lay with you at night. We'll watch the shooting stars, love, and hold each other tight. I'll catch a star for you, love, I'll catch a star for you, and you'll catch one for me, my dear, and you'll catch one for me; I'll put it with my heart, love, and give it back to you."

Mir was smiling now, his eyes glowing softly in the gray winter light. Smiling at her. "It's one of my favorite songs," Eva explained, a little bit sheepishly. She cleared her throat and focused on the road ahead of her.

Suddenly Eva gasped and pulled over, veering the truck's front wheels onto the hard-packed snow. "Mir, look!" She unbuckled her seat and climbed out of the car. Mir did the same and they met in front of the truck.

"Eva, what—" Mir began, but was cut off as Eva pointed at the sky.

"Look," she breathed. There was a break in the clouds and slowly they revealed not blue sky, but gold. Golden light. "It's the sun, Mir."

He stared up at the sky, rays of sunlight spreading and reaching to gild the clouds and touch the snow beneath. It brightened, but he did not close his eyes or even lift his hand to cover them.

Eva watched his face, amazed at how something she saw every day of her life could be such a miracle to another person. She let out a breath that held a laugh simply because, at that moment, she had no worries. There was only her and Mir and the sun. She reached over and took his loose hand in hers, shading her eyes with her other hand before looking up at the sun.

"It *is* beautiful," she said aloud to herself, the cold air biting her nose. Mir's hand was warm in hers.

"Perfect," said Mir, the light in his eyes more brilliant to her than anything in the sky. They were wet with tears and there, caught in the light, they looked clear. "It's perfect."

"Yes," Eva agreed, lifting his good arm and putting it around her shoulders so she could lean against him. "It is."

Chapter Thirty-Four

They stood and watched the sun until it disappeared behind a fresh tide of gray clouds. Mir said nothing and Eva did not break the silence in the car. He wore an expression of profound bliss, and it was an expression Eva had never seen on him. She did not want to disturb it, so she listened as quiet songs came over the radio and hummed along with them.

At the first glimpse of tall silver buildings, Mir leaned forward as far as his seat belt would allow, staring in wide-eyed wonder. "What are those?"

"Buildings, like the – well, like the facility," said Eva. "But for different things. People work in them."

"What do they do?"

"Oh, everything. There are stores and banks and….you'll see." They reached the city in less than ten minutes and Eva parked at a sidewalk with enough quarters in the meter for two hours of shopping. "That should be enough." She glanced up and saw Mir watching her actions, the tip of his tongue just visible at the corner of his mouth in an intrigued look.

"I put money in," she said, then paused. "You know what money is, don't you?"

He nodded, his expression quiet and grave. "Money is how much things are worth. My father said I was not worth anything, but there were some things that were worth a lot. He said the experiments cost a lot of money."

Eva wondered how many times this man could make her heart break. He only knew money in terms of how much Dr. Ross had told him he was worth. "Mir, you—" she took a deep breath and walked close, stepping up onto the sidewalk so she could look him in the eye. "You," she repeated, "are worth so much more than money. You are worth so much; there isn't enough money in the world to equal what you're worth to me. Do you understand?"

He smiled and put his hands on her waist, his sapphire eyes looking into her own. "Yes, but you are worth more."

Eva was not sure how to respond, so she decided not to say anything. She reached around his neck and hugged him, and he hugged her back; she could feel he was being careful with his wounded arm, and she laughed into his neck – a laugh that was salty with suppressed tears. For Mir, for Fyodor, for June... for everything. "Okay," she said after a moment, swiping her hand across her eyes to rid them of tearful evidence and surveying the street. "Clothes first, I think."

"Okay," said Mir, sticking his hands in the pockets of his jacket. "I don't know where to go."

Eva took his hand and he followed her across the street into a Ruggedwear clothing store. "It smells strange," Mir remarked.

"Don't worry about it," said Eva, taking him to the back of the store. "Now, we need to find a shirt that fits you and get a few different colors."

A look of thrilled excitement came over Mir's face. "What colors?"

Smiling at his enthusiasm, Eva looked him up and down. "Well, your eyes are blue, so I'd try blue. Also, maybe a charcoal and black. I think darker colors would look good with your eyes."

Mir squinted at her, obviously not understanding the connection between colors and eyes, but shrugged. "Okay," he said cheerfully. "Is that a shirt?"

"Yes. It's like the one I'm wearing, but for men. Bigger," she clarified. It was just a tee, sporting a v-neck and short sleeves, and it was a navy blue. She held it up to him, trying to judge how it would fit. "I think it'll work," she said. "You need an extra large; you're well built."

His curious expression gained a puzzled edge. "It…well, it means physically you are…" She paused. What phrases would he understand? "You look good," she said finally, at a loss for anything else.

"Thank you."

She grinned. "We may want to try it on for size, though."

She found the dressing room and pulled him in, locking the door. "Okay, quickly, take the jacket off and try this on."

He seemed to sense the hush-hush tone in her voice because he asked as he unzipped, "Is this okay?"

"Ah – I'm sure it's fine," she said, waving a hand and laughing. "It won't hurt anything."

That seemed to satisfy him, and he carefully eased the jacket off. Eva stared. "Oh, shoot."

"Shoot?" Mir gently took the shirt from her, but his tone held alarm.

"Oh." She laughed, a little embarrassed. "I – never mind me. Forget it. It's just an exclamation and I probably shouldn't say it. I'd forgotten you had stitches." The black X still cut across Mir's stomach.

He looked down at it indifferently. "Stitches come out," he said, glancing at the way Eva wore her shirt before carefully working a sleeve over his arm.

"I know," Eva groaned, folding her arms and watching as he pulled the shirt on. "But I can't take you to a doctor...I'll have to do it myself, at Pocky's house."

"Is something wrong with doing it? Do you not want to?" Mir paused half way through tugging his shirt down, as if he was so worried about her feelings that everything else would have to wait.

"No, I want to," she assured him. "I just don't want to hurt you."

"It doesn't hurt very bad, taking them out," he said, his tone that of a comforting parent. "Does it work?"

Eva walked around him, studying the shirt. "Yes," she said after a moment, an approving smile tugging her mouth up the corners. "It looks very good on you, Mir."

He looked down. "I still don't understand why I have to have one."

Oh. Right. "Well, it's... just something people do, Mir. The doctors at the facility all did it, you know. Everyone did."

"I know," he nodded, "I just don't know why. Can I take it off now?"

"Sure. I'll grab a few more in other colors." She waited as he removed it and put the jacket back on, then unlocked the door and walked out of the changing room. "People wear shirts, Mir, because… well, propriety." She heard him stop and turned around to see what the matter was. "Mir?"

He was looking at the floor, his white hair not completely obscured by the hood. "I don't know enough."

Eva walked back to him, slowly, and took his arm. "What do you mean, you don't know enough?"

"I don't belong here." He looked at her, his face devoid of any expression, his voice flat. "I…" His lips drew together in frustration.

"Wait." Eva felt her heart begin to pound for seemingly no reason at all. What was Mir thinking? "You think you don't know enough about the world out here to live in it, is that right?"

"Yes." His eyes were sad, but his expression was uncaring; stating a fact. "I'm sorry, Eva. You don't have to take care of me."

"Mir!" Eva's voice snapped in the air like a branch breaking under a burden of snow. "I'm not doing this because I have to, all right? I want to. I like you, Mir. I like you a lot, and I want to be with you." She reached up and tilted his face so he was looking at her, not the floor. "You are so intelligent, Mir. You have so much more than I do, in here. Where it matters." She tapped her heart, realizing

248

that what she was saying just to keep him here was true.

It was all true.

She took a deep breath – Mir was right, it did smell strange in here. "Listen to me. You have a lot to learn, but that's not your fault. You were raised away from all this, and it had nothing to do with you. And *you* have taught *me* so much – don't ever think that you can't make it out here, because you can.

"And anyway, you can't give up," she added, feeling more confident in her stance. "You have June. You have to take care of her."

Mir's face softened as her words sank in. "June."

And me. "Yes," she said softly, but firmly. "June. Do this for her, if not for you. All right?" Quiet country music spilled from the speakers in the ceiling. "Can you do that?"

"Yes," said Mir, then louder, more firmly, "Yes. I will."

Eva wondered if her relief showed on her face. It was probably impossible for it not to – she felt as if she had been dangled over the edge of a cliff and then pulled back just in time. "Come on, let's get you some boots. Then we have to go to the drugstore."

"A store for drugs?" Mir's voice held its usual mix of wary curiosity again, and Eva could have hugged him for it. "Why do you want drugs?"

"Not – not the kind of drugs you're used to, Mir. And I'm not getting drugs – we need to get things for the babies, and we need to get dye for your hair."

"Explain."

Eva laughed when the demand took her by surprise. "Explain? Okay, well, a dye is something that turns your hair a different color. Most people your age don't have your hair color, and we don't want people to notice you."

"Ah." He nodded, and Eva knew that he really did grasp the importance of not being noticed. He smiled at her, and his smile held no trace of the dark moment before. "Let's do it."

They bought a few more pairs of shirts, two pairs of jeans and a pair of boots the same size as the ones Mir wore. They put the clothes in the truck and then Eva took Mir farther down the sidewalk to the drug store, where she led him past rows of everything from cameras to notebooks and cosmetics until she found the section with hair dyes.

Mir stood and looked up at the mirrored ceiling, then at the various boxes lining the shelves.

"They're all females," he noted, looking at the pictures on them. "And their hair is longer than mine."

"That's fine," said Eva offhandedly, giving him a quick smile. "It works for men and women, and we don't have to use all of it." Finally she decided on two colors and held them up. "What do you think?" She held up the first color; a light honey brown, and the second, a darker reddish brown.

"For me?"

She nodded. "For you." She held them out for closer inspection. "I think they would both look good on you, and give you a little more color than you have at the moment. We're going to have to work on your tan."

"Tan?" He peered at both boxes.

"You know how pale your skin is?" He nodded without bothering to look at it. "Well, that's because your body hasn't been getting sunlight. Once you're out in the sun for a while, your skin will get darker. You'll look... healthier." *Even if you aren't.*

"Okay," he said, then took the box of darker hair dye. "This one."

"Chestnut?"

He nodded. Eva smiled. "Good choice." She put the other color back on the shelf and said "Now, let's get to the babies' things."

"Pocky," Eva called as she kicked the door open with her foot, "we're back!"

"I'm in the kitchen," was the return shout.

"Surprise, surprise." Eva managed to hop out of her boots without dropping any of the grocery bags. "He's probably making tea." Then she stopped. "Mir! What are you going to eat?" She looked at him, her eyes wide with panic and horror. "You've never eaten real food, and we don't have the supplies to feed you intravenously!"

"You mean a system treatment?" he asked, adjusting the bags in his good arm.

"Right, a system treatment. All we have is normal food – I didn't even think of that while we were out!" Eva could have hit her head against the wall, she was so angry at herself. She growled and stomped into the kitchen, setting the bags down on the island without bothering to be gentle.

Pocky looked at her, his eyebrows raised in good-humored incredulity. "Well, I'm glad to see you came back in a good mood," he said, stirring a pot on the stove.

"I forgot that Mir hasn't eaten solid food. Ever. In his entire life." Eva rested her elbows on the counter and put her face in her hands. "How could I have forgotten that? He's probably starving. His last system treatment was three days ago!"

Pocky looked at her, then at Mir, who had just entered the kitchen and was quietly setting bags down on the island. "You know his system better than I do," he said pointedly. "Do you think he can handle a small amount of food? We could use the technique that recovering Holocaust survivors used – just feed them miniscule amounts and slowly build until they can intake normal portions."

Eva looked over at Mir. "I don't know," she said slowly. "I…. think so. But we should start him on something easily digested."

"Yogurt?" suggested Pocky.

"I think that might work," Eva agreed. "Mir, what do you think?"

He looked up from pulling the box of hair dye and his clothes out of their bags. "I don't know what yogurt is," he said finally. "But if you think so, I'll try some."

Eva smiled. "All right." She opened the fridge and pulled out a small container of vanilla yogurt. She tore the foil lid off, got a spoon out of the silverware drawer, and handed it to Mir. "Try a bite."

He took it as if it was an alien object. He looked at the spoon for a moment - then surprised Eva by using it correctly. It was a small thing, but she felt it was really much larger. It was a signal, telling her what she already knew.

He was intelligent, she knew he was – he had a capacity for figuring things out, putting pieces together, for learning. He would make it. "Pocky," she said suddenly, realizing what felt wrong in the house, "where are the babies?"

"Oh!" Pocky stopped stirring. "The Kregs came while you were out and took them away."

Mir slammed the yogurt down and looked at Pocky, his eyes blazing and his mouth pulling into something furious that shocked Eva. "Where is June?" he growled. Eva thought he might leap over the counter and tackle Pocky – and he could do it, too.

"Calm down, my boy. June is asleep in a crib I dragged out of the attic," said Pocky, showing an admirable amount of calmness considering the volatile young man not ten feet away. "I spoke to the Kregs and delicately explained the situation to them – or a version of it, at least. They were the couple I told you was so interested in adoption," he continued, pulling out a couple well-used mugs from the cabinet. "They cannot have children of their own, you see, and were eager for a family, especially when I told them we had found the babies abandoned by the roadside."

Mir had relaxed considerably, but tension still radiated in the way he held his shoulders and clenched his hands. "But we didn't find them there," he objected. "They were from the facility."

"I know that," said Pocky patiently. He sighed. "I felt this was an extenuating circumstance, God forgive me. Rather like hiding Jews from the Nazis." Seeing Mir's puzzled expression, he said, "You will learn about that eventually. In any case, they still had plenty of baby things from when Miranda had her miscarriage, and they were so excited that I let them take the infants directly. Except June," he added.

"What's a miscarriage?" asked Mir, studying the spoonful of yogurt.

Eva and Pocky exchanged looks. "A miscarriage... it's..." Eva coughed and began pulling food out of the grocery bags so she could put them in the refrigerator. "When a female is going to have a baby..." *A female? I'm beginning to speak like Mir!* "Sometimes, things go wrong and the baby dies. Sometimes the mother dies, too, and sometimes they both die. Not usually, but... it happens."

Mir's lips parted slightly, like he was going to say something, but his eyes were so pained that Eva wondered if he was unable. "Her baby died? Miranda's baby?"

"Yes. It did."

"But she – the mother – she lived?"

Eva nodded. "Yes."

Mir closed his mouth and his eyes took on a faraway expression. The line drawn between his eyebrows deepened and he looked down at his hand, spread on the smooth surface of the island. "Does the baby kill her?"

"Kill who? The mother?" Eva frowned, trying to work out Mir's question. "Not always, remember?"

"Sometimes it does." Mir looked up at her, tears muddying the lower rims of his eyes, caught between spilling over and fading. "Would she have stayed alive if I hadn't?"

"Stay – who? Alive? What?" Confused, Eva looked at Pocky to see if he had any better idea of what Mir was saying than she did.

He shrugged. Obviously not.

Mir looked up at her, not bothering to blink away the tears that finally spilled over and left watery scars down his face. "I didn't want to," he said, his voice steady in spite of his shaking hands. He leaned his weight on the island, his concentration not on Eva or Pocky or anyone else. It seemed almost as if he was having a conversation with someone invisible. *Could it be the memories?* Eva wondered. *The memories from that woman?*

"I didn't mean to kill her," Mir pleaded with the air. He shut his eyes and bowed his head to the island, clutching at his hair with his hands. "I didn't mean to!" His voice, torn between screaming and crying, was as raw as an open wound. "I'm sorry, I'm sorry, I'm sorry."

"Mir!" Eva grabbed his hand and pulled it away from his head. "What are you talking about? What's wrong? Why are you sorry?"

He looked at her, his eyes bright, his serial number pulsing just above the zipper on his chest. "My mother." His voice was slurred, painful. "I killed her."

Chapter Thirty-Five

"Mir," Eva exclaimed, staring. "No, you didn't! Who told you that? Doctor Ross?"

"My dear boy," said Pocky, handing Eva a mug of hot chocolate even as he moved toward Mir, "Your father lied to you rather frequently, I'm afraid." He leaned his elbow on the counter, watching the pale young man with grave eyes. "And I am by no means devoid of proof. I know where your mother is."

Eva's eyes widened farther than she had thought possible, and she turned her stare onto the professor. "You *what?*"

"I know," said Pocky evenly, "where Mir's mother is. However..." he smoothed a hand over his fringe of unruly white hair. "I'm sorry, Mir."

"Why?" Mir leaned forward, his voice strained, face taught. "Where is she?"

Eva had a feeling she knew what Pocky was going to say before he said it. "She's at the Providence Hospital."

"Why?" Mir's voice demanded to know. "Why is she there?"

"She has cancer."

Eva was grateful for Pocky's ability to state harsh, cruel facts in a gentle, calm way. She knew that if she had been the one to tell Mir, she would have torn a bigger hole in his spirit and caused serious damage. As it was, she felt as if the hole were threatening her own soul, not Mir's.

She expected to have to explain cancer to Mir, and was surprised when he said quietly, his voice salty with tears, "How bad is it?"

"I have not personally gone to see her," Pocky answered, looking at the ceiling as if drawing strength from it. "But after I was fired..." He paused and looked at Eva. "He doesn't know about all that, does he?"

"I don't think so," Eva answered, wondering how many more shattering revelations Mir could handle.

"Right. Well." Pocky cleared his throat and looked faintly uncomfortable. "Mir, do you know why you grew up in WorldCure?"

He nodded, carefully rubbing the bullet wound underneath his jacket. "Father told me after he gave me the drug to stop my talking. I couldn't talk, but I listened. He said my mother died when I was born, that I killed her. He said he hated me and I was born wrong. I was non-human, so it was alright for him to hurt me."

Eva covered her mouth to keep back the small sob that wanted to escape. Mir spoke so factually. She knew that, no matter how much she told him otherwise, his upbringing had damaged him beyond complete repair. He believed what Dr. Ross had told him, and something of that would remain with him the rest of his life.

The rest of his life...

"Pocky," said Eva quietly. She pushed her hot chocolate away, suddenly feeling physically sick. "Can you come into the living room for a minute?"

"Certainly." Pocky gave her a concerned look, then patted Mir's arm. "We'll be back in a moment. Try the yogurt, but only a bite."

Mir nodded as Pocky followed Eva into the living room.

"What is it?" Pocky asked, settling himself on the ottoman opposite Eva as she sat heavily on the couch. "You look pale."

Eva nodded, wishing she could laugh or do anything besides feel like her world had been smashed like a window and all the little shards were caught in her heart. "All right, well... yesterday, right before Igorov..." she cleared her throat as Pocky leaned forward and patted her knee. "Right before Fyodor came in," she continued, willing herself to get through this without breaking down for what felt like the twentieth time that month, "I had been analyzing Mir's blood."

"Right."

"And I found... um." She blinked rapidly and swallowed hard. *No tears, Eva. No tears, no tears!* "I had thought his heart would be weak from everything – did you know that he's officially died thirteen times now, Pocky?"

He shook his head, a faint smile coming onto his face even though his eyes remained concerned. "He has something special."

"I know." Eva could feel her eyes watering. "So I was expecting a weak heart. But, um... Pocky..." She could not help it. She leaned forward, her shoulders shaking and tears sliding down her face, as if a dam had broken. She felt Pocky's arms go around her, felt him rubbing her back, heard

"There, there, Eva, it's going to be all right. Dear Lord, help her."

She tried to speak, but her voice choked on itself and she could only cry, feeling as if she was a small girl again, being told her family had been killed by Morbus and she was alone, so alone.

It took several minutes for her to regain a semblance of control over herself. Her breath shuddered out of her and she swallowed her remaining tears. Pocky produced an old-fashioned handkerchief from his pocket and dried her face with it, his worry written in the deepening wrinkles on his face.

Once her face was dried and she felt she could finish what she had begun to say, Eva took a deep breath and unleashed "He's going to die, Pocky."

The professor sat back, his eyes sad. "We... should not be surprised," he said slowly, his voice heavy. "It's a miracle he has survived this long."

"I know, but..." Eva spread her hands as words left her. "I had hoped we could... fix him. I don't know. He has a bad heart, Pocky, and... I know what kind of cancer his mother has. Bone marrow." She shut her eyes, another wave of sickness twisting her stomach. "Mir has it, too."

"I've tried thinking of every possible way out of it," Eva said, after several moments of silence. "Nothing will work. Chemotherapy, radiation – physically, he's too... he's too much of a mess. His heart will kill him before the cancer does. I would try and apply for a heart transplant, but it wouldn't do any good."

Pocky hugged her again, and she was so, so glad that she had someone who could comfort her. She knew that without Pocky, no matter how much he could annoy or anger her, she would be adrift with no land in sight.

"I don't know what to do," she murmured, her voice muffled against the sleeve of his cardigan. "I love him, Pocky. I love him more than I've ever loved anyone, and I don't even... how – why did it have to be him? Why couldn't I have fallen in love with a normal guy at college or a normal guy at work or..." Her words trailed off as her mind supplied the answer to her questions.

She did not want someone normal.

She wanted Mir.

"He loves you, Eva."

She looked up, but Pocky's hand did not leave off stroking her hair in a way that made Eva feel as if it was her heart being stroked and soothed, not her head. "What – how do you know?"

Pocky smiled a sad but genuine smile. "I used to look at Margaret that way," he said, his voice gentle and quiet. "The way he looks at you. He sees you as more than just his savior, Eva. He sees *you*."

Eva stared at him, her hair straggling out of its ponytail, knowing her face was red and swollen from crying. "He can't love me," she protested. "Even my voice sounds awful." She blew into the handkerchief. *Yes, Eva, you're so lovely and loveable.* "I was so horrible to him, Pocky – I *experimented on* him, and stood by and watched while he was hurt and crying and I didn't even care. Pocky..." she leaned her head against him again and he continued to pat her messy brown hair. "I'm a horrible person," came out somewhere between a laugh and a sob.

"Eva, if you are a horrible person, then so am I," said Pocky, his eyes scanning the room as if seeing all of his past deeds surrounded there. "I let WorldCure frighten me into meeting their demands, and I stood by and did nothing while evil stole people and ruined their lives numerous times. Eva, you and I are not horrible people, but neither are we perfect. We just... are." He sighed, and Eva felt his hand go still, though it remained on her head. She thought she heard him speak in words so low she could not catch them, and looked up.

"What?" she sniffed.

He looked at her and cleared his throat. "Oh. 'For all have sinned, and come short of the glory of God.'" He shrugged and looked down. "It's a verse I use," he continued, giving her a brief smile Eva knew was forced. "To remind myself."

"To remind yourself of what?" Eva could hardly believe that Pocky would think he was nearly as bad a person as she was.

"That I am a sinner," he said matter-of-factly, shrugging. "And that it is only by God's grace that I am sitting here, today, with you, in the living room of my house, talking to you like I am now." He smiled again, and it was a bit more genuine.

"Pocky..." Eva shook her head. "A loving God wouldn't let something like this happen to Mir. He just wouldn't. It isn't fair."

"Did I teach you to believe that life was fair?" Pocky's eyebrows rose as Eva folded her hands in her lap and stared down at them. "Life isn't fair, Eva."

"What good is an unfair God?" She looked up, leveling her green-eyed gaze at him. "Tell me."

The sad smile came back, touching his face like clouds on a sunny day. "I never said God wasn't fair, dear. I said life wasn't."

"But don't you believe that God created life?" Eva demanded. She had not planned on confronting Pocky today, at this time, when she was in this state, but the words punched out of her like air through a popped balloon.

"Yes, I do." He nodded; sighed thoughtfully. "And I believe, that no matter how difficult, how *unfair* things around us seem, that all things work together for His good. We simply do not always understand."

Something about that sounded familiar to Eva and she fell silent, trying to think of where she had heard it before. *All things work together for...* She stood up, the crumpled handkerchief falling to the ground. "The book you gave me," she said quietly, her hands curling into fists at her sides. "It was the Bible, wasn't it?"

"Verses, yes," Pocky conceded, and Eva was angered by the fact that, while his face was resigned, it was not apologetic.

"You know I don't believe in that *trash*, Pocky!" Eva's voice escalated, reaching for the wooden beams above. "How could you – I trusted you! I thought you were giving me *your* words, Pocky, *your* help. Not someone else's!"

"But Eva," Pocky interrupted gently, looking up at her with quiet pleading on his face. "Those *were* my words. Everything that I have taught you has been based on those words."

Eva felt as if her one last refuge, her one safe haven from the relentless storm that had consumed her life, had been washed away. "I…" She groped for words to hurl at him, but she had nothing left. She turned and ran from the room, shaking her head, crying. She pounded up the stairs to her room and almost slammed the door – only the afterthought *I'll wake June* kept her from shoving it closed with everything she had.

She collapsed on the bed, staining the comforter with a storm of tears until her body, overwhelmed and exhausted, pulled her into a deep and dreamless sleep.

When she awoke, the green numbers on the digital clock read 12:14 am. She groaned and sat up, her stiff muscles protesting at the sudden movement. She felt grimy and unkempt. She snatched her extra clothes from the dresser and took a long, hot shower, wishing the water could wash away the tension that seemed to have sunk into her very soul.

She stood underneath the shower head and let it rain down on her, too tired to cry anymore. "Nothing makes sense," she said to the steam around her. "Nothing, not the big things like Mir and Pocky and not the little things like my feelings and WorldCure and…" She closed her eyes and leaned her head against the shower wall. The water reminded her of the first time she had realized Mir was beautiful, and the thought seemed to leave a gaping hole where her heart should have been.

Had been, a month or so ago.

When she finally stepped out of the shower and got dressed, she looked at her pale face in the mirror and sighed. "No makeup." She shook her head. "I didn't think of that, either." Her purse had been left at the facility when they left… barking a quiet laugh, she spoke out loud again, her reflection mimicking her every move. "You know, I used to think that I would die if I lost my purse. I mean, it has everything in it; my ID, my phone, my money, my credit card. My extra makeup."

She gave another short, self-deprecating laugh and looked toward the door. "Even those things don't seem important anymore," she added quietly. She knew what she truly cared about, and they were all right in this house.

Who knew how long before the roof caved in; before WorldCure pounded the door down and the press screamed from all sides. It would be soon, of that she was sure. There was nothing she could do but wait, and she hated waiting.

Waiting meant doing nothing. It meant sitting back and letting fate or Providence or destiny take control of your life and lead it down the path it chose, leaving you helpless in the back seat.

There was a quiet knock on her door. She checked her faded jeans and blouse and crossed to the door, opening it quietly.

It was Mir, the dim light from her room highlighting the shadows under his cheekbones, the dark circles under his brilliant eyes. He held up the box of hair dye with a smile that held no trace of embarrassment. "You had light," he said, nodding toward the bathroom.

"Do you need help dyeing your hair?" asked Eva, looking at the box.

He bit his lower lip, his expression hopeful. "Do you mind?"

"No," she said warmly. "Come on in. It shouldn't take too long; I'll give your hair a trim while I'm at it."

He walked obediently into the room and followed her into the bathroom, where she positioned him in front of the mirror. "Take off your shirt," she instructed. "We don't want to get dye on it."

He obediently pulled it off, bending over so that he did not have to stretch his wounded arm. "Oh," said Eva. "Right. Let me have a look at your stitches."

He straightened and looked down as she peered closely at the delicate black thread. "Does this hurt?" she asked, pressing gently against one of them.

"Only a little," he said, watching with an interested expression. "They feel ready to come out."

Eva wondered how many times he had been stitched up in his lifetime. "All right," she said, "I'll do that after we do your hair."

"All right," he said, his voice quiet but cheerful. Eva fetched a pair of scissors and gave Mir a haircut; keeping it long enough that it still looked tousled, but did not pass the nape of his neck. Then she filled the tube with dye, put on the pair of plastic gloves that came with the box, and spent the next half-hour carefully turning Mir's colorless hair a deep red-brown shade.

When she had finally finished, she said, "Okay, now, we have to leave it for a while so the dye sets in. I'll do your stitches."

Mir followed her into the bedroom. Eva got a towel from the linen closet and spread it on the bed. "Put your head there."

He complied, lying on his back and putting his head on the towel so none of the dye marked the blanket underneath. Eva rinsed off the scissors she had used to trim his hair – they were small enough to use for this sort of work. She was used to stitches.

She carefully snipped away the first one and tugged the tiny thread out, checking the skin underneath. It was still raised and reddish, healing, but it was closed. "They're ready to take out," she told him, moving on to the next one, "but you have to be careful. Don't do anything that will re-open the cuts."

"Okay," he answered, focusing on the ceiling.

It took Eva almost another half-hour to take the stitches out. There were sixty-two of them. "All done," she sighed, stretching. Her back had stiffened from hunching over that long, and the muscles in her shoulders felt like springs coiled too tight.

Mir sat up and looked at the cross mark on his stomach. "Thank you."

"You're welcome." Eva climbed off the bed, wishing Pocky knew chiropractics. "Come on; let's rinse out your hair."

With Mir bending over the deep sink, Eva poured water over his hair, glad to see that her dye job was worthy of a professional salon. When she was convinced all the excess dye had been washed down the drain, she told him to stand up and bend over again.

"I can dry my own hair," he said, looking at her from his halfway-bent position.

"Not with that arm, you can't," she said shortly. Mir paused, then acquiesced and allowed Eva to rub his hair dry.

"That felt good," he said after she told him she was done and tossed the towel onto the counter. He shook his head wildly for a moment, tossed his head back, and gave her the guileless, unpracticed smile that threw an unexpected butterfly into her stomach.

"Yes," Eva agreed, crossing her arms and smiling faintly back at him. "It does feel good."

Mir looked into the mirror and studied his reflection, looking surprised but not displeased. "It's different."

"It looks good on you," she assured him, standing next to him and looking at his reflection. "You're tall."

"You are short," he answered, then grinned at her when she pretended to gasp.

"I am not short," she protested, tossing her head. "I am five feet and six inches tall. I am not short."

One corner of his mouth quirked; he looked her up and down before saying "No. You're short, Eva."

Eva laughed. She felt her body needed to laugh; her soul needed it. It was short, but it was real and strangely refreshing. "Ah," she sighed, a small, quiet laugh bubbling up again from somewhere as she sat on the edge of the counter, "I love you."

She stiffened instantly.

She had said it out loud.

Before her mind could pull itself together well enough for her to give him a reasonable excuse for what she had just said, Mir said, "I love you more."

Her heart stopped.

"I know," she whispered. She had not meant for her voice to be a whisper, but it seemed determined to disobey her.

"I want to kiss you," said Mir, looking down at the tee shirt held in his hands.

Eva looked at him, her face scrunched slightly in confusion. "Why don't you?"

He raised his eyes to hers, and his voice sounded a little sad. "You didn't want me to."

"What…." Eva's eyes widened. "Mir, what happened in the cell…I – it wasn't your fault, not all of it. I kissed you, too."

"Why, if you didn't like it?"

Eva tried not to be taken aback by the frank questions. She had to remember his innocence - he was being open and honest with her, and it would be cruel of her not to be open and honest in return. "I didn't think you would know when to stop," she said finally, releasing a breath she had held for nearly half a minute.

"Eva didn't trust me."

"I didn't *know* you very well," she exclaimed, trying to explain and failing completely. He had slipped back into third person, she noticed somewhere in the back of her mind. "I didn't…"

"Does Eva trust me yet?"

She looked away, her hands curling around the counter's edge. "Yes." She looked back at him, into those wide, phosphorescent eyes. "I trust you."

"Do you have music?"

"What?" She blinked, startled. *Music?* "There's a radio in the bedroom, why?"

He grinned and took her hand. "Could you turn it on?"

Watching him suspiciously from the corner of her eye, Eva crossed the room and turned the radio on, then fiddled with the tuner until she found a music station. It was all orchestra classical; not what she usually listened to, but pretty. "Is this good?"

"It's good," he affirmed. He held out his hand. "Come here."

She walked over to him, feeling very small in her bare feet. "All right, what is this?"

Mir leaned down and took her left hand in his right, placing his right hand around her waist. With a gentle tug, he pulled her close to him and she automatically tilted her head and leaned against his chest. And slowly, carefully, he began to move. Swaying, stepping, and taking her with him across the wooden floor.

"Mir, are you dancing?" Eva asked in amazement, looking up at him with a shocked expression on her face. "How on earth do you know how to dance?"

"I don't," he said, his breath ruffling the thin fringe of hair on her forehead. "The woman did."

Her memories, Eva realized. She had thought her heart would be pounding, but it beat at a slow, steady rhythm, as if this was supposed to happen. Like it was meant to. *A dead woman taught him how to dance.*

She leaned against him again and for a time that was short but eternal, there was only the music and Mir's heartbeat and the extraordinary ballroom around them.

Eva closed her eyes and smiled.

Chapter Thirty-Six

When the song finally ended – and Eva knew it had to, some time – they sat down on the edge of the bed as the next song came onto the radio. Eva recognized it from a ballet, but she could not remember the name.

She looked over at Mir and smiled. "You're something else, you know that?"

His eyebrows drew together, just a little. "Everybody is something else," he said; his tone telling her that he wasn't debating, just stating something he knew to be true.

"You're probably right," said Eva with a quiet laugh. "Hey, Mir?"

He looked at her over the curve of his shoulder. "Eva?"

"Do you trust me?"

He did not smile, but something in his expression was soft, acknowledging. "Yes."

Eva leaned up and her lips found his mouth. He turned his head and returned the kiss, softly, his eyes watching hers under lashes so pale they looked as if they had been touched with snow.

Kissing Mir was different for Eva; different than when she had kissed boyfriends in college. There was feeling behind this one. There was love, and not just the kind that twisted her stomach into flighty knots.

The love she had explained to Mir in the cell, what felt like years ago.

Mir's hands gently cupped her face, the side of her head, as if keeping her in position. As if she was going to move.

One of her hands crept up to his hair, still damp under her fingers, and the other hand remained firmly on the bed, bracing herself.

"A*hem!*"

Eva jumped.

Pocky stood in the doorway, eyeing them both. "If you are going to engage in such...*friendly* activities, then I am afraid you must do it somewhere other than Eva's bedroom," he said firmly.

Eva could tell that, while he meant what he said, he was not angry. The twinkle in his eyes gave it away. "Yes, sir," she said dutifully, feeling a mixture of guilt and relief at the fact that he seemed to have forgotten about her outburst earlier.

"Why?" Mir turned so he could see the professor fully. It was not a teasing or belligerent question, Eva knew. He really did not understand.

"Propriety," said Pocky, looking at Mir's hair. "Excellent color choice," he added. "You look far less vampiric."

Eva smothered a laugh and pushed her hair out of her face before pulling it back into a ponytail. "Did you come in here to just to check on us or was there a good reason?" she asked.

"Oh, yes," said Pocky, straightening and looking back at Mir. "June is crying." He held out a bottle of milk, suddenly looking tired. "It's two o'clock."

Mir did not hesitate. He stood up, took the bottle, and walked past Pocky out the door. Curious to see how Mir took care of two o'clock feedings, Eva stood up and followed.

Pocky caught her arm. "As overjoyed as I am," he said with a yawn, "to see you two getting along, I must continue to play the concerned grandfather and let you know that I will be watching you." He whistled a few eerie strains that sounded like they came from a horror movie and released her arm, patting it. "Good night."

"Good night, Pocky," said Eva with a tired giggle. "And Pocky?" she asked before he went into his room down the hall.

"Yes, duck?"

She swallowed. "I'm sorry. I didn't mean what I said."

He paused, one hand on the doorframe. "I know." He smiled. "You will try and get at least ten minutes of sleep before morning, won't you?"

She placed her hand over her heart. "I will," she said gravely.

"I will hold you to that," he answered just as gravely, and shut his door.

Eva slipped into Mir's bedroom, leaving the door open wide enough to send a slanting shaft of light from the hallway onto the rug. Mir stood at the crib, positioned by the window, and lifting June out.

"Don't cry," he murmured. His deep voice was soft and soothing. "I've got what you want." He cradled her in his arm and began to feed her, walking around the room as if he could not bear the thought of standing still.

Eva stood, watching Mir and his daughter as the moonlight from the window spilled into the room and made them seem almost phantomlike. He was a good father. It surprised her, considering the father he had been cursed with, that he knew anything about parenting at all.

Then again, she thought, *maybe it wasn't just about rules and training. Mir has a capacity for love of any kind, and that's the most important thing.* She felt her heart turn over in her chest and clutched at it without thinking.

Mir would never get to see June grow up.

The knowledge was too much for her to think about. "Good night, Mir," she whispered, and left the room as quietly as she had entered it.

Eva was awoken the next morning by raised voices below. She was in a panic almost before she sat up. She had fallen asleep in her jeans and blouse but her appearance did not even rank as a worry as she ran out of her room and down the stairs.

Pocky stood at the front door arguing with two —

Policemen.

Eva's heart sank and skipped a beat at the same time. She smoothed her layers behind her ears and walked forward, trying to look calm and put-together in spite of herself. "Hello."

Pocky turned around, his face drawn. "Good morning, Eva, dear, I would like you to meet officers Duarte and Traci. This is Eva Stewart."

They nodded in her direction and the darker one, Duarte, said "Ma'am, we have good reason to believe you are holding a non-human inside this house."

A *non-human*. They did not know about June. "May I ask who gave you this…information?" Eva asked, her mind racing. She had to think of something to say that would get them away from Mir, away from his life. *Their* life.

"We got an anonymous tip," said Traci.

Shocker.

Duarte said "The non-human – Thirteen, I believe it's called – was seen with you yesterday, Miss Stewart. In Anchorage."

Eva felt as if she was going to be sick. "I…"

"If you do not comply, then we have full authority to search the house and use any means necessary to find it." Traci looked at her with cold brown eyes.

"It's all right, Eva," the familiar, beautiful voice said behind her.

No. No, no, no, no.

Mir walked forward to the officers. "I'm Thirteen."

Traci and Duarte were taken aback, it was obvious. They had expected a crazed, deformed thing and instead saw a tall, strong young man, dressed in a tee, jeans, and boots. "You're Thirteen?"

"His name is Mir," Eva snapped before she thought better of it. "Do you have a warrant for arrest?" She folded her arms, but that only emphasized the shaking she felt in her hands, so she stuck them in her pockets. *Breathe. Just breathe.*

Mir looked at her with an expression she had seen on his face once before; in the prepping room, when there was nothing she could do but watch as bruisers riled him up for attack.

Why wasn't there some way for them to switch places?

"Yes, ma'am."

Eva's attention was jerked toward Duarte as he held out a thick, expensive-looking piece of paper to her. She read it even though she knew it would be in order.

"You can't take him," she said, tearing her eyes away from the warrant.

"It's okay," Mir said softly, squeezing her hand as he walked past her, past Pocky, and down the front steps. He turned around and Eva saw him mouth the word *June.*

She nodded, her vision blurred by a sudden sheen of tears. "Where are you taking him?"

"Dimond Prison, about thirty miles from here," said Duarte, glancing at Traci. There was a note of sympathy in his voice. "You can visit tomorrow between eleven and three."

Eva nodded, her hand still clinging to the memory of Mir's. "Thank you," she whispered, her voice hoarse. She watched, unable to move or say anything, as the police officers cuffed Mir and shoved him into the back seat of their car.

The windows were darkened, and she did not know if Mir looked back.

Chapter Thirty-Seven

Eva felt numb as she turned to go inside.

Mir was gone.

Taken.

She had felt so close, so close to safety. So close to being far away from WorldCure and... She heard Pocky talking to her but did not pay attention to what he said. She walked upstairs, her footsteps slow and heavy, dragging her to Mir's bedroom and the crib.

She walked straight to June and lifted the baby out of the crib. She felt so small and light, but she was real. She was real, no matter how fragile she looked. Eva held June close, feeling a tiny, bewildered yawn against her neck. "It's all right." Her voice was muffled, hot tears burning down her face. "Daddy will be back. It's going to be all right."

"Eva?"

She turned around to face Pocky. He crossed the room and she let him hug her and June as she wished, desperately, that she could hug Mir as well. "Prison, Pocky."

"At least they aren't transporting him to another facility," said Pocky. There were bags under his eyes from lack of sleep. "And you can visit him tomorrow, remember? We'll bring June."

"But he didn't do anything." Eva felt a headache pushing against her temples, like fists beating against a door. "He's innocent. It's Doctor Ross and Jude and people like me who should be locked up, not him."

"He has murdered people, Eva," said Pocky, and the truth of his words stung Eva like a whip.

She raised her head. "It wasn't his fault – they tormented him into that; they abused him and mistreated him until he didn't know right from wrong!" She would have wiped her face dry, but she was holding the baby and could only blink rapidly and sniff. "I know." Pocky rubbed her back in slow, soothing circles as she hiccupped. "I know, and I pray that God will work this out. Faith, Eva. It's all we have right now."

Eva closed her eyes. "God."

"You can choose not to believe it, if you like," said Pocky affably, still rubbing her back. "However, it truly is the more comforting option."

She sniffed, laughing in a heartless way. "Well, you believe it for me, then," she said with a small smile as a tiny, contended sound came from June. "And Pocky?"

"Yes?"

"I guess praying for Mir wouldn't be too ridiculous, would it?"

He smiled kindly. "I already do, duck. I already do."

I look down at the metal restraining devices on my wrists. The officers smell afraid, but only a little. They are not used to me. They are like the bruisers at the facility – fear won't stop them from doing their job. I look out the window and watch the world pass by my reflection. I will not fight or hurt them, I promise myself. For Eva. And June, and

Pocky. I will let them take me to prison. I think it is like a cell. I wonder if they'll hurt me there.

My reflection smiles and I touch where its mouth turns up. The glass is cold.

I liked being a human.

I wish I was.

Eva spent the day in a state of half-consciousness. Noises, smells, sensations still registered in her mind, but she ignored them. Her mind felt as if it had been frozen over; inside it was still alive, still functioning, but the outside was enclosed in a thin layer of ice that made it impossible to feel anything more than the cold.

She took care of June and tried to help Pocky with some paperwork, but the professor grew exasperated with her and ordered her to drink some strong black coffee and take a nap. She drank the coffee, but sleep was impossible. She did not shut her eyes for more than five minutes that day, not until four in the morning when sheer exhaustion drove her into a shallow and unrestful sleep.

"Eva!"

She felt as if she were on a ship at sea during a storm. Something was rocking her back and forth, and it was calling her name.

"Eva! Duck, wake up! Rise and shine! Greet the morning!"

She mumbled something unintelligible and rolled over, nearly suffocating herself in the pillow. And then she remembered everything, just as Pocky said "It's ten o'clock, Eva! We're leaving to go visit Mir in half an hour!"

She sat up – she had fallen asleep on top of the blankets – and rubbed the sleep from her eyes. "I'm up," she said, standing. She grabbed the edge of the bedside table to keep from falling over.

Pocky handed her a cup of coffee. "Hurry and make yourself presentable," he said, eyeing her hair. "Your hair resembles a bird's nest after a twister."

She smiled. "Thank you, Pocky."

"You're welcome, dear." He left the room, pulling the door closed behind him.

Eva took a quick shower, ran a brush through her hair, and changed her clothes into something cleaner and less wrinkled. Her mind was already on Mir, in a strange series of past memories and wondering how the visit to Dimond Prison would go.

She went downstairs and found Pocky feeding June in the kitchen, alternately feeding her from one of the new bottles and taking sips of his own Earl Gray.

"Good morning, nice to see you looking alive," said Pocky, motioning toward her breakfast of pancakes and sausage on the table.

"Thanks," said Eva, sitting down and taking a bite. She swallowed and looked at Pocky. "Did Mir ever try the yogurt?" she asked as the thought sprang to mind.

Pocky looked thoughtful as he rocked June back and forth in his arms. "You know," he said slowly, "I don't know."

Eva rubbed her temples. "Pocky, I..." She was quiet for a minute, then shrugged. "I don't know."

Pocky made a sympathetic noise and looked at his watch. "If you want to be there when visitation hours begin, we'd better leave."

Eva did not even bother to take one more bite, though the meal was delicious. "I'm ready."

They had no car seat for June, so Eva held her carefully during the forty-five minute drive to Dimond. June was a strangely quiet baby; she cried, yes, but for the most part she was the silent, observant type, searching the world with her wide blue eyes.

She was painfully like her father.

Eva tried not to think about it.

Dimond Prison was a large, ugly building made from sand-colored stone that rose six stories above the landscape. Eva saw it a mile before they reached it, but something seemed odd about it.

"Why are there so many cars?" She looked over at Pocky, whose surprised expression seemed to mirror her own.

"Perhaps there's a gala," he said dryly.

Eva looked down at June. The baby was asleep, her small hands clenched into fists. "You'll get to see your daddy soon," Eva said quietly, brushing a fairy-like wisp of pale hair away from June's forehead.

They pulled up to the electronic gates at the front, marveling at the amount of cars lined outside the fence and down the road. Pocky showed his ID card to the scanner and the gate opened with a friendly electronic reminder that "Visiting hours are from eleven to three. Thank you for your consideration."

They had to park on the snow. Every parking space was taken.

"This is weird," said Eva, climbing out of the car and holding June close against the cold breeze.

"Indeed." Pocky wrapped his scarf and looked around. They could see security cameras and armed guards everywhere they looked, and the effect was unnerving.

They walked through the front doors and were greeted with warm air and chaos. There were people everywhere. "What's going on?" Eva looked at Pocky, bewildered.

"Excuse me!"

They turned to see a prison guard making his way toward them through the crowd. "Excuse me - are you here for visiting hours?" His face was red and he had a harried look about him, like a mother who had been trying to clean the house with a dozen children interrupting.

"Yes," said Eva, glancing again at Pocky. "We're here to visit – ah, the – the Subject. From WorldCure," she added, hating the taste of those words in her mouth. It felt like years since she had used them.

"Right, we were expecting you." He motioned them with a hand while his attention was jerked aside by the excited yell from a young woman. "Please, come with me."

Chapter Thirty-Eight

"Who are all these people?" Eva asked as the guard led them down a blessedly empty hallway.

"Protesters, mostly. And the press," was the glum answer. "We've been trying to keep them off our backs since yesterday afternoon, once word got out we had the Subject here."

Eva looked behind her at Pocky and exchanged a shocked expression with him. "Word got... wait, people are interested in it?"

"Interested?" He barked a one-syllable laugh that was closer to a yelp. "That's one word for it. Here." He opened the door at the end of the hallway and ushered them inside. It wasn't a very large room, and it was divided by a wall. A small glass partition made the other half of the room – and a door – visible, and there was a chair on either side.

"The Subject will be brought here in a minute," said the guard. "I'll be right outside."

"Thank you," said Eva as the door closed. She turned to stare at Pocky. "Protesters? The press? Are they protesting Mir's imprisonment, or are they protesting Mir?"

"I know no more than you do, dear," said Pocky.

The door beyond the glass partition opened and Eva sat down in the chair as two guards brought Mir, still handcuffed, into the room. He looked haggard, but his face lit up when he saw Eva.

She put a smile on her face as he was seated opposite the glass. "Hello, Mir," she said softly. She held up June. She could not mention that June was Mir's daughter – not when their conversation was being listened to – so she only said "Look, we brought another visitor."

Mir leaned forward. "Hi, June!"

The baby cooed and reached for the glass. Eva lifted her and pressed June's tiny hand against it.

Mir lifted his own hand and pressed it against the other side, dwarfing his daughter's much smaller one. "Hi, June," he said again, his voice reduced to a clogged whisper.

Eva placed her own hand, fingers splayed, over June's. "Hi, Mir." She noticed that the darkness under his eyes seemed darker, and he looked...

Starved.

"Did you ever try the yogurt?"

He shook his head. "No."

She blinked. "Why not?" She could understand being hesitant to try something you had never tried before, but it was not worth going hungry for.

"I couldn't swallow it." He shrugged, a half-grin tilting his face.

Her heart ached. "You must be hungry."

He looked back down at June and drummed his fingers across the glass, amusing her. "Is Eva all right?"

She smiled. She liked it when he used third-person; it reminded her of their first conversations in his cell. So much time had happened since then. "I'm worried about you. I mean," she said hastily, remembering how adamant he had been that she *not* worry about him, "I... I want you to be well." She knew it was an odd turn of phrase, but it was like trying to speak to someone who had a basic grasp of a foreign tongue.

"I *am* well," he said, his voice eager. He leaned forward and met her eyes with such an intense, straightforward gaze that she was compelled to meet it. They kept contact for several seconds before Mir seemed to relax a little. "How is June?" he asked, looking again at his daughter.

"She misses you." Eva smiled and rubbed the infant girl's head. "I miss you," she added. "Are they treating you all right?"

His smile did not falter, but she thought she saw a shadow flirt with his eyes for half a heartbeat. "Yes. I'm fine."

Oh, Mir. I wish you could tell me. "Oh – Pocky's here," she said, turning and motioning the professor over.

"Lovely to see you," said Pocky, beaming benevolently.

Mir's smile widened. "You too."

The door behind Eva opened. "Time's up."

She turned. "That can't be right. It's only been—"

"Time. Is. Up." It was a different guard than the one who had escorted them here, and he reminded her of Brenton.

Mir stood up, his chained hands held in front of him. "Good-bye, Eva."

"I'll come again tomorrow, Mir," she said, raising her voice so he could hear her as the guards led him away. "I'll see you tomorrow!"

The back door closed and Eva, holding June tightly in her arms, glowered at the guard at the door. "Why weren't we allowed more time?" she demanded.

"For security purposes, ma'am," was the emotionless response. "I'll show you out." He turned and walked away from them with brisk steps. Eva wanted to shout at him, but she felt Pocky's hand on her arm.

"It's not worth making a fuss over," he said. "We shall come back tomorrow."

Eva nodded and walked down the hall, her footsteps echoing faintly around the walls. As they pushed open the doors that led out into the main area, Eva was accosted by flashing lights and voices overlapping each other, shouting.

"Doctor Stewart! Is it true you called Humanity International down on WorldCure?"

"Weren't you in charge of a Subject there?"

"Is it true that the Subject is being held here right now?"

Panic flared inside Eva's chest like a firework, but she did her best to keep a calm expression on her face. "Everyone, please," she called, hoping her voice was loud enough to silence them.

"It's all right, duck," said Pocky's voice directly behind her.

Eva took a deep breath, reassured that the professor was there. She looked down at June, whose face was scrunched up and on the verge of crying. *What should I say?* It seemed the silence that had abruptly fallen was mocking her. All those waiting faces, the cameras...

She heard Pocky whispering behind her, his voice barely audible. "Lord, give her strength. Give her the words to say, as you did for Moses when he stood before the people of Israel. Help her."

Eva shut her eyes and took a deep breath. Then she opened them. "It's true. I called Humanity International, hoping they would investigate WorldCure and find out for themselves what *I* found."

Several questions rang out, but the nearest reporter, a young man with an eager face, was the loudest. "And what was that, Doctor Stewart?"

A single heartbeat. Then, "The Subjects are human."

The world became an explosion of light and screaming voices.

Trying to drown out the noise and think, Eva turned to Pocky and handed June to him. "Get her outside!" She was only inches away from him, forced to shout over the chaos around her. She heard a loud whistle and saw guards moving through the crowd, trying to keep the reporters and civilians calm and at bay; spreading their arms to keep them back.

Something clamped around her arm. She jumped.

"This way, please," said the Brenton-copy.

Grateful to escape the mob, Eva was pulled through the crowd and through a thick steel door that reminded her of the one leading from the Facility to Beneath. "Where are we going?" Her voice felt as if it was coming from someone else. She had no reason to be this frightened, she told herself. No reason.

"In here, please, ma'am." Another door – ordinary wood this time – was opened and she was ushered into an office. Three people occupied the room already.

One was behind the desk, sitting with his hands folded and looking at Eva with the vaguely interested expression of someone watching a slow movie.

The second was a woman in her mid-forties, dressed in a professional suit, her hair pulled back. She smiled at Eva, but even the smile looked government-issued.

The third was Devon Ross.

Chapter Thirty-Nine

"It's a pleasure to see you again, Doctor Stewart." Dr. Ross smiled at her, a thin smile that sent a wave of chills up her arms.

She stood and stared. "What – Doctor Ross." She cleared her throat, her mind spinning. "What are you doing here?"

"You needn't worry, I am... under surveillance, as it were." His smile seemed to slip a little, betraying the collected expression on his face.

"Doctor Ross is here," said the man behind the desk, "Because he and the entire WorldCure facility are under investigation." The plaque on the front of his desk read Jon Morgen, *Warden.*

Eva had no idea whether this was a good thing or a bad thing. It was quite possible it was both. "Oh?"

The woman stepped forward and held out her hand, brown lipstick-covered lips parting in a white-toothed smile. "Eva, my name is Dagney Hart from Humanity International."

Eva shook Dagney's hand, barely able to drag her gaze away from Dr. Ross. "Hello."

"I would say it's nice to meet you, but under the circumstances..." Dagney shrugged. "I was sent to investigate WorldCure."

"Ah," said Eva, her thoughts finally forming into words. "If that's true, then why is he standing in this room?" She looked at Dr. Ross, her eyes narrowed. She swallowed hard, unable to believe that Mir was locked in a cell while this monster stood, free, in front of her.

Dagney glanced at the warden, who leaned back in his seat with his hands folded. She looked back at Eva. "It's… complicated. Far more complicated than we could have thought."

"Why?" Eva's voice slapped the air. "It's been proven that the facility, under the direction of Doctor Ross, was illegally abducting people and using them as Subjects! What could possibly be complicated about it?"

"Doctor Stewart," said Dagney, apparently deciding that 'Eva' was too familiar a term, "You yourself were part of that system."

"I know." Eva thought it ironic that those words struck her harder than any meaningless insult directed her way before. "But didn't you see – he and the guards and the warden *killed* every non-staff person in the facility before you arrived! Do *not* tell me you couldn't see the evidence."

"We did find the evidence." Dagney hesitated. "Unfortunately, we have no solid proof that they were not simply non-humans and therefore, able to be treated however the facility deemed."

Eva felt sick. "You can't be serious."

"We are."

Behind Dagney, Dr. Ross smiled again, his cold gaze sending a shiver down Eva's back.

"He," she said, her voice shaking with anger as she pointed at Dr. Ross, "is a murderer. He was buying favors from the HRI – favors that included turning innocent human beings into experimental lab rats. Just ask Mir."

Dagney's penciled eyebrows rose. "Who is Mir?"

It took a moment before Eva replied. She knew she could not take back what she had said, and things could not possibly get any worse than they were right now. "Subject Thirteen. His name is Mir."

"He – it – has a name?" Dagney's voice curled with incredulity.

"Yes." Eva met Dr. Ross's gaze with defiance. "I gave it to him."

Dagney rubbed her forehead. "Doctor Stewart, you must understand that we do not know if Subject Thirteen is a human or a non-human."

"There *is* no such thing as a non-human!"

Eva's shout spread a blanket of silence over the room. She could not even feel her own heart beating. She thought of Mir. "Doctor Ross," she continued in a quiet, even tone, "had him labeled a non-human when he was born to cover up the fact he had an affair. Mir's mother was told he died at birth. When Mir was old enough to talk, Doctor Ross gave him a drug called Cortoxica to shut down the pathways in his brain that controlled speech. Sixteen years later, I gave him the antidote."

She could feel tears pressing at her throat. "He's as human as I am. He's more human, because…" She pressed a hand over her mouth, her chest heaving with the effort of suppressing a sob. She removed her hand and smiled at Dagney as the tears came, running down her face and neck.

"Because when I met him, I had no soul. And he did."

Dagney looked torn between crying along with Eva and demanding another set of handcuffs. "I...." she cleared her throat. "I will have to take your statement. Doctor Ross is going to be held here, under surveillance, until the public trial."

"Trial?" Eva looked at the warden, then back to Dagney. "What trial?"

The Humanity International representative took a deep breath. "The trial to decide Mir's...humanity. And, in effect," she added, pausing before she reached the door, "The humanity of every Subject in WorldCure."

I am led back down the hall. It smells different than the facility – less chemical – but some things are the same. It still smells like fear and anger and darkness. I don't see why it smells like darkness when white light pours in from barred windows. These guards don't carry tranquilizer guns, and they don't call me Tiger. They don't call me anything, they don't speak; they just take me back to my cell and put me in.

This cell is different than my cell at the facility. It's the same size, but there is a window. A small window, as wide as my hand when I hold it up sideways, but it's there. It has a steel shutter that goes over it at night, but during the day it's left open.

I can see out into something the guards called the 'yard' – I haven't been there, but I can watch when the other prisoners are. One man is mean to the others. He shoves and hits them. Most of the men walk slowly, like their joints are stiff. Some seem to play, like they're happy to be there. Outside.

Yesterday, I watched one man who seemed different from all the others. He kept looking up at my window, and he smiled. I smiled back, and he just stood near the wall and kept looking up at me. The air was cold, but it was a nice cold. Like breath.

So I watched him, and he watched me, for almost an hour. I wondered what his name was, and as I walk over to my window now, I wonder if he would be there again this afternoon.

I slide down the wall and think of Eva.

And June.

I can still feel her touch on my hand, such soft skin. My daughter. She is so beautiful… how could something so perfect be mine? For once I didn't destroy a life. I helped create one. It feels so good to hold her, to see her and hear her and smell her. I love her. I know I love her. I would go through anything to keep her safe, to make her happy.

I would even go back to Doctor Ross.

I look at my wall and run my fingers across something scratched there.

Lines.

Four lines, another long line through them.

This same picture is all over the wall, the same picture over and over except one.

There are only three lines. I wonder where the other ones are. Why they weren't finished.

I remember when Eva gave me a name. I remember the way she said it, like she was holding something fragile, something that would break if she spoke too loud. I didn't know what to think. I had never had a name. I almost didn't know what to do with it. It wasn't until later that I realized that the name wasn't for me, it was for her.

A name isn't something for you; it's for the people who use it. It helps them see you.

Am I going to die here? I want to know, but I don't.

If I am, I want to see Eva again. I want to kiss her. I want to hold June and tell her what love is.

Everyone should know.

Eva leaned her head against the cold glass of the car window and paid no attention to the world flashing by outside. Explaining everything to Pocky had been easy – the words had poured out of her mouth like water from a gushing fountain until they slowed to a trickle and finally, stopped. She had offered to drive, but Pocky had only said that if the expression on her face was any judge of how she felt, he'd rather she didn't.

June was asleep, and Eva held her carefully in her arms. She felt as if she was holding a small piece of Mir. She guessed she was.

"I can't believe that Mir is the one behind bars, and Ross is walking around free." She hit her head against the window in frustration, wincing at the dull pain. Her mind flashed back to Mir, slamming his skull against the walls of his cell, and hoped he was not doing that now.

"You did say he was under surveillance," Pocky reminded her.

"That's what he said." Eva shook her head. "I don't understand how life can be so unfair. First my parents and then Jude turning out to be a jerk, and then Ross and Mir…what did I do to earn myself this much bad…bad…"

"Luck?" Pocky guessed, his voice kind but neutral. "Karma?"

"I don't know." She groaned. "Do you believe in destiny, Pocky?"

He made a soft thoughtful noise in the back of his throat. "I believe in Providence."

"And what's the difference between providence and fate or destiny?" She raised an eyebrow, her voice laced with just enough bitterness to make it taste sour in her mouth.

He smiled, and Eva watched the wrinkles surround his clear blue eyes. Most of the men in her life, for better or worse, had blue eyes, she realized. "Providence is fate with hope." He looked over at her, and his smile deepened. "Providence is believing that Someone greater is in control."

"That must be nice," Eva murmured. Her head felt like it was stuffed with cotton. From the corner of her eye, she saw concern mingle with Pocky's smile.

"Eva, are you…all right?"

"All right?" She straightened, careful to keep her voice quiet and not wake June. "No," she said firmly. "No, I am not all right. The man I love is in prison, the man I hate is out of it, and I don't know what's going to happen. At least when my parents died I had some idea of what to do, of where to go. Now I just feel…lost." The last word came out soft, almost a whisper, as if she was talking to herself and no longer to the professor.

"I didn't mean 'all right' with your circumstances, my girl." Pocky's voice was also gentle. "I meant are *you* all right – with yourself."

"With myself?" Eva blinked. It struck her as an odd question, but the longer she thought about it the more complex it became.

The professor was silent, giving her time to gather her thoughts and answer. She looked back out the window. Everything was white and gray. No sun peered from behind the covering of clouds; no spot of color brightened the landscape.

"I suppose I'm all right," she answered after a few minutes of silence had passed. "I don't see why I shouldn't be. I may be in for a legal mess, but at least I'm not in prison yet. And I have you, and Mir, even though I can't see him for more than two minutes a day, and he's dying. And then I have June, and Mir doesn't know he's dying and I don't know where Jude is or what happened once we left WorldCure—" She came up for a breath and realized she was crying.

I've turned into a crybaby, she realized with the taste of saltwater on her lips. She wiped them away with her free hand, then again. It was an angry movement, quick and hard. "I'm fine."

She did not know whether she was grateful for Pocky's silence, or if it irritated her because she wanted the silence broken. "Does it help you?" she asked quietly, "Believing there's a God up there?"

"Immensely." Pocky still wore a smile, but it was faint around his face, like frost on a window. "He knows what He's doing, even when I do not. It's rather impossible for that knowledge *not* to be comforting."

Eva looked down at June and brushed the baby's round cheek with her finger. Her skin was soft and smooth, unmarked by WorldCure's procedures. Mir had unknowingly saved his daughter just in time.

It would not be too far fetched, she thought, *to believe that something greater created such a perfect thing, would it? To believe in some sort of Plan, where everyone's life had a purpose?* She was intelligent enough to realize that life had to begin somewhere, but *where?* There were too many theories.

"Why do unspeakably horrific things happen to people who are good, like Mir?" It took Eva a moment to realize she had spoken the question out loud, but once she realized it she looked at Pocky and waited for an answer.

"It hardly seems fair, does it?"

Eva's eyebrows rose a little in surprise. He sounded as if he were agreeing with her. "No, it doesn't."

"A question people have asked since creation is 'why would a loving God allow this to happen.' I asked it myself, after Margaret died."

Eva sat up straighter. Pocky, her unshakable professor, had questioned the God he believed so strongly in? "Really?"

"Really. We humans are not very good at accepting adversity with grace."

"Most of us," said Eva, a faint smile lifting the corner of her mouth just slightly. *Not everyone...* "That doesn't explain why those things happen, though."

"To tell the truth, I don't know. Nobody does."

That was not what Eva had expected him to say. "Then it makes the whole question pointless."

"Accepting that Someone greater is in control releases us from having to worry about the future," said Pocky, glancing at June and smiling. "It is very freeing."

"Freeing." Eva looked back out the windshield, thinking. "I guess it would be, being able to hand over your life like that."

Pocky laughed. "You make it sound as if 'handing it over' required it to end."

"Not *end*," said Eva, faintly protesting. "Just... it seems hard to imagine... losing control of your life."

"You may lose control, but you gain direction," was all Pocky said for the rest of the drive home.

I am woken up by the door to my cell opening. Two guards stand there. I look at the guns and tasers in their belts, then at their faces.

"Come on," says the taller one. "Exercise hour."

I'm not sure what exercise hour is. "What?"

300

"You've been cleared for an hour in the yard, with the other inmates."

I get to go out? I stand up and walk over to them.

"Hold out your wrists," says one. He sounds tired. I hold my wrists out and the restraints – handcuffs, they're called – go around them.

I am led down the hallway. A door opens at the end and even though I know it isn't the Procedure Room I freeze up just enough to make the shorter guard shove me.

"If you don't want to go out, you can stay inside."

I pause. It's only outside. I want to see the man from yesterday. I walk forward; out into the pale sunlight so bright it hurts my eyes. The air smells like the whiteness that Eva says is snow.

Other inmates are already there. A few of them are talking in the far corner. Others are playing some sort of game with a ball. I look up and see the tower, where I know we're being watched. The walls are high, too high even for me to jump.

I do not see the man from yesterday.

I walk over to the wall and slide down it, sitting on a patch of dry ground. It's cold, but I like cold. I like heat. Even pain can be good. It lets me know I'm alive.

Guards walk around the prisoners, keeping an eye on them.

On me.

I sit for a long time, searching without seeing him.

I look down and see something by my hand. A plant, with green leaves. The flower is bright purple, the color of the shirt Eva wore when we danced. I brush it with my finger, surprised at the sharpness.

"It's a thistle."

I look up at the new voice and see that it's him, the man I wanted to meet. He has a kind look on his face. He is older than me, but not as old as my father. He crouches down and looks at the thistle.

"They're amazing plants," he continues. "Some people think they're weeds. They don't like them; they want to get rid of them. But thistles...they'll grow anywhere. Even right through a stone wall."

He smiles at me.

I smile back, my mind confused. He is speaking to me like I am a normal person. He does not smell afraid, he does not feel evil.

"My name is Paul," he says, and holds out his hand.

I have seen people do this, but I have never done it to anyone. I reach out and shake his hand. "I'm... Mir," I say after a moment. I wondered whether I should call myself Thirteen, but Mir is my name. "I saw you yesterday."

He smiles again. "I wanted to meet you, believe it or not," he says, sitting down beside me and leaning his head against the wall. His eyes watch the men playing with the ball. "I heard you were from a facility north of here."

I nod. "I am."

He looks at me, long and hard. I look back at him and wonder what he wants. "I knew someone who was taken to the facility."

"You did?" My question breathes mist into the air.

He folds his hands around his knees. "Yes. She was never…quite right in the head, you know what I mean?"

"Insane?" I ask.

A smile twists his mouth like it was a joke, but his eyes remain serious, sad. "A little, I guess. But she was the sweetest thing I'd ever met."

"Was she…" I swallow. "Was she a non-human?"

"She was labeled one, yeah. Taken away only a few years after graduating college." He looks up at the sky. It is the same gray as his eyes. "I was told I would be able to visit her."

"None of the Subjects ever had visitors," I say, surprised.

"I found that out." He re-folds his hands and turns his head to look at me. "Being there was not easy." He said it as a statement. As if he knew.

Slowly, I shake my head. "No," I agree, almost whispering. "It wasn't."

"And yet here you are."

I am silent for a few seconds. "Yes."

"Ever wonder why?" He shifts, continues to meet my gaze.

"Why what?"

"Why you're here. The purpose of it all. Don't you think half the men in this yard wonder

303

every minute of their lives how they ended up here?"

I look at all the men walking, running, shouting around me. "They're here because they did bad things."

"Did you?" he asks.

"Yes." I look at my fingers, curled toward my palms. I remember. I remember my hands around Eva's throat, squeezing. I remember the deaths before that. Yes, I did that. Then I wonder. "Why are you here?"

"Me? I'm a murderer." He is quiet, and then smiles again. A calm, quiet smile.

I am confused. "Are you happy about it?"

"No."

"You seem happy."

The smile shifts, like he is smiling at a secret. "I'm...not worried," he says finally.

"About what?"

He shrugs. "Death. Guilt."

My eyes widen. "How can you not be guilty about taking a life from someone?"

"I regret it," he says, his words slow. "But a while ago, I – I put things right. With everyone. And they forgave me. So," he shrugs, "I'm content to be here. I deserve it."

"Who forgave you?" A cold wind prickles across my skin.

"His family. The man I killed." His eyes look like they are somewhere else as he talks, but he does *look content. "And God."*

"His family forgave you?" My eyebrows draw together. "How do you know?"

He laughs. *"I apologized. It took me a long time, but I finally saw what I had done. I said I was sorry."* He shrugs his shoulders.

"Were you?" I ask, watching his face. *"Were you sorry?"*

"Oh," he sighs. *"Yes. Guilty, sorry...I wondered why I'd done it. Why I was still alive and he was dead."*

"But they forgave you? And God forgave you?"

He nods his head. *"Yes."*

"How did you apologize to God?"

"The same way I apologized to the family. I couldn't take it anymore, I broke down, I confessed. I probably cried more than any grown man should," he adds.

"How do you know God forgave you?" I lean forward. *I'm not sure what to think – only Pocky talks about God like this, and Pocky never killed anyone.*

"Because He said He would."

The answer is simpler than I had thought it would be. *"He talked to you?"* I ask, amazed.

"Not directly, but in a way." He looks at me, his smile reaching his eyes now. *"I could give you a Bible, if you want."*

"What's a Bible?"

"It's..." He squints at the thistle on the ground. *"It's a lot of things. I only have a New Testament, but—"*

"What's a New Testament?" I know I am asking a lot of questions, but I can't help it. I'm curious; I have to know.

He pulls something out of the pocket on the front of the jacket, just like every other inmate wears. Just like mine. "Here." He hands it to me. It's a book, very small. It fits into the palm of my hand. "Read it later, if you want."

"Okay." I run my thumb over the gold-embossed words on the cover.

He looks at me. "You can read, can't you?"

"Yes."

He looks a little surprised, a little impressed, maybe. "How did you learn?"

I try and remember. "I watched," I say. "And I listened. Then I got memories from another woman, and that helped a little."

"Memories from another woman?" he asks, his mouth open. "Was that at the facility?"

"Yes." I remember music, and Eva. "She taught me how to dance, too."

He looks like he wants to ask more questions, but a guard walks toward us, calling "All right, that's enough. Mingle, you two."

We stand up.

Paul looks at me. "I'll see you tomorrow."

I smile in return. "Thank you."

He turns and walks toward the other end of the yard, and I take a deep breath and look down at the book in my hand.

Chapter Forty

When Eva, Pocky and June arrived at Dimond the next morning, they were escorted by the same guard to the visiting room. Mir was already there, and Eva smiled when she saw his face through the glass.

She sat down on the stool. "How are you?"

"Happy to see you," he said, smiling. He looked at June, and Eva put the baby's hand against the glass, like she had done at the last visit.

Again, Mir pressed his palm against the other side for a moment, and Eva knew she would always have this image in her head; her own hand covering the much smaller one underneath, with Mir's hand larger than them both.

"I met someone," said Mir.

"Who?" Eva wondered if she would ever quite get used to the directness of Mir's gaze. Most people did not look directly into her eyes when they talked, but he always had. They were not glowing, so she could look back.

"Paul." Mir shifted a little. "He murdered a man."

Eva's breath caught in her throat. Mir was spending time with a murderer? *Mir has killed people too, Eva,* she reminded herself. Still, it did not seem the same. "Is – is he nice?" she asked, feeling as if it was a ridiculously childish question.

"Yes." Mir continued to smile, as if he liked the very thought of his new acquaintance. "He talked to me yesterday, in the yard."

"What did you talk about?" Eva shifted June in her arms, glad the baby's eyes had closed. She did not want to have to explain the infant's glowing eyes to any of the prison personnel.

"Forgiveness."

Eva stopped moving, her eyebrows knit in confusion. "Forgiveness? What do you mean?"

Mir shrugged. "He told me how he regretted killing, and how the man's family had forgiven him. He said God had forgiven him, too."

"God?" It was ironic; Mir was learning about God from a prison inmate. It hurt, somehow, to think that he was learning things and interacting with other people she did not know. It was a strange thought that Mir might end up believing the same things as Pocky; and she would be the one left out. "Do you believe in God?"

"Eva doesn't?"

She laughed, but it sounded uncomfortable even to her. "Not really, no."

Mir's face was quiet, listening. Eva tried to think of something else to say, something to explain herself. "He just... hasn't ever done anything for me."

Now Mir's eyebrows drew together, the corner of his mouth puckering in a bewildered frown. "Didn't He make you?"

Eva had not expected such a barrage of religion to come from Mir. "That's debatable," she said, her voice sharper than she had intended. "I personally don't think so."

"Oh." His expression was not condemning, just interested. "Why not?"

"You've become as frustrating as Pocky," she said with another short, forced laugh.

"I'm sorry," said Mir, looking genuinely contrite.

"Wait – turn your head," Eva instructed, leaning closer.

Mir obeyed, tilting his head to the right. "Why?"

Eva noticed that his jawbone, naturally well-defined, seemed sharper than usual. "Mir," she asked, sudden alarm in her voice, "Don't they feed you here?"

He straightened. "Yes."

Eva's eyes narrowed. "But?"

Even as he answered "I can't eat it," Eva remembered. He had not been able to eat the yogurt, either; his body physically could not force food down after a lifetime of system treatments. She turned to look at Pocky, who had been silent up till now; watching.

"Pocky, could you please get the guard?" She kept her voice calm, masking the anger she felt.

"Eva, I'm all right," said Mir, leaning closer; the lighting highlighting the earnest expression on his face. "I'm only four days behind."

"How…" Eva cleared her throat. "How long have you gone without system treatments before?"

"Six days," he said, putting his hands on the counter. Eva saw the handcuffs and felt her entire body tense with anger at the injustice of it all.

"I'm not letting you go six days without food again," she said firmly, making sure he knew that she meant what she said.

Pocky re-entered the room, guard in tow. "Is there a problem, ma'am?"

Eva stood up, holding June close. She could feel angry heat blossoming across her face as she said, her voice low and steady, "Do you have an intravenous feeding system here?"

The guard blinked. "Uh...I don't think so, ma'am."

"Could. You. Please. Check."

He seemed to sense that the question was really a command. "Yes, ma'am," he said, his eye twitching nervously. He turned and left the room with hurried steps.

"You scared him," said Mir, his voice tinny through the speaker.

"I meant to," said Eva, sitting back down on the stool. She propped one foot on the lowest rung. "Mir, I'm sorry about all this."

"It isn't bad, Eva."

To a normal person it would be, Eva thought silently. It was only to someone like Mir that prison and starvation were not considered 'bad.' "I think June might be close to talking," she said, switching the subject. "I think she almost said a word last night."

Mir's face lit up, his smile turning into a wide grin as he looked at June. "Really?"

Eva had to smile at his excitement. "Yes. I hope she waits until you're able to hear it, though."

A shadow came over Mir's face for the briefest of moments. "Me, too."

The door behind Eva opened and she turned, half-expecting to be told her time was already up.

"Miss Stewart?" the guard said. "I spoke to the warden. We *do* have an intravenous system."

Eva felt her muscles relax in relief. "Thank you." She gave him her warmest smile to make up for her icy tone earlier. "What solutions do you have?"

"I...don't-know?" His words were stinted; he shuffled awkwardly on his feet.

Eva's smile slipped and she could not help but sound disgusted at his lack of knowledge. "Let me see it."

"I – ah, I don't know if that's allowed."

Eva put her free hand on her hip, making sure June was secure in the other. "Then let me speak to the warden myself. Unless you're authorized and trained to feed someone intravenously?"

"No, ma'am," he said, reddening.

"Then it only makes sense for me to be the one to do it. You can stand by and oversee, if it would make you feel better." She felt, for a brief moment, as if she were back in the Procedure Room.

"I..." His eyes bounced from Mir to Pocky and back to Eva. "I think that would be fine."

"Thank you." She looked back at Mir, who was watching everything through the glass with wide, interested eyes. She smiled at him before turning back to the guard. "Where do we hook him up?"

"Does he need a special room or something?" The guard suddenly looked alarmed.

Eva sighed. "He needs to be able to recline. That's about it, as long as you have the correct tools."

"Maybe the therapy room? It has a reclining chair, and it isn't in use," he said, his expression hopeful.

"That would be perfect," said Eva, relieved. "Take him there, please, and show me the equipment you have."

Five minutes later, Mir was lying back on the therapy chair, watching as Eva hooked the bag of solution to the pole and checked to make sure the needle was working. "You know the routine," she said to Mir, smiling a little.

He smiled and looked back at June. Eva had set her on his lap for a few minutes while she got the IV ready. The baby's fists were curled around Mir's fingers as he played with her, talking to her in a soft voice.

"I'm ready," said Eva.

"All right." Pocky gently lifted June away from her father and held her while Eva looked down at Mir.

She said nothing as she put the needle into his subclavian vein below his collarbone. Every doctor had their vein of choice; arm, jugular, but she had always preferred the subclavian. She personally thought it was the most convenient.

She put a piece of surgical tape over the needle to keep it in place and sat down on the edge of the chair. She wondered if Mir knew that Dr. Ross had been in the same building yesterday, and may still be there. Did he know about the trial? She had not been authorized to tell him about it, so she did not mention it.

Mir reached up with his right hand and played with June's hand, just within reach. Eva smiled, even though it was a sight she had not gotten used to. She had mixed feelings about seeing Mir with his daughter. Pride that Mir was such a loving father. Anger that June had been bred, not conceived from matrimony like a baby should be. Heartbreak that Mir would never see June live to be a woman. Worry that June would suffer health complications from her parents.

She looked at the IV, watched the clear liquid drain from the bag into Mir's body.

Life.

For however long.

Chapter Forty-One

On her way out through the reception area, Eva heard her name called.

"Miss Stewart!"

She turned and saw Dagney striding toward her, that brown-lipped smile stuck to her face.

"Oh," said Eva. "Hello."

"How is Mir?" Dagney said the word 'Mir' with a mixture of condescension and something that might have been genuine interest.

"Well, he's no longer starving," said Eva, feeling unexpected anger at Dagney's appearance. Every time the Humanity International representative spoke, she felt like a dog whose fur was being petted in the wrong direction.

Dagney's smile did not move. "Good. I'm glad to hear it. He's become quite the subject of interest, if you'll pardon the pun."

Eva fought the urge to smack the woman. For someone from Humanity International, she was disturbingly insensitive. "Oh? How so?"

"Haven't you seen the newspaper?" Dagney asked, blinking wide-eyed. She pulled a rolled-up paper from her purse and handed it to Eva.

The headline read **"Are Subjects Really Human?"**

Beneath it was a picture of Mir. It was low-quality; grainy and blurry; taken as Mir was being escorted into the prison. Eva was surprised by the calm expression on his face as he looked at the photographer. At her.

"This Subject of yours has caused quite a stir in news circles," said Dagney as Eva scanned the article, her eyes widening with every printed word.

"Pocky, listen to this," said Eva, turning to face the professor. Aloud, she read the eloquent article, "*Since the early twenty-first century, it has been believed that there are two kinds of people: humans and non-humans. But the arrival of former WorldCure Subject Thirteen has sparked a debate that asks the question 'what defines human?' A crowd gathered outside Dimond Prison, Alaska was shocked at the sight of the proven non-human Subject as it was taken into custody – not because of a grotesque or monstrous appearance, but because of Thirteen's apparent normalcy. Thirteen's former Handler, WorldCure Doctor Eva Stewart, has even given the Subject a name. She calls him Mir, and many people have adopted the name as well. 'Mir' is still in prison awaiting trial that will take place on Thursday at the Anchorage Courthouse—*"

Eva broke off and turned to face Dagney. "Why wasn't I informed that a date had been set for the trial?"

"The trial will begin at 11 AM," said Dagney primly, extracting the newspaper from Eva's hands. She looked at Pocky. "You must both be there. I can have an escort—"

"We will be there," said Eva, grinding her teeth. "Thank you very much. I assume Doctor Ross will be put on trial as well?"

"Yes," said Dagney, hesitating. "We discovered evidence this morning that…well, never mind. You, Professor Pock, Doctor Ross and Subject Thirteen will all testify."

For a moment, Eva could think of nothing to say. She could not even be certain the trial would be a fair one, not in today's political climate. "How do I know that justice will be dealt instead of discarded?"

Dagney looked shocked. "Are you suggesting that a court of law would purposefully—"

"Yes," said Eva without flinching. "I am."

Dagney straightened to her full height, her expression that of someone who had been personally insulted. "I can assure you, Miss Stewart—"

"No," said Eva, interrupting for the third time. "You can't." She turned to Pocky. "Come on." She walked out the front door, feeling that the sharp winter air was warmer than Dagney's glare.

The book tells me I have 'sinned.' It says I'm not good enough by myself. I know this already, but the book tells me a way to make everything right again. It says I can be forgiven.

I want to be forgiven. I want to be forgiven by the people I killed. I want to be forgiven by Eva for trying to hurt her. I want to be able to forgive myself.

God will forgive me, the book says. It has instructions, it tells me what to do.

I prayed for the first time last night. I talked to God.

I hope He heard me.

I look up as the door to my cell opens. It creaks a little, like the hinges are rusting and I shiver somewhere in the back of my mind.

"I'm taking you to the visitation room," says the guard. "There's someone who wants to talk to you."

I am handcuffed and led down the hall, back from where I came only this morning. I wonder who it is. Eva already came and visited me today. Who else would want to talk to me? I sit down on the stool and the door closes behind me.

I wait, rubbing my arms. They hurt lately. Everywhere hurts, even without prepping. My chest hurts more; even breathing is uncomfortable. I lean forward, making it a little easier.

The door opens and someone walks in.

I know I'm starting to glow. I can't feel it, but I know it happens when my heart beats faster.

I thought he was dead.

Father sits down on the other side of the glass and I can see my own reflection there. Yes. My eyes are narrowed, glowing.

Past them, my father smiles and I tense.

"How are you doing, son? Homesick?"

I don't have a home, unless it's Eva. My heart lives with Eva. I'm homesick for her.

I shake my head. "No."

He smiles, sharp as broken glass. "You've made quite an impression on Doctor Stewart."

"She is kind to me," I say quietly. I don't like talking about Eva with my father.

"Kind to you?" If he had had an eyebrow, it would have risen. "I was kinder to you than she

was. After all," he says, re-positioning himself more comfortably, "I let you live."

"No, you didn't," I say after a moment of silence. I tilt my head; look at him through the glass. "You kept me breathing, but you let me die."

He spreads his hands, still smiling. "It was for science."

The words cut even though I don't know why. I wonder if I am going to bleed. "Why didn't you die?" I ask, my voice soft from the tears welling in my throat.

"Why? Do you wish I had?" He leans forward, squinting; still smiling, but waiting for my answer.

I feel almost trapped. That he wants me to say something specific. I say the only true answer that comes to me. "I only wish you hadn't hurt people."

He opens his mouth, like he's going to answer, but nothing comes out. His smile fades before coming back. "You can't fool me, 'Mir.'" He spits my name, but I don't interrupt him. "You may have fooled some people into thinking you're not a threat. That you're a 'good person.' Would you like me to remind you of what you've done?"

His tone is nice, helpful. I feel my hackles rise. "I know what I've done."

He acts like he didn't hear me. "I saw the video feed, you know. I watched what you did to those people. I heard them scream for help. 'Oh, God, no.' Do you remember hearing that?" His eyes gaze into me.

It is difficult to breathe. "I remember." My pulse pounds heavily but I feel calm in a way that surprises me. "Do you?"

He blinks, taken aback.

"Do you remember my screams? What you did to me?" I am smiling, but my eyes are crying. "What you did to everyone?"

"See, there's the thing," he says, straightening his tie. "They're non-humans. So are you." His voice is polite and civilized. It's amazing how painful it can be. "And no matter how much you want to be..." he leans forward, his voice even softer, "you will never, ever be a human being."

"Aren't you?"

"Excuse me?" Dr. Ross asks with a surprised look and tone.

"If I'm your son, then I must be human. Unless you aren't."

He stands up. One eye twitches in a wink and he walks toward the door.

His fingers are wrapped around the door handle before I speak again.

"Doctor Ross."

He turns, looks at me with something glinting in his eyes. "Yes?" he asks, pronouncing the word clear and cold.

There are so many things I could say. Scream, cry at him.

"Sleep well," I say, and walk away from the glass partition.

Chapter Forty-Two

Eva had just fallen asleep on the couch when her cell phone rang. She fumbled to find it in her pocket and answered. "Hello, this is Eva Stewart."

"Miss Stewart, this is Jon Morgen, the warden at Dimond Prison."

Eva sat up, worry pushing sleep away. "Yes, what is it? Did something happen?"

"If you would, please come to the prison, Miss Stewart."

A thousand possible reasons behind the request flew through Eva's mind. "I'll be there as soon as I can," she assured the warden. She shoved the phone in her pocket and hurried into Pocky's study. Books lined the shelves and a large oak desk graced the far corner by the window. Pocky was seated comfortably in a large leather chair at the other end reading an old book.

The room was so old-fashioned that every time Eva entered it she felt as if she had been transported through time. "Pocky, I have to go to prison."

He looked up from his book, blinking behind his glasses. "Whatever did you do?"

"I just got a call from the warden." She held up her cell phone, sinking her teeth into her lower lip until it hurt. "He said to come there, I don't know why. Where's June?"

"She's asleep in the crib upstairs," said Pocky, laying his book down on the arm of the chair. "Are you going alone, or would you like company?"

"No, no," Eva assured him, hoping he believed her. "I don't want to wake June. I'll be fine."

He nodded. "Call me if you need me to drive up. In case of...anything. You know."

She nodded. "I know." She gave him a false smile and left. She drove faster than she felt comfortable with in her rush, kicking up piles of snow and ice and hoping that nothing horrible had happened at the prison.

Eva entered the reception area and saw the warden talking to the receptionist. She walked up, the heels of her boots clicking on the polished floor. "What happened? Where is he?"

He straightened and set his cup of coffee on the counter. "Come with me."

Eva followed him down the hallway. They took a different branch and he opened the door for her with a half-hearted sweep of his arm. "In there."

She strode in. It was a small room with a table and chairs at one side. A barred window cast slanted shades of light across it.

Mir sat in a chair at one side of the table, and another inmate Eva had never seen before sat at the other.

"Mir," exclaimed Eva when she caught a better glimpse of his face.

His eyes were downcast as he shifted in his chair. A cut graced his lower lip and a bruise covered his cheekbone.

The other inmate's arms were folded, and his scowling face looked no better than Mir's.

Eva turned. "What happened?" she asked the warden. "Was it a fight?"

"Yes, ma'am." The warden nodded, exasperation in his voice. "I can't get either of them to say who started it, though."

"So you called me?" Eva raised her eyebrows. She was glad she had been informed of the fight, and she would seize any opportunity to see Mir, but she had never heard of friends and relatives being called to a prison because of a fight before.

"Not exactly," said the warden, looking at the inmates. "Miss Hart and I wanted to talk to you about Thirteen's release until the trial on Thursday."

"Release?" Eva leaned forward. Had she heard correctly? "You're going to release him?"

"Well, we *were*." Jon Morgen sighed. "Until this happened. If we can't get either of them to say who started it, then Thirteen might be guilty and we won't be able to let him out on good behavior."

"Oh." Eva rubbed her forehead, thinking. "Can I have a minute alone with him?" She could see that Mir's hands, resting on his lap, were cuffed.

"Not alone," said the warden. "But I can have a guard sit at the other end of the room while you talk."

It was better than nothing. "All right. Thank you."

She stood by and waited while the unfamiliar inmate was taken out and the warden left, replaced by a tall, thin guard who sat down in a chair near the door and nodded at her.

"Go ahead."

Eva gave him a thin smile. She walked over and sat down across the table from Mir, whose eyes remained lowered. "So," she said after a moment where the only sound was the ticking of the clock on the wall. "What happened?"

"I'm sorry." Mir's voice was faint, hoarse. He looked up and spoke again, more clearly. "I'm sorry."

"For what?" Eva leaned forward, her hands on the table. "I don't know what happened."

Mir leaned back in his seat and looked as uncomfortable as Eva had ever seen him. "Fighting," he mumbled. "I shouldn't have done it."

"What were you fighting about?" Eva tilted her head, trying to look at his eyes. "Mir?"

He sighed and lifted his gaze to the ceiling. "He was being mean to Paul."

Paul. The murderer Mir had made friends with. "So you got into a fight?" She made sure her voice was not angry or irritated.

"He was trying to start a fight with Paul." Mir pulled his gaze down and looked Eva in the eyes. "He called Paul a liar. He said he wasn't really sorry for what he had done."

"Did Paul hit the other guy first?"

"No." Mir ran his thumb along the circle of metal around his left wrist. "I did."

"Why?" This time, Eva could not keep a little exasperation out of her voice. She knew that unless he was tormented and threatened, Mir was not the sort to start fights.

Mir licked his lips and looked as if he was going to answer, but decided against it.

Eva clasped her hands together and asked the only plausible question that came into her head. "Were you defending him?"

More silence. More ticking of the clock, and then Mir nodded. "I shouldn't have hit him."

"I..." Eva shut her eyes and felt something between a smile and a laugh inside her. "Mir, you're a good friend. Hitting someone isn't the way to settle an argument, but you were sticking up for Paul."

"I'm supposed to let myself be hit, Eva! Not hit someone else first." Mir's fist thumped lightly on the table, a half-hearted pound like a tired judge's gavel.

Eva smoothed her hair back, confused. "Mir, you didn't really do anything wrong."

He clenched his hands into fists, his eyes burning with suppressed anger. "Eva," he said calmly and evenly, "I can't hit people. You don't understand. I get angry and if I hit them..." His voice trailed off and he took a deep breath, jaw muscles clenched.

He changed the subject with an abrupt, "How is June?"

Eva was now fairly certain she understood. Mir was afraid of losing himself again, of hurting someone in such a way they could not recover. "She's fine," she said with a faltering smile. "Beautiful."

Mir smiled; a sad smile that touched his eyes with longing.

"You're going to have a trial, Mir. Did you know that?"

"Trial," he repeated, the expression on his face stating he knew nothing about it.

"You and..." She cut her sentence short. Did he know about Dr. Ross?

Her face must have clearly shown her thoughts, because Mir said in a low voice "I know about Father."

"You do?" Eva's stomach knotted in concern. "How?"

"He came to see me."

"He..." Eva's tone was quizzical, but Mir's face seemed to shut the door to any questions. "Well. You, Doctor Ross and I will testify, and a jury will decide...well, everything," she finished, twisting her mouth in distaste. The idea of strangers deciding Mir's fate worried her more than she could let on.

Mir's eyes widened and worry lent a note of strain to his voice. "What will happen to June?"

"I don't know. The point is, they might release you from prison until the trial. Up until today, you had shown model behavior. Plus, I don't think they want the press hounding them any more than they already are," she added.

Mir leaned forward, his face a mixture of hope and regret. "Will I be able to come home?"

"I hope," said Eva, with all the true feeling she felt. She looked over her shoulder at the guard who sat at the other end of the room, flipping through a magazine. "The fight may have altered our options."

"Can you ask?"

She nodded. "I'll ask."

Pages rustled from the other end of the room. The guard cleared his throat and said, "Time to go, Miss."

Reluctantly, Eva stood up and pushed her chair back in its place. "I'll get this sorted out, Mir." Turning her head so that the guard could not see her face, she mouthed 'I love you.'

Mir's eyes smiled back.

Chapter Forty-Three

As Eva stepped out the door she saw that Mr. Morgen was waiting for her.

"Well?" he asked.

"He was defending another inmate."

The warden's eyebrows rose. "He was?"

"You can ask the guard inside if you don't believe me," said Eva, a polite smile forcing itself across her face. "All I know is what Mir said, but I have never known him to lie." As she watched the conflict play out across the warden's face, she wondered why Dr. Ross had not done everything in his power to make sure Mir stayed in prison until the trial.

As much as she hated to think about it, she could not help but entertain the idea that somehow, Dr. Ross was working the situation toward his own ends. Whatever those ends were.

"I'll speak to Miss Hart," he said finally, doubt lacing his voice.

"May I come with you?"

He nodded and led the way to his office. Eva smiled at Dagney, who rose from her seat as they entered.

"Doctor Stewart," said Dagney.

"Miss Hart."

"How is our little Thirteen today?"

Eva bristled at the condescension in the woman's voice. "Concerning the fight, there is really nothing to tell. He was defending another inmate, and no one was seriously hurt."

Dagney opened her mouth, but Eva interrupted. "How would one go about securing a pre-trial release?"

"I hardly think that after his display of violence—"

"What would she have to do," Jon Morgen calmly cut her off, "to secure a release?"

Dagney blinked rapidly. "You aren't serious."

"From what I've seen of Thirteen, he's surprisingly mild-mannered." Eva felt her liking for the man increasing as he continued. "I know forty-seven, the inmate he hit. I think with the proper precautions, he could leave Dimond till Thursday."

Dagney's mouth opened and closed several times before she stammered, "Well, that's – that's just – that's ridiculous!"

"I thought you worked for Humanity International." Eva could feel her eyes narrowing and lips thinning, an expression of displeasure she could not control.

"Yes, but the 'humanity' in this case has yet to be decided," said Dagney in a honey-coated voice.

"We'll give Thirteen a tracking bracelet," said the warden, his tone warning them both to stop before an argument erupted. "He will not be able to take it off, and it will tell us where he is at all times."

Eva nodded, trying to relax. "Are there any other conditions?"

"No," Jon said evenly, "just that one."

Eva wanted to ask if Dr. Ross had said anything about Mir's release, but she knew better and kept her mouth closed. "Thank you. When can I take him home?"

Dagney huffed.

The warden glanced at her with something that was almost a smile. Eva had the feeling he was enjoying irritating the Humanity International representative. "You have to fill out the release papers."

"How long should that take?" Eva inquired.

"Half an hour at the most, and then you can take Thirteen."

"Can I make a quick phone call first?"

He nodded. "Go ahead; come back here when you're ready."

She nodded and walked outside, dialing Pocky's number.

"I can hardly believe it," he said when she told him about Mir's release.

"I know. It's either miraculous, or Ross is up to something."

"Both are completely plausible, but there is nothing we can do except enjoy the fact that you have two more days with Mir before the trial."

Eva smiled. "I will. We should be home in a little while; are you all right?"

"Oh, we're fine; 'holding down the fort,' I believe is the expression. How is Mir holding up?"

Eva switched the phone to her other ear. "He's going to have to wear a tracking bracelet, but that seems reasonable."

"More than reasonable."

Eva looked at the wall in front of her, rubbing her forehead. "Well...I'll see you soon, Pocky."

"I look forward to it."

Thirty-three minutes later, Eva watched as the warden clamped a bracelet around Mir's wrist. It locked automatically with a small click, and Mir turned his arm this way and that as if fascinated by the thing. "What is it?"

"It's a tracking bracelet." Eva smiled reassuringly at him. "It's the reason you're able to be released. They'll know where you are if you try to…" she paused. Mir would not try to run away, she knew that; but she was afraid of saying anything that would make him think she mistrusted him.

"Escape?"

"Is my face really that readable?" she asked with a tense laugh.

Mir's face held that profound naïveté Eva had come to love and even look strangely forward to. "You say a lot when you stop talking," he said, looking back down at the bracelet.

Eva rubbed his arm with a smile that was no longer forced. "Come on, let's go see June."

He looked so eager that she laughed. "Whoa, boy, hold your horses; we have to sign out first."

They were in the parking lot, and Eva felt the familiar presence before she saw him.

Sunglasses covered his eyes, but there was no mistaking the shaved head and confident stride. "Doctor Stewart," he said pleasantly.

"Doctor Ross," said Eva, far less pleasantly.

"Thirteen. Or is it Mir now?"

"My name is Mir."

Eva looked at the young man who rubbed his tracking bracelet with a thumb, watching his father with caution in his eyes.

"I see they released you." Dr. Ross's sunglasses looked at the bracelet.

Eva could not stand to be around the man any longer than was absolutely necessary, and she did not think this conversation fit into the category of 'necessary.' "Good day," she said with a stiff, almost old-fashioned politeness.

"I'll see you in court." Dr. Ross held out his hand. Eva was more than half-tempted to smack it away, but it was not directed at her.

Mir hesitated before grasping his father's hand and accepting the gesture, but it was clear that every fiber of his being wanted to recoil. The handshake was brief; Mir let go as though he did not want his skin to be in contact with his father's any longer than it had to.

Dr. Ross's expression was unreadable, his son's eyes reflected in his sunglasses. He turned to Eva. "Have a nice day," he said before walking away toward a black convertible parked a few hundred yards away.

Eva felt an involuntary shiver claw across her back. She looked at Mir, who was following his father with his eyes as the other man climbed into his car and shut the door with a *bang*.

As the convertible drove away, Eva lifted her hand to shade her eyes against the brightness of the snow and met Mir's gaze. "Are you all right?"

Mir took a deep breath, blew it out, and nodded. "Let's go home."

The instant the front door was opened by Pocky, Mir crossed to the living room, dropped to his knees and lifted his daughter. "June!"

Eva felt a ray of happiness pierce the burden of the worry that was her constant companion these days. "How are you?" she asked, watching June and Mir. Mir rolled onto his back and set his daughter on his stomach, holding her hands to keep her from falling over.

"Tired." She rubbed her face. "I haven't gotten any real sleep in...I don't know. Too long."

"Go on upstairs and have a bit of a lie down," the professor urged gently, pulling her coat off and hanging it on a peg. "We can manage to keep the world together until you wake up."

Eva almost protested – she wanted to spend time with Mir, explain trials and court systems, and ask about his visit with his father – but she found herself nodding instead. "All right," she said, covering a large yawn with her hand.

Pocky patted her back. "There's a good girl. Do you want me to wake you when dinner's ready?"

She shook her head. "I'll eat something whenever I get up." The sounds of June's baby squeals mingling with Mir's laughter followed her up to her room.

Chapter Forty-Four

Eva was up sitting at the kitchen counter searching the internet when Mir walked in. She glanced up and smiled warmly.

"You're up early," she remarked as he opened a cabinet and withdrew a mug.

"So are you."

"Hmm." She tapped the 'x' in the corner of the screen and the tab closed. She turned slightly on her stool to watch as Mir poured coffee into the cup. His hair was still tousled from sleep, like a lion's mane, and his habit of sleeping shirtless was threatening to give her face an uncharacteristic blush. "Did you sleep well?" she asked, diverting her current train of thought.

He looked up and smiled. "Yes. Did you?"

"I slept well enough, but not long enough. I woke up about half an hour ago and couldn't go back to sleep." She rubbed her bare arm below the sleeve. "Did June sleep well?"

He nodded and sipped his coffee, then set the cup on the counter and watched her, the pale dawn light from the window reflecting off his eyes like shards of crystal. "Are you all right?"

Eva straightened. "Why? Do I look sick?"

"Not sick." He ran his tongue along his lower lip, something Eva had noticed he did when he was deep in thought.

Eva was about to ask what when she noticed his fingers wrapped around the handle of the mug. "You're drinking coffee?" She could feel her mouth open in a half-formed vowel of surprise.

"I had a little yesterday. It seems to be all right; I haven't had much," he said with a half-smile. "You fed me water a few times. I guess it's the same."

The sight of Mir doing something completely normal like drinking coffee warmed a place deep inside Eva. She clasped her hands and felt a smile tugging at her mouth. She wished every glimpse of happiness were not darkened by the shadow of Mir's illness, the awful truth she could not bring herself to tell him.

Was it fair, to keep the truth to herself? Or was it kinder to let him live as long as he could without knowing? Her smile slipped and her eyebrows drew together as her thoughts turned inward in turmoil.

She did not hear Mir set his coffee down and walk over to her; not until she felt fingers running through her hair with gentle strokes.

"Is Eva worried?" he asked.

Eva savored the voice; the third-person, the deep softness of it. That he really cared. "I was wondering…" she hesitated. Was this a good idea? She was her only judge. And there was not much time. "I was thinking we could go to Providence Hospital today," she said slowly. "To see – to see her."

Mir sat down on the stool next to her. "My mother?" he asked after a long moment.

Eva nodded, watching the war of emotions cross his face as fear gave way to longing. "We don't have to go," she said, her voice soft in the quiet kitchen. "But I thought you might want to."

"She's sick." It was spoken as a statement, but Eva read the underlying question.

"Yes." She took Mir's hand, larger and paler even than hers. Tracing a vein with her thumb, she said, "She's very sick."

"She is going to die."

Oh, heavens. He's going to make me cry already. She sniffed as subtly as she knew how and answered, "Yes."

The silence around them seemed to grow thicker, broken only by a lone bird chirping somewhere on the other side of the window-glass.

"I want to see my mother."

I thought you would. "We'll go as soon as everyone's up."

He nodded, his lips pressed together. "I..." He looked at the ceiling, blinking rapidly. His voice was choked into a whisper and he took a deep, shuddering breath before meeting her eyes. "I'm scared."

Eva felt strangely small, sitting there with her feet propped up on the lowest rung of the stool, next to the young man whose very presence was a puzzle. "Why?" she asked, tightening her grip on his hand to reassure him. *I'm here.*

"What if she doesn't want to see me?"

Eva looked at him with all the earnestness she could push through her gaze. "Mir...I don't see how she could possibly *not* want to see you. She thought you died, and if..." she swallowed, forcing herself to talk past the lump in her throat, "if she's anything like my mother, then she'll be very, very happy to see you." Her last words were whispered; a tear rolled down her cheek, a saltwater raindrop on her skin.

Mir wiped it away.

"Are you sure this is a good idea?"

Eva looked up at Pocky as she popped the seal shut on her travel mug of coffee. "Is what a good idea?"

"Taking him to see his mother."

"Of course it is." Eva picked up the mug and walked out of the kitchen. Pocky's voice stopped her.

"On top of everything else?"

Eva shut her eyes and took a deep breath. "Pocky..." She turned to face him. "Look. I think – with everything that's happening, Mir has a right to see his mother. Even if something happens and we can't see her, or she's not even awake. These may be his last few days free, and I don't intend to let them go to waste."

Pocky nodded and zipped up the front of his coat. As he pulled gloves onto his hands, he asked quietly "Have you told him yet?"

"No." Eva gripped the travel mug tightly. "Not yet. I can't."

She knew from the look in his kind eyes that he understood – and that sooner or later, she would have to tell Mir. "I don't want to have to do it," she said in a low voice, glancing up the stairs. Mir was readying June in his room, and she could hear the faint sounds of talking and laughter from behind the closed door.

"Frequently, the things we need to do are also the hardest." Pocky stuck his hands in his pockets and sighed. "But that doesn't alter the fact that we have to do them."

"I know!" Eva snapped. She felt an invisible, constant weight sink harder onto her shoulders. "I'm sorry. It's just...not now. We'll talk about it later."

Pocky walked over to her and patted her shoulder. "All right," he agreed, letting the subject fall away.

"You know what the funny thing is?"

He turned as she laughed, a laugh with no humor. "What, duck?"

She tried to fit her thoughts, like fractured puzzle pieces, into something she could recognize. "A part of me is still back in that lab, and it doesn't want WorldCure to shut down. It wants to keep everything hidden, because..." she took a deep breath and felt an involuntary shudder shiver down her frame.

"Because how else will you find the cure for Morbus," Pocky finished, his papery voice soft.

Eva lifted her eyes to his and nodded. She could feel a blush of shame and guilt firing her face, as if the room around her had suddenly grown hot. "I know that it isn't right, and I know that whatever happens, I will see this thing through. I'll do everything I can to stop WorldCure, to stop Doctor Ross, but I will *not* stop trying to find a cure. Mom and Dad wouldn't quit on me." She felt her expression melt into something fierce. "I am *not* going to quit on them."

"Of course not, Eva," said Pocky in that caring yet firm way of his. He wrapped a knitted scarf around her neck. "I wouldn't expect you to give up, no indeed. But using humans like lab rats – that must stop. I know you know that."

Eva nodded. "I could never do that again. Even thinking about it makes me sick." She shut her eyes and wished she could shut her brain as bits of memories – Mir screaming, crying, wretched – forced themselves into her thoughts.

She looked up the stairs again as a door opened and Mir came down, holding June. Eva had to smile at the sight of the baby, bundled in a coat, mittens, a hat, scarf, and boots. "She looks like me, when my mom used to dress me for playing in the snow," she remarked.

Mir grinned. He wore only a coat, but Eva reminded herself that he was used to cooler temperatures. "I don't want her to be cold," he explained, kissing his daughter's rosy cheek.

Eva wanted to kiss both of them, but she restrained herself and headed for the door instead. "Come on, you guys. We don't want to miss visiting hours."

Mir opted to sit in the back with June, so Eva sat in the passenger seat beside Pocky for the trip. She kept her eyes on the scenery outside the window with something small inside her hoping – perhaps even praying – that the visit went well. That was all she asked; that no hearts were broken, that it was an easy-in, easy-out.

She glanced at Pocky out of the corner of her eye and he returned the glance. "It's going to be fine," he mouthed. "Breathe." He moved his hand in a 'wave' motion to indicate breathing.

Eva humphed a little but obeyed, and felt a little better after a few deep breaths, though her worry was far from gone. "How much longer until we reach the hospital?"

"Not long. I thought children were supposed to outgrow the 'are we there yet' question."

"I don't think we ever outgrow it," said Eva, tugging at the strap of her seat belt. "We just stop asking it."

Pocky laughed quietly and Eva turned in her seat to look at Mir. He had one hand in June's lap, and the baby's own were curled around two of his fingers. He was staring through the window unblinking. He looked as if his mind had abandoned his body and was thousands of miles away.

"Hey." Eva tapped his knee.

He blinked slowly and looked at her, eyes widening as he smiled. "What?"

"Are you all right? You were a little zoned out." She realized that he might not grasp the phrase 'zoned out,' but he seemed to put the pieces together because he shook his head once, deep chestnut strands falling over the tops of his eyebrows.

"Just thinking."

Eva wanted to ask what he had been thinking about, but only turned around in her seat and stared through the windshield, much the way Mir had done before the moment.

She wished they had longer to drive.

They walked into the hospital, Mir carrying June in his arms and looking around the place with the corner of his mouth pulled inward.

"Is something wrong?" She felt as if she asked him a version of that question every time she turned around, but it felt too insensitive – too much like Doctor Eva Stewart – not to ask.

He looked at her, thinly-masked displeasure on his face. "It reminds me of the facility."

Oh. Eva had felt as if the hospital was a familiar face: the sterile smell, the white walls, nurses and orderlies walking everywhere.

For Mir it must feel like a return to prison.

Eva put her hand on his arm, even though all she could feel was the fabric of her gloves and his coat. She saw the way he held one hand to the side of June's head, as if protecting her from her surroundings. "This is a place for healing, not experimentation. We'll be fine."

He nodded and breathed out through his nose, his lips still pressed tightly together. "I know."

Eva left him and went to inquire at the front desk. "We're here to visit…" She realized she did not know the woman's name and gestured to Pocky.

"Ah," he stepped forward, "Da-Hye Song."

Well, thought Eva, *I guess that explains the shape of Mir's eyes.*

The nurse ran her finger along the computer screen. "What is your relation to Miss Song?"

"Her son came to see her." Eva waved Mir over.

The nurse looked him up and down with one over-plucked eyebrow raised. "Her son," she repeated.

Eva nodded once. "Yes."

"There is no mention of a son in her family records."

Eva's eyes shifted over to Pocky, but the professor looked as worried as she did. "There...he..." *Stop tripping over your words, woman! That only makes you seem less credible!*

"My name is Mir." Eva stepped to the side and allowed Mir to lean into the front desk, June asleep in his arms. "I was raised by my father. I know my mother is sick, and I wanted her..." his voice caught, and for a moment Eva wondered if he would be able to continue. "To be able to see her granddaughter before..." he stopped again, his lips pressed together and his eyes unblinking.

"Please," Eva interjected on his behalf. She knew that he was close to screaming or weeping, and it hurt her too much to watch either one.

The nurse wavered, her hand poised above the 'allow' button on the computer. "It really isn't allowed without the right papers," she said feebly.

Just then, as if by miracle, June opened her eyes and yawned. She blinked her big, blue eyes at the nurse and gave her a smile that spread across her tiny mouth like early-morning sunlight.

The nurse's face melted into a smile of its own and she cooed, "Hello, there. What's your name?"

"June," Mir supplied, switching arms that the nurse could better see his daughter. Over the baby's hat, he glanced at Eva and smiled.

Eva grinned, but dropped the expression into something more serious when the nurse looked at her.

"All right, you can go in, but not for long. Miss Song has her treatment soon." The nurse pressed 'allow' and smiled at them, waving at June. "She's in room 208."

"Thank you," said Mir, all politeness.

The nurse smiled before turning away to answer the ringing phone.

They walked down the halls, passing closed door after closed door, and Eva began to realize that the similarities between the hospital and the WorldCure facility were beginning to wear on her as well as Mir.

His nervousness was so obvious she could almost touch it, and it was with clear relief that Eva announced, "Here we are, room 208." She turned to look at Mir. "If you want, I'll take June and you can go in first."

He looked at the door, the familiar phosphorescent glow brightening his eyes. Eva could see the same glow spilling faintly from his shoulder blades and chest, even under his jacket. "Eva," he hesitated.

She reached up and lifted June from him. "It's fine." She moved so she could look into his eyes. "Everything will be fine. You said you trusted me, right?"

"I do."

She brushed his cheek with her lips. "We'll be right out here."

His face set with determination, Mir pushed the door open and walked into the room.

The Facility smell is even stronger in here, but it's easy to ignore it when all I can see is a woman lying on a bed, her eyes closed. I hear a beeping sound; I know it's a heart monitor. I've been hooked up to them before.

I know the person on the bed is my mother. My mind knows it, but my heart has a hard time believing it. I think this is just another hallucination and I'll wake up and this will never have happened – but I haven't woken up from Eva yet.

There is a chair by the bed and I walk over to it, afraid I'll be too loud and wake her up. She's beautiful. She has black hair and looks young, younger than Pocky. Father once told me that my mother had been young when she gave birth to me, and now I believe him.

I sit down in the chair and watch her.

My mother.

She is pale and too thin. She looks like the other Subjects at the Facility looked whenever I saw them.

I suddenly want to run from the room and as far away from the hospital as I can. What am I going to do if she wakes up? What if she's been happy without knowing she has a son, or a granddaughter? What if I make her sad or angry?

No.

I can't leave.

I don't have the time.

She turns her head toward me. Her eyes are still closed, but as I watch she opens them. We look at each other as the monitor beeps softly in the corner.

"Who are you?" *Her voice is brittle, quiet.*

Mine is, too. "Mir."

A shade of confusion passes over her face as she looks at me. "Do you work here?"

"No. I'm—" *My hands shake. I clench them into fists and feel my breathing grow faster. I shake my head, trying to ease it of the pounding that fills it.*

"Are you all right?" *She tries to sit up and I want to stop her, but my body fights me. I feel like I'm going to have a fit – I haven't had one in weeks, it can't happen now! –I try to calm down.*

Soon my breathing is deeper, slower. She is looking at me.

I think she's worried.

"Are you sick? Do you need a nurse?"

I shake my head again.

"Well..." *She looks helpless.*

I make myself look at her, and it makes it hard to breathe, but in a different way. My heart hurts; a sharp, stabbing pain and black crowds the edges of my vision. "I wanted to see you."

"Why?" *She is so pale, almost the color of the sheets around her.* "Are you a patient here?"

"No." *My voice is a gasp, not like my normal voice at all.*

I know not to be frightened of it.

"Then who are you?"

The pain fades into the background. Who am I?

"I'm your son."

Her breath catches, and the monitor beeps faster. For a moment, she says nothing and I'm afraid that I've hurt her.

"I don't have a son," she says. She looks like she might fall apart and break if I talk too loud.

"Yes, you do." I lean forward and for the first time since I can remember, I feel cold. "I never died."

"I never. Had. A child." She says it like she's trying to convince herself, like each word is forced out of her against her will. She's crying and I realize that I am, too.

I stand up and sit down on the edge of her bed. "Twenty-four years ago you had a baby and you were told it died."

She stares at me. "How could you know that," she whispers. "Nobody knew that except..."

"My father, Doctor Ross," I finish when her voice goes silent.

"Devon." Her voice sounded faint, emerging through layers of buried memories.

My father's name was Devon? "Devon," I say aloud; softly, but the word is sharp and angry.

I feel a hand on my face and flinch. She is looking at me, her brown eyes leaking. Crying. "What—" she takes a breath. "What's your name again?"

I'm so shocked by the touch of my mother that I almost forget to answer. "Mir."

"Mir." She nods and seems very calm. And then she is crying harder and hugging me, so fragile and small. I wrap my arms around her, holding her together.

And I cry, too.

Chapter Forty-Five

Eva sat outside the door, holding June as the baby faded in and out of sleep. She looked up at Pocky. "How long has it been?"

"Nine minutes," he replied after glancing at his watch.

"Maybe we should—"

The door opened and Mir stepped out. Eva stood up. "Is everything all right?" she asked immediately. She saw his eyes were smudged dark with tears.

"She…" He spread his arms, at a loss. "She's my mother."

Eva hugged him with her free arm. *Thank you, thank you, thank you.* She did not know who she was thanking; she only knew she was grateful, so grateful that Mir was happy. "Do you want June?"

He smoothed a hand over the top of his sleeping daughter's head. "Yes, please." He took the baby as Eva slid her into his arms. "Do…" He paused and turned to search her face. "Do you want to come with me? I'd like her to m-meet you."

Eva felt her face warm. "I'd like that. I'll only be a few minutes, all right, Pocky?"

He smiled. "Go right ahead."

"Wait." She pulled her sleeve over her thumb, the dark liquid staining the edges. "Did she see your tears?"

His eyes widened in alarm. "She didn't say anything."

"It's okay. We'll explain everything to her in time."

She walked into the room a little behind Mir. This felt surreal. She was meeting Mir's mother. Mir, the Subject; Mir, her living experiment.

"Hello, Mrs. Song," Eva smiled, walking forward and taking the thin hand. "It's wonderful to finally meet you."

"Just Miss; I was never married." Da-Hye smiled, though her eyes shone a little confused. Eva noticed that her hair was still thick and black – research may not have been able to cure cancer, but at least it took away some of the side-affects of treatment. "I'm always glad to meet someone new, but who are you?"

"My name is Doctor Eva Stewart," said Eva, wondering how much introduction she should give the petite woman. She looked paper-thin, and she did not want to say anything that would tear her around the edges.

"Ah, you work here?"

Eva glanced sideways at Mir, desperate to know how much he had told his mother. He shook his head, just a fraction, and turned back to Da-Hye. "No, I work at another facility. I'm a friend of Mir's."

At those words, the woman's face seemed to soften, smooth out until she almost looked young. "I'm so glad he has friends," she whispered.

Two, to be exact, Eva thought. *And a daughter.*

"Who's the baby?"

There we go. Eva turned around and looked at June, held safely in Mir's arms. Trying to speak as well as she could without words, she eyed him. *What should we tell her?*

"She's your granddaughter, June." Mir walked forward and placed the baby in his mother's arms; they seemed to outstretch almost automatically, her eyes wide with surprise.

"You have a daughter?" Amazement filled her voice, weak though it was.

Mir nodded and looked at Eva, who was not quite sure how to handle this. She should have known Mir would not lie, but a fabrication couldn't have hurt, could it?

"Yes."

Eva knew the question that was coming next.

"Are...are you married?"

She shut her eyes, praying he could come up with a good answer.

"No."

She wasn't sure whether she wanted to hit him for being an idiot, or hug him for being so honest he couldn't bring himself to lie. She looked at Da-Hye and watched as confusion and deep concern for the son she did not really know crossed over her face.

"Who is the mother?" she asked, leaning forward, her voice soft.

Mir looked down at his mother and daughter and, for the first time, seemed lost.

"I am," said Eva before giving herself time to think about the words leaving her mouth.

Da-Hye did not look as surprised as Eva had thought she would. "Ah."

Mir's eyes were so wide, staring at Eva in shock, that she was tempted to laugh in the middle of the absurdity. "We're getting married," she said, trying to ease Da-Hye's worry. "Soon."

Mir's astonishment grew plainer. "Eva—"

"It was an unplanned mistake," she interrupted before he could break her stride. His expression was as if she had struck him.

Da-Hye nodded her head, but as Eva watched, the color seemed to wash from her face like wet paint in rain, leaving behind only white. "Miss Song?"

"What happened?" Mir ran forward, lifting June and feeling for his mother's pulse as his had been felt for many times before.

"I don't know!" Eva felt the woman's face as her eyes fluttered shut. "Get the nurse!"

Mir obeyed without hesitation and ran to the door, opening it and grabbing the arm of a passing nurse. When the surprised girl asked what the matter was, Mir hauled her into the room and to his mother's bedside.

Eva looked up. "She fell unconscious," she explained, her heart pounding uncomfortably hard.

The nurse nodded. "Ah – uh, would you please leave the room?"

"Will she be all right?"

Eva could hardly stand to see Mir so panicked. "Come on, Mir, let's go."

He followed her with reluctance, craning his neck to look at his mother as two more nurses walked past them into the room and shut the door behind them. Pocky turned and walked over to them, his smile switching to concern.

"Is everything all right?" he asked, looking from one face to the other.

Mir's eyes caught the florescent lights that lit the hall and for a moment Eva mistook the shine for phosphorescence. "She's going to die."

"What?" Eva and Pocky asked in unison.

Mir took a deep breath and bent his head over June with an anguished tenderness that tore the never-healing place in Eva's heart. "Why would you say that?" she asked, her voice soft.

Lifting his head, the pain on Mir's face – etched there as firmly as chiseled stone – told Eva he was nothing but serious. "Because she is." His voice trembled, high with pent-in grief. "It smells...different."

Eva put a hand on his shoulder and felt the faint shaking of his muscles under the fabric of his shirt. "What does?"

"Death." He took a deep breath, as if sniffing back tears and his own weakness at the same time. "Death smells different."

Pocky's eyes were wide, but grave. "I had a friend once, who could smell death. He worked in a medical facility." He was looking at Eva, and she read the unspoken message. *Believe him, Eva. He's telling the truth.*

"What do you want to do?"

Mir looked from Eva to Pocky. "Stay," he said after a moment in which the only sound was hospital buzz in the background. "I want to stay with my mother."

"I'll stay with you." Eva looked at Pocky, who nodded.

"We'll all stay," he said.

"Come on." Eva tapped Mir's arm. "I'll go ask a nurse if you can be with your mom."

Chapter Forty-Six

Eva sat with Pocky and June in the waiting room. Her legs, tired from being in the same position for almost two hours, tingled like a thousand pinpricks. The nurse had allowed only Mir to be in the room with his mother, and it was now halfway through the afternoon.

Eva unfolded her legs, winced at the stiffness, and looked at the sleeping baby in her arms. "Pocky?"

"Hmm?" He blinked sleepily and adjusted his glasses. "What?"

"Did you really know someone who could smell death?"

He nodded. "It's not uncommon. Many hospice workers and the like learn to recognize it, since their careers surround them with it."

Eva thought back to the Facility. The place must have stunk with death, and she had never noticed it. Mir was sensitive to it, and she could see why. "I wonder if the reason I never noticed was because I was causing it," she asked aloud, her voice clinging to memories of her 'work'.

Pocky patted her hand with his own wrinkled one. "You were not responsible for any deaths there, duck, you know that."

She shook her head. "I helped. I was just as bad – I would have killed him if I'd been given enough time, Pocky." The knowledge turned her stomach.

"Eva, I love you as if you were my own daughter, therefore I am going to tell you what I would tell my daughter if I had one." She nodded. "You are not doing any favors, for yourself or anyone else, by this continual mental beating."

Eva straightened and started to protest, but he cut her off with, "Now, now." He waggled a finger. "Everyone makes mistakes, some more than others, some bigger than others. And I'm sorry to say, you cannot move forward in life if you are continually looking over your shoulder."

Her mounting arguments dissipated with his last sentence as it struck the rawness inside her. As much as she hated admitting she was ever wrong, she knew he was right. "I can't just let it go," she whispered, filling her gaze with the angel face of sleeping June.

"You are presented with a choice, Eva." Pocky tapped the arm of her chair. "Don't disappoint me by making the wrong one."

"I'm not trying to—"

Something ripped through the air, breaking it apart with a sound that shot electricity through every fiber in Eva's body.

"Mir!"

She shot up, handed June to Pocky and ran from the waiting room, her footsteps pounding on the squeaky white floor. She knew that sound, and she hated it.

Mir was in pain.

"Out of my way!" Eva pushed a nurse aside and pushed open the door to room 208. The door opened and she was barely had time to dodge out of the way as a nurse ran out screaming, "Get security! Get security to room 208 *now!*"

Mir crouched in the center of the room, one hand gripping the rail on the side of the bed until the veins on the back of his hand stood out. His eyes were gone, replaced by burning holes of fire in a face that chilled Eva with fear.

His mouth opened and unleashed another scream; a painful scream, as if his heart had shattered and the fragments were cutting away inside his chest.

She knew she had to stop him, calm him down before security arrived. She had only seconds. Eva inched forward, feeling a fear she tried to tell herself was unreasonable. There was no need for it.

Except there was.

Turned inside out...broke the spine of another...

He wouldn't do that to me, she thought, but her shaking hands betrayed her false confidence. *I don't have time for this; I have to stop him before someone else comes in.*

The second his scream died down, she began to sing, "Baby mine, don't you cry, baby mine, dry your eyes; rest your head close to my heart, never to part, baby of mine."

She could not tell if Mir's eyes were on her or not; with no iris to show direction, she could not be certain if her song was having an effect. "Let those eyes sparkle and shine, never a tear, baby of mine." She walked forward, feeling like a little girl moving to assuage the monster in the closet. It was an old song she sang, one she could only remember half of the words. "All those people who scold you, what they'd give just for the right to hold you..." Her eyes landed on the bed, at Da-Hye.

There was no movement.

"You're so precious...to..."

The heart monitor had flatlined.

Mir's mother was dead.

"Oh, Mir, I'm so sorry," she whispered, getting down on her knees in front of him. Growling sobs shook his large frame and tears streaked down his face to clash darkly with the white floor.

"Ma'am, please back away," a deep voice boomed from the doorway.

Eva looked over her shoulder at the huge man standing behind her, a tag that read 'security' pinned to his vest. His hand gripped a level-three Taser, pointed at the floor but hissing with electricity. "Wait!" She held out her hand. "Please," she added, her heart beating urgently in her chest. "I can calm him down. Please wait."

She could see past the tough expression on his face the nervousness hiding there, just like the bruisers at the facility. "It isn't safe, ma'am." Tiny beads of sweat dotted his forehead as his eyes flitted from Mir to Eva. "Its eyes – it isn't natural!"

"He's my friend. Just wait."

Two seconds stretched for two hours before he nodded. "Hurry and do something, ma'am," he added, trying to command and succeeding in pleading. "Before I have to take him in."

"I've got him," Eva insisted. She turned to Mir and wrapped an arm around his back. "Mir, listen to me, okay? You *have* to calm down."

He lifted a fist to his mouth and she could tell he was struggling to gain control over his outburst. Eva knew that it was very possible he was going to fly into a long overdue rage, but in a hospital – no. She had to get him out of the building, away from people. "Mir, come on. You have to stand up and come with me *now.*"

She grabbed his arm and tried to pull him to his feet. For a second she thought he was going to remain there, a dead weight, but then she felt something give and he moved, half-standing and half-scrambling for the door as if he understood the urgency of the situation.

She ran after him, yelling directions as he ran down the hall with strides that reminded her of a wildcat chasing its prey. "Straight! Turn left!"

Eva ran past the waiting room without bothering to call to Pocky. She knew everyone was staring at them as they ran out the front doors. The pounding of her heart drowned out the pounding of her feet as she tore across the parking lot behind Mir, who was now running blindly away from the hospital behind them.

"Don't go onto the road!" Eva screamed as Mir swerved toward the street. Headlights swerved around the corner and she felt time stop for a brief moment as the vehicle's brakes slammed on as Mir jumped, frightened, off the road and onto the snow by the side of it.

The car window lowered and someone called out, "Are you trying to die or something? Stay off the road!"

"It's all right!" Eva shouted, nearing the car. "Go on, it's okay!"

A hand waved flippantly from the window and the car accelerated, moving away at a speed faster than the limit. Lungs threatening to collapse, Eva stopped ten feet away from Mir and watched as he lay on his back on the snow, staring up at the sky with eyes that tried to match the stars.

"It's all right, Mir," Eva called, wishing she could believe her own words. "We're away from people; just…get it out."

He flung one arm over his face and it was then that Eva realized he was not screaming or exploding in a fit of rage.

He was crying.

Fingers curled into a fist that pounded the snow, his body heaving in small movements as if he was trying to contain emotion that would rip him apart if he unleashed it.

Once she realized that he was no longer volatile, Eva walked over to Mir, wet snow soaking the bottom of her jeans. Kneeling down next to him, she said nothing; just watched him as something she could only describe as anguish tore him from the inside out.

Her legs began to numb after several minutes kneeling in the snow, but she did not want to get up. She couldn't leave Mir out here like this.

Why did his mother have to die on the very day we found her? She looked up at the sky. If there was a God behind all this, He seemed to have a lousy sense of justice. *Why couldn't she have made it? If You're the One that brought us here, why couldn't You have waited until we were gone to kill her, instead of making Mir watch it? Why couldn't my parents have made it? Why...?*

Her own voice broke into a scream. "Why? *Why?"* Her scream lingered in the air, surrounding her as it faded. Something inside her chest had released, just enough so she could breathe. Perhaps it really did help Mir. She ran her hand along her eyes, clearing away tears that had somehow snuck down her face without her noticing.

"Eva?"

She raised her head and met Mir's blue eyes, muddied by tears. "Are you all right?" she asked, sniffing deeply.

"No." His voice was soft, wreathed by a cloud of cold white air. "Are you?"

I'm fine, she opened her mouth to say. "Not really," she said.

They reached for each other at the same time with a fierceness that surprised Eva and for the next several minutes they knelt in the snow and hugged each other, as if they could transfer strength to the other person through touch.

"I am so, so sorry," Eva breathed finally, the soft texture of Mir's hair pressed against her cheek. "So sorry."

"Me too," said Mir, one hand rubbing up and down her back in a soothing motion. "Me too."

Chapter Forty-Seven

"We should go inside," Eva said after several minutes, once her tears had dried into frozen streaks down her face.

Mir stood and pulled Eva up. Once they were both standing, he looked at her with a face full of honest distress. "What do I do?"

Eva pushed her hands up through her hair and shook her head. "We'll find out when we get back to the hospital."

"Will Doctor Ross find out?" Mir asked as they began the walk back toward the hospital, now a quarter of a mile in the distance.

"I don't know. He might – I don't know if he's kept in touch with her or not," said Eva, her legs freezing inside her wet denim jeans. "I doubt it, but it will probably be mentioned during the trial."

"The trial," Mir repeated in a dull voice.

Eva looked over at him. "Don't worry. Trials happen every day. We'll win."

"I'm not stupid, Eva. The chance that we'll win the trial is small."

"No, it isn't!" Her voice came out with a vehemence that surprised her. "We are going to win, Mir, so help me God."

"You don't believe in God."

Her footsteps slowed until she was no longer walking. She hadn't meant – she was only using a metaphor, wasn't she? "That's not what I really meant."

He turned to face her, crossing his arms. "I know."

Those two words were so sad that Eva felt another piece of herself crumble inside. "Mir, just because I don't believe in God doesn't mean that we won't win the trial. It doesn't have anything to do with—"

"Yes, it does, Eva!" Mir shouted.

Eva stared. Mir never shouted at her, it simply was not like him. "What...?"

"It does matter!" He walked back toward her with long strides until he stood only a foot away, bending down with a mixture of sadness and anger in his eyes. In a softer voice, he repeated, "It does matter."

"Why?" Eva's face was hot. "Why does it matter? It's just religion, Mir! How do you know God even exists? I didn't expect this from you, of all people!"

"Eva!"

Her heart hammered with adrenaline, frustration, and now surprise.

"Please don't." His voice was still soft, but now his face held something Eva could not stand to see on it.

Disappointment.

"You – you cannot order me around, Mir!" Eva realized she was almost shouting too, but lowering her voice seemed impossible. It could only get louder, higher with her anger. "*I saved your life!* You have no right to tell me what to do!"

"And you have the right to tell me."

He did not ask it as a question, but even in her mounting anger Eva realized that there was much more behind the statement than what he spoke.

She was staggered with the awful realization – she loved Mir, and yet she never stopped treating him as if she was better than he was. How was she supposed to defend him at the trial – defend him to anyone! – if she herself was still a product of the humanistic beliefs she had grown up with? The foundation of everything she thought, no matter how open she tried to keep her mind, was that she was inherently better than Mir was.

On the surface, she knew he was just as special and important and human as she was. Probably more so, because he had retained the heart of humanity, the thing that could not be put into words.

She was a product of what she had been taught.

Eva realized she was staring at Mir with her mouth open, cheeks flushed. She had even forgotten to breathe. How many times, she wondered, could everything she knew about her life shatter around her, only to reveal a truth she did not have the courage to face?

She wanted to apologize. She wanted to say she was sorry, so sorry, and she wanted to repeat it over and over until it covered the amount of transgressions she had made against the man in front of her.

But the only thing that she could do was spread her hands and feel her eyes fill with cold water, unable to say a thing.

"I'm sorry."

She stared at Mir. "Wha – why would you be sorry?" She sniffed.

"I made you sad." He reached out and smoothed the hair down the side of her head. "I was mean."

"No, Mir, you weren't mean!" She grabbed his wrist and lifted it away from her head. She did not deserve comfort, not now, not yet. "I've looked down on you ever since I met you. Even after I fell in love with you, something – I didn't…"

He glanced at her hand, clamped around his wrist, and then back at her eyes. "Unlearning is harder than learning. I've never minded how you treated me, Eva. I love you. You did save my life, and I wish I could save yours."

She shook her head, holding on to his wrist now not to keep it away, but to keep contact with him. "You did, Mir. I swear, you already did."

Pocky was pacing around the lobby when Eva and Mir arrived back at the hospital. As soon as his eyes landed on them he cried, "The next time you decide to take an impromptu vacation, DO be kind enough to let me know!"

"You'll wake June," Eva shushed.

"I'm sorry," said Mir. "I didn't mean to." He took his daughter from the professor's arms, smoothing her head with a large hand.

"What happened?" Pocky looked into Eva's face, his own wrinkled with concern.

Eva glanced over at Mir, but he seemed absorbed in June. "His mother is…she died."

Pocky nodded. "I know, I threatened the nurse with my lecture on bioethics. I meant to ask what happened out there." He nodded in the direction of the doors behind her.

"Oh. That…" Eva ran her fingers through her hair as she tried to figure out what to say. "We…it was…interesting."

"Undoubtedly."

"Pocky, do I treat Mir – no, never mind. I know I do. Just – will you help me?"

"With what, duck?"

She could still see the disappointment on Mir's face. "I realized out there that I'm the non-human. It was…it frightened me, Pocky." She took a deep breath. "I'm the one who sees the world wrong. I'm the monster, not him. I knew it, but it never really hit me until I was standing out there."

He nodded. "It's hard to outgrow something you've been taught."

She smiled a tired smile. "True." She began to turn, but stopped. "Do you think we have a chance at the trial tomorrow?"

"A chance? Of course. A small chance is still a chance."

"But it isn't good enough."

"It has been frequently thought that God works best in hopeless situations."

"God again. I'm getting tired of hearing about Him." Eva combed her hair with her fingers again, at a loss as to what to do with her hands. "Honestly, He's never done anything to help me out, and I don't feel like I owe Him any particular favors."

"I thought you didn't believe He existed."

Eva shrugged. "I don't think we can really know."

"Can't we? Would you like some evidence?" The professor's pale blue eyes held such strength of conviction that without really meaning to, Eva replied, "Yes, I would."

"Very well." He turned and looked at Mir and June. "I'm looking at two miracles this very second, if you would care to join me."

"They're people, Pocky. Not miracles."

His eyebrows rose. "Do you really believe that?"

"I don't tend to say things I don't mean," she responded, tilting her chin up.

"You're a doctor, Eva. A scientist of a kind."

She nodded. "So?"

"So how, in all honesty, can you look at a human being and not believe it is a miracle? All the information processed, the cells created, the electrical pulses – do you really believe it came from nowhere?"

Eva studied Mir. It was a task she was never averse to, but she had never thought about him as an example of possible scientific evidence for religion. "We're all born, Pocky. Life begets life begets life. Cells beget cells. It's the way the world works."

"Yes." He smiled. "But have you ever thought about why life works that way? Do you believe it all appeared out of nowhere? Surely you are too logical and intelligent a being to believe that."

Eva opened her mouth, then closed it. "It...this isn't really my field of expertise, Pocky. I'm not a theorist, I'm a medical doctor."

"And as a medical doctor, you see hard evidence every day for the existence of a Creator. Look at Mir – you ran tests on him, dissected him, did you not? Do you believe that he is simply a collection of lucky accidents? That we are all nothing more than freaks of nature?"

"No, of course not," she said quickly, but realized as soon as the words left her mouth that she did not know how to continue. She decided to switch positions. "Isn't it sillier to believe that a God created everything than to believe it came about through natural process?"

"What natural process? Where did the natural process come from?"

Eva wondered if this was how a gazelle felt, cornered by its predators after running itself to exhaustion. Except this predator had a valid point. "Where did God come from, then?" she challenged.

He held up a finger. "That is a question of the wrong category."

Eva frowned. "What?"

"You cannot ask 'how much does the smell of a rose weigh,' or 'how many inches long is the flavor of ice cream.' God exists out of space-time, therefore we cannot ask where He came from."

Eva's mind felt as if it had been pulled apart and tied in knots until the process of untangling them seemed next to impossible. "But it's not an unreasonable question, is it?"

"Not unreasonable, no; just misguided. You ask for evidence of His existence, when it is everywhere around you. Those who choose not to see it are without excuse."

It should have been ridiculous. It defied what Eva had been taught – except it did not. She had been taught reason, logic, and intelligent thought. This argument was all of those – logical, intelligent. It was as if she had just been told a fairy tale was true, and then given an entire library of evidence to support the claim. "How could I believe in a God who allowed good people to suffer? I can't do that. If God really is in control of everything, then He killed my parents and He killed Mir's mother. He tormented Mir for twenty-four years, not to mention every other Subject ever placed in a Facility." She shook her head. "I'd like to believe you, Pocky, and I almost could. I just can't believe in a tyrannical God."

"I feel as if we have had this conversation before," said Pocky, his voice gentle and a kind smile on his elderly face.

"Well, how about you give me an answer that makes sense? Then I'll think about believing in God."

"It goes far beyond simply believing in Him, Eva. He does not accept half-hearted devotion. It is better to be cold than lukewarm."

"Fine. I'll seriously look into the Christian thing if you can give me one good reason why He would destroy lives like He has."

"The answer is simple." He shrugged his cardigan-clad shoulders. "He doesn't destroy life. We do."

Eva stared. "What kind of an answer is that? Pocky, you're struggling here."

"Am I?" he asked in a musing tone. "Because it makes complete sense to me."

She adopted a defensive stance, her hand on her hip. "How?"

"If God exists outside our finite realm of knowledge, then is it unreasonable to assume He has a greater knowledge of how present circumstances will affect the future? We see so little of time, Eva."

She nodded, pursing her lips in thought. "This is a lot," she said finally. A headache pounded behind her temples. "I'll get back to you, okay?"

He smiled and walked across the lobby toward Mir and June. June had woken up and was being oohed and ahhed at by a young nurse.

"Excuse me, Doctor Stewart?"

She turned and saw the receptionist standing behind her with a computer pad in her hand. "Yes?"

"Would you please sign these release papers for Miss Song's body? Her son told me to come to you. He seemed at a loss."

Eva could well understand that. "Sure." She took the pad and the electronic pen and signed her name on the three indicated lines. "Did he say whether he wants the body buried or cremated?"

"He chose buried. Once I print the form, I'll include a list of recommended funeral homes."

Eva nodded with a vague smile as she looked back at Mir. "All right. Thank you."

Chapter Forty-Eight

"They'll hold the body for up to three days, until we call them and tell them where to transport it," Eva explained to Mir as they sat at Pocky's around the dining room table that evening.

Pocky and June were asleep; Eva and Mir remained awake, staring at the empty space in front of them without saying much.

Mir nodded. "Thank you."

He had been silent, almost depressed since they came back from the hospital, and Eva could not blame him. *Pain now for a better future,* she thought to herself, recalling Pocky's words earlier. Was there really something good behind the death of Mir's mother?

Eva swallowed a drink of her coffee. It had long since cooled past lukewarm, but she did not feel like walking into the kitchen to pour herself another cup. "Mir, I want to apologize to you," she said after another stretch of silence.

"You don't have to, Eva."

"I know, but…it would make me feel better, all right?"

He tilted his head and nodded. "I forgive you."

"Why?" The question popped out of Eva, fueled by surprise and natural curiosity.

His eyes grew a little wider. "Because I do. Eva, do you want to know why I'm worried about the trial tomorrow?"

Eva did not point out that it was technically today – it was 1:36 am. "Why are you?"

"I'm worried because, even if they decide I'm a real person, I've still killed other people." His eyes were hollow, his face leaner in the dim light of the dining-room lamp. "I'm a murderer. I stole their lives and I can't give them back. So even if we win the trial, I lose."

Eva leaned forward and laid her hand on top of his. "Can you even remember killing them?"

He shook his head. "No. But I did."

"You were under the influence of drugs and torment! You aren't responsible! Even if you had succeeded in strangling me, it would not have been your fault."

He lifted his eyes to hers, and for the first time to her, Mir looked old. "But I do remember that, Eva," he said softly, as if he were afraid raising his voice would make his admittance all the more terrible. "I remember *you*."

Eva leaned back in her chair. His confession felt like a stake through her heart. "I guess I was special, then," she said with a humorless smile.

"I don't remember the first time, only the second time." He tilted his gaze up to look at the lamp hanging low from the ceiling. "I thought that if I killed you, you would stop hurting me. I wanted the pain to go away."

Eva swallowed. Mir saw it as his fault, but she knew it was hers, more or less. "I'm so sorry."

"For living?" He stared at her. "I'm glad you're alive. I'm very glad." He did not smile, but there was such sincerity in his tone and expression that Eva could not have doubted him even if she wanted to.

"I meant it when I said I was sorry." She touched his hand again, running her thumb back and forth across the vein across the top of it. "I'm sorry for every needle I put in you and every time I thought of you as an animal and for treating you like I was somehow better."

"I know." He watched her thumb and smiled. "I know. Eva?"

She looked up. "Yes?"

"If I go back to a facility tomorrow, please take care of June?" His question was simple, and yet she knew he was asking her a question that meant the world to him.

"Of course," she whispered. She cleared her throat and spoke louder. "But chances are good that I'll go to prison, you know." She tried to laugh it off. "I don't know what will happen to Pocky."

"God will take care of June," he said with confidence. He nodded once; a motion that made Eva wonder if he was reassuring himself. "She'll be fine."

Eva wondered if his fears were the same as hers – after all, if June's father was sent to another facility, then so would June. She clenched her free hand into a fist and hoped with every breath in her body that June's parentage would not be brought to light.

"Everything will be fine," she said aloud.

Nevertheless, neither of them slept at all that night.

"This is the courthouse?" Mir looked up at the glass-walled building, so tall it seemed to scrape the bottom of the sky.

"This is it." Eva straightened her blouse and inspected Mir for the last time. His hair had been combed back and he wore a suit they had purchased after they left the hospital the day before, the dark blue setting off his eyes. "I hope I look half as good as you."

"This feels weird," he said, rotating his shoulders inside the jacket.

"I'm sorry," said Eva. "If it's any consolation, this may be the only time you have to wear a suit."

"You look pretty."

Eva looked down at herself; a white blouse and close-fitting slacks paired with high heels. She never wore this sort of outfit to work – her work was more suited to a lab coat and gloves – and so to her, it did not seem so much 'pretty' as 'I am going to what may possibly be the last public event of my life and I want to look professional.' "Thank you."

"You look splendid, Albert. Why thank you, Albert, so do you."

Eva and Mir looked at Pocky, who was nodding at his reflection in the front door.

Eva laughed out loud. "You look quite sharp, Prof."

"Thank you, dear, you both look excellent. Even June is dressed for the occasion." He smiled at the baby, who Mir had refused to let go of the entire trip. In spite of his proclaimed confidence the night before, he seemed to feel that this was his last chance to hold his daughter.

"I think I had better take her now," the professor said, indicating June.

Mir nodded and kissed the baby before handing her to the older man. "I love you," he whispered, his eyes locked on June.

Eva took his arm. "Pocky will take good care of her, and you'll be able to see her in the stands the entire trial, okay?"

He nodded. "Okay."

They walked inside the building, Pocky taking a different route to deflect attention, and were immediately dwarfed by the giant lobby. There must have been at least fifty press gathered, all of whom turned at their arrival and swarmed around them with loud voices.

"Doctor Stewart, are you regretting your stance?"

"Thirteen, is it true that you glow in the dark?"

"Did Miss Stewart really give you a name?"

Just as Eva was beginning to wonder if they were going to escape the crowd before Mir panicked, two security guards appeared and the press instinctively backed away, though the questions did not stop being called after them as Eva and Mir were escorted through the lobby into the main auditorium.

"Walk right up the middle aisle into the arena," were their instructions as the doors into the auditorium opened.

Eva hated the term 'arena' – it brought to mind barbaric images of ancient cultures. Then again, it felt ironically correct for the day – she knew they were going to get torn apart by the lions of the public, and there was nothing she could do but try to defend herself with whatever meager opportunities she had.

The auditorium was vast; if it had been oblong rather than circular it would have taken up the space of a football field. Rows of benches curved around either side of the room, and in the middle was an open circular space with three stands for the defendants. Lawyers had stopped being used almost three decades ago.

With the new system, everyone on trial had their place in the arena and was allowed to call one witness at the appointed time. The jury consisted of twenty-four random citizens who sat high in balcony stands. There were three judges. Each judge could form their own opinion, and they would take the jury's evaluation before deciding the outcome. The majority agreement of the judges at the end of the trial would determine the outcome.

The judge's stands were at the far end of the room, their faces plastered to the rising walls by huge screens so that everyone could see them.

Eva had explained all of this to Mir the night before, but now, walking down the row toward the stands where everyone would gaze upon and judge them, she wished she had someone to comfort her.

The benches were already filled with people like sardines in a tin. The jury was present —only the judges had not yet arrived. They would not arrive for seven minutes, when the trial officially began.

Eva walked to her podium and watched as Mir stepped up on to his. The remaining podium was empty, but they knew Dr. Ross would soon arrive.

She saw Mir searching the stands and knew he was looking for Pocky and June. He smiled when he saw them and Eva followed his gaze – they were at the back, in the highest row. The sight of them encouraged her, and she gripped both sides of the podium and took a deep, cleansing breath.

She had not yet told Pocky, but she had come to a decision as dawn began to take over the sky that morning. If they won this trial, she would accept Pocky's faith as her own, no matter what the requirements.

The incoherent buzzing of the crowd grew louder and Eva turned to see Dr. Ross striding up the aisle, his face unsmiling but confident. He raised his hand toward the crowd, like a benevolent god acknowledging the presence of his Subjects.

A chill shivered down Eva's spin, and she saw Mir swallow and follow his father with his eyes as he took the last podium.

Dr. Ross met Eva's eyes and smiled as if they were old friends.

The only expression she could return to him was one of hardened indifference. *Don't let him intimidate you, Mir.*

The minutes wound down with excruciating lethargy, until Eva felt like a time bomb about to detonate. Mir's stance was surprisingly calm, but his eyes held a glow that, while faint, was unmistakable. He was nervous, and an experiment with phosphorous made it obvious.

Then the speakers around the hall crackled to life, and three faces filled the projection screens. They were unsmiling and solemn; from left to right, the displayed faces were that of the Honorable Carl Whitley, a man in his sixties; the Honorable Amanda Sheif, a stern-faced woman in her forties, and the Honorable Patrick Ness, the youngest judge at thirty-nine.

They were an imposing trio; giants glaring down at Eva and shaking her core with sudden doubts in her own stance.

From the middle screen, Amanda Sheif boomed, "The court recognizes the defendants Devon Ross, Eva Stewart, and Subject Thirteen sometimes called Mir."

The session had begun. Eva took another deep breath to steady herself.

"Devon Ross is accused of crimes both bioethical and humanitarian. Eva Stewart is accused of radical action opposite the law. Subject Thirteen is accused of humanity."

Accused of humanity. Eva wished she could wake up from this nightmare, but it had only just begun. She listened as the summary of events that had led up to the trial was laid out for the audience and the jury in a manner as impartially as possible. Even condensed, it took twelve minutes by the enormous digital clock above the judges' stands to cover it.

"Eva Stewart, please state your accusation against Devon Ross," Judge Sheif ordered.

Eva felt her mouth go dry, but she focused on the screen. "I accuse him of abducting legal humans and labeling them non-humans in order to perform experimentations on them, including his birth son, Subject Thirteen."

The room gave a collective gasp of shock at the last statement.

Pushing ahead, Eva added, "He had the baby labeled from birth and told the mother the child had died. She never knew the existence of her son until yesterday, when we went to visit her at the hospital."

"And what happened at the hospital?"

"We arrived less than an hour before she died of bone cancer," said Eva, hoping Mir was doing all right. She could not afford to take her eyes of the judges.

"This is true," said Judge Whitley. "We can confirm both Thirteen's parentage as well as the proceedings at the hospital yesterday."

Judge Sheif nodded. "Devon Ross, what have you to say?"

He seemed remarkably unmoved by the news of Da-Hye's death.

"Subject Thirteen is not a human. It never has been. When it was born, it was discovered it had an unusual form of retardism and was therefore legally a non-human."

Eva felt her breath catch in her throat. 'Retardism.' There was nothing retarded about Mir. "With all due respect, your honor, many people with so-called 'mental problems' have functioned perfectly and become respected citizens."

"Thirteen was different," snapped Dr. Ross. "As his legal parent, the choice was given to me to either have the infant euthanized or put to better use. I chose the latter."

"Having been exposed to Subject Thirteen for a substantial amount of time, I can argue that he is perfectly capable of living in the normal world," Eva retorted, her pulse quickening.

"Whether or not it can function in society is not the question!" Dr. Ross's voice was strained with anger. "I was presented with options, both of which were entirely legal, and I chose one. You may not agree with my decision, but it was my decision to make. In order to provide a valid argument against my case, you would have to disagree with the entire non-human act!"

She knew he was baiting her, hoping to draw her into an argument she would undoubtedly lose. Instead of the panic she had expected, she felt strangely calm as she replied, "I do."

Even the judges appeared taken aback at her statement. "You now state that the Non-Human Act is unethical?" inquired Judge Whitley.

"I do," Eva repeated. She allowed herself a glance at Mir, and her heart swelled at his expression of complete pride in her.

"Outrageous!" Dr. Ross slammed his hand down onto his podium. "Your girlish infatuation has caused you to abandon reason for emotion!"

"That is—"

He cut her off with a swipe of his hand. "Your honor, this woman's relationship with Subject Thirteen is demented and nothing short of bestial."

Eva felt something inside her explode. "He is more human than you could ever hope to be!" Her voice echoed through the arena thanks to the microphone in front of her. "Your honors, I request permission to ask you a question."

The judges nodded. "Go ahead," said Judge Ness.

"Do you believe in the existence of souls?" Eva's fingers gripped the podium so hard she could feel the edges cutting into her skin.

"Souls have long been acknowledged as fact to some extent, so yes," said Judge Sheif. Judges Whitley and Ness nodded.

"And 'non-humans' are deemed animals, so technically, they should not have the complex souls humans have, correct?"

"Yes."

"Where are you planning on taking this, Doctor Stewart?" Dr. Ross asked, his hand covering the microphone.

Eva ignored him, her eyes on the judges. "Are your honors aware of the five states of consciousness?"

"Please familiarize us."

Time for Pocky's lectures to come into play, she thought with an equal mixture of trepidation and confidence. "The first stage is that of sensation such as pain, an emotion, or a sound. A sensation cannot be false."

The faces on the screens nodded, and she continued.

"The second stage is a thought, a mental content than can be expressed in a sentence. It can be true, or it can be false. It's a state of consciousness." She could imagine the look of surprise on Pocky's face when he realized she had been paying attention all those times she rolled her eyes and acted as if she was mentally miles away.

"The third stage is a belief, a mental content that we take to be true to some degree or other. The fourth stage is a desire, a felt inclination toward or away from something. A desire cannot be true or false, but can be appropriate or inappropriate."

"Go on."

She could feel Dr. Ross's pale eyes drilling into her sharply and steeled herself. "The fifth and last stage is an act of volition or free choice. If I were to give you an example of these states, it would be a man waking up in a hospital. He hears a heart monitor beeping. He wonders where he is. He realizes he's thirsty. He wants a drink. Because of this, he chooses to ask for a glass of water."

"What is your point, Miss Stewart?" asked Judge Ness.

She knew everything rode on her defense, and the thought terrified her. "I witnessed Mir go through every one of these stages while he was my Subject. Now, these five states of consciousness lead to a simple conclusion: anyone capable of going through the five states of consciousness has a soul. So I ask you, how is it possible for a non-human to go through these five stages and not have a soul?"

She wondered if she imagined the faint expression of impressed surprise on Judge Sheif's face as she asked, "Devon Ross, have you a rebuttal for Miss Stewart's argument?"

"A rebuttal?" His eyes narrowed even farther in her direction. "Yes, I do. I am a medical doctor and scientist, not a philosopher. I knew the hard evidence in front of me, and I do not have to delve into spiritual psychology to know the truth when I see it. A Subject may very well display these 'states of consciousness,' but there is no evidence that they have a soul since we can neither see it, read it, hear it, or know it with any other sense. It is scientifically improvable."

"Doctor Ross." Eva leveled her gaze at him and hoped it let him know that she was not about to be trifled with. Too much rode on her ability to win this argument. "Do you believe that animals are capable of second-level thoughts?"

To her relief, he looked slightly perplexed. "Clarify your question."

"Do you believe that animals have the ability to think about their thoughts?"

"Of course not. That requires higher intelligence," he answered in a tone that left no question as to what he thought of her.

"And yet Mir is completely capable of second-level thought, and I have witnessed it. How can he be non-human and still be capable of the human range of thought and consciousness?" Eva pressed.

"I don't have to answer this."

"Your honors, Mir – Subject Thirteen – has shown himself capable of second-level thought, of remorse, of love, of protection, and every human range of emotion, thought, and feeling. There is nothing about him that suggests non-human. I witnessed and even partook in experimenting on him, and the only actions he took that appeared non-human were the result of emotional and physical torment and extreme pain. No human would react in any less way."

There was silence from the stands and the screens. Finally Judge Sheif said, "Subject Thirteen."

Mir looked up at the screens.

"Have you any defense for yourself?" The question was not confident, but curious.

Mir's eyes widened in panic and he looked to Eva for help. She gave him an encouraging smile and mouthed, 'Tell them.'

He looked back at the judges and leaned into his microphone, mimicking Eva. "I...I don't understand what you mean. Eva has already defended me."

The judges exchanged glances, visible enlarged on the screens over the defendants' heads. "You want us to believe you are human," said Judge Whitley. "Prove it."

Mir's hands lifted briefly from the podium before coming back to rest on it. He looked frightened, and Eva began to wonder if he was going to be able to do this. "I was never really treated as a human," he began, his voice unsteady. "I still don't know a lot of things that people talk about, and I feel stupid. Eva has helped me as much as she can, but I can't learn twenty-four years of knowledge in a few months, so I know I still have a long way to go. When you talk about being human, I think of my father." He looked at Dr. Ross, but there was no malice in his face. "If it weren't for him, I wouldn't have felt human. He made me feel very human, every time he came to see me. I knew the bad side of being human thanks to him. I knew what it was like to be angry and alone and afraid and what it meant to hate someone."

Dr. Ross was watching his son with a wary interest, as if he was watching a dangerous animal and waiting for it to attack.

"It was Eva who showed me the good side of being human, and I...I didn't think there would be more good than bad. But there was." Mir took a deep breath that echoed through the hall and added to the tension already thick in the air. "She showed me what kindness was, and that meant more than all the bad I'd learned from Doctor Ross. I was raised like an animal and sometimes I thought I was one, but then I would remember.

"When I was little, my father gave me something that made it so I couldn't talk. I could think, and I would want to say something, but I couldn't. After that, I tried everything I could to make myself heard. Nothing worked, not until Eva came. I hated her at first, because she hurt me. It was only her job, but I wanted her to stop hurting me and I thought she would if I killed her.

"I almost did, twice. But after the second time, I realized I didn't want to kill her. I would have hated myself if I did, because she was just as scared of me as I was of her. Eva made me realize I had a soul."

Eva felt her heart swelling again, to the point of being gloriously painful. Even if they lost the trial, she would not feel it had all been in vain.

"I love Eva."

She stared at Mir.

The hall was silent, stunned out of speech.

Mir pressed his lips together and looked at the hundreds of people surrounding him. "That's how I know I'm human."

Eva took advantage of the continued silence following his words. She lifted her hands to the microphone and said, "I love you, too."

"Well," said Judge Sheif after several seconds. "This is an unusual development, actually."

"You can't let their emotional attachment sway the facts!" exclaimed Dr. Ross so suddenly that it started Eva.

"If emotions aren't real, then what is?" This question came from Judge Ness, and made Eva stare at the screen with his face. "Emotion is one of the largest evidences toward humanity."

Dr. Ross opened his mouth and closed it, opened it and closed it again. He seemed shocked that one of the judges would defend Eva and Mir, and it rendered him temporarily unable to protest.

"True," said Judge Whitley, "but emotions are not proof."

"Not proof, perhaps, but evidence of a soul. The echo proves the sound."

"Devon Ross, would you like to refute anything Mir has just said?"

Didn't he already? Eva wondered, glancing at Mir. The glow in his eyes had increased and his hands gripped the sides of the podium. She wanted to step down from her place and walk over to him, tell him he was doing magnificently and everything would be fine.

"Refute? Give me a real, intelligent argument and then I will find something to refute," said Dr. Ross.

Eva smiled inwardly. He may as well have said he *had* no argument. "Just because someone's stance disagrees with yours does not make it incorrect," she stated. "That's why it's called a *disagreement.*"

Chuckles rippled through the spectators.

"I believe we know where the defendants stand," said Judge Sheif. "Now you are all given the opportunity to call upon a witness or someone who can help you defend your position. You may call on only one person, and your choice cannot be changed. Miss Stewart, you may proceed."

Eva nodded and looked into the stands at Pocky. "Professor Albert Pock?"

Pocky stood up and waved from the back as a guard walked through the stands to help him around the building and into the arena. Eva wondered if he would bring June – she hoped he would find someone else to take care of her. The baby's identity was crucial in the event they lost the trial.

Moments later, Pocky hurried down the aisle without June. She assumed a nearby caretaker – mandatory at trials – had accepted responsibility of the baby during his public appearance.

"Professor Albert Pock," said Judge Sheif, speaking as if she was reading from a biography, which she probably was. "You were quite renowned among the scientific community in previous years, were you not?"

"I was," he said into Eva's microphone. They exchanged smiles – Eva felt comforted by his being so near.

"Your popularity dropped drastically after you took what some would call a radical anti-HRI stance. Did you know the consequences of your actions?"

"I did," he replied.

"And yet you had been a WorldCure employee. What caused you to change your mind?"

Pocky looked over at Mir. "That young man did."

"Subject Thirteen?" The judge sounded surprised. Eva wondered if the woman had ever been surprised this many times during one trial before. "How so?"

"I was there when Devon gave an eight-year-old boy a drug that would keep him from asking for help from the guards. I had already begun to doubt the morality of WorldCure and the non-human system, and that action confirmed it. I knew I could not support something as barbaric as that, even if it was legal barbarism."

"What is the name of that drug?"

"Cortoxica."

"And what purpose did it serve?"

"It scrambled the electric brain-to-speech signals, rendering a perfectly intelligent child

386

unable to speak. Now that I look back on my days at WorldCure, I find it sickening that I could ever have thought it even remotely acceptable."

"You are a Christian, are you not?"

"I am."

"Did your religious belief affect your decision?"

"Certainly."

"How so?"

"I came to believe firmly in the equality of all humans during my time at WorldCure, regardless of what some would call 'defects.' Everyone was created by God and for His pleasure, and it is not up to us to decide on what our flawed minds would call perfect or imperfect."

The judges exchanged looks again. Eva hoped Pocky had not ruined anything by bringing religion into the conversation, even though it was the judge who had begun it. She bit her lip and focused on the professor's face. He seemed calm and assured, which gave her even more comfort.

"Do you agree with Miss Stewart's defense?"

"I do."

"Is there anything you would like to add?"

"I believe Mir to be physically, mentally, spiritually, and in all other ways completely human. I believe every so-called 'Subject' is, and though everyone has differences, we cannot change the fact that we are all fundamentally human. I have seen the best of good and the worst of evil in my life and the evil has not been in those labeled as non-humans but in those who believe that they have the right to brutally torture other human beings under the guise of furthering science. No matter how noble the cause – curing Morbus, for example – barbaric means are never justifiable."

There was a silence that, while short, had an air of reverence. "Thank you, Professor. Miss Stewart, is there anything else you would like to ask him?"

Eva looked at Pocky and felt a small smile on her mouth. "No," she said finally. "No, I think he's said it all."

"You may step down, professor."

"Thank you, your honor." He turned and caught Eva's eye. With a wink, he said, "Give them what's right, duck. God will work out the rest."

"Devon Ross, you may now call your witness to the podium."

The man glanced up at the stands, leaned in toward the microphone, and said with confidence, "Jude Harborn."

Shock bloomed in Eva and she turned around, searching for the familiar face. Jude. She should have known he would end up on the wrong side of the argument, but when had he gotten so close to Dr. Ross that he would call on him as a trial witness? She saw him, walking down the aisle toward the arena, and a sickening feeling took over her stomach.

Her expression couldn't have been anything other than a glare if she had wished it. "You're sick," she muttered, her eyes on the young man walking up to Dr. Ross's podium as if he owned the building.

"Greetings, ladies and gentlemen," Jude spoke into the mic, waving both his hands briefly at the crowds.

"Jude Harborn, you are a medical doctor working in a WorldCure research facility, are you not?"

"Yes, your honor."

"What is your view on the non-human act?"

He shrugged his broad shoulders. "I believe it's perfectly understandable and reasonable. If we can't root out the weeds, how will those of us worth living be able to spread our roots? We have to pick and choose."

"But what gives us the right to pick and choose?" Eva interjected, wondering if she would be thrown in jail if she walked across the arena and strangled Jude with her bare hands.

"Superior beings have always had the right to rule over lesser beings," said Jude, smiling at her as if they were the best of friends. Only she could read the contempt behind the grin.

"That's what the Nazis thought, and their beliefs caused the holocaust," she said, her spine rigid.

He shrugged again. "But they had the right idea. The holocaust was a necessary evil, like the non-human act."

"But it isn't a necessary evil. There will always be people with flaws, we can't change that. The thing is, they're still people. Killing them isn't going to make things better, it's only going to add more death and pain to an already brutal society."

"It follows a reasonable line of thought that if you weed out imperfections from a society, only perfection will remain."

"That didn't work out very well for Germany," Eva snapped. She could not believe what was coming out of Jude's mouth – and yet at the same time, she could.

He laughed. "Actually, it turned out very well. They created a system and it worked, until we stepped in and overthrew it."

"I don't think the Jews and blacks would think it worked very well," she responded dryly. The thought of strangling him was becoming more and more appealing.

"They were the lesser beings; it wasn't up to them."

Eva looked over at Mir and let out a long, deep breath before she said something that lost her the trial. She was thankful when Judge Whitley spoke.

"Mr. Harborn, were you ever present while Thirteen underwent experimentation?"

"I was."

"Did you ever perform experimentations on the Subject yourself?"

"I researched on it, but I didn't experiment. That was Doctor Stewart's line of work." He winked at Eva, sending a shiver down her spine.

"Did the Subject ever display signs of humanity?"

"Not that I could see. It behaved very much like the animal it was." He leveled his gaze at Mir, who remained expressionless except to swallow.

"Your honor," said Eva, feeling lines of pain in her hands where they were dented by the podium, "I walked in on Mr. Harborn once while he was researching on Mir. I was not completely swayed against the non-human act at that time, but what I saw was enough to convince me it was wrong in every possible way."

"What was it you saw?" asked Judge Sheif.

Eva fought against nausea as she recalled the memory that had seared itself into her brain. "Mir was strapped to an examination table, completely awake, while being cut open and probed by Mr. Harborn." An acidic flavor filled her mouth and she swallowed it back down, wishing she could have a drink of water.

The enormous face on the screen turned to look at Jude. "Is it not normal procedure for the Subjects to be sedated and given painkiller?"

"It is usual, yes, but Thirteen proved resistant to both sedatives and painkillers, so there wasn't really anything I could do."

"WorldCure policy has always been to treat their Subjects with humanity." Judge Sheif did not sound pleased with Jude, and a faint ray of hope lit in Eva's mind.

"Thirteen was too valuable a Subject to leave alone, so we were forced to operate without drugs. I did try, it just didn't work."

Judge Ness leaned forward. "While I can see your point, I find the image Miss Stewart just portrayed to be frankly, a bit disturbing. Surely there was a more humane way to operate."

"Not really," said Jude.

"Can you explain what sets non-humans apart from humans?" asked Judge Sheif.

Jude smiled easily. "Abortion has been legal for almost a century; I don't think the non-human act is very different from that. It gives a parent the right to choose whether their child is fit to live or not. If someone cannot have a good life, then it makes sense to put them down or to use them to further science."

Eva wanted to throw up. *How did I ever agree with him?*

"If you could ask a baby whether or not it wanted to live, do you think it would say no?" asked a voice that surprised Eva.

Mir was looking at Jude with an expression of determination and intelligence that Eva hoped the judges would see as a very human expression.

Jude laughed a little, but it faded into incredulity. "Excuse me?"

"If you had been born with something wrong with you, and someone asked you if you wanted to be killed or not, what would you have picked?"

Eva could hardly believe it. Mir was not only defending himself on trial, he was entering into a debate with the man who had given him the x-shaped scar across his torso.

"If – that isn't the question." Jude seemed to have lost his ability to create a well thought-out argument in the face of such a blunt question. Eva gave an inward cheer.

"It's because you would choose life." Mir looked up at the judges. "If any of you had been born with a defect, would you have offered yourself up to be killed just because your 'quality of life' wasn't what other people thought it should be?"

Eva wondered where Mir had heard the phrase 'quality of life.' She thought she might burst with pride. *Go, Mir. Tell them the truth.*

"I'd like to waive that question," said Jude stiffly.

"Is there anything else you would like to add before you step down?"

Jude smirked and Eva wondered, not for the first time, how she could ever have dated the man. "I think Devon Ross is a brilliant doctor, and everything he did was for the good of collective mankind. If a few non-humans get hurt in the process, it may be regrettable but since it's for the greater good I believe it's worth it."

Barely-suppressed rage coated Eva's face as Jude stepped down, and as he turned to leave the arena, he caught her eye.

The look in them was something she could not name, but she felt as if he knew something she did not. She wanted to run across the circle and grab him, make him tell her what it was he was goading her with, but she shut her eyes and took one, two, three deep breaths.

"Subject Thirteen, is there anyone you want to call to the arena?"

She looked over at Mir and realized he had no one to call. He was alone in defending himself, unless her arguments in his favor counted.

He was silent, and the entire hall felt as if it was holding its breath until something was bound to burst.

Eva tried to read him. He was debating inside himself, but it was what he was debating that worried her. She thought her nerves, stretched as tightly as violin strings, would fray and snap if he did not say something soon.

"I–I would like to c-call..." His voice faded and Eva watched, helpless, as he leaned against the podium, breathing heavily. She wondered what was wrong – he looked as if he might collapse.

"Is Subject Thirteen all right?" asked Judge Sheif.

Mir straightened, his face set. Eva could see the faint shine of sweat on his face as he set it in determination and said in a voice that held a slight tremor, "June."

Eva's foot slipped off the pedestal and she almost fell. She hopped back up, her ankle throbbing now. "What?" She stared at him, unable to stop herself. "Mir! What are you doing?"

For the first time she could clearly remember, he ignored her. In a louder voice, firmer, he announced, "I call June."

Eva shot her gaze back up at Pocky in the stands. He was half-standing, June back in his arms and looking as bewildered as he possibly could.

"And who is June?" asked Jude Whitley.

Mir swallowed and looked at Pocky. "Please bring her," he said, his voice directed toward the professor in the stands.

"You are re-calling Professor Pock to the stage?" the judge asked in disbelief.

"No. I'm re-calling the baby he's holding."

394

"A baby?" Judge Ness's eyebrows rose almost to his reddish hair.

Mir, what are you doing? Eva felt her heartbeat racing faster as a guard appeared next to Pocky once again and escorted him from her view.

"You're calling on an infant to defend you?" Dr. Ross's hairless eyebrows raised incredulously, his mouth turning upward at one corner.

Mir's simple answer was, "Yes."

Eva turned as the doors to the arena opened and Pocky walked down the aisle, his eyes locked on Eva and his expression asking the question she was wondering herself: had Mir lost his mind?

Pocky reached Mir and handed June over to the tall young man, who took the tiny human being as carefully as if she were made of glass.

"Who is this child?" asked Judge Sheif.

"Her name is June."

Mir's voice was strained and nervous, but Eva got the feeling he knew what he was doing. She only wished she knew as much.

"And what bearing does she have on this trial?"

Don't say it, don't say it, don't say it, don't say it, Eva's mind pleaded in rhythm during the short silence that followed the judges' question.

"She...," Mir took a deep breath. "June is my daughter."

The hall became alive with voices; incredulous, shocked, buzzing like an upset hive of bees. Eva felt her knees go weak and grabbed the podium to support her.

Judge Ness leaned forward. "How is it possible you have a daughter? According to our sources, you have been kept in a WorldCure facility the entirety of your life."

Mir nodded; Eva saw his chest heaving faster as his breathing became more nervous. Still, he held June in a way that made it obvious she was the most precious thing in the world to him. "I know. I...."

Eva, though shocked at the turn of events, hoped – hoped beyond anything – that something – God, even – would give him strength. This was one of the hardest things that had ever happened to him, and he had to tell it to a crowd of hundreds upon hundreds of people.

"I don't remember much of it," he began. His voice was faint, but he continued talking. "I was drugged and taken to a closed room. There was a female Subject and..." He shook his head. "I still don't remember much."

Eva couldn't help but feel glad. Who would want to remember something like that in detail?

"It was all monitored. There were people outside even though we couldn't see them. I don't remember what she looked like. So much happened afterward that I forgot about it until the Facility was being destroyed and I saved June and three other babies. Eva read June's ID bracelet and saw she was my baby. I don't know where her mother is."

Eva had expected the buzz of voices to grow louder, but instead it fell silent. The room might as well have been a tomb.

"You were *bred* with another Subject?" Judge Ness asked, finally shattering the shroud of quiet.

Mir nodded.

Judge Sheif's sharp eyebrows were drawn. "What was that about the facility being destroyed?"

Eva stared. The judges had not known? How was that possible?

Dr. Ross spoke. "Before Humanity International arrived, the facility was Subject to an unfortunate chemical fire. We lost most of the Subjects. It was a tragedy, yes, to lose so much research, but we could not stop it."

"That's not true." Eva's voice was so hard she thought it might break. "You blew up the facility on purpose to destroy evidence of the fact you were grotesquely misusing those Subjects! And what about Fyodor? The specialist you hired to personally keep Mir in line – you would have shot us if he hadn't been there to protect us."

"Ah, yes. The Russian. He turned on me with a gun and there was no choice but to protect myself. Why would I have shot one of my own doctors and our most valuable Subject? It doesn't make sense." He was no longer smiling.

"He saved us. You would have shot us both, as well as the babies, if he hadn't blocked your way."

Ross scoffed and looked at the judges. "Surely you don't believe this raving."

Judge Ness smiled. "I never said that I did believe it, so why would you ask?"

"Where is this specialist now?" Judge Whitley leaned into the microphone.

"He was murdered by Doctor Ross," said Eva.

"I was forced to shoot him in order to defend myself!" Dr. Ross pounded his fists on the podium so hard that it wobbled a little to the side.

"You killed the specialist you hired to keep Subject Thirteen under control?" Judge Whitley asked in disbelief.

"It was a clear case of self defense!" Dr. Ross looked as if he was on the verge of screaming.

Eva hoped, for the sake of the trial, that he did.

Judge Ness rubbed his chin. "It makes sense to me that if I was performing illegal operations – including the breeding of Subjects which is, for numerous reasons, strictly forbidden – and someone was coming by to inspect my work, I would certainly want to get rid of the evidence in any way I could."

"Doctor Ross murdered every Subject in the facility except Mir and the three babies he saved." Eva did not want to think about all the others he had not been able to save.

"Where are the other two infants now?"

"They were taken in by some of our neighbors. As the infants were healthy and had not yet been induced to tests or experiments, we told them that the babies had been found by the road and needed a home."

"But if the children are non-human, then they will need to be transferred," said Judge Whitley.

Eva shook her head. "They were born in the facility, but they were perfectly fine. Judges, I have already told you my stance. Every Subject everywhere in the world is completely human."

"That is a very broad statement," remarked Judge Sheif.

"It's one I stand by."

The judges all looked at each other, their oversized faces exchanging subtle messages on screen. "The first phase of this trial is over," said Judge Sheif. "The jury will please go into the deliberation room and make your decision. You have fifteen minutes."

Eva shook her head and stared through the clear podium at the floor. It seemed impossible that something this important was now in the hands of twenty-four individuals.

She caught Mir's eye and smiled, hoping it covered up the churning in her stomach. He returned a thin-lipped smile, one that lifted the right corner of his mouth higher than the left. It was a smile that said 'there isn't anything more we can do.'

The fifteen minutes stretched longer than any fifteen minutes should. Every second felt as long as a minute, every minute as long as ten.

She heard Mir groan and looked over at him. He was leaning against the podium again, and she could hear his labored breathing from her stand fifteen feet away.

"Mir." She whispered loudly, trying to catch his attention. "Mir!"

He looked up at her, his eyes strangely dull.

"Are you all right?" Eva knew he was not, but she had to know if it was serious. It was a bad time for anything to happen that would interrupt phase two of the trial, but Mir was more important.

He said nothing, only nodded.

Eva's fingers curled into fists. She needed to have a look at him, but she could not do it now. "Be careful," she mouthed, even though she had no idea what she was really saying. Be careful for what?

The clock on the far wall beeped.

The fifteen minutes were up.

Chapter Forty-Nine

Eva watched without blinking, without breathing, as the twenty-four members of the jury walked back into the hall and resumed their seats. She knew their decisions would have already been sent to the judges, who would look over the jury's response and then come to their own conclusion.

The judges' screens went blank.

This was it. This last decision. Their lives were held in the hands of three judges, who had not seemed particularly swayed in either direction. Judge Ness, perhaps, was more forgiving toward their side. Judge Whitley seemed more inclined to believe Dr. Ross. Judge Sheif...she was the wild card.

The screens came back on.

Eva had not expected their decision to be made so quickly. Her heart stopped beating.

"The body of judges has come to a decision," said Judge Sheif.

Please, please, please, please. Please...God. Please let us win this. God, I swear if you let us win this, I will follow You. I will.

"Devon Ross, you are charged with taking illegal actions with non-humans including breeding and killing them at your own whim."

Ross's face was red, the vein on his forehead standing out as a throbbing line.

Eva lifted a hand to cover her mouth. She could hardly believe it.

"Eva Stewart, you are charged with insubordination to your superior and behaving without authorization."

She nodded, shocked that was the only thing she was charged with. She wondered if she was so afraid she was hallucinating.

"Mir."

Eva heard blood roar in her ears and her heartbeat came back, pounding. They had called him Mir. Did that mean...?

"It has been unanimously agreed that both you and your daughter are human."

Mir's mouth opened, but the only sound that came out was something between a choke and a gasp. A black tear rolled from his eye and Eva wanted to cry too, because his was a tear of joy. She ran from her podium and wrapped her arms around him, crying and laughing and feeling for the first time she could remember that a miracle had happened. There was no way the verdict should have been what it was; there was too much against them. There had to be a catch.

"However."

Judge Sheif was smiling, but it was a cautious smile as she continued. "Mir, you are going to have to live under surveillance. We know you are guilty of killing several guards at the Facility but we are not holding them against you because they were the result of torment and drugs."

Mir nodded.

"Eva Stewart."

She kept her arm securely around Mir but looked up at the screen.

"Mir will have to be placed under professional security."

Eva opened her mouth to protest, but her words were left hanging in midair as the judge finished, "Unless you wish to oversee him yourself."

Eva felt her own eyes filling with tears of grateful disbelief. "Yes," she managed hoarsely. "Yes, I would."

"Your penalty for unauthorized proceedings is suspension from the medical community for two years."

The sentence struck her heavily, but she was surprised that it was not as heavy as she would have thought. "Thank you."

"Devon Ross, your superiors have asked custody of you, and we have granted their wish. You will be handed over to them for discipline." A loud bang filled the hall as a gavel was lifted and slammed down for the first and last time of the trial. "This case is closed."

The room exploded with flashing lights and voices. Some were outraged, but they were drowned out as a cheer swept the room. The sound sent a shiver across Eva's skin and she buried her head in Mir's shoulder and laughed.

Two guards grabbed their arms. "We'd better get out of here before you're trampled," called one over the din.

Eva walked with them, but kept a grasp on Mir. After this, she never wanted to let him go.

They reached the lobby, which was ringed off by more guards to keep the dozens of reporters and bystanders from getting through.

A tall man in a steel gray suit approached them. "Congratulations, to both of you." He smiled, faint lines appearing around his green eyes as he held out his hand.

Eva shook it. "Thank you," she said with genuine feeling. She felt as if she had seen him before, but she could not place it.

"My name is Edward Nolan."

"The talk show host?" She stared in surprise. "From Know It with Nolan?"

"That's right." His grin displayed two rows of perfect white teeth. "I am very interested in getting both sides of the non-human act out and available for the public. I was wondering if you and Mir would be interested in coming on to my show for a live interview."

Eva turned to stare at Mir, who blinked at her. "Should we?" he asked.

"I...I'm sorry, so much has happened today – do you have a card or something so I could contact you later?" Eva knew she wanted to accept his offer, but there were too many things to think about at the moment to give an immediate answer.

"Of course." He pulled a card from his pocket and handed it to her. "I'm very impressed with you both. I hope you give me a call."

"Thank you so much," she said, smiling so wide she was glad her face could not crack or break in two.

Edward Nolan smiled and walked away, lifting a hand in farewell. "I can hardly believe it," said Eva, turning around, looking for Pocky. "Know It With Nolan – I watched that show in college!"

"Eva?"

"What?"

She turned and was seized with panic. "Mir?" He was doubled over, his skin a pale gray. "Get help!" Eva ordered the nearer of the guards.

"Yes, ma'am!" He turned and ran toward another set of doors.

Eva took June and handed her to the other guard. "Please hold her," she asked, breathless, and turned to grab Mir as he stumbled forward.

"Mir! Somebody help me!"

Eva tried to catch him as he fell but he was too heavy. He hit the ground and lay still, his eyes closed.

"His condition is progressing rapidly. At this rate, I'd give him thirty-six months at the most."

Eva sat outside the hospital room with her head in her hands. Thirty-six months…that was less than she had hoped. When he woke up, she would have to tell him.

She felt a hand pat her shoulder and knew, without looking up, that it was Pocky. "I think I'm more afraid of hearing myself say it out loud again," she said through her hands.

"I know," he said softly.

She looked up and sniffed. "It was so sudden – I had thought we would all be in prison by now. Instead we're given the most amazing answer we could wish for, and then he collapses right after – I just…" She shook her head and wanted to cry again, but for the moment all her tears had been wrung out of her and she felt like a limp rag.

"I'm so sorry, duck. I know it's a very different kind of love, but I love Mir too. Grief is the only thing we can expect for a while now."

Eva nodded and took a deep, shuddering breath. "Pocky, there's something I didn't tell you."

"What is it, my girl?"

Her smile felt painful inside her, stretching a wider hole inside her chest. "I told God that if we won the trial, I would accept Him."

There was no cheering or shouting. Only a quiet look of relief on Pocky's face, as if ten years has fallen from his age and he was left with feelings he could not put into words. "Eva, as light as this news makes my heart…do not accept Him simply because you feel bound by a promise to yourself. Faith in God goes much farther than that."

"I know." She straightened and stared at her hands, folded in her lap. "I mean, don't expect me to be perfect right off or anything," she said with a one-syllable laugh. "But I'm going to try."

Pocky hugged her and she returned it, holding onto him as tightly as she could. She leaned her cheek against the soft texture of his sweater and let it calm her. "How long have you thought this way?"

"I'm not sure. Maybe years of you annoying me kicked in." She gave his arm a weak but playful punch.

As they pulled apart, a nurse walked out of the door to the right. "Miss Stewart? He would like to see you now."

Eva felt the shaking begin again, deep inside her veins. "All right." She stood up, briefly touching the wall for support. She forced a smile at Pocky. "Pray for me," she said, half-joking.

His expression was serious. "I will."

Eva walked into the room and heard the nurse close the door behind her. "Hey."

"Hello."

She looked down at him, her smile struggling to stay up. "How are you feeling?"

His eyes were half-closed; his skin still pale but less gray. An IV dripped into his arm and the familiar beep-beep-beep of the heart monitor sounded faint in the background. "It hurts," he murmured, his voice half-gone.

"I know." Eva sat down on the edge of the bed and took his hand in hers. "But you'll be better, I promise."

He blinked and opened his eyes a little wider, his pale lashes reminding her of how different he looked with his hair dyed darker. "It's all right."

"Did the nurse tell you anything?"

"No."

A lump the size of a golf ball formed in Eva's throat. "Mir...you know, um, that..." She knew if she let herself stop and think about what she was going to say, she would not be able to get the words out. "You're very sick, Mir. And...it doesn't look good."

"Eva—"

"Please hear me out, Mir, or I'll never be able to finish. It's taken me too long to tell you this in the first place." She filled her lungs with sterile hospital air. "You've got bone cancer, Mir, and your heart is too weak to keep working for much longer."

"Eva."

"You're dying." There. Those two words that seemed like a death sentence, even if it was not at her hands. The two words she had tried to fool herself into not believing until the weight of the lie was too much to bear.

"I know."

Eva's breath caught. "What?"

His voice was still quiet, almost a whisper as painkiller dripped into his veins. "I know," he repeated. A faint smile touched his face.

"How?" Eva realized she was clutching his hand with ferocity, but she could not bring herself to loosen her grip.

"I heard when you told Pocky," he replied, shifting a little under the white sheets. "I'd thought so before that, but…" His eyes fluttered closed briefly before re-opening. "I'm sorry for not letting you know."

He had known all along? Since the day when she brought Pocky into the living room and told him…and he had never said a word. He had never let on, never given her any clue. "Why didn't you tell me?"

"I thought it would make you sadder."

Unable to speak for fear a sob would overtake words; she leaned down and kissed him softly. He did not return the kiss; his eyes closed again and she knew he was asleep. She laid her head on his chest and listened to the faint but deceitfully steady beat of his heart. Warm memories of the night he danced with her flooded through her mind and she let them come.

Thirty-six months.

She would make them the best of Mir's life.

Chapter Fifty

Eva looked up and smiled at Mir as he entered the kitchen. "How do you feel this morning?"

"Better." He rubbed the top of her head as he passed her to open the cabinet and pour himself a cup of coffee.

Eva watched him. It was different, watching somebody you knew you did not have very much time with. You paid attention to detail, as if even the smallest, most insignificant thing about them was wildly important. Because it was. The curve of his neck when he turned his head, the way his eyes squinted when he smiled, the excitement in his voice when he played with June.

He had been released from the hospital three days ago with orders for Eva to keep him under close observation and for him to take it easy. They had offered several drugs that, they said, could prolong his life by perhaps a few months; and if not they would at least ease the pain of the degenerative process.

Mir had disagreed, and Eva had not stood in his way. She wanted as much time with him as she was allowed, but he was done with drugs. "I'm not going to live any longer than I'm supposed to," he had told Eva, and, through tears, she had agreed.

She was still getting used to the idea of death. She had not been prepared for Morbus to take her parents, but this time, she told herself she would be ready. She had to. "Is June still asleep?"

"Yeah, she was up late last night." Mir sat on the counter and took a sip of his coffee. "What was she doing again?"

"Teething," said Eva, grinning.

"I wonder what she'll look like with teeth."

"She'll still be adorable; she'll just be able to bite. Until they fall back out, anyway." She stood up and reached past Mir to pour herself a refill. She looked up at him. "Do you remember losing your baby teeth?"

He shook his head. "No."

Eva stirred sugar into her cup, willing herself not to think about all the things Mir would miss in his daughter's life. From trivial things such as teeth to her first love, her graduation, her wedding…something splashed into the coffee and Eva realized it was a tear. She glanced up and was grateful that Mir had not seen it.

"So," she said, "today's a big day."

His face was bright even though it did not wear a smile. It was as if he could do nothing with his joy except hold it inside.

"Are you nervous?" she asked.

"No. I'm excited. You?"

"A little nervous," she laughed. "But I'm excited, too." She looked at the clock above the stove. "Hey, we're leaving in half an hour. I've got to get ready to go."

She left the kitchen and as she walked up the stairs, wondered how it was possible life could move this fast. Only three days ago…she shook her head and smiled. For the next thirty-six months, life would go by too fast; and the only thing she could do was accept it. There would be time for memories later.

Pocky drove them to the beach. There were no clouds in the sky; the sun lit everything with gold, turning snow into cloud and water into liquid diamond.

The air was still cold, but Mir had insisted he wanted to do this as soon as possible. Eva was worried about the shock it might put on his heart, but she had decided to trust him. He could make his own decisions. It was his life, for however long he had it.

Mir lifted June, still strapped in her car seat, from the car and carried her as the four of them walked down to the water's edge.

"You're sure you understand this?" Pocky asked, looking at Mir and Eva in turn.

"Yes," said Mir.

Eva repeated, "Yes."

"Then Mir, please come over here?" Pocky waved a hand.

The young man set June's seat down on the ground and waded with Pocky into the water. They were less than twenty feet out, up to their waists. Eva stood next to June, shielding her eyes from the sunlight.

Pocky put a hand on Mir's broad shoulder. "Mir, do you believe that Jesus is the Christ, the son of the living God?"

"I do."

"Have you, Mir, accepted Jesus Christ as your personal Savior and Lord?"

"I have."

Eva's heart swelled.

"Then, in the name of the Father, the Son, and the Holy Spirit, I baptize you into new life."

As Mir emerged from the water, dripping and shining like the sun through the clouds, Eva knew. This was right.

"Come, duck!" Pocky waved at Eva as Mir walked out of the water, soaked and radiant. "You're next!"

Eva walked toward the water, the stones smooth under her bare feet. It felt like something out of a dream, but the fluttering in her chest told her it was real. The water was cold, very cold.

She felt very wide awake as she moved through the water; everything caught her eye. The ripples around her, the smell of salt and snow in the air, the glittering of sunlight on water, even the flash of a bird drifting in the sky overhead.

She faced Pocky, shivers prickling her skin. Her upper body felt colder in the air than the rest of her did under the water. "I don't really know what to do with myself."

His eyes, always so kind and warm, smiled at her. "Do you want to continue, or shall we wait?"

She shook her head. "No. I want to do it today. I want to…I want to re-start." She smiled and inhaled a deep breath. "I'm ready."

As she sank under the water, she felt two things.

The cold embrace of the salty water around her, as if everything on earth had wrapped its arms around her, and something warm that settled inside her.

Then water streamed from her vision and she was above the water, choking a little and smiling so wide she thought her face would not be able to hold it.

"Well done," said Pocky, taking her hands in his. "Well done."

Epilogue

"So how does it feel to be on this show?"

Edward Nolan looked at Eva and Mir, his signature smile wide on his clean-shaven face.

"I'm glad to be here," said Eva, smiling.

"And I'm glad to have you here," said Edward cordially. "What about you, Mir?"

Mir glanced at the people sitting in stands that surrounded the outer semi-circle of the show stage. "I'm a little nervous," he admitted. "I don't know what to do."

A camera swung around them, filming their faces. Mir watched it for a brief moment before returning his gaze to Edward.

"Don't worry," the man reassured him. "It's a friendly show; I'll ask questions, you supply answers. Just talk."

They sat on a couch in the center of the stage. They had microphones clipped to their shirts so their hands could remain free.

Before sitting down, Edward raised his arms toward the studio guests. "Everyone, please welcome Eva Stewart and Mir, the couple who defied all odds!"

Cheers overwhelmed Eva and she stared, hardly able to take it all in. It was surreal, something from a perfect dream.

"You have quite a lot of fans," said Edward, seating himself on the edge of the couch and facing them. "How does it feel to see yourselves on the covers of news magazines?"

Eva glanced at Mir. "Well, at first it felt like an invasion of privacy," she said, choosing her words carefully. "But then we realized that we could use the attention to help people understand the issues we're fighting for."

"Such as repealing the non-human act?"

She nodded. "Mir has already spoken at several conferences."

"So I heard!" Edward turned his attention to Mir. "Is it strange, to give your testimony in front of so many people?"

Mir nodded. "Yes," he said quietly.

"Now, there's a delicate subject we've all been wondering about." The host motioned toward the spectators and looked back at Mir. "Is it really true that you've been given less than three years to live?"

Eva had known this question would be asked, but hearing it was no less difficult.

"Thirty-six months," said Mir. His voice did not shake; he spoke with soft confidence. "Thirty-five now, I guess."

"And have you prepared yourselves for this? What about your daughter?"

Eva glanced at Mir again. "We're working on it," she said with a faint smile. "I don't think it's something you can totally prepare for. God doesn't give you grace ahead of when you need it."

"Then it's true that you both became Christians?"

"It is."

Edward laughed. "I bet that surprised a lot of people. What made you decide to take that route?"

"There was someone at prison, when I was there," said Mir, rubbing his hands together slowly, deliberately. "He was a good man. I don't know what happened to him, but he…helped me. A lot."

"I see." Edward's face was sympathetic. "What about you, Eva?"

"Well, I'd heard about Christianity from Professor Pock for much of my life. But the day before the trial, I decided that if God let us win, then I'd accept Christ too."

"Interesting," said Edward, squinting at them. Then, as if religion was an uncomfortable Subject, he asked, "So what about June? Where is she right now?"

Mir smiled. "She's at home with the professor."

"And how old is she now?"

"A little over ten months."

"She's teething," interjected Eva, causing laughter and sympathetic groans from women in the crowd.

Edward smiled and leaned his elbow on his knee, lowering his voice in a conspiratorial manner. "I hear Doctor Harborn was promoted to head of the research department in the new facility here in Alaska."

"Yes." Eva kept the word short and razor-edged, exactly how she felt. *He deserves to be in prison with Ross.*

"Wasn't he an ex-boyfriend of yours?" Edward winked at the crowd.

Eva took a sharp breath but felt Mir's hand brush her leg. She smiled instead. "A long time ago," she said, and clapped her hands together once. *Open and shut, please don't ask more.* To her relief, he did not.

"And now, to the biggest question everyone's been waiting for." Edward shifted, leaning forward and looking at them both with a friendly intensity. "You two have more or less become the couple of the year, in spite of the hardships you've been through. Are you two in an official relationship now?"

Eva looked at Mir and felt a blush warm her face. She smiled; she couldn't help it. Instead of answering, she held up her hand.

A delicate silver ring wrapped round her finger.

The spectators rose, cheering and clapping and drowning out Eva's laughter.

As soon as the noise died down enough for his voice to be heard, Edward exclaimed, "You're engaged! Congratulations, you two! This must have been a hard decision, all things considered."

Eva twined her fingers in Mir's and leaned her head against his shoulder. "Actually," she said, "it wasn't."

Acknowledgements

Mom and Dad, for their honest feedback and constant encouragement, and for teaching me what life is all about.

For every Awesome who read each new chapter of Monster with enthusiasm. Your threats to kill me if I hurt Mir, your excitement for more, and your hardcore fangirling. To the guys who didn't fangirl so much as nod appreciatively – thank you just as much.

To Amanda Bradburn, Stella Velox, Raquel Z. Duarte, and Katherine Sophia for being both editors and friends.

To Kelsey, for giving me an actual research scientist's point of view. It was absolutely invaluable, and I couldn't have done it without you.

To Jessica, for such a glorious cover. I have no words.

And, most of all, to my awesome God, who dropped everything into place as only He can.

I love you all.

Mirriam Neal has been writing seriously since she was thirteen, although 'seriously' might be taking it a bit far. She loves unique people, unique stories, unique music, and plans to continue writing a wide variety of books for the rest of her life.